EMPRESS OF ASIA

Empress of Asia

A NOVEL

ADAM LEWIS SCHROEDER

THOMAS DUNNE BOOKS
ST. MARTIN'S PRESS ☙ NEW YORK

THOMAS DUNNE BOOKS.
An imprint of St. Martin's Press.

www.thomasdunnebooks.com
www.stmartins.com

Library of Congress Cataloging-in-Publication Data

Schroeder, Adam Lewis, 1972–
    Empress of Asia / Adam Lewis Schroeder.—1st U.S. ed.
       p. cm.
    ISBN-13: 978-0-312-37640-6
    ISBN-10: 0-312-37640-5
 I. Title.

PR9199.4.S39 E47 2008
813'.6—dc22

2007043036

First published in Canada by Raincoast Books

First U.S. Edition: March 2008

10 9 8 7 6 5 4 3 2 1

This book is dedicated to
Frank Emery Schroeder & Harold Lewis Sutton,
my grandfathers.

One

A beefy-faced guy was pushing the gurney when they came to get you; he rolled it up the driveway and must've caught the corner of the Taurus just above the headlight because now there's a pretty good gouge in the paint. I didn't notice until the next morning, and what grated me most was that as soon as I saw it, I thought, goddamn that beefy-faced guy, it'll cost two hundred bucks to patch that! I was peeved at the paramedic who'd come to save your life. Then I wished that the gouge had been a hundred times bigger just to teach me a lesson, I wished the Taurus had its roof stoved in and a crater through its seat and all four tires melted down, like that car I hid under in Singapore on the day we met.

Now I'm staring at it again as I wait for the taxi, the same as every morning, standing here next to the driveway with my heels on the grass and the toes of my shoes on the asphalt and jingling the change in my pocket. Dr. Cavallo told me the Temazepam probably won't ever wear off before ten-thirty. Temazepam — *Tasmanian*, you call it. I'm trying to remember what else happened when the ambulance came to the house but it's all a blur. I remember I just stood inside the front door and pointed them down the hallway because I knew I could never cover the distance faster than they could. I must have told them your condition, too, they must have asked about that. Didn't they? They must have. That's how things have always been for me, and maybe that's how it is for everybody: these bursts of activity that happen so quickly that we can't even tell exactly what's happening, and once it's over everything's been changed and we're left with these empty stretches of time with nothing else to do but try to figure out what the hell happened. Maybe it's like that for everybody. Maybe there's really nothing special about you and me.

The Taurus hasn't moved since the last time you drove it. You always backed it in, you said at our age you never know when you'll have to leave in a hurry. You must get tired of being right all the time.

There are still yellow spots on the lawn from where you put down the Weed 'n' Feed. The pansies are doing well.

The taxi driver's an oily-looking guy with white skin like he's had the flu, and his car's a Cutlass Sierra. I can't imagine how he makes a living with the mileage they get.

"St. Paul's Hospital," I say.

He says, "Yezzir."

There are a lot of those Vietnamese kids on the corner, eating popsicles.

Now I'm too tired. The old CN station is going by on the right, we must be at Main and Terminal, which isn't the way a cab usually goes; they usually take the Cambie Bridge. The CN station has been fixed up so the Greyhound buses will use it now, polished up so the granite looks nice and clean, pillars and cornices just as good as in the old days, and if a bus station can rise again I figure maybe we can too.

You remember when I turned seventy-three and I needed to renew my driver's licence? I had to get that note from Dr. Clarke saying I was fit to drive, and he passed the buck to that horse-faced optometrist who said no, I wasn't. Every morning in the taxi, I think about that. Dr. Nickerson had just retired; he'd been our eye doctor since we first got back here. He'd just been de-mobbed out of the army like every-body else so he knew what had gone on out in the world, what we had come back from. He got my eyesight almost to the way it had been. But that young horse-faced one didn't give two shakes as to *why* my eyes get so tired. I could've told him it was just Imperial Japanese Army-style malnutrition that had done my eyes in, but these young guys don't want to hear about that. Every time you tell somebody how rough you had it they figure you're just accusing them of having had it easy. They get their back up, and then a guy will never get ahead with them.

"Hospital." We pull up in the loading zone and the cabbie looks at me in the rearview mirror. "May I ask, is it your wife you are going to see?"

I can't think of how to describe your situation exactly, so I just nod to him. Am I riding around collecting sympathy?

"You are quiet," he says, "so I have a feeling. Make sure to give her my best."

So I'll extend that to you now, from the cabbie who had the flu.

St Paul's. To get to room 407 a guy gets off the elevator at the fourth floor, turns right, right again at the nurses' station and your door's the second on the left.

That nurse with the ponytail — Molly? Brenda. She leans over the counter as I go by.

"Too bad you missed Gwen," Brenda says. "She was just in to see her!"

"How are things today?"

"Oh, she's doing okay."

I wonder if she knows how bad *okay* sounds. But it's my fault for asking. As if you, Lily, were something they could quantify. Like monthly sales.

I carry on into 407. I can quantify this much: today is Wednesday, July 12, 1995, which means that you've been in this room for exactly three weeks and they've taken you out of it a grand total of five times for one test or another. There's one unopened Sun-Rype apple juice box on your bedside table, along with the water jug and your glass and a paperback called *The Bridges of Madison County* with the bookmark still inside the front cover. There's a purple balloon up in the corner of the room, that's from Rudy, with a yellow cat on it saying *Better Get Better*. And there's the two pots of African violets from Gwen, I've been watering them off and on but they don't seem too taken with the place, maybe I ought to hustle them down to Cardiac for a change of scene. Oh, there's a little purple bear propped on your headboard, that's new — Gwen must've left it. All those bouquets from the church ladies have been gone for a week, the only other thing left is that potted daisy the

Winnipeg Browns sent out, that's doing just fine. Brenda's been picking the dead heads off it. And in the bed: you, my girl. That much I can tell you without a hitch.

I take my usual seat with my back to the window. It's 10:16 in the morning. The clock radio's there on your bedside table. The time drags when you're out, sweetheart, it's faster when you're awake and telling me the odd thing. I mean, I prefer to read a story where things move along at a fair clip, guys on horseback, making a break for it, that kind of thing. I don't read a lot of books about two people sitting in a hospital room.

When I watch you sleep I can't help but imagine when you won't be here at all. I know that that's the last thing I should talk about but you're a smart girl and I'm sure you've figured out that that time might come. Can pneumonia really kill somebody in this day and age? Doesn't seem likely, does it? That Dr. Cavallo's a cagey one, whenever she starts listing off tests and regimens and facts and figures I know that what she really means to say is that there's no black and white to speak of when it comes to you old people, all bets are off. And that's fair enough. I understand that life is like that. Even so she took that breathing tube out of your throat last night which was sure a giant step for mankind, and if you feel like waking up I'll tell you as much.

Look at that, 10:18. Why do they keep cutting your hair? Looks like it's about an inch long now, and it doesn't help that it's so patchy on the one side. And I still want to pull those tubes out of your nose even though I've stared at them ten thousand times and ought to be used to them, but from that noise you make with your mouth hanging open I figure they've got to be strangling you. I asked Dr. Cavallo and she said of course they weren't, it was quite the opposite. Now don't get embarrassed, I needed to ask.

You haven't been this skinny since we came out of the camps, when we looked like a couple of rakes wearing dishrags. How much have you lost now, thirty pounds? At least that. And where did it go? I don't see how so much of a human being could just disappear. But once upon a time I didn't know what happened to the oil once it went in the crankcase, either, it wasn't fuel for the car so where could it go? Friction burns it up, of course. Duress.

The seat of this chair always cuts a line into my backside. I lean my elbow on the arm, fold one leg over the other, show off some freckled skin above my sock. I can hear the doctor announcements out in the hall. Sometimes a family walks by looking for their grandma's room, all with bovine looks on their faces — it's the look a hospital stamps on a person. Albert Einstein walking through a hospital would look like a moron. And the clothes some of these people put on, tracksuits and that, baseball caps, those sure as hell don't make them look any smarter. Who're they visiting, their gym coach? I've seen them a hundred times, rattling car keys in their hands, and if there's a kid then the mom has her hand on the kid's shoulder, and the kid is always fat. Yes, dear, even here I can sit and judge people. I've got a knack for it.

My watch ticks, and your oxygen machine ticks too, only not as often. It ticks about every second and three-quarters. I can hear the traffic going by down on Burrard Street but it's so constant it's like listening to a stream, except sometimes there's a motorcycle without a muffler that sounds like it's going to come through the window. But you can't be rattled once you've had your Tasmanian. Remember Rudy talked about getting a *Hog* once and forever after you called them "pigs," and I'd say, "No, they're called *Hogs*," and you'd say, "Oh, how silly of me," like I'd really opened your eyes. But I knew you were pulling a fast one.

You're sitting up now. Looking right at me.

"I'm terribly thirsty," you say.

I get up too fast and the front legs of the chair go up and come back down with a *bang* and I see you blink at that. I'm pouring water into the glass.

"Here we are."

You wrap both hands around it and manage to navigate to your mouth without knocking it against the tubes coming out of your nose, then I take it out of your hands and get it back across to the nightstand without having it smash all over the floor, which I know the glass would like to do, and there, another routine by the magnificent performing Winslows! I realize, after all that, it's a plastic glass anyway. It would've survived better than I have. I take your hand. I can feel the little scars all around the palm.

"You must promise to do something very important," you say.

I figure that all the time in bed has changed your perspective on what's 'very important,' and you're going to ask me to clean out the eavestroughs.

"Anything," I say.

One of your shoulders starts to sag and I imagine that in half a minute the pillows and everything will tip over and you'll bang your head on the metal rail, so I want to get up and hold up that shoulder but I don't because you can't stand for me to fuss. I look back at your face and you're three times more tired than you were a moment ago.

"I should have told you years ago," you say, and your voice is so thin it sounds like someone else is whispering from under the bed. "I had every intention."

"What's this you're telling me?"

Your hand reaches up like it always does, feels the tube across your cheek, just touches it, sees where it goes, then feels the tube on the other side. And you always talk about something else at the same time like you're not even aware of it, like your hand's taken it upon itself to see what's going on.

"Michel is still alive," you say. "Michel Ney. You really must go to Thailand and see him."

"He … he what?"

Because you can't mean the same guy that I used to know — I figure the nurses must've slipped you a newspaper and you saw the name of a tourist who fell onto his head off an elephant. You stretch your hand toward the side drawer but you can't reach. I open it. There are all your folded pairs of socks, and a torn-out page from your little notebook sitting on top.

"There," you say.

I put the paper beside the water jug where we can both see it, then I take your hand again. You've written a long address that says *Michel Ney* at the top and *Kanchanaburi Province* at the bottom, and that was where a lot of the railway guys did end up, so only now does it cross my mind that we might be talking about the same person.

"But this isn't the same guy I used to know."

"He certainly is."

"Then where'd his address come from?"

You squeeze my hand.

"I've had it memorized."

You're going to fall asleep before we can sort this out.

"All right, dynamite gag so far," I say. "How come you have it memorized?"

"I've been there."

"To see him?"

I see that fraction of a nod that wouldn't have meant anything a month ago but these days I know is a full-fledged nod, it means yes, yes.

"Sweetheart," I say, "when were you ever in Thailand?"

You grin — you actually grin! You look like yourself again.

"When I told you I'd gone to Singapore. Not every time." You tilt your head back on the pillow. "Only the last few times."

I feel the blood drain out of my face, you know that feeling? Hell, you must have that feeling all day long.

"It's a dynamite gag," I say. "But if it's the same guy, how come I never heard from him?"

"Because." Your hand is feeling your cheek again. "I asked him not to."

"We'll hash it out when you get out of here, how about that?"

But you've shut your eyes. The way every conversation has ended for the last two weeks. I pick up the little page and hold it in one hand and keep your scarred little hand in the other. I can feel my own pulse in the ends of my fingers. Your printing used to look like it'd come off a typewriter, but it's chicken-scratch now.

Michel Ney
Coudreaux Guesthouse
32/5 Moo 1 Tumbon Nong Luu
71240 Sangkhlaburi
Kanchanaburi Province, Thailand

And I imagine that tall, bald Michel Ney really is there, drinking coffee and going to the bathroom, but I only play that game for about two seconds because I know for a fact that he's been dead fifty years, and even when he was alive I'd given up on him being my friend. So why would you give me this, and this story? To shake me out of my complacency. Since I retired I've been on a decline, that's seems to be the consensus, and last night you lay there listening to nurses walk by and concocted this scheme.

And now I wonder if it's not just a word game. If I take every third letter of his name it spells CLY … Clydesdale? No, the address doesn't spell Clydesdale.

You squeeze my hand, and I look up to see your eyes are open and a nurse is standing on the other side of the bed, her fingers around the rail. Her nails are painted yellow. I've never seen this nurse before — her name tag says *Yuriko*, and when I read that I feel like someone's given me a tap in the middle of the chest.

"You must have had a good sleep," she tells you.

That's a Japanese name, of course, but she doesn't seem entirely Japanese, not according to my rules of Orientals: Chinese look half-asleep, Japanese look like they want to bite you and the Koreans tend to be taller than the other two and look a bit confused.

"Mr. Winslow?" she says. "Dr. Chase is just making a phone call then he's coming in to see your wife, and I think he prefers if family waits outside. It'll only be about ten minutes.".

"Who's this?"

"Dr. Chase. The pulmonary specialist."

"Uh-huh."

"He'll just be a few minutes."

You're asleep again anyway. I have to pull at your fingers to get my hand free. I climb to my feet. Yuriko is over by the bedside table. She drops a daisy head in the garbage. I go around the end of the bed, my legs have stiffened up as usual.

"Which doctor is it again?" I say.

"Dr. Chase," says Yuriko.

"Okay."

I go out in the hall. I've forgotten the name already. I wander down to the elevators and stand there looking at the different makes of soda in the vending machine.

Then I come back to the nurses' station, and the one with the cardigan is there. I have a pretty good idea that she's the supervisor because once I heard her tearing a strip off old Brenda.

"Excuse me," I say. "I'd like to make a request regarding personnel."

She stops what she's writing and looks at me over her glasses.

"Yes?" she says.

"It's this Japanese gal in there," I say.

"Yes?"

"That's not helping anybody."

"How so?"

"She might be a decent enough nurse, but you really —"

"The other night Yuriko sat with her for a full hour when her shift was already over. Your wife didn't seem to have a problem with that, if you —"

"I'll be blunt," I say. "I can't trust people like that."

"Like *what*?"

"Japanese people," I say quietly.

She stands up.

"I'm going to go back here and forget we had this conversation."

She takes her papers and walks to another desk.

"You ought to have some flexibility in your staffing," I say.

She opens up a cabinet and starts jamming in papers.

"Mr. Winslow?"

I turn around. Yuriko is behind me. My heart's beating up in my throat.

"Did you bring that little bear?" she asks. "It's so sweet!"

Gwen telephones to invite me over for macaroni and cheese but instead I spend the evening leafing through all of your old ledgers for some clue that maybe you really did go to Thailand like you said. Most of them have to do with our car lot and even then I don't know what they mean, they're just a bunch of numbers, and now I can't help wondering if it's all in code. But do you know what I find in the bottom of your underwear drawer? I'll bet you do — an old chequebook! And all of the entries at the back just say PO, every one of them. An account with the Granville Street branch of the Bank of Montreal, that was only used for paying PO, whatever that was. Once a year you've been writing a cheque, most recently for $107.50, though cheque #1, written in 1948, was only for $14.75. That's inflation for you. What is it, Peeved Off? Post Office? It can't bode well that you keep it in your underwear drawer. Though you should be tickled that in, what, forty-seven years I never once thought to snoop around in there.

This morning the driver is a big guy in a turban, and these days that's the kind I prefer because they never make a peep. I've been thinking about the Michel Ney days. I'm staring at the black hairs on the back of the driver's neck and trying to remember exactly what happened to that guy who threw his rice bowl at the fence. This is all a scheme of yours to make me to think about something other than St. Paul's room 407.

As I come up to the front doors, two old guys in wheelchairs cut ahead of me. They're in those hospital-issue chairs with SPH scrawled on the back, and one says to the other, "Got your pink slip? We'll race."

That makes me feel better. Remember the party we had when I turned sixty-five? Everybody kept saying, "Don't do something stupid like become a senior citizen." The show must go on! That's what I tell myself every morning when I walk across this foyer, because I hate the sight and sound and smell of this place, but I know that it's better than nothing, Lily, that a day will come when I'll have to be glad that there was at least this much time, and I'll miss this hospital just like I miss our upstairs apartment with the McGintys. Some days I have to stand by this magazine rack before I carry on to the elevators, and say, deep breath, Harry, deep breath. But today I don't have to do that because I'm feeling just that little bit better.

"How are things?" I ask.

"Oh," says Brenda, "she's doing okay."

The old gal in the cardigan doesn't even look up.

They moved my chair around to the foot of the bed sometime last night, and now it feels like you're miles away. Who's sleeping in that bed, anyway? The parts are the girl I know but it's not the girl herself.

Brenda gives me the same look every time. Some kind of glassy optimism. Their faces must always have that expression on this ward, because they know there's not much chance that you'll be walking out with me when this is over. That's what a hospital produces: nothing. That's their industry. Come in with something and walk out with nothing. Unless people are coming in to have children, I suppose, but that was never in the cards for us, and now I can't help wondering if you'd have more piss and vinegar if you were sewing grandkids' ballet costumes the way Gwen does every morning, noon and night. Would everything be different today if we'd just been able to accomplish that one thing?

"Harry," you say.

You don't open your eyes. But you must have woken up. I pick your hand up off the blanket and it's the smallest thing I ever held. It feels a little cold.

You say, "That you, Mister?"

"Sure it is."

Now I'm holding it in both of mine. You open your eyes but they don't find me right away. Now they do. For a while all you do is look. Then you bring up your hand that has the IV in the back of it and touch the tube on your cheek.

"What will we do when we've left this place?" you ask.

"We'll go anyplace you want."

"You should go and see someone else. Besides Michel."

"And who is that?"

"I was thinking about Singapore."

"We'll go anyplace you want."

"I was thinking."

You look up at the ceiling. I wait about a minute. Your breathing's pretty good but I want to press the button. Is it an emergency if all you're doing is not saying anything?

"What were you thinking?" I ask.

You're smiling. I can see that now. Your face hasn't changed one bit, but your eyes have that squint.

"About when you fell and hit your head."

"When who did what?"

"Funniest thing that I had ever seen. And I said it. You were stretched on the floor and I said, 'That was the funniest thing I have ever seen.'"

I can feel every little bone in your hand.

"This was in Raffles? I don't remember that."

"You were unconscious."

Your mouth's trying to smile. Someone has just come in. It's not Dr. Cavallo, it's a bald guy with some curly hair and a white coat and green tie.

"Mrs. Winslow?" he says. "How is everyone in here today?"

Your eyes stay on me. You don't know who's talking. You make a little swallow. But maybe you do know that a doctor is here, you've been waiting for him, in fact, because now your free hand grabs hold of that pink blanket like a good goddamn and the machine that's been ticking away every second and three-quarters goes off like an alarm clock. Your neck arches back to try to get breath in. Jesus Christ. Your hands come up so your tubes bang against the rails, and I try to hold onto your shoulder but a nurse is already there. I get in her way. Nobody says anything to me. No, hell, they probably do. They're talking to each other and hanging IV bags on the rack.

"Lily," I say. I don't say it very loud. I don't want to be standing here screaming at you, and I know you wouldn't want that either.

You fall back on the pillow. Your tongue moves on the roof of your mouth and you blink your eyes a bunch of times and they're this silver colour, like they're covered with something. Then they shut completely. But you're breathing again, sweetheart. You're asleep. The nurse by the IV stand tucks her hair behind her ear. *Alice*, her tag says. I'm standing by the chair again and the doctor walks around the end of the bed to me. Alice folds her arms.

"Listen," the doctor says. "Can we go out in the hall?"

I follow him into the hall.

"This doesn't look too good," the doctor says. "Pardon me, would you like to sit down?"

I fold my arms and lean my shoulder against the wall. I try to look intent on what he's saying. I don't know how the hell I look. Do I even look like me any more? I've been so caught up in whether or not you look like you. I see myself reflected in his name tag. *Dr. Burnett.* My mouth hangs to one side so I make that grumpy face I always make in the mirror, you used to tease me about it.

"Don't worry about me," I say.

"All right." He looks at the floor. "She isn't suffering at this point."

"I'm not the doctor," I say, "but I don't, I don't think she got a great kick out of that, what just happened."

What am I doing? Arguing with him?

"No." He looks at me. "I don't believe she —"

Alice comes out of 407. "Doctor Burnett," she says. Then she runs back in.

The doctor goes in after her.

I don't follow him. I don't want to share you with them; this was never how we spent our time together. For all that time it was just us. I don't want to fight through them to get to you. Sugar, I'd like for us to be someplace else.

After a second I go back into 407 and stand behind the doctor. Alice is on the far side of the bed. She has her hand on your shoulder. Some of your green hospital gown is between her thumb and finger. She's looking at the doctor.

"She's gone," he says.

Alice looks over at me. It's so quiet in here. As far as I'm concerned you look the same as you did five minutes ago. But it's been such a long time since you looked like yourself.

Dr. Burnett says that I shouldn't take a taxi, that I should have someone pick me up, so I try to call Rudy on the phone at the nurses' station but I can't remember his number. I know the number at the lot, of course, but it's Saturday so he won't be over there, he likes to stay home with his kids. I know that much. So I ask for a phone book. They aren't expecting that. A shunt into your belly, sure, but not the white pages.

Most people don't phone for a ride when this happens, I guess, they've seen it coming and they've gathered all the family around. You fooled us good and proper, my dear. Alice asks if I want to sit down. I seem to be wandering back toward 407. Brenda comes out of the elevator and hands me a phone book.

"I'm so sorry," she says.

Laurie answers but I ask if Rudy is there, the son of our dearest friends, Gwen and Gord, though of course Gord passed away years ago. I tell Rudy I'll be on the bench outside. I hang up the phone and Dr. Cavallo's standing there in jeans and a sweater. Her mouth crumples up and she puts her arms around me. The side of her face is wet. She says it must have been something she hadn't expected, they're going to find out what it was. What for, I want to ask. Her car keys dig into my back.

It's warm outside. The sky looks dark blue. The smokers are all around the benches, the same folks I see every morning and night, the skinny girl in the wheelchair, the guy with his IV and the two Indians. I haven't sat down here before so they look me over pretty good. Maybe they can tell. How can I still be the same and you be so different? The girl in the wheelchair holds out her cigarettes.

"They're menthol," she says.

She must weigh ninety pounds.

"Not anymore," I say. "Thanks anyway."

How am I able to hold a conversation?

Rudy comes up the walk in shorts and running shoes. He's a big man these days, and why shouldn't he be? He's been well-fed every day of his life. Thirty-seven years old now, and that strikes me as significant somehow — it makes him half of my age, but he doesn't even seem that. He can't be old enough to be losing his Auntie Lily, the little boy who stole flowers out of our yard to give to his mom, and we wouldn't have even known it if Gwen hadn't made him come back and apologize, hanging his head. We've been the best of friends ever since, of course, but I've always thought it was terrible how Gwen made him do that.

I get up and he puts his arm around me, then his nose starts running and he wipes it with his T-shirt. We walk down to the sidewalk like that. Jesus, the poor kid loved his Auntie Lily an awful lot. His car's right there.

"I found a meter!" he says.

We laugh at the same time, sort of a snort. Thinking of the days when finding a meter would really have been significant. Wondering if days like that can ever come again.

We're in his brand new '96 Cavalier but I don't like sitting in it. As long as I was sitting in a taxi there was a chance. Sitting in the '96 Cavalier brings home what's happened more than anything any doctor or nurse could ever have said to me. Rudy says I should stay with his mother for the time being, that they'd been planning on this.

Gwen isn't any better off than me, we keep trying to play cards and one of us starts sniffling and then the other starts in too, and we're actually crying on each other's shoulders. That yellow housecoat of hers has seen better days. When we finally have the cards back in our hands all we can do is talk about you. The tests they did. The medications. I tell her that I wondered if you were still in the room after it happened and she gets up to start a pot of coffee. "That never sorted anything out," she says. Some things she went through with Gord she doesn't want to get into again. Instead we talk about your tests again. Gwen knows all about them; she was quizzing Dr. Cavallo morning and night.

"But what do you or I really know about it?" she says. "We're helpless."

She doesn't start crying this time, so maybe it's getting easier for her. The next day Rudy brings over my shaving kit and some shirts from home, along with all the vases of flowers that have been left on our doorstep — "The dearest soul we could ever hope to meet," says one of the cards, I can only read a couple at a time — but I keep thinking that I have to get back to the house to water your nasturtiums. Your tender perennials. When you planted them you told me that that was what we were too. We come back every year, like it or not, but we've got a soft side too. You'd seen me mist up during some of the TV commercials. Now I wish you'd never said anything like that. The phone's ringing so Gwen gets up.

"The minister." She's leaning in the doorway with the receiver tucked in her armpit. "Wants to know if there's anything you'd like to say."

"When? Now?"

"At the service."

I'd never thought of that. I shake my head.

Gwen says that the minister wasn't surprised; apparently for the older people the husband or wife never says anything. Rudy is going to say something, though, and some of your church friends.

"I've tried calling Pia half a dozen times. The number in Lil's book doesn't get me anywhere, is that the only one?" Gwen's pulling a thread out of the sleeve of her housecoat. "I must have the wrong code for Singapore. Wouldn't she be over the moon if we could get Pia here? God, the way Lil would drag herself around after those trips, it was like someone had died. Every time, it was just like someone had died. Is that little blue book the only one she had?"

"If it's not in there," I say, "I don't know."

I stay five days with Gwen.

Now Rudy is driving me over to our place at nine o'clock at night, he couldn't get away from the lot any earlier, or maybe it's just that he's like I was and leaves all of his paperwork until the last minute.

"This afternoon a guy traded in a Mazda," Rudy says as we stop at the light. "MX-6. I hadn't even written a price on it when another guy comes in and asks how much. Said he'd been looking down in Richmond and everywhere."

"I wouldn't have carried it," I say.

"All right, sheesh. I shouldn't have mentioned it."

"I'd have told him trade it with Gypsy's up the block. Gypsy wouldn't handle Volkswagens, so it worked out. What's that new one they've got? The Golf?"

"The Japanese are the biggest movers."

He's not the kid who pinched flowers out of our yard anymore; I can't just tell him to bugger off. We sold him our car lot! He started off cleaning toilets. We owned the lot and he cleaned the toilets.

"Only ever some kid trying to pawn a Datsun off on me anyway," I say.

"Nissan."

"Now why would they change it? I tell you Mitsubishi made all of their planes in the war?"

"Yeah."

"The boat I was on, the house your aunt grew up in, blown to smithereens. Everything. Brought to you by Mitsubishi."

"You told me," Rudy says. He pulls up short behind somebody so I have to put out my hand to not whack myself against the dash. "I don't see a lot of Mitsubishis."

"Mazda, Datsun. You know why people buy those cars? Because they have very short memories."

Now it strikes me how ridiculous it is to be having this conversation with the poor goddamn guy who's going to be speaking at your funeral. It's been a few days since I had to dab at my eyes, though, so maybe it is time I got back to walking and talking the way I used to. I'm sorry about that. It's not that you don't deserve crying. If it's any consolation it still feels like I've got a chunk of something blocking up the top of my stomach, I still can't eat more than a bite or two, and I know that's bad. Even Dr. Cavallo could tell me that.

"What do you mean, 'memories'? You carried every German car under the sun!"

He had me there, didn't he? That was always the argument you made too.

"I saw with my own eyes that the Japanese are a hateful people."

"I never heard Aunt Lily say that."

"No, I guess in her camp they had it pretty good."

He does that thing where he pulls his mouth down at one corner — Jesus, it looks terrible! He can't be doing that on the lot or he wouldn't earn enough to feed himself.

"Mom told me you've lost ten pounds," he says out of the blue.

"I don't know about that," I say.

"She must be too polite to say anything about it."

And just like that we're pulling in behind our Taurus at the house where you ought to be but aren't. I smell the cut grass as soon as I'm out of the car. It's all over the sidewalk. Right down the block the colours of the flowers are so bright it's like another planet. Snapdragons and mums. I walk straight into the carport to hook up the hose. The place is filled with your terra-cotta pots and bags of peat moss. I hear Rudy go up on the porch and bang the mailbox open. I hit my head against those sailboat wind chimes that turned all rusty but you refused to throw away.

"Hey, Pop, you've got a lot of cards here," says Rudy.

I'm dragging the hose out onto the lawn. "Must be for my birthday."

"Condolence," he says. "Some nice ones."

I'd thought that five days without water would've killed your nasturtiums, and for that matter I half-expected all the windows in the house to be broken, too, and I'm almost disappointed they aren't. Because otherwise I could have left this place behind. Walked away. But the idiotic show must go on. I switch the nozzle to the softest spray and move it up and down all the vines, the orange flowers and the red ones. They really came out beautifully despite all the fuss I made when you planted them — I didn't want to go to Vander Zalm's because he was still a crook as far as I was concerned even if he did have perennials on sale.

"Something from Vital Statistics here," Rudy says. "Must be forms for you. Just a sec, I'll turn this light on."

He unlocks the door and goes in, and more power to him. I didn't want to be the first one in there. The whole time at Gwen's I had the idea that I should climb on a Greyhound bus and ride off to somewhere where nothing I see means anything, because even Gwen's crossword-puzzle books reminded me of you. Go where I can see a street sign that would just be words on a board, not a street where we'd once lived in a mouldy apartment or delivered a car to a teenage girl in the pouring rain. I see now that the life we made in this city is a trap. A curse. Thank God I never made any of those trips to Asia with you, right? Because I can at least entertain the thought of going back there. Except for Singapore, Jesus — that'd be like riding the elevator up to 407 and feeling around in the sheets.

This is a good setting, it mists up the petals just right.

So can Thailand be a place where nothing I see means anything?

Kanchanaburi Province? No, it wouldn't, because I'd be following your orders and every second of every day and every cloud I'd see floating by I'd wonder what in hell you'd had in mind. You went there *by yourself* to see Michel Ney? Who you met once in, what, '43? I have trouble believing that. This is just a puzzle you've concocted for my benefit. If we'd been able to have a kid or two and you'd been sewing grandkids' ballet costumes you wouldn't be playing this game with me now. Weren't you just going to see Pia in Singapore, wasn't that what you always said? You only did that to take my mind off of things now, to set this up. If you'd been a foul old bird I could be rubbing my hands with glee and wishing you good riddance. Instead I spray water across the front of my pants and don't even notice I've done it.

Now I'm at the lattice that you always said needed a coat of paint, and I never got around to doing it because it's a pain to paint a lattice. Now I don't know if I'd feel worse if I took a brush to it or if I didn't — can't a lattice just be a goddamn lattice?

We used to talk about how rotten it would be to be the one left behind, we'd laugh about it when we did the dishes and say that driving off a cliff together would be the way to go. Of course if old Nickerson hadn't retired and I'd kept my licence that's exactly how it would've gone, but no, that horse-faced eye doctor came along and robbed us of that option. If he shows up at your service I'll throw him out, I *will*, by the seat of his pants. He always had it in for us.

Rudy's going up the walk to the car.

"Just getting the bags," he says.

It really is a beautiful night out here, sweetheart. The sun's set and the air is still warm, these are those few weeks when a guy really knows it's summertime. There's still that glow over the trees. You used to stay outside for hours on a night like this, weeding by flashlight, up to your elbows in squash plants, singing away.

You are my sunshine, my only sunshine
You make me hap-peee when skies are grey

Did they play that in Singapore when you were a kid? It doesn't seem very Singaporean, but everybody in the world must know that song one way or another. I haven't gone back to look at the squash plants yet.

I guess I figured the nasturtiums were more important, out in front of the house where everyone can see them. Maybe I figured you'd think that was important.

"All right." Rudy's coming across the lawn. "The kettle's on. I put the bags in your room but I didn't unpack them. Are you going to need a ride anywhere tomorrow?"

"Can't I decide that tomorrow?"

"But I have to know if I'm going to come and get you."

"Then your mom'll call you and you'll come over, right?"

"But you're staying *here*."

"No."

He undoes his tie and shoves it in his pants pocket.

"Yeah, Pop, you are. That's why we came over here. You and Mom hashed the whole thing out this afternoon and she got your bags ready and you helped me put them in the car, you remember that?"

"Oh, sure. I remember that."

He's looking at me the way Gord used to on the golf course when he figured that I'd written in less strokes than I should have, and it wasn't a look that I cherished seeing because usually Gord had been absolutely right.

"Call if you need anything," he says. "Make sure you eat something."

He gets into the Cavalier and backs out, and I go into the carport and coil the hose onto the plastic rack. Our Taurus is still in the driveway. I should ask Rudy about having one of his guys work on that gouge. I think about putting my hand on the back of the car, as though you were watching me and you'd know I was signalling to you by putting my hand on the back of a 1993 Ford Taurus. Now, in your opinion, would it be crazier to go ahead and do that or to *not* do it because it might be crazy?

I tiptoe up the steps. I look through the screen door and across our dark hallway. The lights are on in the kitchen. I take the plunge, I walk through our front door into the house and bend down to untie my shoes. Now I can feel exactly how wet my pants are.

I go into the kitchen as though everything were the same. The kettle's boiling beside the mug tree. We own four mugs that say *Lily*, each one shows a picture of a lily, you got all of them for various birthdays from various well-meaning souls, and you must have had another dozen that have smashed over the years. But you're never going to have another birthday now and that whole cottage industry is going to collapse.

I unplug the kettle and pour the water into the teapot. The steam rises up my sleeve. I'm having trouble fitting the lid into the top of the pot. I hear the screen door click shut in the foyer. I adjusted the pressure canister so now it takes half a minute to close, and, I know, you think that's too long. It annoys you. I wipe my wet hands on the back of my pants. I open the fridge for the first time in a week and smell the sour milk. I can't help it, I check the top to see what day it expired.

JUL 16.

The same day as you.

All I can think to do now is pour the tea down the sink even though there's a pound of Coffee Mate in the pantry I could use, but I don't want the tea any more, I have to be as busy as possible at all times and I have to find something else to do with my hands. I'll change into dry pants.

I feel my way down the hallway in the dark. I walk past your sewing room and hear the tissue-paper patterns flutter on the table. I turn the light on in our room and my jeans you bought at the Bay are on the top of the laundry basket where I left them on the morning you died. Evidently I'd thought it was as good a day as any to wash a pair of jeans.

I go back to the kitchen. I don't care if I have wet pants. I take the Yellow Pages out of the drawer and open it and start flipping. SPRIN-KLERS. TRAILERS. TRAVEL. There's a million of them. Grace's Travel? That sounds reliable. Or maybe I'm just thinking of Lloyd Grace, because that was what I signed up for way back when, wasn't it? Travelling with Grace.

I pull my wallet out of my back pocket and take out your little note-book page: *Kanchanaburi Province.* Your master plan. I clear my throat.

"I'd like to ask you about flights to Thailand," I say.

I dial the number but after eight rings there's still no answer because it's ten o'clock at night. I wish now that I hadn't thrown that tea down the drain, and I wonder if we have enough crossword puzzles to get me through the night.

Grace's Travel has a big window display showing model ships and maps of South America, and I suck in my belly before I look at my reflection in the glass — I know, I've always done that. You used to shake your head. Who am I trying to impress nowadays, you ask? Any rate, there I am in the window, it's been a hot spell this past week so I have on my blue shorts and those argyle knee socks. I look just as dapper as you please. I go in the door and a little bell rings. A lot of plastic airplanes hang from the ceiling and a lot of people at desks are talking on telephones. A guy in a yellow shirt sees me and holds up one finger. I pick up a magazine, *Princess Cruises*, that shows a woman in a pink bikini with a snorkel on the side of her head. I want a flight to Kanchanaburi Province, Thailand.

What does this have to do with Michel Ney? When we crossed the Java Sea there was no such thing as a snorkel or a bikini. Michel Ney. I hope he knows I'm coming, because somebody has a hell of a lot of explaining to do.

"Can I help you?" This is a tall woman with curly brown hair. She reminds me of Violet Millar, you remember? Those teeth? "Were you interested in a cruise?"

"A trip," I say. "A flight." I put the magazine back on the pile, then I take a second to straighten it out, I'm not sure why. "Do you have the different fares?"

"Certainly, sir," she says. "Come back and have a seat."

I follow her past the desks where everyone is still on the phone, rolling their eyes at whoever it is they're talking to, and she pulls out a chair on wheels so I can sit down facing her.

"I'm Margaret," she says, like she wasn't Margaret until she sat behind the desk. "Can I get you a coffee?"

I take a pen out of a jar and tap it against the palm of my hand.

"Can I get going in the next couple of days?"

"Where did you want to fly into?"

"Thailand," I say.

"Into Bangkok?"

She starts typing. The pen says *Montreal* and there's a little Olympic Stadium inside it that slides back and forth in front of the other buildings. It's a hell of a stadium that can do that.

"And then will you stay in Bangkok, sir?"

She stops typing and looks at me — no, at something over my shoulder. I turn around and the guy at the next desk spins away from us and sits there smirking at his computer. He's done his hair so it all stands up on his head.

"What's the trouble?" I ask.

He looks over like he just noticed I was sitting there.

"Oh," he says. "No problem. Hey, I like your tattoo."

That line between my collar bones — remember how people used to think I'd drawn on myself with ballpoint? 'No, no,' you'd say, 'that's Harry's war wound.'

"Does it signify something?" he asks.

"It's just from the war."

"Cool!"

He gives a big nod. I turn back around and Margaret's waiting, fingers at the ready. I realize that I have to get the address out of my wallet so I stand up and the chair rolls away across the office.

"Kanchanaburi Province." Your paper already looks the worse for wear. "Is that right, I'd go into Bangkok?"

The guy with the hair brings my chair back. I sit down and tap the pen.

"Sangk — Sangkhlaburi?" she says. "I don't know it." She types for a minute. "It won't be straightforward getting there, I'm afraid. Not the least little bit."

"No," I say. "I wouldn't expect it would be."

"Oh, you're going to have a blast," says the guy with the hair.

Two

I grew up in Vernon, B.C., which of course you and I visited every year while my folks were alive and after that a few times while Roberta and her kids were still there. It's dry hills, and orchards, and Kalamalka Lake, and the first time you ever wore a bikini was to go in that lake. You were thirty-two years old and Holy Christ did you look good. Your mother had been a big woman and most times that's how the daughter turns out, but when you walked out on the sand that day I realized once and for all that that was not how you had turned out at all. The Arnotts were with us that trip and I turned around to Les and said Amen. Amen to that.

The Depression was on most of the time I was a kid but we still did okay. That stuff was only in the papers until we saw guys come in off the trains and start knocking on doors. You told me it was the same over in Malaya, you still had your lacy outfits but everybody complained about rubber and tin being in decline. Because nobody could afford a car! But I was a kid, I didn't know anything about that. Of course, after the war they were putting rubber into everything, and one day you walked out on Kalamalka Beach in a bikini with rubber waistband and rubberized bust.

My folks. It always felt like my sister Roberta and I had come in at the tail-end of a hilarious conversation my folks had been having, that as far as they were concerned all the good stuff had already come and gone and it was just too bad for us that we hadn't been around to see it.

When he was a kid my dad had gone on a cattle drive from Montana
up into B.C., fell off his horse and landed on a bunch of cactus. Ma made
so many jokes about it that I figured I'd sit on the first cactus I came
across too. But the first time I ever saw one was on Celebes and by then
it didn't seem nearly as interesting as the fact that Michel and I were
being shot at.

My folks just sat in the house and *read* — he read the *Vernon News*,
unless there was a big story like Jimmy McLarnin becoming welter-
weight champion, then he'd wait until the next day and buy the *Vancouver
Province* from the day before. They never went to a party down the block,
but my dad did go to town council meetings, he loved that, and at elec-
tion time he'd go to the meetings for every single candidate. That was his
idea of high adventure — sitting on a folding chair with his hat still on.
Every time he teased her about her meringue falling flat, Ma would say,
"Why don't you go run for alderman?" He'd lower his newspaper and
wink at Roberta and me because we all knew she'd trumped him —
alderman! What next, pirate captain?

He ran a store called Priest Valley Dry Goods, you remember, where
the Coldstream Hotel is now. It was one of the old stores with the wood
cabinets up to the ceiling on either side, bins in the middle, stacks of
cloth at the back, pickle barrel at the front, crates of matches, ginger ale
in the stone bottles. Meat pies on the counter if the woman remembered
to bring them in. Vernon had been called Priest Valley before it was called
Vernon so with that name it seemed like an old-time store even then.
It smelled like spices. It did a fair business because of its regulars, these
farmers who'd drive into town the same time every week like clockwork, and if Farmer Deleenheer picked up his lamp oil and flour and
fencing nails by eleven o'clock on a Tuesday morning then Dad knew
there'd be no more business that day and he could lock up, walk up the
hill and spend the afternoon on the porch reading the *Vernon News*.
Of course, there was a slim chance some unpredictable woman might
come in to buy three clothespins, but if she was in a real panic she could
always go to another store. Dad calculated that the dollar value of
the good health he achieved through his occasional afternoons at home
outweighed the profit he might recoup on the sale of three clothespins.

Ma didn't like that because oak cabinets right up to the ceiling aren't cheap, so when he'd started the store Dad had graciously let his in-laws cover his overhead and I don't know if he ever paid them back. Whenever he was on the porch Ma would stomp around the kitchen, rolling out pie dough and telling me that after this-many or that-many days the profit on three clothespins *would* add up to something. If he had that much time on his hands he could at least run for alderman. It paid twenty dollars a month! But he just read his newspaper and told us about the Japanese in Manchuria and that; the Japs were starting it even then. Maybe things would've been different somehow if I'd paid attention, but I doubt it. I doubt it.

What surprised me was how much Ma was crying, because she had a reputation as something of a hard case. I stood there in my room, rocking on my heels so the floorboard creaked over and over and over, hands in my coat pockets, looking around the place one last time. My suitcase lay on the bed, bulging at the seams, and I could hear Ma blubbering down at the bottom of the stairs while Dad muttered to her. The whole week previous he'd taken the tack with her that at least I wasn't going to fight a war, it wouldn't be anything like those three Kidston boys who went to France and never came back. Ma had even been stepping out with one of them — Roberta had told me that like it was the best secret in history — and if it hadn't been for this boyfriend of hers getting gassed at Passchendaele maybe my going away wouldn't have been such a tragedy. All I was doing was going to sea, and not even in the navy, just a merchant ship. The worst that could happen would be falling over the side, but of course we weren't exactly a seafaring family.

I could hear her down there, *boo-hoo boo-hoo*, just the same as they cry in the pictures. It reminded me of the part in *Tom Sawyer* when he and Huck pretend to be drowned and sneak back into town to see their own funeral, and all the women are crying and Tom gets a real kick out of that. But I didn't get a kick out of listening to Ma. I could say my heart went out to the old girl, because it did, but phrasing it like that sounded a bit mean. She'd bought me a new suit to wear down to the coast, and a shiny overcoat with pockets on the inside. But I couldn't go back downstairs right then because it would just make things worse. I'd been down already and Dad had sent me back up. So I creaked the floorboard and waited for Roberta to come back with the car; I listened for the gravel under its wheels. She'd gone down the road to pick up Shaw.

My room. A quilt on the bed from Grandma Patterson out in Ontario. Three different handbills over the desk for the Barnes & Sells-Floto Circus that'd camped out on Schubert Street: "The Hindoo Torture Box," showing a guy in a turban sticking a girl full of swords; "More Dead Than Alive — The Human Skeleton," showing this beanpole of a guy with his eyes bugging out; and "The Palace of Illusions," showing this girl in her underwear flying over the jungle. A pile of nails on the desk that I'd found in my pocket after the last day at the packing house.

I heard the car and went around the end of the bed and looked out the window. It was sunny out but cold. A couple of yellow leaves were left on the maple tree. Roberta and Shaw drove up in Dad's Packard with the top pulled down. She was at the wheel wearing her hat with the gauze around the crown that she'd bought with half her Bulman's paycheque. On the canning line they made them wear these oh-so-sturdy white uniforms — "I look like a bohunk," she'd say — so on her days off she really put on the dog. Shaw sat beside her in his check blazer with the green scarf his mother had sent him, wrapped four times around his neck. He wasn't very good-looking, he had a weak chin in my opinion, but he wore his hair in such a way that girls took notice of him. Roberta included. The two of them got out of the car as my folks stepped down off the porch. I watched the tops of their heads.

Eric Shaw had been my best friend for four months, since July, when we'd both started as sorters at the packing house. I had just finished high school then. We filled baskets of grapes, crates of peaches, coffins of celery, then the apple crop started coming in and I was bumped up to box-nailer and got to tie on a leather apron.

Before Shaw came along we'd had to suffer through all the tinny-sounding big bands and garden-party orchestras they had on Radio

CKOV out of Kelowna, but that all changed when he *walked* over the Rocky Mountains, all the way from Manitoba, with a 1926 Phillips phonograph strapped to his back and twenty pounds of records in his suitcase, all of them by one guy. Fats Waller. Old Shaw had all the latest ones out of Minnesota, "Ain't Misbehavin'" and "Lulu's Back In Town" and "The Joint Is Jumpin'" and "Truckin'" and "Honeysuckle Rose" and all of them. My buddy Frank Casorso had a flatbed Ford and we'd set the Phillips up on the back of that and Ted Yakamura would bring his football and we'd toss that around and holler along with Waller. "Truckin'" was our favourite — *We had to have something new, a dance to do way up in Harlem, now eve-ry-body's truckin'* — on account of Frank's truck. Sometimes a few girls would come and stand by the fence, Liz Megaw and Muriel Doherty and some others, and we'd kid them and ask what the heck they wanted and they'd say that they just liked Ted's sweater, that it was a nice colour. Ted Yakamura was taller than the rest of us and he ran up and down the alley a lot, inventing touchdown plays. Most nights we'd wrap it up when Ma threw a shoe at us like we were a pack of alley cats. She thought that was hilarious. The music that I said was plain good jazz she and dad called "jungle music."

Every time I got my pay I'd tell old Shaw which records I'd buy off him, but he'd never bite. But *I* had something that knocked his socks off too, I had all of the *Terry and the Pirates* comic strips for 1936; I'd cut them out of the paper every day of the week and pasted them together. The great thing about *Terry and the Pirates* was that it was one long story that went on and on, so I had the whole thing where Pat Ryan was in Shanghai with the bandit queen, the Dragon Lady they called her, and Connie was there cracking jokes, he was the poor kicked-around Chinese houseboy — "Mist' Terry and Mist' Pat! Flenchy-flied potatums!" Old Shaw read those and he went on and on about sailing on a boat out to China after that, he figured that'd be just jake.

We gave some money to Mr. Casorso to buy a bottle of Black & White whisky to give to our foreman and before long Shaw was a box-nailer too and we were stacking shakes together, cutting the wires, loading the truck, and all the time talking about the same thing.

"I don't care if it *is* a slow boat," he'd say. "We're going."

"'Won Long Hop Took One Long Hop to China,'" I'd say. That was the title of another Fats Waller record; we'd never heard it but we'd seen the name on the back of a sleeve. *Also Available From Bluebird.*

The thing about a packing house is that it's hard work but it doesn't last. They let most everybody go by December, so there was always that light at the end of the tunnel to make it easier to get up at 5:30 in the morning. But all that light really meant was that before long we'd be out of work, and in Shaw's case that meant he'd be living with the hobos in Polson Park. He saved some of his money and sent the rest home, so I saved mine too. I didn't take any girls out or anything. There was one at the packing house who was all right, Agnes, she had a skinny neck but a good figure otherwise; a cardigan hung off her pretty well. She always pinned her hair so it fell over one ear. But I was saving money so I didn't ask her out, even when I overheard her telling one of the girls that she wanted to go down to the Capitol to see "Pygmalion" with Leslie Howard. I also had acne up and down my cheeks so I was pretty nervous around girls.

"Got a letter from my Uncle Lloyd," Shaw said one day. We were loading boxes onto the conveyor belt and it banged like a snare drum every time.

"What uncle's this?"

"My mother wrote to see if he could give me any work."

"What's his business?"

"Wait for it," he said, and gave me a look. I figured that meant his uncle was an outhouse inspector or something. "He runs a boat out of Vancouver, tooling all around the Pacific." He winked. "Says he needs crew."

I must have looked like I was going to faint, because he started laughing and slapping his leg, dancing around with his hammer swinging on his belt. I guess I'd had the desired reaction.

"So I'll write and tell him to wait for us!"

"Tell him to wait for us," I said. "Don't sail one inch without us."

His uncle wrote back to tell us to be there by the 26th of November and to ask if either of us had our Seaman's Ticket. That made me a bit nervous, my folks nervous especially, but Shaw said not to worry, his uncle would go easy on us. Everything had worked out all right for Shaw up to that point so I figured if I kept my wagon hitched to him I'd be all right.

I packed my bag the night before our train, then Shaw and I went down and saw "Suez" starring Tyrone Power. He builds the Suez Canal and tries to make up his mind which girl to marry — that story suited us just fine. Go east, young man, where there are more pretty girls than pickles in a barrel. But that night I had bad dreams. I was on a boat with a lot of guys in rubber boots who were disappointed as hell.

When I came down from my room the four of them were waiting in the hallway, Dad with his arm out to take my suitcase, Ma holding some paper crumpled in her hands, Roberta holding Shaw's arm and Shaw holding his hat. I wouldn't let Dad take the suitcase.

"Here's something," Ma said, and she stuffed an envelope into my pocket. "Look at that coat, you've lint — I'll get the brush."

"Don't fuss him," said Dad.

She opened the closet door to get down the clothes brush.

"Ma," he said quietly. "Don't fuss him."

Ma shut the closet door and turned around. He didn't use that tone with her very often. He must've figured that events in her world were nearing something of a crisis and she needed a firm hand, and she gave me that defeated look of hers, with the eyebrows up a little. She realized that a job was a job and even if she abhorred the thought of a sailor for a son she abhorred the thought of him begging at back doors even more. Which was how I felt too, despite Tyrone Power and *Terry and the Pirates* and the rest. It hit me all of a sudden. She put her arms around my waist. We'd didn't hug very often in our family, so every time it happened I was surprised at how small Ma was. She barely came up to my armpit.

"That's for emergencies."

She meant there was money in the envelope. But I would've been happy to have given the money back and gone back up to the room and climbed into bed. No, I *did* want to go, that was only Ma's foolishness getting to me. My buddy and I were going to sea!

"Departure is 4:23 p.m.," said Dad.

Ma let go of my waist. Shaw and Roberta were out on the porch again, Shaw making a big show of looking at his watch. Ma put her hand on the small of my back and steered me down the hallway. We stopped at the hat-rack and she took mine down and put it on my head so the brim fell over my eyes. I didn't touch it.

"How's that?" she said. It was a joke of long standing.

"Just fine," I told her.

Then she pushed it up and we went out on the porch.

Roberta looked Ma over. "Where's your coat?" she said.

"We won't be going." Dad was buttoning his vest. "We'll see you off here."

Ma stood next to him and Dad put his arm around her. She stared at Shaw without blinking.

"Tickets?" Dad said.

I stood up straight, thumped my chest. They were in the inside pocket of the shiny new coat.

"Wooden nickels?" he said.

"Got em," I said.

"Marbles?"

"Don't got em."

"Just fine," he said.

Then he put out his hand and we shook.

"Anthony Adverse," he said.

Ma hugged me again. Dad shook hands with Shaw. We all said polite things but I was ready for that part to be over. I went down the steps behind Shaw and Roberta, who was pulling on her driving gloves for the three-minute trip to the station. I climbed into the back and put the suitcase on the seat next to me. Roberta started the engine. Ma was on the porch at the top of the steps.

"Don't forget to eat!" she called.

I waved to her. I had been out with Roberta and Shaw in the Packard before, just the three of us, but never with all of us bundled up in hats and coats. That made it strange. It wasn't summer any more, it was something brand new. We backed onto the street and turned down the hill towards the CP station, and after a couple of blocks who should we see standing on the corner of Connaught Street and Price but old Bob Fitzgerald and his brother Wilf, shivering away in their shirt sleeves, holding a piece of cardboard over their heads that said GOOD LUCK SEAMAN WINSLOW! The green paint was still running down off the letters so they must have done it up about a minute before. I could see their mother in the house behind them, glaring out the front window.

I kneeled up on the seat and waved my hat as we went by.

"Abyssinia!" I yelled.

"Abyssinia!" they hollered back.

And Wilf dropped his end of the sign and hopped up and down with his hands in the air. He was fourteen years old and must have thought that sailing away to China sounded like the greatest thing in the world. Hell, I thought so too, and I was eighteen.

We bumped over the tracks and turned right on Railway Avenue toward the station. Starboard. I pointed with my right hand. The train whistled somewhere behind us, coming in from Okanagan Landing. Roberta drove the front wheel over the curb.

"Hurry it up," she said.

I jumped out and turned around to get the suitcase but it got jammed behind the seat and when I finally got it loose Roberta and Shaw were in a pretty tight clinch. As far as I knew nothing had ever gone on between them and maybe now they felt bad about that. He had the 1926 Phillips slung over his back and two suitcases still in the trunk, one of them stuffed with twenty pounds of Fats Waller records. She let him go and grabbed onto me. She was wiry as an electric eel.

"Don't you bring any China dolls back here," she said in my ear. "I'll kick you both in the pants."

"You don't scare me," I said.

Shaw had gone up the steps and was turned around looking at us. Roberta spun around and jumped back into the car, wiping her nose with the back of her driving glove. She put the Packard in gear, dropped off the curb and roared away down the street like there was a three-handed cribbage game at home that she could not stay away from. I went up the wooden steps. A gang of women with scarves on their heads watched us over their shoulders. I wanted to tell them so long, that I was going away and they might not see me for a while, and I realized that one of them was even blonde Mrs. Belaney, the best-looking teacher at our primary school, but the train was pulling into the station and Shaw had already gone ahead. Instead I just nodded to them and felt for the tickets in that inside pocket. Old Harry Winslow won't be around anymore, I wanted to yell out. Look all you want but you won't find him.

At 6:15 that evening the train came to the end of the line at Sicamous. Shaw and I didn't need to go to the baggage car so we just hopped out onto the platform and asked the first conductor when the train to Vancouver would be by, we were ready to go, boy, and the conductor said that it wouldn't be by for an hour. A couple of women bundled their kids indoors and then we were the only guys out there. They'd built a nice hotel right on top of the station, the whole thing looked out on Shuswap Lake. Dad and Ma had come up once for their anniversary because the hotel served "lovely meals," but I'd never been before. It would've been nice to go inside and have a look around but right then I was concentrating on the next thing, on what was coming. I might be missing out on the right-then but at least I'd be ready for the next, that was how I looked at it. We stood under the electric bulbs out there in the cold.

There are all these movies where the hero meets a pretty girl who's travelling all alone on the train and she's nervous so he takes her under his wing and by the end of the trip they fall in love, I'd seen that a hundred times and imagined how the pretty girl would feel snuggled up tight against my ribs, her head on my shoulder, the two of us getting drowsy as the train rattles along. But there weren't any girls waiting for that train.

"Smell that," said Shaw.

"Smell what?" I said. Of course I was sniffing as I said it, the cold air tingling my nostrils. I had my scarf tight around my neck.

He slid the Phillips off his shoulder, down to the boards.

"In the trees there."

I saw an orange light flickering under the trees opposite, and shapes moving around in the dark. It was a hell of a spot for a hobo jungle — right next to the train tracks, sure, but with that cold, cold wind off the lake. What exactly could they be thinking? You can't judge them until you're in their shoes, that's what Ma would've said.

It was like I missed her, the way I kept thinking of stuff like that.

"They won't hop the train here," Shaw said. "They'll wait for it to roll a bit. Just at a crawl, then you hop on. If you get in a car before it's moving you never know if a bull's going to climb in for a look, in some of these places they wait as long as they can. It's probably some old guy who has to hustle over from his dinner table. They wouldn't pay a full-time detective in a town this size. Soon as those wheels turn he'll head home again. Back to bed."

He spat, bright white under the lights until it disappeared out in the dark. I heard it land out there.

"You ever ride the rails?" I said.

"Edmonton to here." He opened one of his cases, checked that the towels were still wrapped around his records. I saw the pink corner of that Waller set with the five records in it. "The bulls don't even look for you any more after Rocky Mountain House, this time of year anyway. *They* know that *you* know that you'll freeze the hell to death if you go up in the mountains at night. That's instant death, buddy. Ming's ray of instant death."

"That wasn't instant death," I said. "It sucked nitron out of the atmosphere."

"I ended up in a freight car with a horse in it, he was lying down, that's how I lived through that. But I couldn't feel my feet afterward. I tried shoving my boots under him but he didn't like that."

"Why don't we listen to some of those records?" I said.

He dropped the lid and latched the case.

"The cold's no good for them."

"Let's go in."

"Too late for that now. Going into the hot'll just warp them. And bringing them back out's even worse, turn em brittle, don't you know anything about records?"

"Can you take them out to sea anyway?"

"You can take them out to sea."

"You said you walked over the mountains. You told me that when we were unloading celery and we dropped that crate, you remember? It was that first morning. You've got to remember that."

"I didn't walk the whole way," he said. "Not the whole way."

"What do you know," I said.

Right then seemed like a hell of a time for him to be saying that things weren't exactly as he'd made them out to be. It occurred to me that it was only fifty miles back to Vernon and I could live at home for the winter and get work running logs down off of Tillicum because I knew the guy who had the horse teams. If you looked at the globe in the geography room it would only take one little dot to cover up Vernon and Sicamous both, I was still at home, virtually, whereas we were about to sail off who knows where and spin that globe in all directions. Maybe he was telling me that one thing as a hint of other things to come, before it was once-and-for-all too late to turn around. But that's how a little kid thinks, 'Gotta get home before dark, gee, fellas, I don't think we ought to,' looking for the first sign of trouble so he can run back to Ma. But what does a man do? He rolls with the punches, that's what.

"I need a smoke," I said.

Shaw was down on one knee, checking the straps on the Phillips.

"Get me a pack, will you?" he said.

"Not Sweet Caps."

"Best believe it."

I set my suitcase down beside him. I didn't bother asking him to watch it, because who else was around? I pulled the old brass handle and went into the station. Five guys in hats sat there smoking on the benches, one knee folded over the other, and all with cases the size of bathtubs up on the benches next to them. Salesmen. Brushes and shoes and missionary funds. I went over to the counter and asked the guy for a pack of Consuls and, when he'd already turned around to the rack, for some Sweet Caps too.

"Oh, sure." He wore a wool sweater with a hole in the elbow. "There you go." He winked and dropped them on the counter. I gave him the thirty cents and stuffed the Sweet Caps in my pocket. Those guys were all watching me out of the corners of their eyes. I made such a big show of ripping the top off those Consuls that some cardboard landed on the floor, then as I went back out the door I could hear them giggling and thrashing their newspapers around behind me. Shaw was brushing something off the sleeve of his coat and wearing a grin that went from there to Timbuktu.

"You get the Sweet Caps all right?" he said.

They came in a white pack with red letters and a sun rising, there weren't any flowers or frolicking lambs on the pack and they tasted the same as anything else, but there was a common conception that Sweet Caps were only for women. Shaw always smoked them because he liked to ask for a pack in the drugstore and then hand the guy a line like, 'My old lady, first she wants one thing, and once we're done she wants another,' winking from under the brim of his hat. The other reason he smoked them was that he liked to send me in to buy them, because he knew that I couldn't do all of that stuff with the finger-snapping and winking, I'd tried it and knocked over a whole display of nylon toothbrushes, so every time I'd end up stuffing them in my pocket and hustling out so the counter guy must've figured I was a girl of the first order. I mean, if a guy could buy a pack of Sweet Caps and look slick about it then he was slick, period. That was as good a test of being slick as you'd ever find.

I finished my first smoke and threw the filter out on the tracks, then turned my collar up over my ears and pulled my gloves on and stuck my hands in my armpits. Jesus, there was a wind off that lake! Shaw walked up and down the platform like a tin soldier, taking big steps. It was strange that it was the end of November and there still wasn't snow on the ground, because I had it in my head that the first snowfall was always supposed to be on November 16th. When there's no snow to insulate everything the world's just barren. I kept wiping the sides of my mouth with my cuff because I figured if I had any saliva out there it would freeze solid.

"This must be like the prairies," I said. "This cold."

He stopped walking and just gave me this strange look from under his eyebrow.

"It's about the only thing the same."

Then a guy walked into the light out of the woods and stood there blinking at us. He wore an old overcoat and had another one draped over his head, and his eyes looked like they were bugging out because his face was so black and filthy. He picked up my cigarette butt and nodded to us and went back into the trees, the branches snapping behind him.

"The only difference between us and him is he can't find work," said Shaw.

"Got to get a half a buck somewhere," I said. "Shine my shoes and slick my hair."

"Got to get myself a boutonniere." Shaw lit one of his goddamn Sweet Caps and put the matches back in his pocket. "Lulu's back in town."

A porter came up the platform pushing a hand-truck in front of him. He wore a ratty old suit, a pair of little spectacles, a scarf wrapped up to his nose and a cap with a brass plaque that said "Canadian Pacific."

"Said you were out here." He stopped next to our luggage, put his fist on his hip and leaned against the hand-truck. "You're going right down to Vancouver? Some of this rig'll have to go in the bag car."

Shaw tapped his suitcase full of records with his toe.

"These can't go in the warm," he said. "They'll warp."

The porter already had the Phillips on the truck. "Don't even worry, bag room's colder than Christ. What about these, you need these for sleeping? All right." He gave two stubs of paper to Shaw. "Claim tickets. You can smoke inside as well as out, you know." Then he pointed his head at the woods. "And watch out for those hunkie sons-of-bitches."

He left the two suitcases on the boards and rolled the hand-truck around the corner. Shaw folded his arms and looked down the platform after his record player. He walked in a circle and I lit another Consul. When it was done I threw it out on the tracks for our friend, but he didn't come out. I wanted the in-between stages to be over, I wanted to get on the boat and take my medicine and be done with it.

"I wish he hadn't taken that Phillips," said Shaw.

The train came in, brakes squealing. There was a big light on the front of the locomotive and under the light it said 5911. After that two dining cars went by, windows steamed up, but I could see silhouettes of the people inside. I thought of the girl who might be travelling by herself. All day I'd been expecting to see signs that my leaving for the coast was a good idea, like the world was a big clock and I was a little second hand doing just what I was supposed to, but as far as I could tell the number 5911 didn't signify anything. I was born May 22, 1920, and this was November 25, 1938. Maybe one of my grandparents had been born in November 1859, that would've been 59 - 11, but when *had* they been born? I'd never bothered to find out. We'd been in car number 40 from Vernon to Sicamous but I didn't see how that could mean anything either.

"This one's ours," said Shaw. "Let's go."

Our car was called *Sudbury*. I hadn't expected them all to have names. A CPR train was brand new to me, every nut and rivet — not to mention a Negro porter! He stood at the top of the steps in a white jacket, waving his hand so that everybody would come in and go down the aisle. He nodded to each of us but he had this grimace on his face like he figured we were about to bad-mouth him. Hell, I was in love with Fats Waller, I didn't have anything against the Negroes! The seats were red and yellow leather with wooden armrests, arranged in pairs, one facing the other, down either side of the car. We were seats 23 and 24 but a couple of salesmen were in them already with their feet up on their cases. Across the aisle was a blonde girl in a blue jacket, twisting some hair around her finger and gazing out at the platform, not paying attention to anybody.

"This is us," said Shaw.

"We're here," said the first salesman. "We like the view."

The other salesman put his hat over his eyes and pretended to go to sleep.

"These are the ones we paid for," said Shaw. "Go get in your own."

"Drop dead."

"Excuse me," said Shaw. "But my buddy and I are in a line of work where it doesn't much matter if we've got two black eyes."

"Easy." The one who'd been sleeping pushed his hat up on his head and got to his feet. "Take it easy."

The first one straightened up too, but they weren't standing up to us, not by any means, just collecting their tickets and matchbooks and checking that they still had their wallets in their inside pockets.

"Let me guess," the first one said. "You must be schoolteachers."

The blonde took a notebook out of her bag. She looked up at the four of us and wrote something down.

"Evening," Shaw said to her.

She kept writing. The salesmen picked up their cases and went down the aisle. They got to the end and went right out the door — they weren't even in that car! We took our coats off and settled in. A lot of hissing and clanking noises came from underneath us. Guys were still pushing hand-trucks across the platform — the Phillips rolled past.

"Excuse me," said Shaw. He leaned out into the aisle. "What you writing?"

"My impressions," the girl said. She didn't even look up. I figured if she were in a movie she'd play the studious older sister.

"Hold on." I picked up my coat and felt through the pockets. "I thought Dad bought tickets for a sleeper. We going to sit up all night?"

"They make up the beds." She pointed with her pencil at the cabinet above her head. "Herman comes around. Have you never been on a train before?"

"Not for the night," I said.

"I never paid money to sleep on one," said Shaw. "That's all I'll say."

He sat back and spun his hat between his hands.

"Did you work for the railroad?" She scrunched her nose up every time she asked a question.

"Not that either."

I guess she didn't think much of our answers because she went back to her notebook. Or maybe she thought so much of them she had to write them down. The train still wasn't moving. I looked out our window at the black trees and sure enough there was our man with the overcoat on his head standing beside the tracks, the light from our window across his face. He had a carpet bag in his hand.

"That's pathetic," said Shaw. He rubbed the glass with his sleeve. "There aren't any drags on this. There's no place to ride."

A drag? He'd never talked like that before.

"What are you talking about?" I said.

"A freight car. No drag, no place to ride."

Maybe our man heard that, because he looked back towards the rear of the train then spun around and ran straight back into the bush. A second later that porter we'd talked to ran through the patch of light over the tracks and into the bush, waving a hunk of wood over his head. Then a couple of big guys wearing blue went in after him.

"Jesus Christ!" Shaw jumped to his feet, still peering out at the dark. "Three bulls at one station!"

"Why, what's happened?" asked the girl. She held her pencil in mid-air.

We started to move, *chuka, chuka, chuka*, and if it wasn't for that hissing and the light fixtures rattling I'd have believed that the platform was moving behind her while we stayed still. Shaw sat down again.

"My, my, my," he said.

"Yas, yas, yas," I said, because that's what Waller says at the beginning of "Lulu's Back In Town."

"If you ever in your lives read an article that mentions two strange boys who got on at Sicamous," she said, "you'll know who it's about."

"I wish they'd let me carry the Phillips on," said Shaw.

She twisted some of her hair again, then let it drop.

"Would you really have fought those two men? They looked a lot bigger than you."

"All for your sake," said Shaw. He kicked his feet out into the aisle and the rest of him landed out there with them, it looked funny as hell. He held out his hand to shake. "I'm Eric and this is Harry."

"Hullo," I said.

"Lorraine Brindley," she said. "Is it true you're schoolteachers?"

"Tree surgeons." He dropped back into his seat. "Those trees don't care if you've got two heads or a game knee, trees are just glad for the help."

"Are you from this area?"

"Old Harry is."

She looked right at me but all I could do was nod. He'd spoken the truth.

"I'm from out in Manitoba myself," he said.

"Winnipeg? I was out there not long ago."

Most everybody around us had blankets pulled up to their chins and their eyes shut, but it couldn't have been too easy to fall asleep sitting up with all the lights on and a bunch of jokers gabbing away. A skinny lady with freckles gave me a very dirty look. She had bags under her eyes like hockey pucks. By then the train had a good rhythm going, *cha-chuka, cha-chuka, cha-chuka, cha-chuka*, and in my head I started to hear it as *you want it - you got it, you want it - you got it.*

"Down south of the Peg," Shaw said. "My folks have got a farm. But I came out west to help the trees. There's more of them out here."

I looked for a sign in our seat numbers. If my birthday was the 22nd then it followed that we were sitting in 23 and 24, right? Sure it did.

"I expected snow in this part of the world," she said. "Wouldn't there usually be snow?"

"Ask the expert," said Shaw.

"Sure," I said. "There ought to be heaps by now. Course, that's a sign right there, no blizzard today."

"What's this?" asked Shaw.

"Well, the tracks could have been snowed under, could've kept us in Vernon. That's a sign right there."

They both looked at me for a minute. Lorraine started to write something down but then she lifted up her pencil and closed her book. Shaw winked at me.

"Oh!" Lorraine looked up the aisle. "Here's Herman."

Herman was that Negro porter. He was pushing a cart piled with white linen.

"Miss Brindley, I know you like to go to bed early," he said. "I'll turn it down now if you like."

"I'd adore it if you would," she said. She took a long stretch, holding that notebook over her head. "Could you do my friends' as well? That way we can all go for a drink. This is Eric and Henry."

"Harry," I said.

"Evening, Harry," said Herman.

Lorraine stepped into the aisle and Herman pulled a latch above his head so her bunk dropped down to eye level. Shaw collected his coat.

"Say, Herman," I said. "Are you familiar with a recording artist named Thomas 'Fats' Waller?"

He took a pillow slip from the cart and held it under his armpit while he reached for the pillow.

"Come on, Harry." Shaw had his hat on.

"I know I know that name from somewhere," Herman said. "Who is it?"

"He's a piano player from Harlem," I said. "I heard he was something like the Mayor of Harlem."

Herman shrugged and threw the pillow on the bunk.

"I've never been east of Montreal," he said. "I'll see you boys in a minute."

Shaw and Lorraine rolled their eyes, then we trudged up the aisle. I didn't think it was as stupid a question as all that — if Harry Winslow of Vernon BC had heard of him, why shouldn't Herman of the CPR? I liked that; it sounded like a movie serial. He'd turn down beds and solve crimes.

"Fats must ride on trains," I said. "He could've met him that way."

We walked through three more cars, *Windermere*, *Albion* and *Kathleen*. In the lounge a lot of people sat on loveseats smoking cigarettes while a waiter brought drinks around. It was very impressive.

"Do you expect every Negro to be on intimate terms with every other one?" Lorraine asked. "Like they were in some sort of club?" She sat down and crossed her legs. "What if he'd asked what you thought of Bela Bartok?"

"I'd have said she's very talented."

"Scotch and soda," she told the waiter. She took her jacket off and underneath she was skinny as a rail. "Make it three. Why don't you two get comfortable?"

That was the first night I ever got good and drunk, and you've probably heard all the gory details before. Lorraine was pretty chummy with that waiter so he never asked Shaw and me how old we were. She was coming out from Toronto to write a travel article for a magazine or a newspaper back east, maybe it was both, so we provided her with our life stories up to that moment. We thought it would help her article.

"I must say I'm relieved you're not tree surgeons."

After she paid for the first couple of rounds Shaw suggested that we pony up too and reminded me of the envelope from Ma. I hadn't exactly forgotten about it, of course, but I knew I shouldn't be dipping in on the very first night. I was supposed to be saving it for an emergency. What emergency I didn't know, but what constitutes an emergency is when a guy doesn't know it's coming. I explained all this to Shaw and he just rattled his ice cubes. *Cha-chuka, cha-chuka, cha-chuka, cha-chuka.* Once I had a third drink in me, though, it became an emergency to get another.

"To the landlubbers," said Lorraine. We clinked glasses. The waiter had gone to have a cigarette so he'd left the seltzer and scotch on the table. There was no more ice. I wasn't too sure about Lorraine, whether she was my type or not, whatever they mean by that. She was a girl, wasn't she? And whenever she looked at old Shaw I wanted her to be looking at me. I imagined what sort of underwear she might have on. She said we needed to celebrate our last night of freedom before we signed our ship's articles. She seemed to know an awful lot more about it than we did.

"Eric." She put her hand on his knee. "Once you've set down your name, there will be no turning back. No more of your wandering ways. Think of Manitoba. Tell me. When will you see your mother again?"

Old Shaw sat on that loveseat with his arms against his sides and didn't say one word. I knew better than to mention his mother to him — that was guaranteed to bring the evening to a grinding halt. Lorraine took out her notebook and started playing naughts and crosses with herself. Herman of the CPR came in and stood over us. He folded his arms. His jacket looked very white in the lamplight. *Cha-chuka, cha-chuka, cha-chuka, cha-chuka.* Sometimes I forgot we were on a train, then all of a sudden I'd remember.

"There you all are," he said. "It's late."

"The elms are my favourite," said Shaw. "The way they smile when I bring out the saw."

We followed Herman back to our car. I focused on the white of his jacket. The seats in the passenger cars had all disappeared, there were just black curtains down either side of the aisles, and even over the *cha-chuka, cha-chuka* you could hear fat guys snoring. Herman didn't say anything, he just kept waving us on. I figured he couldn't get in bed himself until we were tucked in. Good old Herman. I thought maybe we could get into the baggage car and play some Fats for him after all.

I knew we'd come to our beds because they were the only ones empty and with the curtains still hooked open. Turned from seats into beds, just like that! I figured I'd turn into a seaman just as easily, slide, push, lock, one thing into another. It was a good sign how those bunks had once been seats.

Lorraine fell onto her bunk and Herman closed the curtains behind her. But then her foot slid out through the gap and her shoe dropped off into the aisle. We stood there gawking. She wore brown stockings. She pulled her foot back in.

"Get in bed!" Herman whispered at us.

"You want top or bottom?"

"Don't matter," said Shaw.

"I'll give you a leg up," said Herman. I put my foot in his hands and the next thing I knew I was lying in bed with the aisle about a mile below me. "I'll put your shoes down here on the floor," he said. "You look for them there."

"I don't want to."

"In the morning," he said.

His hands came up and closed the curtains and that made it dark, and I had a little room all to myself. I pulled my trousers and jacket off and only knocked my head against the wall three times.

I woke up. The train was going around a curve and everything swayed in that top bunk. Up in the crow's nest. The curtains had slid open an inch so a band of light lay across my blanket, and it crossed my mind that if mine had then maybe Lorraine's had as well. I remembered how her foot had looked coming out of that shoe. It hadn't looked like much, really, but a foot's attached to a leg and so on and so on. I rolled onto my knees with the back of my head pressed against the ceiling, and I peered out through the gap. Shaw was standing in the aisle, looking at me.

"What are you doing?" he whispered.

I couldn't think of what to say.

"I brought your coat," he said. "You left it there."

He put my overcoat through the gap. I laid it on my other things.

"Go to sleep."

"All right," I said.

I put my head back on the pillow.

I woke up on my side. *Cha-chuka, cha-chuka, cha-chuka.* I was in my little cocoon, and my head hurt. The curtains swayed. I pulled my knees up to my chest. There was an ashtray in the wall above my head.

The curtains slid open and it was very bright. Shaw stood there in his hat and coat. He put some stubs of paper in my hand. His hand was hot.

"I'm not going to pack them any farther," he said.

I figured he meant the stubs of paper.

"We're almost at Hope." He took off his hat, looked at it in his hands, then put it back on. "You'll be a hell of a sailor," he said. "Hell of a sailor. Look at you."

I couldn't keep my eyes open. The light fixture was so bright yellow — didn't they ever shut off the current? He pulled the curtain across again.

"Anyway," he whispered. "So long."

"G'night," I said.

A while after that I heard the brakes squealing and old 5911 slowing down, *cha-chuka, cha-chuka. Chu.* I rolled on my back. That was a good time to sleep.

"Rise and shine." I could hear Herman moving past. "Ten past six. Breakfast in the dining car. Rise and shine."

The sound of the train was so steady I almost confused it with being asleep, like the kind of dream that sits in your brain after you've woken up, so as I woke I expected the sound of the wheels to fade away too.

My mouth was very dry. I felt a weight on my chest like I'd been strapped down. Not exactly nausea, but close.

"What's for breakfast?" somebody asked.

"Beefsteak and eggs. Broiled beefsteak. De-licious."

Lorraine groaned from across the aisle.

"Here's your shoes," Herman said. He was right beside my head. "Don't forget I told you."

"All right," I said.

He must've gone because after that all I could hear was the other passengers yawning and their curtains sliding open, the rings riding down the rails. The consensus among the ladies and gentlemen was that it was too cold to be out of their beds. But when isn't it? If it wasn't cold out of bed it would be too hot in bed, and that wouldn't be comfortable.

"Will I see the two of you at breakfast?" Now it was Lorraine talking right next to my head. "I'm going for a wash."

"I'm getting up," I said.

Shaw didn't say anything.

"I'll see the one of you at any rate," she said.

There was a lot of coughing and nose-blowing elsewhere in the car. I sat up and untangled my clothes from the blankets. My suit looked like a yak had been wearing it. I wrestled my trousers on and got the curtain open and managed to find the little ladder at the foot of the bed. The rungs were damn cold, I couldn't argue with that. Shaw's curtains were still shut so I peeked in. The sheets were in knots but he wasn't there.

I put my feet into my shoes and walked up the train to the dining car. It was still dark outside. Some guys were smoking up on their top bunks, their feet dangling out of their pyjama legs. Maybe on the boat it would be like that, maybe we'd have curtains on our beds and we'd sit around smoking. Would they smoke Consuls or something else? Shaw would know. I'd ask him. I almost asked the other passengers for a glass of water as I walked along, I was that thirsty.

"There you are." Lorraine was drinking coffee at a little table. She was dressed in green and her hair was in a bun. I put my overcoat over the back of a chair.

"You can ask Herman to press your jacket," she said.

A waiter brought me a cup. Some parents told their little boy to at least eat something. Everyone moved quickly and laughed too loud.

"No sign of him?" Lorraine asked.

"He'll be in the bathroom," I said. "He's a great one for the bathroom. Spent half his life there the last job we had."

"So today's the day. Your port of call. You must be nervous."

"We'll fumble through."

I finally quit blowing on the coffee and took a sip. She looked out the window and tapped her book with her pencil.

"I should make this trip in summer," she said. "There'd be more daylight."

"Excuse me, sir. Is it Winslow?"

A conductor stood behind me, his clipboard next to my ear.

"Shoot," I said.

"I thought I'd better let you know," he said. "The poop is that your friend from 24 is not eligible for any refund for the untravelled portion of his ticket. If he'd wanted that your friend should have contacted a ticket agent 48 hours beforehand."

"Oh," I said. "Sure." There are enough guys named Winslow in the world, who knows which one he figured he had. "And who exactly's my friend?"

The conductor moved his finger down the page.

"Eric Shaw."

Well, that didn't sound right.

"What's happened?" said Lorraine.

"You know this fella, Eric Shaw?" asked the conductor.

"Of course we know him!" She flipped through her notebook, God knows why. "What's happened to him?"

"He's just in the bathroom," I said.

"No, sir, he is not. He disembarked at Hope. We put out the mail and when we were set to go he said he was staying. That's the real poop, I was the one that asked him. I'd assumed that you knew all about it."

Lorraine stopped flipping, she looked up at him. Then she flipped one page more.

"He's still in Hope right now?" I said.

"I'd assume so." He tapped the clipboard against his leg. "Next train going east from there's not until ten o'clock."

"And he won't get a refund," I said.

"That's right."

He turned around and muttered something to a waiter, and the waiter looked back at him and whistled. Then the conductor walked out of the car. Everybody watched us as they stirred their coffee.

"The lousy." Lorraine put her elbows on the table. "He jumped off the train!"

"Not likely."

"Where does that leave you? This is nearly Vancouver now."

The sky was turning yellow. I could see mountains away on the horizon and the peaked roofs of houses going by. I still had Ma's money to buy a ticket back. I figured this would qualify as an emergency. When we got off the train I wouldn't even know what boat to look for.

"It'd be an interesting story," she said, "if only it hadn't left you in the lurch. A boy and his mother. Huh."

I got up and put my coat back on. I still figured the whole thing was a mistake — that conductor was just confused as to which guy he'd talked to. But I had talked to Shaw, hadn't I, and he'd certainly looked like he'd been going somewhere. Son of a bitch, I wanted to say. Son of a bitch, I was the only one, out of all the dandies on that train, who was on his way to turn seaman. If I could find my boat. And if I couldn't, what were my options then? Walk around Vancouver with a bunch of hobos, fight over which of us wears the overcoat on his head. And I knew that in Vancouver a guy couldn't earn a bite to eat by chopping wood because they all used sawdust or coal furnaces. Now I did have the nausea. Now it was exactly like nausea.

When I was halfway through *Albion* I took the envelope out of my inside pocket. The porters were turning all the beds back into seats and everybody was standing around the aisle so I accidentally elbowed a guy in the side as he was lighting his pipe. The envelope didn't feel very heavy. There was a slip of paper inside that said "Much love," in Ma's printing, but that was all. The money was gone. I took that as something of a bad sign.

"You'd better clear out of here," said the pipe lighter.

Numbers 23 and 24 in old *Sudbury* were already turned back into seats, and somebody had left my hat on 24 with two stubs of paper tucked in the band. Of course — Shaw had handed me those. My suitcase was on the floor under the window. Only mine. I sat down in his seat. I knew by then that the conductor had been on the level and that there was no point in looking over my shoulder to see if he was coming up the aisle. But I did anyway. At the end of the car the porters were still working on a bunk that wouldn't go back into the wall.

Then I had a look at those stubs of paper: *CP Railways*, they said, *Luggage Claim*, numbers 11701 and 11702, the Fats Waller records and the Phillips player. That was something anyway. I put my feet up on my suitcase and lit a cigarette.

We went under a bridge and I saw the campfires from the guys living under it. I sucked on that cigarette and pretended it didn't matter, we were just passing through another town and my own destination was still a long way down the line, some place with blue sky and leafy trees where I knew everybody. Where I had a lot of friends. The train carried on, *cha-chuka, cha-chuka*, but I knew that it would slow down in a minute and when it did the nausea would come back. The lights in all the fixtures went off, but outside it was daylight now. A lady up the aisle had a book on her knee, *The Diary of a Country Priest* by George Bernanos, with a picture of a steeple. The train started to slow down. I took a deep breath.

Chuka. Clunk. *Chuka*. Something tried to come up my throat so I waved my cigarette around in front of my face and concentrated on that, I watched the heat eat up the paper little by little. Being a seaman, how terrible could that be? A million guys made their living that way. Might get wet. Might get yelled at. That wouldn't be so bad. But while that happened I wouldn't want to feel that I was all alone, that was the thing. I would want to feel that I was friends with one person.

Lorraine came up the aisle and gave a forced little smile. She lifted her suitcase onto her seat and took out a tiny pair of gloves. I tried to think of something really snappy to say to her.

"So where am I supposed to go?" I asked.

She pulled on the gloves and looked down at me. She folded her arms.

"Go to the ship. You're not an idiot."

"Sure, but what ship? There's got to be a million. I'm not going to walk —"

Everything went black. We were in a tunnel or somewhere, and the train had slowed down to just about nothing. It was like we were in a broom closet. A lot of people felt their way past us, bumping their cases against the armrests.

"Didn't he say it was the *Harbour Lion*?" asked Lorraine. "He must have said it fifty times."

"Really? The *Harbour Lion*? That doesn't sound right."

"What did you think it was?"

That was a lesson against the dangers of drink if I've ever had one. I threw down the end of my cigarette and watched it glow there on the floor. Yellow light flooded in the windows as we pulled up to a platform. Lorraine had already picked up her suitcase.

"I have to send a telegram," she said. "Lots of luck."

She shuffled up the aisle. A lot of people followed her. I waited for them all to get off, then I stared out the window at the porters stacking trunks, hatboxes and canvas sacks on the platform, and the passengers handing over their claim stubs and the station porters loading their carts up and rolling them away. The station porters were all Oriental and most of them looked pretty old. I sat there with my hat in my lap and watched them skitter away. I didn't know if they were all Japanese or Chinese or which, some people said that their eyes slanted different directions but I didn't hold with that. I knew that old Ted Yakamura was Japanese because he told us he was, not because we measured his head or anything. What would he be doing right then? He'd be at home eating pancakes. The porters hollered back and forth at each other and it sounded a lot like Ted's house, so maybe they were Japanese after all.

All of a sudden it came to me that Shaw had my money. Not just that I didn't have it any more, that had sunk in, but that he'd reached into that pocket and taken it. I realized he wasn't the guy I thought I'd known. Whatever he was having for breakfast I hoped he choked on it.

But it was strange, handing those claim tickets over and hauling the Phillips up onto my back. It was hard to stay mad at him then. He'd hauled the thing right across the damn country, and now it was mine, I could set it down anywhere and listen to any record I wanted to. I could listen to "Lulu's Back In Town." I picked up the case of records with my free hand and followed after the last of the porters. My arm stretched down from my shoulder; twenty pounds of records is heavier than you'd think.

We rode a freight elevator up to the waiting room where a flock of taxi drivers in black caps was hanging around. The room must have been fifty feet high with paintings of mountains and rivers up by the ceiling, and tucked between the benches were glass cases showing models of steamships. *Empress of Russia*, one of them was called. *Empress of Japan* was another. It was warm in there but everybody had coats on.

"Where you going?"

This was a taxi driver who had no eyebrows to speak of.

"I don't know, where *you* going?"

He walked alongside me. It was better, being off the train. It had been no good sitting there stewing. It was better to stretch my legs and feel like I was going somewhere.

"Where are the boats?" I asked.

"Where you going, down to the States? San Francisco. They're down the way. Twenty cents'll get you there."

"I want this one, the *Harbour Lion*. I've got a job on it."

He stopped walking. He knew I was no customer. Two girls sat on a bench in front of us, one of them putting on lipstick.

"Sounds like a name for a towboat," he said. "Is that right?"

"Could be."

"That could be anywhere. You don't know?"

"No."

The girl dropped the lipstick into her handbag. She was something!

"Huh. Try down off Carrall maybe. Take a left out here, hoof it down to Carrall. You'll see. You don't want a ride, do you?"

I shook my head. "I'm much obliged for the help."

Then I walked out the front door. It wasn't any colder outside but everything smelled of car exhaust. A newsboy stood on the sidewalk next to his stack of papers, but he wasn't hollering "Wuxtry!" like they did in detective stories. I figured maybe he only said it every minute or so, so I waited, looking up at the tall buildings while my arms got longer. He sold somebody a paper. It was the *Vancouver News-Herald* — a Vancouver paper on the very day it was printed!

"Wuxtry," I whispered.

The newsboy just stuffed his hands back in his pockets and looked about as worn out as everybody else, with the exception of that girl with the lipstick. I came up to an intersection, Cambie Street and something else, and on every corner there were guys in caps holding out tin cans. I had no money for them, but maybe that was what everybody told them. If it came to that, where was I going to get my hands on a tin can?

The buildings didn't look much different than in Vernon, there were just a lot more of them and they were taller and looked pressed together, but I knew if I stood there gawking some wiseacre was going to come up and ask if I'd fallen off a turnip truck. Instead I marched in a straight line like I was there on business. Everybody else seemed to swing from side to side as they walked along and seemed to be looking about three guys ahead of them like they were trying to see what was around the next corner. I tried to do it too but it was too much work with the Phillips on my back. All I could do was hunch along like a turtle.

I set the cases down and got out my Consuls and my matches. This was on the corner of Hastings and Carrall — I was right under the street signs so I knew that much. In front of me an old lady sat on a folding chair next to a cart full of chestnuts, they looked roasted but they must've been ice-cold.

"Who's a chestnut?" she said. "Who's a chestnut?"

She looked right at me but I didn't say a word — I wasn't a chestnut, I knew that much. The building across the way said DR. LOWE CANADA'S GREATEST DENTIST, in these tiny letters, like it was a fact that he was the greatest and there was no sense in making a big deal about it. Downstairs from the dentist were signs for Union Cigar and the Baltimore Oyster Saloon. Oysters! I'd never had one.

I could see water ahead of me down Carrall, and sure enough I came to Water Street and had to stop for the traffic under a big maple that had dumped orange leaves all over the sidewalk. Those leaves were a bit like home. I ran across the road when the signal changed, then past a long brick warehouse and out onto the train tracks, eleven lines to hop over, one after another, cinders crunching under my feet, and the Phillips trying to pull me over backwards all the while. I could smell cedar; I must've been downwind from the mills. And right ahead of me the pilings for the docks rose up. A lot of trucks and sedans were parked in front of a warehouse with a wooden sign that said UNION STEAMSHIPS LTD. and a metal sign under it that said AUTHORIZED PERSONNEL ONLY PASSENGERS REPORT TO TICKET OFFICE. Was my ship a Union Steamship?

Two guys hopped out of a truck and stood looking at me. One of them had on blue coveralls and a duffel bag over his shoulder, and the other was wearing striped trousers and a black sweater. The one in the sweater was eating a bacon sandwich. I could smell it a mile off.

"What's this, the one-man band?" he asked.

"Where you headed, pal?" said Coveralls. "If you wanted Powell River it's gone."

Jesus, I could have used a bite of that sandwich!

"I want the *Harbour Lion*," I said. "Name of a boat."

"Not here," said Sweater. The bread mashed around in his mouth. "'Lenore,' 'Skidegate.' We got deluxe names like that."

"So where's the *Harbour Lion*?"

They both shrugged and kind of grimaced and started to walk away, past the sign that said AUTHORIZED PERSONNEL ONLY PASSENGERS REPORT TO TICKET OFFICE. Coveralls changed his grip on the duffel bag.

"Hold up," he said. "*Harbour Lion*, isn't that Hoffman's towboat. Down there by Ballantyne."

"Hoffman sold that." Sweater took another bite then rubbed his eye with his knuckle.

"Who to?"

"Grace. Down at Ballantyne."

"There it is! Lloyd Grace! Sorry, Junior, it's been a long night.

Your boat's down at Ballantyne."

"Not *right* at Ballantyne," said Sweater.

"You walk thataway, ask for Lloyd Grace. Don't say we sent you."

Lloyd Grace, of course, Uncle Lloyd! I liked the sound of that name, Grace. Like kindness. That was a good sign.

I looked right across the inlet to the mountains on the other side. There were ships all over the water, tugs pulling barges, big liners with three and four smokestacks — maybe they were the *Empress of Russia* and *Empress of Japan*. There was even a big navy boat docked down the way, solid grey with big artillery cannons at the front and back like the *Hood* or the *Prince of Wales*. Those boats were always in magazines. The gunboat was tied up to a big long pier with a long white shed, it really was a beautiful set-up so I figured that must be Ballantyne Pier. Nobody was around to tell me otherwise. There was another pier right before it with tugboats tied on either side, so I walked down that ramp, all on my own, no Shaw there to hold my hand. My choice was to eat or not eat, walk down the ramp or don't. I stretched my arms out like a tightrope-walker and the two guys in the bow of the first boat stared at me the same as we used to stare at poor old Benny Wadsworth.

The taller guy in the bow was writing in a notebook. He wore a tweed jacket with grease stains right up to the elbows, and the other one wore a pair of overalls with a yellow sweater underneath. It stank of fish down there, and it also smelled like the mossy ground around a duck pond. I didn't want to talk to the guys who'd been staring but just to be sure I checked the name of the boat, it was painted in yellow right under where they were standing. It was the *Harbour Lion*. Jesus, it was cold down there by the water.

"Mr. Grace?" I said.

The one in the tweed didn't even glance my way, but his buddy in the yellow sweater looked up with his mouth open. He was an ugly one — stumpy little nose and hardly any hair.

"Mr. Grace?" I said again. "I'm Harold Winslow. Here to join the crew."

Mr. Grace finished what he was writing and handed the book to the ugly one. He had a long wrinkled face and a lot of pomade in his hair, and since he was Shaw's uncle that made sense. His eyes were just little slits, and they only got slittier when he looked at me. The dock bobbed underneath me. Where were all the fish I could smell? I started thinking it was the ugly one that smelled like that. Uncle Lloyd — if it was Uncle Lloyd — took a pipe out of his pocket and stuck it in the side of his mouth. He didn't have any teeth just there.

"Where the Christ's Eric?" he asked.

I finally set down the case of records. Fats was with me if no one else.

"Mr. Grace, I tell you what," I said. "That's what I'd like to know."

So I went away to sea. But the farthest we ever got was Port Hardy. We'd putter across to these two-bit towns, tie up to a log boom and spend a couple of days towing it back to Van. But it was never a "log boom," Grace told me it was a "Davis raft." It took me a while to learn the ropes, with actual ropes, too, and considering I was green as a bean I didn't do all that badly. The pug-nose crewman was named Overend, and the first time it got stormy he gave me an old rain slicker of his that someone had written "Rube" on in red crayon, so he wouldn't wear it anymore. The first bad water we hit I vomited three times.

"My people are from the interior," I told Grace. "I think maybe my physiology's unfit for the sea."

He took his pipe out of his mouth and hollered at me until the embers fell down his sleeve, and he made me darn his shirt afterwards, too. He was a pretty good teacher, though; the tweed brought it out in him.

"He's a royal son of a bitch," I'd say to Overend, but of course Overend never said anything back. He just sat next to the engine or lay on his bunk and hardly said a word. He *looked* like a monkey but other than that he wasn't anything like one, because a monkey at least would've climbed around on the pipes or thrown bananas or something. If I was lucky he'd pick his nose and wipe it on the wall above his head, or if I was really lucky he'd repeat whatever gems of knowledge he'd picked up in the July 1933 *Reader's Digest* that he kept under his pillow.

"The art of being a bore," he'd say, "is to tell everything."

One Friday afternoon we towed a hulk across from Nanaimo and I told Overend that when we got back we'd go up to the White Lunch for roast chicken sandwiches. We could cook on-board but all we ever had was oatmeal or beans or tinned stew, or all three together if we felt flush, so I'd try to get up to the White Lunch every week or so. We were going up the ramp in our good clothes when Grace took me by the elbow and said that if I was going to backsplice a rope so that it was such a god-forsaken lump it wouldn't even slide through the block then I might as well not do it at all. The trick, I learned, is to weed out half the strands.

"Get your knife and come back in here," he said.

So that meant no White Lunch for Overend either; without me as a chaperone he'd head straight to one of the bars off of Carrall or around the Seaman's Manning Pool up on Dunsmuir, though it wasn't likely he'd make it that far. I'd go to those places with him if Grace told him to take me along, though all the other seamen ever did was throw back the gin and bang their hands on the table and ask Overend about his girlfriend — meaning yours truly — and listen to hokey songs on the bartender's old Edison turntable, *the memory of love's re-fraiiin!* They never once sang "Blow the Man Down" like I'd figured they would, and the gin never sat well with me. On the first night we went out Overend said, "If anybody hands you a pipe you hand it straight back," meaning opium, I figured. Like in *Terry and the Pirates*. Once I went into the Gents and found Overend staring at himself in the mirror, not even blinking, while some old seaman with two fingers on each hand tried to take a leak in the sink. Most of the other guys worked tugs and freighters out of Van but some were from Norway or New Zealand or places like that. I never once heard Overend telling *them* the art of being a bore, in fact he said even less than he did on-board. A gallon of gin couldn't warm him up, until a certain point in the night when he'd accuse some guy of being a patsy, and whether that meant he was a thief or a stoolie or a queer I was never sure. As far as he was concerned there was probably no distinction. But more than once I got knocked on the side of the head from trying to pry these guys' fingers off Overend's throat, he always picked the biggest guy, and then I'd pick myself up from under the bar,

watching Overend's boot trying to kick the guy in the knee, and I'd hear
a bottle break and I'd crawl out and who would it be but Captain Grace.
Even the guys from Portugal seemed to know him, they'd put Overend
back down on his feet and Grace would say something real quiet and set
his bottleneck down on the bar, and then the three of us would walk out
of there. Who knows how Grace ever found us, but I figured he must've
known that Overend was an odd sort of Cinderella who had to get
himself killed come midnight. Once we got in sight of the boat I'd start
teasing old Grace, telling him he was like Cap'n Easy from the comics,
the way he always rescued Overend, and that Overend was like pudgy
old Wash Tubbs. I'd sing them a song to the tune of "I Got Rhythm"
only I'd change it to "Cap-tain Gracey," until one morning Grace took
me into the wheelhouse and told me that he would put up with certain
things only to a point, and only then because he remembered being
young once himself.

"I would love it if the world were only full of wise old gentlemen,
but I know that can never be the case because for the species to continue
there will always have to be young bucks, and unfortunately that will
always mean a certain percentage of the populace are going to be
morons. I accept that. All the same I'd rather you didn't sing a goddamn
song about me, savvy?"

I might still be working on the *Harbour Lion* to this day if Hitler
hadn't invaded Poland in September of '39. The papers said DOMINION
FIGHTS HUNS FOR SECOND TIME IN 21 YEARS in letters that took
up the whole front page, but the newsboys still wouldn't say "Wuxtry"
even if you begged them.

"I'm going to see if I can't join up," Grace told us. "I'll sell to Island
Tug & Barge if they take me."

He was in our little cabin, with his hands up on the crossbeam so I
could see the rip in the armpit of his jacket. Would I still have to mend
it if the army took him?

"So you two ought to come as well," he said.

The next day a letter came special delivery from Ma, saying that I "should avoid enlisting like the plague." As if my life depended on it, because it did. "There is no cowardice in being your own man, even if that means not fighting," she told me. "All of these lemmings are just afraid to do otherwise. The Fitzgerald boys have signed up."

Grace was leaving for the recruiting office in a double-breasted grey suit we'd never seen before, and came back just about hopping out of his skin — they'd made him an officer. Apparently he'd been in the Great War already, to France and everything, but had failed to ever mention that to us.

The next morning the guy from Island Tug & Barge Ltd. came aboard with all the paperwork, he said they'd be happy to have me and Overend stay on as crewmen except that we wouldn't be allowed to live onboard anymore. I knew the boat pretty well by then — in ten months we'd taken the engine apart three times — so I figured I'd try to get a few laughs out of Island Tug & Barge Ltd.

In parting Grace gave me a good long squint.

"Davis raft," he said.

The Dunsmuir Hotel was cheap and halfway clean so I moved in there. I never found out where Overend was living; I'd see him on the *Harbour Lion* but he didn't say any more than usual. One night he came up to my room with some bottles of beer and said he missed hearing my "minstrel records" — maybe he picked that up in the July 1933 *Readers Digest* too — so we listened to *I'm going to sit right down and write myself a letter, And make believe it came from you*, then he picked up the rest of the beer and went off down the stairs. At seven the next morning our new chief, Captain Draper, told me that a beat cop had found Overend stretched out on Powell Street, and that somebody had used a brick to knock his brains in. And Captain Draper was pretty annoyed about it because he'd been planning to have us oil the gear boxes that day.

So I quit and went to work on the *Skidegate* for Union Steamship. Ma wrote me in December asking if I would come home for Christmas. I didn't get the letter until Christmas Eve because I'd been waiting around Port Hardy for a new engine, hanging around the pier with a lot of spaniel dogs and guys with their shirt lapels out over their jackets, even in that weather. So I missed Christmas at home in 1939. I also missed 1940 because one of *Skidegate*'s cooks told me that Fats Waller would be playing in Seattle on December 22nd, so I begged a ride on the *Princess Charlotte* and jumped onto the dock as she pulled up and ran right across Seattle to the 411 Club because I didn't know how taxis would work there and I ran in with sweat soaked right through the front of my hat even though it was below zero, and who was on the bill at the 411 Club? The Gay Jones Orchestra. When I got back to the *Charlotte* they told me I'd just missed hearing Waller on the radio, live from Chicago.

I telephoned Ma from Vancouver and told her our ship had nearly sunk, there'd been an explosion, and that was why I wouldn't be able to make it home. Another seaman named Ray overheard me saying that, he was on the phone next to mine.

"You can't lie about a ship sinking." He was a tall guy with his eyes set far apart. "There's powers that control these things. They'll think you're wishing for it."

We got to be buddies after that. He liked the Ink Spots a hell of a lot — we'd listen to their song "The Java Jive" and then have to run straight up to the galley to guzzle coffee. It wasn't Waller, granted, but it wasn't that Gay Jones Orchestra big band stuff either.

In the first week I knew him Ray grew a full beard, and I tried to grow one to cover up my pimples but had no luck. One of the mates picked a fight with Ray right after New Year's, so Ray and I both quit. We knew it wouldn't take much to find a new berth because so many guys had gone back east to convoy across the Atlantic, except that we wanted to stay on the Pacific. Japan was only at war with China then, which was no concern of ours, whereas floating anywhere on the Atlantic would mean being in a war.

Sure enough, we went down to the Seaman's Manning Pool the next week and they'd written our names on the blackboard under *E. of Asia*, an Empress boat owned by Canadian Pacific just like the train I'd first come to Vancouver on, so that was a good sign. Mr. Seidensticker at the Manning Pool told us that *E. of Asia* was six hundred feet long — two-thirds the size of *Titanic*, which meant she was pretty damn big —

and that she'd been the last word in opulent luxury twenty years before, when any rich guy who needed a new dressing gown from Yokohama had sailed on her.

"Three funnels," he said. "Eight hundred portholes."

"That is a touch bigger than I'm used to." I was breathing in everybody's cigarette smoke and rocking back on my heels, trying keep a cool head — this boat would take us clear to Japan! "But it does sound like a better job of work than skipping rocks in Port Hardy."

"Oh, she's not much to look at now. Get down to Pier C like they told you." Seidensticker was putting the laces back in his shoes. "You'll get an eyeful."

So before we went for our trunks Ray and I decided to take a look at the biggest thing on the West Coast. She was bleeding rust out of every seam and when the crane landed a skid of flour on her deck she groaned like an old lady with arthritis.

"Like my Aunt Sally," Ray said. "Except they put Aunt Sally in hospital."

A tall guy with a bald head glared down at us from the top of the ladder; he didn't have a sweater on even though it was January.

"You sightseers or what?"

On his arm a tattooed snake swallowed a tattooed anchor.

"Yeah." Ray ran his fingers through his beard. "The Manning Pool sent us down for a look."

"You're the twosome. My name is Mitchell. Petty Officer. And the one thing I won't take is bullshit."

Three hundred Chinese guys were already on board. They all lived in two big rooms down in the steerage, so that all any of them had space for was a hammock and a pot to piss in. We needed three hundred of them because *Asia* still ran on coal like a big locomotive, and the only guys who'd shovel coal at those wages were Chinese. The ship's boilers weren't running so it was cold as a meat locker in steerage.

"That's not fit for human beings."

"They'll survive," said Ray.

Seidensticker had said that before the war there'd been whole families and pretty little girls running around on *Asia*, but from the smell of her that was hard to believe. I looked in a bathroom up in the old first class, though, and sure enough there were plaster cherubs set right up in the corners. But the cabin they'd reserved for Ray and me was two decks below steerage, farther down than even the Chinamen, so all it had for air was a vent in the ceiling.

Ray's mother came to see us on the day we embarked and gave me a kiss on the cheek that was dry as toast. He was put to work on the deck crew, coiling ropes and hawsers and such, while I, one month short of Able Seaman, was put on detail with a bunch of Chinese guys scraping and repainting decks, except for every third week when I had to scrub toilets. The glamour never let up! Worse yet, we couldn't loiter around the tidy Pacific — they told us we were headed for Panama and through to the Atlantic, and I discovered that the worst thing about scrubbing toilets, besides the fact that they're toilets, was the amount of time it gave a guy to fret over the packs of U-boats waiting for him. At least when I was working down on our deck I could leave our cabin door open and play "I Got Rhythm," and that gave me something else to think about: Harlem was on the Atlantic, just waiting for me to stop in.

We got all the way north to Glasgow in Scotland, and how the U-boats missed us, sweetheart, I will never know. Then down to Liverpool for an entire month to put on coal and load up Limey troops. That was Ray's word for everything over there — "There's a Limey with a Limey belt holding up his Limey trousers."

"Be sure to follow the local air raid protocol," Ma wrote. "They will know their business. We have learned from Mrs. F. that the English asked one of our divisions to cut a lot of timber for them (assuming Canadians would be adept!) and that Wilf was badly injured. I urge you to avoid becoming involved if you can possibly help it. Your sister has studied the photo and I am supposed to report that you look 'some salty.'"

During the day we packed sandbags around the bridge and wireless office and at night we went to the Manchester Arms and drank Yates Nut Brown and pretended that packing sandbags around a wireless office was just routine maintenance. It didn't have anything to do with the war.

We carried a lot of Limey soldiers down to Freetown and Durban then up the east coast of Africa, and once we got to Egypt they put ashore in a long line of tin barges. It was hot as blazes. Ray and I stood on deck and saw our own reflections down on the water, and it seemed like we were a mile in the air. We looked across at the town and the desert out beyond it, and nothing looked the least bit familiar even though I'd seen *Suez* with Tyrone Power. Guys wearing turbans came alongside in boats, trying to sell us junky little camels full of sawdust. We called every one of those guys Sinbad — we yelled, "Hey, Sinbad One," "Sinbad Two," and so on.

When we were back in Liverpool I bought a new Waller record, "All That Meat And No Potatoes" b/w "Do You Have To Go?" at Lewis' Department Store and played it in our cabin while the other guys were down at the Manchester Arms, and the air-raid sirens wailed all night so I had to listen with my head stuffed in the horn. That was my highlight of 1941. The next day I went back to Lewis's to see if "I Wanna Hear Swing Songs" b/w "Let's Get Away From It All" had arrived, but Lewis' wasn't there any more because the Krauts had bombed it during the night. All that was left was part of the wall that faced the street. The guy from their music department was in the crowd out front.

"Those records you were after were on the loading dock," he said. "Weren't even out of their boxes."

So I was more annoyed with Hitler than ever. We loaded *Asia* up with Limeys again and went all the way back around to Suez, and if I ever saw a soldier standing having a smoke I'd stop and wish him good luck, and every time I came off watch I'd lay on my bunk thinking about the submarines swimming under us like schools of fish.

But when I found out we'd be docking in New York I quit fretting over those Liverpool records and everything else, and as soon as my twelve hours' leave started I went straight to Harlem. I even took the "A" Train like in the song!

I found a whole block of record stores with guys roller skating out in front of them. The only new Waller record any of them had, though, was "Sad Sap Sucker Am I" — they had "All That Meat And No Potatoes" b/w "Do You Have To Go?" on the counter but of course

I had *that* — and one store let me play "Sad Sap Sucker Am I" two or three times until I had to tell them it was not his best work. One of the clerks agreed with me, he played "The Joint Is Jumpin'" and "I Got Rhythm," the real good stuff, but then the other guy put on a record of this saxophone music that couldn't swing if its life depended on it, and my clerk banged the counter and called it Chinese music, but this other clerk — I'd never heard Negroes arguing before — said it was the new thing and we'd better get used to it. My clerk gave up after that, he started doing a word-find puzzle and eating a bowl of soup, and the other one told me that Waller wasn't even in Harlem that week because he was out on the road.

"With a *big* band, you know. Just like ol' Benny Goodman."

If that wasn't bad enough, a new guy named Bunny came aboard in New York, taking up space in the bunk above Ray's. He looked like Clark Gable except he was even taller.

"Pleased to make your acquaintance," Ray told him. "Our names are both Smith."

The joke there was that the chief officer and captain of *Asia* were both Scotsmen named Smith, so Ray and I had been having a giggle telling guys that we were both Smiths as well. But Bunny didn't know about the real Smiths so he didn't laugh at the joke. He unpacked a stack of letter paper with little zeppelins in the corners.

"I'm sick of New York fog," he said. "I want to catch some sun."

By then Ray and I had been to Suez twice already, so at least in that respect we had a leg up on him.

When we got back to Liverpool all the black-faced Chinese stokers who'd been aboard *Asia* for ten years were told to pack up and go across to these British battleships — that was a military decision — and then the only guys Captain Smith could find to shovel our coal were Irishmen. Ma had Irish in her so I've got nothing but affection for the race at large, but these stokers they brought on were crazier than a box of cats. The captain let them bunk in the cabins so that the troops could take over the hammocks in steerage, but of course there were so many Irishmen they had to sleep in rotation. A guy called Jimmy claimed to be in charge so he had the empty bunk under mine all to himself.

He had a pot-belly and long arms and legs and didn't smell quite right, and he started shouting mumbo-jumbo as soon as he dragged his trunk in.

"And I refuse outright — outright! — to let these bastards drag us east of Bombay. We are politically neutral and refuse therefore to enter into any theatre of war."

Which was more than anyone in our cabin had said in a month. The only war we knew about was in Europe and North Africa, so he must've known something we didn't. Ray said he'd heard that Captain Smith already thought the new stokers were *unruly* — this was as we sailed out of Liverpool with 15,000 nautical miles between us and Bombay.

"He needs his coal shovelled, don't he?" said Jimmy. "Smith can kiss my arsehole and watch it winking!"

On the eighth of December we were off the coast of Africa and the public address system came on just as those of us on night watch sat down to our second mess of bacon and stewed tomatoes.

"This is the captain speaking. We've received the following bulletin." Captain Smith sounded even more Scottish on that particular day. "Yesterday, Japanese aircraft destroyed the American fleet stationed at Pearl Harbor, Honolulu, Hawaii. In light of these events, Great Britain, Canada and the United States have each declared war on Japan effective this morning. As have the following: —"

We all looked at each other. Some guys raised their eyebrows.

"— Costa Rica, the Dominican Republic, Haiti, Honduras, Nicaragua, El Salvador, South Africa, the Free French and the governments-in-exile of the Netherlands, Czechoslovakia, Luxembourg and Yugoslavia."

Somebody dropped their tin cup and it banged across the floor.

"Now I will tell you men that this information will in no way affect our schedule, as I do not expect to meet with enemy forces at this time."

We sailed into Bombay without a hitch, sure enough, then we stewed in the heat there while the boats in our next convoy took on fresh troops and tins of tomatoes. I stood watch the last morning we were there, wiping black dust out of the corners of my eyes and studying the lines of coolies packing coal up skinny little gangplanks, all of them in loincloths like a bunch of Indians. Of course they *were* Indians. And I didn't hold it against them because we stripped to our underwear to hose the decks down every afternoon. The coal dust hung like a thundercloud over that whole end of town. Most times I was excited as we pulled out of a port, but not that day out of Bombay. I had hiccups that I couldn't get rid of and felt like I had a ball of paper stuck in my chest.

My watch ended just as we were pulling out, and I went down to the cabin but the only one there was Jimmy, wearing the purple blazer that he always went ashore in. I started to read my book so he wouldn't bother me, but of course he went on and on about how his favourite thing about Bombay was how far away it was from England.

"Me motherland's a fine place, cepting it's just across from George the Six." He was drunk and he kept winking at me to make sure I was in on the joke, whichever joke that was. "Are you aware your face is checkered like a Eye-talian table cloth?"

It was good of him to remind me that I still had so many pimples. The ship's whistle sounded; we could hear it six decks down, even over the racket of the screws and compressors and my hiccups.

"Now, Eye-talian." He came right in close so all I could see was that purple shore blazer. "What colour's this, then? The *worst* colour a sailor could wear."

He stunk like a kerosene lamp. He kept his whisky bottles wrapped in long underwear inside the trunk he'd brought from home; there wasn't much else he could've done with long underwear in Bombay. He'd soaked through the armpits of his blazer.

"Leave me alone," I said. "Can't you see I've got hiccups?"

I concentrated on the page I was reading.

"*Maroon*," he said. "Now let's off to find a dusky maid who'll slap you with her titties." He nearly fell over and grabbed my shoulder. "That's the way, Eye-talian, we Catholics'll set this business right. Think of Udham Singh shooting. Shooting bloody O'Dwyer."

Bunny came in and slid up on his bunk like a mongoose. The ends of his *Gone with the Wind* moustache had bleached blond by then.

"Jimmy, get off him," he said. "You're not in the goddamn navy."

We had this joke that they all buggered each other in the navy. Maybe they did — I hadn't ever been in the regular navy.

"We all on siesta?" Bunny had the worst sunburn I'd ever seen, the colour of raspberry jam. He'd been sunning starkers on top of the wireless office.

Jimmy lurched away from me and leaned on Bunny's bunk.

"England's difficulty is Ireland's opportunity," he said.

I went back to reading my book, *Cannibal Quest*, written by a guy named Gordon Sinclair from Islington, Ontario, who'd gone around Asia having adventures. My cousin Edgar from St. Catharines, Ontario, had sent it to me. I'd never even met him, the only reason he'd sent me anything was that he was laid up with polio — "just like dear Roosevelt," as Ma said — so that by writing to a merchant seaman he figured he was contributing to the war effort. He wrote that I was a real hero for risking death by U-boat every minute of the day but I didn't much care to hear that so I just read *Cannibal Quest* over and over and gave his letters to Mitchell for rolling papers. I was lucky I hadn't gone blind reading down there as we only had a 40-watt bulb, but at least Jimmy had quit blocking my light.

He sat down to pull on a pair of saddle shoes he'd bought in Egypt or somewhere.

"Jesus, Jimmy," Bunny said. "Where in hell you going duded up like that?"

"Not wasting precious time." Even sitting down he couldn't keep his balance, he swung all over the place. "Dusky maids."

"Listen, the pilot's on the bridge. We been under weigh ten minutes."

"Shore leave finished last night," I said.

Jimmy gave me a look. His eyelids must've weighed ten pounds apiece.

"You go clean the loo," he said.

Then he keeled over on his bunk.

"Did they tell where we're going?" I asked Bunny.

"Not saying."

"It'll be back to Suez," I said. "All the way out here just for a field trip."

"Hell, the Japanazis'll do what they want to us."

And just like that my hiccups quit. The four turbines boomed away under us and like always the pipes banged like somebody was hitting them with a hammer.

"When they circumcise these boys out east." Jimmy talked with his arm over his face. "The whole town turns out to see."

"At least get his shoes off him," Bunny said.

"I'm not touching the guy."

Jimmy rolled over so his face was against the bed frame.

"Read me something out of that," said Bunny.

"Which part you want to hear?"

"Just the part you're on."

"'The quickening of advanced civilization brings on mental collapse, worry, insanity, fear and breakdown.'"

"He doesn't like jazz either?"

"This is the section about New Guinea."

He lifted his legs and put his feet against the ceiling. He had rough skin all over his elbows.

"Find a part that talks about women."

"'Why does the Borneo woman consider herself brazen and immodest if the nipples of her breasts are covered? This weird fantasy and extravaganza faces the prowler of the 1930s who strikes off the beaten South Sea and Asiatic path in quest of voodoo, black magic and cannibal lore. Are there human man-eaters in 1933 you ask? I answer thousands; and most of them are women!'"

"They'll suck you dry," Bunny said. "That's the truth. Do that bit with the virgins."

Chapter Four was called *Voluptuous Virgins* so I was always reading it aloud.

"'I know I've gone right off the deep end where these Balinese beauties are concerned, but you should see them. Tawny skinned with dark, flirting eyes. They have proud red mouths and firm, tawny breasts.'"

That Gordon Sinclair really knew how to write.

"Leave me there a minute," said Bunny.

Ray came crashing in — he'd been on anchor detail. He pulled off his boots and put on these rubber sandals that he called his wog slippers.

"You should've heard the new Limeys going into steerage," he said. "Like they hadn't ever seen a cockroach. Just loads of them. Limeys, I mean."

"They say where to yet?" asked Bunny.

"Not a peep," said Ray. "Christ, he pissed himself! Look at that."

The front of Jimmy's trousers looked pretty wet.

"That's just sweat," I said.

"You think he'll make like a bagpipe?"

Ray put his wog slipper down on Jimmy's stomach and Jimmy let out this kind of moan. Ray's teeth looked real white through his beard.

"This part of the world smells like an armpit." Bunny took a long pull on his own goddamn armpit. "Not a woman's of course. Theirs is kind of tangy."

"That true?" I said.

Jimmy's gut let out a rumble and he rolled over. Ray pulled his feet out of the way just as Jimmy lifted his head and heaved all over the floor — it looked like a potful of pea soup. Then he dropped on his face. And who did he remind me of then? Old Overend, rest his soul.

"That's great." Bunny put his pillow over his face, so we could barely hear him. "You fellas throw one hell of a party."

It really stunk to high heaven. Some of it dripped off Jimmy's hand. Ray looked at the bottom of his wog slipper.

"So clean it up," he said.

Jimmy didn't budge.

"You, Windsock," said Ray.

"I'm not cleaning that up," I said. "I'm the last guy should be cleaning that up. It's you should —"

"It's all over your goddamn ladder! You want to put your foot in it?"

"Somebody better." Bunny still had his pillow over his face.

"Listen." Ray tugged on his beard. "I go up and tell Mitchell that I just came off anchor and we got a hell of a mess down in our cabin, who's he going to detail to clean it up? You think Bunny's going to do it?"

"Won't be," said Bunny.

The puddle shifted back and forth with the boat. There were hunks of sausage meat in it. Jimmy breathed in and out. Overend had at least mopped up after himself.

I got up off the stool.

"How long am I supposed to clean up after you?"

"A while yet," Ray said.

I went out in the passage and got the bucket and mop out of the locker.

"There's still some under there," said Ray.

An Irishman named Mikey hustled in and knocked the mop out of my hands with the side of the door. He wore his pants pulled halfway to his neck.

"You're wanted on deck, you and you, some officer said." He tossed his smoke on the floor and took a look at Jimmy. "What's the matter with him?"

"Homesick," said Ray.

Even in the tropics Mitchell never wore a hat, so his head was always peeling and sometimes he'd pull off a hunk of skin right in front of you. He'd changed all the schedules after shore leave so it turned out he'd wanted me on deck a half-hour before, and all those Limey soldiers laying up on the deckheads got a real kick out of watching him take me down a peg.

"Just scrape the goddamn deck down so we can get painting!" said Mitchell.

"The *entire* deck?"

We were an hour out of Bombay, with old India still hazy off one side, when they sparked up the public address system to welcome everybody aboard. The deck was cooking through the knees of my trousers. I scraped with the wire brush at a rusty patch shaped like an umbrella and my hair was full of fly ash because I was behind the funnels, and after some bigwig Limey had muttered instructions over the PA they put on the worst record in the world, "Perfidia" by Xavier Cugat. "Dooo dooo — do do do do do *doooo*." The Limeys sang along, and it was an instrumental!

"Let's not wait around here," one Limey told another. They leaned on the rail chewing tobacco and must've figured they were real sailors. "Let's *go* to the fight. I'm not bothered if it's just the *Japs*."

Then he spat in the wind so it went all down my arm.

Eight more boats stretched out around us and we all steered in zigzag patterns and sounded our whistles every seven minutes, even *Emerald*, the big destroyer. That was how a convoy worked. The hot wind blew under the rail, the string section on "Perfidia" sounded tinny and horrible, and all eight whistles blew across the water at once. It seemed sad as hell.

By the time I'd worked my way back to the stern the sun was going down red behind us, which meant that I'd been dead wrong and we weren't sailing towards Suez after all.

"Here's to North Africa." Some Limey clinked bottles with his buddy. "Kicking Rommel in the Panzers."

"The sun goes down in the west," I said.

So they looked back at the sun, which was still behind us, then pointed their fingers back and forth and finally figured out that meant we were sailing east. They watched me scraping away down there.

"You bugger," they said.

That night Jimmy came in at 2300 and leaned against my bunk looking pleased as punch, blinking like hell. He wore a ragged old T-shirt with sweaty armpits but of course that was all any of us had on.

"Let's have it," I said.

Bunny tapped his teeth with his pencil. He was a great one for the letters home.

"Been mixing with these soldiers," Jimmy said. "And a good lot of them are the *Ninth*, they say. It says so on their gear, 'the Ninth.' They're quite taken with being the Ninth. But I'll let you in on a secret."

Ray was on his bottom bunk leafing through some Hindoo magazine.

"You're also in the Ninth," he said.

"I am *not*. The Ninth Regiment *escorted* provisions from County Down and back to England in 1847, that's all, during a potato blight and cholera outbreak. Sons of whores'll follow you anywhere."

He disappeared under me, bedsprings honking like a trombone.

"Relieved none of you's British Army, I can tell you that much. I'd have to ask just what you reckoned you were fighting for."

"Mussolini," Ray said. "He wears these terrific shirts."

"Jimmy. Here, I got something for you." Bunny pulled some kind of stick-pin button out of his junk pile, tossed it down to Jimmy. "That's the Yellow Kid on there, genuine New York City. Used to be in all the papers. See, he always had something written on his shirt there, read that out."

"'I am jist as Irish as you are if me dress *is* yaller.'" Jimmy didn't sound too impressed. "And the wee bird on his arm says, 'You ain't so many.' That's really fine."

His arm came out and the button landed on my bunk. It had a cartoon of a bald-headed kid in a yellow nightshirt, with a parrot on his arm.

"'Jist as Irish as you are,'" said Ray.

Jimmy just gave a sad-ass sigh from down below me.

"Guys want the light out?" asked Bunny.

He unscrewed the bulb before anybody could say anything. I always thought that was funny as hell.

"Ray, they run 'Terry and the Pirates' in that?" I asked.

I heard his magazine hit the floor. It was real cozy in the dark like that, with the strip of light showing around the door. I slept right under the ventilation grate but enough sweat still came out of my pores to qualify me as a bucket of water.

"I talked to that madman Bowlin." Bunny always started talking once the light was off, it was like having a radio playing. "Talked my ear off, in fact. What's he, Third Engineer?"

"Fourth," said Ray. "Please shut your yap."

"Scuttlebutt is we're headed east."

I took off my T-shirt and bunched it under my neck. I figured that might be cooler. I ran my fingers over the grate. The air had to travel down through six decks so it was swampy no matter what we did. I flexed my feet a couple times to see if that would put me to sleep. Dad had told me to try it when I'd been in bed with the flu — to just keep flexing my feet until the sandman came.

The next afternoon old Mitchell appeared and asked if I'd ever stoked coal.

"No," I told him. "Donkeyman short of guys?" The chief stoker was referred to as the Donkeyman — I sure laughed the first time I heard that.

"Never mind," Mitchell said.

We had our underwear hanging up all over the cabin and not a single pair was clean. A guy had to line up for an hour for the wash taps, so instead we just aired things out now and then. He put his handkerchief over his mouth and went out into the passage.

"This isn't a meeting hall," he hollered at somebody. "Make yourselves scarce."

I stuck my head out — a gang of Irishmen were having a smoke at the bottom of the ladder.

"Have some manners," Mikey told him back.

"I shouldn't see you unless you're at your job," said Mitchell.

"I believe you'll hear from us all the same."

"Regarding what?"

"We've no plans to stoke ourselves into your theatre of operations."

"Go tell the army."

I hustled back in and cranked the record player. "Lulu's Back in Town" was already on the turntable and even just starting with drum and guitar, Slick Jones and Al Casey, it *swung* right off the bat. *My-my-my,* Fats said, and right away it went quiet out in the hall. *Yes-yes-yes.* When the horns came in I looked out again and Mitchell was gone and the Irish were all tapping their feet. Waller did that to everybody. Except for the Krauts — if you sat them down with a record like that it wouldn't even touch them. They weren't quite human. That was the reason we were at war.

Bunny came in with engine grease down one side of his head and wanted to hear "The Spider and the Fly," so I cranked it for a while and we lay there fanning ourselves with our hats. Some guys could get crazy on a boat after a while, but so long as I had a couple of records I was a goat in clover. Jimmy came in, black from head to toe, and blinked at us.

"Spill," Bunny said.

"Singapore," said Jimmy. "They told all them soldiers. Sending us to war against the Japanese nation. But once they've put a hole through my belly I can't quite go and explain that I'm an Irish citizen and therefore bloody neutral and would they please shoot no more torpedoes, can I?"

"The Krauts would've done the same to you," said Bunny. "If you don't like to get wet you should've stayed home in bed."

"Babes to feed." Jimmy slid down the door, which put a smear on it a foot wide. "Puts you against your bloody principles. We've been under attack eight hundred years, so I couldn't expect you to understand it."

"Guys at Pearl might disagree with you."

"Oh, apologies. *Hawaii*. There must've been some *suffering* there. What a hellish place." Jimmy rubbed his eye with his thumb. "Have a look at my trunk, I've seen the world."

"'I'm jist as Irish as you are,'" said Bunny.

We went down the west coast of Sumatra and the Limeys all ran around the boat making bucktoothed faces at each other.

"And what's more, them Japs is all nearsighted! It's fact. They can't see at night owing to how their eyes are shaped."

"Won't even see us coming."

"I feel sorry for them. I do!"

"No, it doesn't seem fair."

They even accused one of the messboys of being Japanese and shoved him around a bit till the other Chinese came out of the mess with cleavers.

Mitchell brought me and eight other guys up to the capstan to coil a lot of hawsers, and he kept scratching his snake tattoo on the head.

"Now I don't need to tell you to keep your eyes peeled. Your mind on your work and your eyes peeled. If you see planes, you come tell me. I will brook no bullshit in this. This is nearly the Indies."

I looked out at *Emerald* and all those boats and I couldn't help but imagine each of them exploding at the waterline and sinking bow first.

We went through Sunda Strait — Java on the right and Sumatra on the left. I stood on deck with my scraper and watched them go by, though there were a lot of little islands scattered around between us and Java proper.

I love coffee, I love tea
I love the Java Jive and it loves me

They assigned more guys to the 0400 watch because we were getting close to Singapore and nobody knew if the Japs were that far south or not. I didn't mind the idea of getting up at 0400 until I had to feel around in the pitch black for my trousers.

"Windsock. The Japs can't see in the dark."

Ray sounded like his old grey mother when he was half-asleep.

Every light on board was blacked out, but there was a moon so I could see all right. I had to walk along the tops of the houses, which was as high on the boat as a guy could get except for the funnels a mile above my head. The smoke trailed away behind us. The air was warm as a bath — that's when a cigarette tastes really delicious. I looked down through the glass dome into the ballroom, at the hundreds of Limeys crowded on the floor like it was relief camp. I watched them for a while. In that green light they could've been all dead bodies. I'd almost convinced myself that they were, that they'd been gassed while they slept and I should run and tell Mitchell, but then one sat up and lit a cigarette.

The next day Sumatra was still off our port bow, greener than Africa but just as hot. It was the beginning of February. It'd been cold when we left Liverpool in November but then we'd sailed past South Africa in the middle of their summer, then Bombay and all the rest, which meant I'd had sweat running down the insides of my legs for two months straight and I figured that was about as long as I could stand. Sometimes I'd think about Shaw and me freezing to death on that CPR platform and feel better for all of three seconds.

The Limeys wanted to move their Vickers gun around on the stern so they sent a gang of us up with sandbags. The gun was only about four feet long but they were trying to keep as many guys busy as possible. They showed us their boxes full of ammunition belts.

"Singapore tomorrow," the Limeys said. "It might get hot."

Six guys were giving us orders at once, and I was holding a sandbag between my knees when I saw a triangle of planes way up above us. They looked more like a flight of ducks than anything else.

"Are those Japs?" I asked.

Everybody said *Oh Christ* and started pointing in the wrong direction. The planes didn't seem to be flying at us so much as alongside us and half a mile up. Mitchell was supposed to go and report someplace but instead he took his wallet out of his back pocket and looked at it there in his hand. The sirens all went off.

"Under cover!" Mitchell said.

Then gun-toting Limeys were all around us, elbowing us in the kidneys so they could get their rifles to the rail and be the first to kill a Jap. *Emerald* fired a couple of shots just off our starboard — I saw the smoke go up then heard the thud a second later. I couldn't say exactly which scientific principle was at work there, but for some reason the effect filled me with confidence, as though *Emerald* could choose when and where her guns were going to be heard and the Japs would just have to take their chances. The planes flew away over Sumatra then turned back. I still didn't know whether they were Japs. I hunkered down behind a crane.

"You see red suns on the wings?" asked Ray.

"Couldn't tell."

"*I* saw them."

Mitchell tugged on my sleeve and we followed him under the deck-head and down a passage until we were all crammed in front of the barber shop. A bottle of Palmolive still sat in the window.

"You'd better put that down," Mitchell said.

I still had my sandbag; it had left marks like little waffles in my hands.

The planes must've come back a lot lower because we heard them buzz past, then the Limeys' rifles popping away. And, "Get your tin hat on, you!" — I heard that distinctly. Then the planes must've started dropping bombs because I heard one thud after another though all I could see while I crouched there was the door to the purser's office and a piece of blue sky at the end of the passage. The thuds got further apart and I patted my hands together between them, *pap-pap-pap-pap-pap*, just listening to the syncopation, but I quit when I saw Mitchell watching me.

After five minutes the sirens stopped, and I realized I'd had my hands over my ears. But had the planes gone or had the Japs disabled the sirens?

"There'll be a mess to clean up. You." Mitchell looked at me. "Pliers."

Steel bomb fragments had jammed into the wooden deck on the promenade. I was conscripted to yank them out and spent the whole time wondering how Mitchell had known it would need doing even while he scratched his anchor tattoo in front of the barber shop. After an hour they'd figured out that one of the lifeboats beside the Vickers gun had been blown up but that not one guy had been hurt. Those Limeys sure were blue, boy — they hadn't shot down a single Jap. They grabbed my broom to demonstrate how it was supposed to be done, leaning on the rail with the bristles stuffed in their armpits.

"Exactly the same as shooting skeet," one kept saying, his cigarette dangling from his lip.

I found Jimmy packing his gear in our cabin. When he was sober he carried himself straight as a pallbearer.

"I've found a free berth with the stokers," he said.

Ray lay on his stomach reading his Hindoo magazine and he looked back at me.

"But he promises he'll come back and yodel in a bucket."

Jimmy lifted up his mattress and pulled a black suit on a hanger off of the springs, then he stood up very straight while he picked the bits of cockroach off it.

"I've got far more important things to worry about than you," he said.

"I don't follow you." Ray rolled on his back. "Are you saying you have more to worry about than I do or that what you're worrying about is more important than me?"

"Both," said Jimmy. "In equal measure."

I opened the Phillips, put "Lulu's Back In Town" down over the post, wound up the handle and let that guitar clip along. Brushes on the snare. Jimmy was taking real pains to fold a couple of dirty shirts. Waller bounced in on his piano.

Gotta get my old tuxedo pressed, gotta sew a button on my vest

"You're like a daft little child," Jimmy told me.

This from the guy who'd wanted to get slapped by dusky maids' titties.

I took a nap and woke up with my head already off the pillow. The boilers had stopped — the pipes didn't sound like somebody was hitting them with a hammer. That meant we were floating off the coast of Sumatra. My watch said it was five in the afternoon, which meant enough daylight for even a Jap to see by.

"Maybe Jimmy's given up on stoking." Ray's head appeared from under my bunk. "His whole black gang."

There must've been at least a hundred of those stokers because I tripped over at least that many shovels as I climbed to the promenade. Did every guy have his own shovel? I went up one flight of stairs after another until I found myself on the big red staircase in the first-class foyer, like it was the Ritz or somewhere, with brass banisters and a swaying chandelier. Mitchell took hold of my arm. I could see the stokers milling around at the top of the stairs, their backsides pressed against the railings above our heads, jostling like they were watching a bout. I couldn't see who they were shouting at.

"Pick up a shovel," said Mitchell. "I need you to stoke."

"Where am I going to find a shovel?"

I turned around to head down to the boiler when a great clomping of boots came up the stairs behind us. Limey soldiers, a hundred or so — a division, a platoon, I don't know — coming up in a column eight guys wide, all wearing helmets covered in green netting, their rifles propped on their shoulders with long bayonets on the ends that belonged in a butcher shop, not on the *Empress of Asia*. It had been a high-class boat! These guys all sneered the way only Limeys can, marching up the stairs towards me and Mitchell like an able seaman and a petty officer were the cause of all their problems. What were they going to do, kill all the stokers? That wouldn't get us back up to twenty knots.

"Sweet bullshit," said Mitchell.

Somebody blew a whistle. The soldiers stopped in their tracks and stood up straight on whichever stair they were on, then looked starboard at one of their tubby officers running up another flight of stairs to the landing. He had shiny boots and a tight jacket and blew that whistle like it was the only way he could keep his heart beating. I backed up the stairs one at a time.

"On — whose — orders?" asked the officer.

The Limeys all went to attention with their chins in the air.

"On our own recognizance, sir!" said one.

"*This* is no time to turn on *white* men!"

"No, sir!"

The straps on their helmets sat just below their noses.

"Can any of you guys shovel coal?" asked Mitchell.

A bunch of hands went up like they'd been waiting all their lives to be asked.

I turned around and ran the rest of the way up the Ritz staircase to see exactly what our stokers were accomplishing up on the promenade. Why go looking for trouble, you might ask? Because after more than a year on that boat any sort of change was welcome. And I figured it might make a good letter home. Dad loved to read about labour unrest. At the top step I came up against the backs of their black necks, so I went up on my toes to see old Jimmy standing up above the crowd on the rim of a big brass pot, one arm around the trunk of a palm tree.

"Citizens of Ireland!" he said.

He held onto his tree and they hollered back so loud that I couldn't make out a single word of what was said.

Chief Officer Smith and Captain Smith stepped in from the deck through the stained-glass doors, both looking like they'd eaten something that wasn't sitting well. The stokers by the door all stepped back a couple of feet. Captain Smith was fastening his brass buttons. For a second the whole black gang stood staring at them.

"Have your Royal Navy stoke your fires!" hollered Jimmy.

The other stokers loved that, they hollered along with him. One turned around to grin at me. His nose was full of black snot.

"If I may have one word!" said Chief Officer Smith. "We *all* cash in if we do not make Singapore! Be aware of that!"

"I tell you this for the last time," said Jimmy. "We are bloody neutral!"

Mikey climbed up beside Jimmy. "Ask your Royal Navy in!"

"You stoke or you die," said Captain Smith.

Then he pulled out a revolver and pointed it right in some poor sap's face, and even under his coal dust that sap went white. I went down a step.

"Either you stoke or you die."

They hadn't made him captain for telling jokes. Chief Officer Smith took a pistol out of his pocket too, but he didn't point it at anything. Captain Smith stayed just as he was. The stokers didn't back up but they didn't charge them either.

"We won't!" said Jimmy. "We're bloody neutral!"

"How about you, lad?"

Captain Smith looked at the kid at the end of his pistol.

"Will you stoke our engines?"

"He won't!" said Mikey.

"Yes, I will," the kid said. "I will."

The captain lowered his gun. And that was it. The stokers started moving past me down the stairs. Jimmy climbed down off the pot.

"My friends," he called, "I apologize."

The rest of the convoy waited around for us out on the sea, zigzagging like hell, their guns pointed at the sky, and whenever a zigzag brought them close enough we'd see heads in white hats looking across at us, trying to figure out what in hell we were doing. A gunboat painted in zebra stripes swung in off starboard. Must've come from a gunboat costume party — no, just a joke. It was supposed to make them harder to see.

After an hour we'd climbed back up to eight or nine knots. Everybody was saying that the soldiers who'd volunteered to shovel coal deserved medals.

"Bowlin was in ruddy heaven when they came down that ladder,"

Bunny said. "Told them he'd sailed around the world with all their grandfathers."

"Some guys' time has come and gone," said Ray.

He pulled off his wog slipper and killed a couple of roaches that were humping the bejesus out of each other.

I tried to wash my hands before we went to mess but only a thimbleful of water came out of the faucet. The boilers had been down for too long and the pressure had gone out of the pipes. We had rice for supper that night instead of the usual potatoes, which must've been to teach Jimmy a lesson. Scuttlebutt was that he'd be arrested once we made shore.

The next morning the other ships were all a long way ahead of us, and Bunny pointed out a British destroyer that'd come alongside, *Exeter*, said it was famous for sinking a Kraut boat in South America. We plowed past a lot of low islands just as green as Sumatra had been. I could see stretches of white beach and little boats with triangle sails. Mitchell told us that as soon as the Limeys disembarked at Singapore we'd have to sweep out the steerage because women and kids would be coming on.

"Japs have all of Singapore on the run," he said. "Can't say anybody expected this."

"These lads we're bringing will fix their wagons," said Baker.

"We could get the ladies and kiddies to shovel coal," said Ray.

"They'll shovel *you*." Half the buttons on Mitchell's shirt were missing. "Where in hell's Sherman?"

Old bald Sherman ran in with his one lock of hair flying out from the side of his head. He grabbed Mitchell and pulled him up on deck. We all stood at the rail. A green line lay across the horizon with a column of black smoke rising out of the middle of it.

"That's a volcano," I said. What'd they call that one? Krakatoa.

"That's Singapore!" Sherman patted his hair across the top of his head. "For Pete's sake!"

I went down to the cabin and took apart my record player and wiped off each of the pieces with a towel that I used exclusively for that purpose, then I polished all the records and put them back in their box. I found a scratch on "It's A Sin To Tell A Lie." That was a hell of a thing.

I would've asked Bunny about it but he was still at the boilers, trying to get our pressure back up. I moved it back and forth under the light, and there was a scratch all right. I couldn't imagine where or when I'd be able to replace it.

Then sirens went off. I fastened the lid of the trunk and stuffed it into my locker. *Then* I ran for the ladder. Each landing had another siren that almost knocked my head off. I still had that towel in my hand so I draped it over my head.

"Baby Snooks!" some guy hollered.

Baby Snooks was this girl who was sometimes on the radio with Bob Hope, I'd never thought she was funny and who would bring up Baby Snooks at a time like that? Even with the sirens I could hear the gunboats going *thud thud thud* on either side of us.

The ladder was solid with guys, and we weren't quite to the shelter deck when the boat pitched backward and the shoe of the guy above me came back and hit me in the mouth. I cut my upper lip on my front teeth. I pulled my hand free to see if there was any blood, and there was. I felt annoyed at the guy above me, so when the boat pitched forward I pushed my chest into the backs of his legs, hard, so his shinbones said hello to those old steel rungs. I never found out who he was because once I got up to the shelter deck there was nothing but smoke and guys running in all directions.

I didn't even wonder where that smoke was coming from. All I could think of was my records down in the cabin.

At my action station I found a lot of guys elbowing and yelling — one of them had his sportcoat on like we were already at Singapore and it was time to go for supper — but then I saw Mitchell so I followed him into the second-class dining room where the Limeys messed. The ceiling was on fire, flames running right across the flowery designs in the plaster. Then it was just like a drill — he opened the firehose cabinet and unrolled the thing and I went and stood at the switch. It was a relief to do something I'd done before. He pointed the hose up at the ceiling.

"One!" he said.

I turned the switch all the way and crouched out of the way of the flames.

"Turn it, Winslow!"

But he could see from the switch that I had already. A teaspoon of water dribbled out of the end of his hose. No pressure in the pipes. He kept it pointed up at the deckhead and I couldn't help but grin. Just as he turned and tossed the end of the hose at me the boat pitched forward and I fell on my elbow. A couple of timbers dropped out of the ceiling towards him so he had to roll over to where I was with sparks flying everywhere. I could see right through to the deck above us, into two WCs at once — two bathtubs sitting right next to each other! A toilet fell out of the ceiling and smashed into a pile of chairs. It's funny how things are so fascinating when they're on fire. The doorway out to the deck was full of smoke, so Mitchell put one end of my towel over his face and I took the other and squinted like hell and ran out with him.

We got out into the passage but just about fell ass-over-teakettle on bullet casings rolling around like so many marbles. A hundred Limeys knelt at the rail, blasting away with their rifles, at what exactly I couldn't tell, hollering in each others' ears all the while and working their bolts like mad so the brass flew around everywhere. Then a bomb fell past the railing — it looked like a fence post dropping past — and three seconds later a column of seawater shot up in front of us though we were fifty feet above the waterline. The Limeys had to spit out their cigarettes because they were soaking wet.

Then I saw the planes themselves, two hundred feet out beside us. They were dark green. It looked like a dozen in the formation. They all turned together over the water to come back towards us, and then I saw the red circles on their wings. Our sirens drowned out the sound of everything — the Limeys might've fired their guns a hundred times but I barely heard them. I was trying to pay attention to things because in the movies it's always some little detail that saves a guy's life, the rusty bolt that he's able to unscrew with his fingernails or the scarecrow Terry managed to build so that Captain Blaze's men wouldn't shoot him dead. And concentrating on one thing at a time at least kept me from running around screaming, which I knew Mitchell wouldn't like. The Jap planes swung back towards our bow. Then I couldn't see them.

I crouched down against the steel bulkhead but that was hotter than hell and I just about set my behind on fire.

The sirens cut out all at once. I heard the empty shells roll across the deck. A fist clenched in my stomach because the silence might mean that the Japs had come aboard, and then I imagined fifty of them hustling down to divvy up my Waller records. But I only had twenty-six and that wouldn't divide into fifty — I couldn't help but do arithmetic at a time like that. The Limeys were looking back and forth for the planes. After a second we heard a crackle from the public address.

"This is the captain." He didn't sound sad or excited or anything, he just sounded like the captain, and I thought, good for him. "All hands to muster stations."

To abandon ship. From the heat coming through that bulkhead I couldn't much argue with him, but that meant the last chance to collect the records had come — poor Waller sweating down there, all twenty-six getting warped as clamshells. I wrapped the towel around my head and looked for the ladder down but somebody took hold of my arm, his hands felt hot and sticky, and I tried to turn around and kick him but my feet rolled on all those casings so I wound up on the ground with Limey boots running past on either side of me. Old Mitchell stood over me.

"Them decks is gone!" he said. "Get aft!"

He made a good argument but a guy couldn't access the stern from the shelter deck, I had to climb one deck higher, so I ran past the engineers' cabins, then straight into the galley. One of the walls in there was on fire and the messboys were throwing boiling water at it. I carried on into the pantry and tripped over a sack of white flour and tumbled onto the floor. I had flour all over me and a sore wrist. Limeys hustled in behind me through the white cloud, knocking their guns against the shelves. For all I knew the boat was already halfway to the bottom. But daylight was sifting down from the stairwell in the corner so I picked myself up and took those stairs three at a time, right up to the bridge deck, where a potted palm was on fire and a Limey was picking up playing cards on his hands and knees. By then I had quite a bit of adrenaline so I ran down that first-class promenade with my fists pumping and my knees up by my chin. The Jap planes buzzed right past me, kicking up a wind that blew the hats off every Limey in sight.

The stern was crammed with guys. The big Vickers gun swung right and then left, trying to follow the planes, and the guys stuffed in around it had to hunker down or lose their heads. Some seamen had a lifeboat hooked to the winch. I leaned over the rail and peered down to the bow, and as far as I could tell our whole ship was on fire. The rest of the convoy steamed straight on toward the tower of smoke that was Singapore. We seemed to be the only boat in any kind of trouble. But we'd been the furthest back, the slowest, so of course that was why they'd picked on us — if Jimmy hadn't thrown his fit we might've been all right. Guys leaned on my shoulders from all sides, breathing on me, and I decided that I would've been happier if someone had walked right in and stolen my Waller records because then there'd at least have been an outside chance of getting them back one day. I imagined each of them melting down and wondering why their father hadn't come for them even after all the times he'd kissed them and told them that he loved them.

Exeter drifted away with the cloud from her guns still sitting around her funnels. The planes circled over us, a long way up now, but the Limeys kept the Vickers rattling so when they came down low one of the planes burst into flame right where its wing met the fuselage, then a second later the wing dropped off and the rest of the plane flipped through the air like a boomerang till it hit the green water.

"Take that, Adolph!" yelled the Limeys.

The water was on fire where it had hit. The other planes flew away towards Singapore. The Limeys picked up the gunner and tried to carry him around on their shoulders, but he held onto the ammunition belt for dear life so they had to put him down. I played my tongue over that cut lip. The first lifeboat dropped into the water and the Limeys started singing "The White Cliffs of Dover" or one of those horseshit songs. I couldn't help but feel annoyed as hell with them because if they hadn't been aboard no one would've bothered with us and we wouldn't have been on fire. It's human nature to blame whoever's nearest at hand. The fire licked around our funnels and even though I was as far astern as I could get I could feel the heat on my forehead. I would've wiped the flour away but I didn't have room to move my hand.

They lowered another lifeboat off the port side but more Limeys kept piling onto that aft deck, running up the promenade with their packs on, so that guys who were already there had to sit up on the rails. A seaman named Chalmers who only ever wore yellow socks climbed up to the top rail, then stepped out into space with his arms flailing like he must've figured that he was Harold Lloyd. He hit the water in a splash of foam and surfaced a couple of seconds later. A little fishing boat tacked over to him and some guys with cloths over their heads and brown backs pulled him out of the water. We watched Chalmers shake hands with them as the water ran off of him, and whichever guys had room to clap their hands did so. We all whistled.

I looked back at the flames spewing out of a porthole somewhere behind the bridge. I felt less anxious since I'd decided that the Waller records were gone for good. It still hadn't occurred to me that the fire might get me too. Burn to death with all that water around us? Of course not.

That zebra gunboat came gliding alongside us. She had an Australian flag on her stern. Absolutely beautiful. I couldn't help it, I cheered. Everybody cheered. She pulled right up next to us but her deck had to be fifty feet lower than ours; some guys put a leg over the rail even the though the Aussie sailors were waving their arms at us not to. A Limey officer pushed through and hooked a rope ladder to our rail, and we watched it unroll right down to the gunboat deck. Guys were sliding down before it even hit bottom. They clipped another ladder onto the rail in front of me and I was first to get my hands on it; I hopped up and did that neat little turn like we'd done in the drill so that my behind was out over the side. I got my feet onto a rung and down I went.

It wasn't all peaches and cream, believe me, because for the first half my knuckles scraped the side of our boat, the metal was bugger hot, too, and the hemp tried to saw through my palms with every rung I went down. But I didn't mind. From that angle I could see the rust leaking out of every bolthead — she was a hell of a mess, old *Asia*. I felt sorry for her. I'd done all that finicky-as-hell work with the goddamn wire brush, sure, but as soon as she had a real problem I was first over the side.

As more guys climbed on above me the whole ladder started to swing like a pendulum and I went back to worrying about myself. Of course *Asia* got narrower as she got closer to the water, so my knuckles were all right once her side started to curve away from me, and once the ladder was really loaded with guys it didn't sway more than an inch. I got a glimpse of the Aussies in their tan uniforms down on the deck, watching me with their hands shielding their eyes because the sun was straight above us and of course our boat was on fire. There were guys on ropes on either side of me but I didn't watch them — I watched my hands on the rope. Bits of hemp dug into my fingers but I carried on, then all of a sudden somebody took me by the arm and I stepped down onto the grey metal deck. It was an Aussie with his cap pushed back on his head.

"She'll be right, mate."

"Okay," I said.

His buddy had a roll of bandages in his hand but I told him I was all right and wandered up towards the bow. Where was I supposed to muster? I didn't see Mitchell or any officers I recognized. I just gazed up at their rows of guns like a tourist.

A minute later a thousand Limeys had piled on and I got shoved into the anchor cable. We started to drift away from *Asia*, and the last man down the ladder was a stoker whose shirt had been burnt right off him — strands of it hung off his shoulder. As we pulled away we heard a thud from somewhere down inside *Asia*, and a second later a bolt popped out of the side and sailed out over us like an arrow, and I wished like hell that it had fallen in front of me. After all the time I'd spent dragging my feet around her decks it seemed a shame to not have a souvenir of some kind, but at least I had my undershirt and pants and boots.

The fire didn't look as bad as we sailed off, the wheelhouse was blazing away but the rest of her looked all right. The Aussie gunboat hadn't been built for so many guys; it wobbled like an egg, and she kept slowing down to drop lines to guys in the water. Boats all around us were doing the same, tugboats and naval ships and the works. I was buried under guys. I couldn't even be bothered to be annoyed with the Limeys any more, I just wanted to get ashore and drink some cool water and get away from all of them. Ray sat down beside me in his yellow coat, running his fingers through his beard.

"Going to fry yourself in butter?" he asked.

When you got up that morning you must've thought it was a cloudy day. I can tell you that it was not, that there was blue sky beyond all that smoke. As we sailed into the smoke we all stood up and craned our necks to see exactly what we were getting into. Big long piers came out into the water — one of them on fire — and hundreds of people stood at the edge of the pavement. Warehouses stood along the water but half of them had fallen over so they looked like a row of busted teeth. That was all of the city we could see because of the smoke. There was a smell in the air that might've been burning tires. I didn't figure I'd find a new record player any time soon.

Little motorboats rattled away from the docks, full of white ladies holding down their floppy hats, and our boat plowed straight on toward the dock so they all had to scatter. The Limey next to me kept cleaning his ear with his finger.

"Looks like frying pan into the fire," he said.

"No, dummy, no," Ray said. "From the *fire* into the fire."

The Limey looked at him the way most people looked at Ray.

"Japs came straight down from Kota Bharu," an Aussie seaman said. He was washed and pressed while we all looked like a pan of burnt sausages. "Sunk the *Repulse*, sunk the *Prince of Wales*, took Kuala Lumpur and everything up north. Bloody incredible. Didn't even have planes half the time. Infantry came south on bloody bicycles."

"How'd you get so wise?" asked Ray.

"Saw my mate in hospital," the Aussie said, "he was in a lather, right — first thing in the morning on the eighth of December he was fighting Japs on the beach at Kota Bharu, and he reckons that was a couple hours before they hit Pearl Harbor. Everyone's saying the war started over there December seventh, but that's not so, there's the International Date Line, see?"

Ray raised his eyebrows.

"You lost us," I said.

Right then some Japanese planes flew over the dock and they must've had machine guns as well as the bombs because a few of the people waiting at the front bent over and dropped into the water. Two ladies in dresses. I had made it over to the rail so I saw it all perfectly. They sank two or three feet below the surface then stayed there with their dresses billowing out around them. One still had a handbag looped over her arm. All the people on the docks seemed to be trying to get away from the water but they were packed so tight that all any of them could do was turn around. We didn't have any place to hide either, I was stuck now at the rail whether I liked it or not.

"Twenty-seven of those planes," said Ray. "That's their formation."

He was right, though they moved so fast it was hard to count them; it seemed like there were fifty of them. They flew in from behind our heads, over and past us, dropped their fence posts on one warehouse and everything around it, and they must've hit gasoline drums or something because the fire that shot up was twice as tall as the warehouse had been. Our boat fired its ack-ack guns a few times and they were so loud that it was like being whacked on the head with a shovel every time they went off, and those long barrels nearly looked alive the way they recoiled and slid back into place. But they didn't knock down one plane.

A wind came up off the water and blew the smoke around so that I could see some long lines of houses with greasy-looking tile roofs, all pushed in together, and way off to the right the smoke was drifting around a lot of big places that all looked like the Marine Building on Hastings Street except that these were grey instead of gold. Of course you know very well what Singapore looked like, but that was how it looked to me. Places seem different when a guy doesn't know what anything is.

I crouched down and held my head against the rail, for all the cover it was going to give me, and watched the Jap planes bob and weave like houseflies over the buildings and the billboards, you remember those big signs you had everywhere: GOLD FLAKE CIGARETTES, PIRELLI TYRES, JOIN THE ARMY AND SEE THE WORLD. Every Limey with ashes up his nose must've been tickled pink to see that one. SEE THE ROAD TO RIO WITH HOPE & CROSBY & LAMOUR. I couldn't even think to insult Crosby because the longer I sat there the blanker my mind went. Sometimes a plane would lower its landing gear and slow down to just

about nothing and then knock the coat of arms off any building it
wanted to. They really seemed to be having a good giggle. A few times
a fence post dropped right out of nowhere like a bolt of lightning
from some plane that must've been a mile up — I saw a car go through
a second-storey window from one of those.

A plane buzzed right above our heads and I leaned back to watch
its white underbelly go over. One of the red suns on its wing blocked
out the real sun, and an instant later it was gone and I had to shade my
eyes again.

They were all gone, in fact. That was the last of them.

"We came in at the start of their fuckin' blitz!" said Ray.

It seemed to me right then that Singapore was the bad-timing
capital of the world. An ambulance was trying to get through the crowds
to the water — a Henney Packard, the same make of ambulance they
used in Liverpool — with a couple of rickshaws pulling in after it loaded
with hatboxes and junk and pulled by skinny little guys from a Charlie
Chan picture. While I was watching the planes I'd forgotten about the
ladies in the water, and to look down at them again while a boy and girl
in little white outfits held hands at the edge of the pavement and looked
down at them too, it made Waller and *Terry* and especially *Cannibal Quest*
seem old-fashioned and ridiculous. Because those ladies down in the
water were the very latest thing. The handbag had worked its way up to
the woman's wrist — it must've had a perfume bottle or something in it
that made it float — and I couldn't decide if I wanted that poor dead
woman to hold onto her handbag or if I wanted the bag to at least save
itself. It bobbed up her hand until only her middle finger had a grip on
it, then it swayed once more and a second later it broke the surface.
People pointed at it. The little kids had been pulled back into the crowd
by then and the newly arrived medics were on hands and knees, peering
down into the water.

I'd been out in the sun for a long time. Three of our Limeys were
taking a leak over the side of the boat and their buddy took their
picture. A few guys just had towels around their waists that said CPR
Empress because that was all the kit they'd had time to grab. One guy
stood there stark naked with his hands on his hips, grinning at one and

all like it was the best day of his life. I was out on the bow so I was one of the last off, and I spent all of that time craning my neck to see if the planes were on their way back, to the point that once I was on the dock I nearly tripped over some guy in a white suit lying on the ground with a hole through his leg. I tried to keep my eyes on our guys in towels as they followed a guy in a turban up the sidewalk.

A lady in a shawl jumped out at me, waving a birdcage in my face.

"Which is the evacuation ship for Java? That one?"

A kid in short pants sat on a stack of crates behind her.

"Our ship's on the bottom of the ocean," I said. It *wasn't* as far as I knew, but if she'd been waiting around for the *Empress of Asia* I wanted to make sure that she gave up on it. Her kid was holding the ugliest vase I'd ever seen, and I'd seen some bad ones.

"How do you mean?" she asked.

We stood there looking at each other. She wore white gloves.

"Do you happen to have a record player in all this?" I asked. I wouldn't have wanted theirs, of course, but all the same that was what came out of my mouth.

"We had to leave our phonograph at home," said the kid.

He was about six but he sounded like Winston Churchill. His mother was staring at a line of women who seemed to be going somewhere.

"Why shouldn't he have it?" the kid asked. His tie blew in his face.

"Yes, of course, help yourself to the phonograph," she said. She seemed pretty distracted. Then she looked right at me. "It's at my sister's at 81 Orchard Road and they've all gone. We've come via the jungle from Terengganu."

"There are a jolly lot of records." The kid kicked his legs. "Even 'Roll Out The Barrel.'"

"Where's your dad?" I asked.

"Typhus," said the mom. "Now I must —"

"Bit by a rat!"

The kid jabbed two fingers up and down. Then his mom helped him down off the crate. They were on their way.

"I'm new to the place," I said. "Afraid I'm not much help."

I spotted Ray's yellow coat across the crowd of people so I started after him. I knocked my kneecap right into the birdcage. Then I had to push through rows of empty baby carriages. A lot of guys in those safari-movie helmets stood smoking cigarettes and waving to people.

All at once the air-raid siren cut out and I realized that it must've been ringing all that time. Then I could hear a hundred boats gunning their engines behind me and warehouses on either side crackling like pans of popcorn. Some Chinese ladies threw cigarette tins full of water onto a burning doorway. After that the crowd thinned out and I could run right up the middle of the street, past a lot of buildings with big wide steps that looked like banks. A guy in a towel disappeared around the next corner but then I had to get out of the way of a truck with soldiers standing in the back, maybe our Limeys off *Asia*, and its exhaust smelled like a cherry lollipop. There were signs in Chinese plastered to every hunk of wall.

Around that corner was a hospital. Some guys were already coming down the steps carrying mugs of something, and it looked like they'd even washed their faces. Chalmers was one of them. I watched him come down.

"What'd you get?" I asked. "Cocoa?"

A Jap plane flew over our heads from behind the hospital. Baker ran back up to the porch but I was still in the driveway so I rolled underneath a car, a little Ford with rust around its doors. I looked out from underneath and saw two black guys cutting the grass next to the flower beds and not budging an inch. They weren't African black, they were Indian black. I had gravel stuck to my chest and a bolt of some kind digging into the back of my leg, and as I peered out I realized that if a bomb landed in front of me I wouldn't even have time to know it. That Ford would be no help at all. But then white squares of paper started to land in the driveway. I stuck out my hand and grabbed one — it was a cartoon of a girl in a nightie hugging a soldier, and across the bottom it said, *Nightmare of your neglected wife: 'Oh Tommy! I am going crazy.'* The plane hadn't been dropping bombs at all! But the guy in the picture didn't look like a Jap, he just looked like a white guy, so I couldn't figure it out. Was Tommy supposed to be remembering what it had been like to hug his wife?

I crawled out again. A Limey came out from behind a bush.

"Why in heavens would you hide there?" he asked. "Petrol tank was right over your head."

One of the black-skinned guys across the way leaned on his scythe, reading a leaflet. He looked up at me, then back at the paper — maybe I looked like Tommy. But my concern right then was cocoa, I didn't care how hot it was so long as it was wet. I ran up the steps. An old nurse stood in the foyer pulling on a cigarette. She had a line of blood across the front of her uniform like someone had shot her with a water pistol, but she stood there like she didn't even know it had happened.

"Comforts Corner is what you're after." She had that sweet old lady voice — if she'd been in a movie I figured she'd have played the maiden aunt run ragged by Andy Hardy and his friends. She must've read on my face that I wanted cocoa. "Down the corridor and up the stairs."

Then before I had turned away two medics burst through front the door, carrying a guy on a stretcher with a bloody bandage around his head. I heard a woman screaming from down another hallway. The medics stood panting while the sweet old nurse walked across the foyer to the ashtray on the wall and crushed out her cigarette.

All of our *Asia* guys were lined up along the hallway at the top of the stairs. The whole place smelled like a hamburger stand — so many guys were cooked black that I couldn't even tell who was a stoker any more. Ray was eight or nine ahead of me and he seemed to have blood leaking out of his ear, but from the way he stood there chatting it didn't seem like anybody had told him. The guy sitting in front of me stretched out his arm and I noticed he had a hole in it just above the elbow. He looked up to make sure I was watching and then he stuck his finger in it. Well! A light came in around the sides of my eyes and I had to lean against the wall.

"Souvenir of Singapore," he said.

A different old lady came around the corner pushing a gurney loaded from one end to the other with cups of tea — they splashed with every step she took. I lifted one off and handed it down to Hole-In-His-Arm, not out of charity so much as to keep his hands full. The tea was too hot to drink at first. She wore those old-lady glasses with the chains that hung down either side.

"I apologize for this tea, but we've done our utmost," she said. "Now the nurse will be by shortly, and if you'd like to know, she's gone out to get married. But you'll have had your tea."

"To Granny!" somebody hollered.

"Hip hip!"

"Hooray!" we all yelled. I meant it, too. I would gladly have given up every other kind of drink if that tea could have gone on forever. Hole-In-His-Arm looked up at me like I was his new best friend.

A siren started to screech right above our heads and my cup jumped six inches.

"That'll be the air raid," Granny said. "Remain as you are."

Then a younger nurse came up the steps. She was tall and good-looking and wore this dark red lipstick that looked a whole lot better than anything I'd seen them wearing in Liverpool. She stopped when she noticed Hole-In-His-Arm and bent over to talk to him. The top button of her uniform was undone so I could look down the front of it and see a breast hanging there in a lacy white cup. She felt Hole-In-His-Arm's forehead then went away up the line, and after that he just stared at his teacup. He must've seen them too. I was twenty-one years old, was I supposed to sit there saying prayers?

The siren cut out after one minute, leaving only the rattle in the mechanism and the ringing of spoons inside teacups. Granny came back down the line, followed by a couple of Chinese guys rolling a cartful of bandages and iodine. They wore long white shirts with *Canadian Pacific* written across the bottom.

"What you guys doing?" I asked.

"No more ship," one of them said. Granny unrolled the gauze and he cut it with his scissors. "We volunteer."

"We *vorunteel*." Ray grinned through his beard at the guys on either side of him.

"And where is your trouble?" Granny asked me.

"All I wanted was the tea."

"You've had it now."

A doctor put his arm around Ray and led him into a room.

Bunny marched down the line towards me with a black patch over his eye.

"Nurse said I got a cinder in it. Good God, what a cutie."

"You ought to ask what time she's off," I said.

"She's the one that just got married."

If Clark Gable had ever worn an eye patch then Bunny would've looked just like him. Most likely he had, but I couldn't think of the movie.

"I need something to eat," I said.

"We'll have to pound the pavement. I've been back there and all they've got's an X-ray machine."

The foyer was packed with Chinese guys hauling people on stretchers. I couldn't even tell if the patients were white or not. A taste like sawdust came up into my throat, and I told myself that I was just hungry. We got out the door and I saw that the car I'd been underneath was on fire with its roof jammed right into the front seat, and there was a hole four feet deep in the ground next to it. Gravel was rolling in even as we walked by.

"That's artillery," Bunny said. "Japs must be gunning right across the island."

"What island?"

"Singapore," he said.

The driveway led into a big main road, and we could see people in blue or in black hustling past, and the buzz in the air was like people going into a circus tent. We came around the last of the hedges and the road was crowded from one side to the other with Chinese people, all walking away from us — old guys with beds strapped to their backs, old ladies pulling rickshaws full of chickens and cookstoves, pairs of little kids dragging pots and pans behind them like they just got married. I couldn't figure out why they were going that way, because the smoke seemed to be in every direction. A truck with soldiers in the back honked like hell to get through — probably that same truck had been driving around all day. The guys were cutting grass further up the road by then.

We tried to travel with the crowd but I tripped over a big kettle on wheels that a woman was pushing, then everybody had to steer around us while I collected myself so we ducked into an alley where two Chinese kids were playing badminton, of all things. They kept the same rally going the whole time we had them in sight.

"So where do you figure we'll find some eats?"

"Chances are they've got an Automat tucked in here."

We ducked under the net. The houses ran together in a long line down either side of the street, with an arch-roofed porch in front of every door and shuttered windows upstairs. About a ton of laundry was hanging on clotheslines between the buildings, so half those people must've run away without their clothes.

"I've got letters to mail," he said. "They were giving out paper in the line and I was fidgety."

On the next street the smoke had turned all of the storefronts grey, so that everything looked more like a black-and-white postcard than like real life. *Scenes from the Japanese Invasion.* Like we were walking through one of the old daguerreotypes Ma inherited from Aunt Isabelle, *Views of Quebec* and *Views of Old Montreal*, except for the odd Chinese guy walking through in black trousers and a long shirt.

"I had to write Beverley and tell her I don't have a clue what's happening next and for all I know I'm not going to be writing any more. I hated doing that. How can that sound good to her? It can't sound good."

"Who's Beverley?"

"My girl, Windsock! Who you think I've been writing to every night?"

"Your folks. You have any money?"

"I've got five American dollars." He felt his shirt pockets. "How much for a stamp here?"

At the corner an old Chinese lady squatted in the storm drain beside a dead horse with its guts spilled out. She had her hand flat on its neck. The sawdust taste came into my mouth again and I decided I'd be better off if I concentrated on that rather than on the smell or what I was seeing. There were so many flies that it sounded like a radio. We stayed on the other side of the street, but even so she jumped up when she saw us like we were going to steal it. Then a couple of kids came around the corner chasing a ball and one slipped and fell and stood up with blood all over the seat of his pants. Then the other kid started pointing and laughing so the first one picked up the ball and ran after him and threw it at the back of his head. Jesus, it was like the Brothers Grimm.

"I've got a pile of them for her."

"For who?"

"Beverley."

I admit I was annoyed at the idea of those letters to Beverley. It would've been dandy to have a girl of one's own and of course I didn't like it that Bunny had what I wanted, but I was even more annoyed that she might eat up all of our Automat money — a slice of pie and a roast beef sandwich, that was what I was getting.

"Why didn't you mail them on-board?"

"It would've put Beverley out quite a bunch if I'd mailed 'em on on-board now, wouldn't it?" He fiddled with his eyepatch. "This might be the post office."

We crossed a yard full of parked cars, surrounded by tall buildings with columns. Bunny pulled a hundred letters out of his pockets. Two black guys in long pants walked past smoking cigarettes — they were Indian black too.

"I'll tell you what's cooked is my record player," I said.

The post office had a statue of Mercury or one of those guys on top of it, and as we got closer I noticed that there was a big hole in its front wall, and a sign across the top that said it was actually Robinson & Co. That didn't sound like the post office. The second storey stuck out over the first storey, and there was one window after another under there with lots of things on display. We walked toward a stone arch that looked like it might lead to the front door. The whole place smelled of booze.

"There's got to be grub in here," I said. "I could eat a horse."

"Gordon's Gin. I know it well," said Bunny.

A cardboard sign in the foyer said *Due to Bomb Damage, Robinson's Café has been Relocated to the Basement.* I looked for the stairs down, but way across the main floor I saw a sign that very clearly said GRAMO-PHONES. I grabbed Bunny's elbow.

"Hold your water," he said. "When the hell was the last time you ate something?"

"But I've got priorities!"

"They're rotten. How much money have you got?"

"Zero."

"Well, the five bucks are coming downstairs with me, if it's any interest to you." He went on down the marble stairs. "Don't forget what the weed of crime bears."

I ran between the rows of chesterfields and cabinet radios anyway. Everything smelled new. The record players were lined up on tables, Phillips and Victor, even an Edison, the arms all straight and silver. I spun the turntables with the flat of my hand. The records were on shelves along the wall, arranged alphabetically — Jesus, that would've been a better job of work than scrubbing toilets! I saw the label *Waller* taped on one shelf and nearly bit through my sore lip. I knocked my hip against a piano on the way there. Waller! He once was lost but now was found.

They didn't have "Ain't Misbehavin'" or "Lulu's Back In Town" or "The Joint Is Jumpin'" or "Honeysuckle Rose." All they had were a half-dozen copies of "Swing Out To Victory" b/w "By the Light of the Silvery Moon," which was a record I'd never heard before. New Waller! I stood there for a minute just looking at the sleeve. I was sweating and my fingers wrinkled it. It had an RCA Bluebird label that said *Foxtrot* but of course anything that wasn't a waltz said that. I pulled it out of its sleeve and laid it down on the Columbia electric player. I flipped the switch.

The song was pretty simple at first, just some mid-tempo piano, but once he started playing the high keys it sounded good. Then the rhythm section came in, everybody swinging all right though it was still just mid-tempo. Then Waller sang.

In the air, on the land, in the sea

Let's swing out to victory

I figured that was trouble. It wasn't a real Waller song. He was supposed to sing about broads and parties.

If you're really with me

Let's get in a tank

With some clarinet looping along under the piano — that sounded good but I still didn't like what it was about. When *everything* started being about the war, then what was the war for in the first place? The drum solo sounded a bit like Gene Krupa so of course that was good, and whoever was playing bass was doing great, probably Cedric Wallace. Then right at the end Waller said:

Double victory, double victory.

And I was too disgusted to even wonder what it meant. My stomach was hollering at me but I told it that for Fats Waller I would need another minute. I turned the record over to "By the Light of the Silvery Moon," but before I could put down the needle I noticed two women hustling towards me across the store and I figured that they were coming to say that Robinson & Co. didn't welcome hobos, so I left Waller there and put my hands in my back pockets and went over to look for Count Basie records as though I had money to spend. And then I couldn't help but wonder if I would ever have money again, because Captain Smith had to sign my articles before I could get paid, and most likely I'd never see Captain Smith again and I'd left my articles in my trunk so by then they probably wouldn't have filled an ashtray. The amount of Paul Whiteman in that store was unbelievable. And the Crosby! It was terrible. There was no Basie, so I started looking for the Ink Spots.

"Pardon me," one of the women said. She was the older of the two and built like a brick outhouse, with her hat tilted over on the side of her head. "Those little men put a hole through the parlour last night. Might you demonstrate some of your radios?"

It was an English accent but she said every word like she was about to burst into song.

"Christ on a bike, Mum," you said. "He doesn't work here."

"I do wish you would not say that," said your mom.

You had curly hair and pearl earrings and black-and-white shoes, and you seemed to have a lot of teeth in your mouth and your ankles looked a little thick. But it's not like I didn't think you were cute as the dickens.

"I may not work here," I said. "But I can show you the radios."

I offered my arm to walk you the six feet to the radios, and you didn't take it, you just walked past, but you smiled to beat anything.

Your chest looked pretty well put together. You were wearing a blue dress that was tight in the waist, maybe you remember the one.

"Where is it you come from?" your mother asked.

Jesus, she was British as the Rock of Gibraltar!

"Canada," I said. "I'm a seaman."

"What's happened to your clothes?" you asked.

It's funny what a guy won't even notice until a girl walks up — my pants were shredded to the knee and my shirt had a rip that went up one shoulder and down the other side. But my boots were still all right.

"Our ship burned up out in the harbour," I said.

"Poor man!" said your mother. "You've brought reinforcements, haven't you? The ship of reinforcements, that's —"

"What's your name?" you asked.

"Harold Winslow. Harry."

"Oh, forgive us, aren't we terrible?" said your mother. "I'm Marguerita Brown and this is my daughter Lily."

We shook hands. Yours felt as small as a kid's, and my grimy paw left a smear on it like you'd just been cleaning a chimney. I saw you wipe it on your hip.

"Reinforcements to drive the little men back into the sea," your mother was saying. "Are you a lieutenant?" *Leftenant*, she said. "I can always tell. A naval lieutenant. And a fire, that must have been horrible. Can your quartermaster not find you a change of clothes?"

"He didn't make it."

"Oh, I am sorry."

"I was just looking around for the men's department."

"Certainly we must find you *something* to put on."

"Weren't we going to see the radios?" you asked.

You probably don't remember but there were a lot of tabletop sets — a couple of Philcos, a Fairbanks-Morse, a crappy plastic Zenith and a nice wooden Belmont. I flicked it on and some Limey guy's voice came out as clear as a bell:

"It's no use telling people in Singapore that Malta has had thousands of air raids and has stuck it out. They have ideal shelters. Singapore has nothing but —"

Your mother shut it off.

"Panic," she said. "That is most unseemly."

"We had a cabinet radio at any rate," you said.

"When I looked out and saw how they had *decimated* my garden, I was this near to charging up the road after them, wasn't I, dear? And they wouldn't have known how to stop me, either."

"You're much too fearsome, Mum."

"I am."

Bunny walked up as I leaned against a big Grunow. He handed me a sandwich on a china plate.

"I fixed that myself, Slow Poke." He had one of his own, and took a bite. "How are you ladies? Nobody came to work today so it's a smorgasbord down there."

"I beg your pardon, a what?" asked your mother.

He had crumbs on the side of his mouth.

"A buffet."

"These are the Browns," I said. I had to chew with my mouth shut because you kept looking over at me. It took quite a bit of effort. "Missus and Lily. Japs blew up their radio. This is my buddy, Bunny."

I figured you'd look him over and ask whether he was related to Clark Gable.

"Buddy Bunny," you said.

"*Sort of* my buddy."

"You choke on that," said Bunny.

I could've eaten six of those sandwiches. Even though the food in the mess had been awful I was still accustomed to getting it three times a day.

"Once your belly's full, what say we find a boat?" asked Bunny.

Your mother was turning knobs.

"I understood that your boat was on fire."

"Oh, you hit the nail on the head, ma'am," he said. "That's why we need a new one. So where's Mr. Brown? He in the service?"

"Your lieutenant needs a fresh set of clothes. And we mean to buy them."

"Oh, I've got money," I said.

"The who needs what?" asked Bunny.

"What happened to your eye?" you asked.

"Cinder," said Bunny.

"Thanks for the chow." I handed him the plate. "Looks like I'm on the go."

You put your arm through mine. Your mother was already ahead of us.

"What this?" he said. "I can't tag along?"

"Thought you'd be mailing letters."

We were walking between the floor lamps and the double beds. I looked back at him over my shoulder.

"Where we staying tonight?" he called.

You pulled my arm closer. That blue dress felt scratchy against my elbow.

"Tell him the YMCA."

"The crummy Y," I hollered back.

The three of us went up the stairs. I could see Bunny down at the other end of the store, studying the Zenith with the lightning bolt down the front. I'd lied to the both of you by letting you believe that I was a *leftenant* and I'd abandoned Bunny, neither of which I was proud of, but now as much as then I feel like it couldn't have happened otherwise. He picked up the two plates and wandered back toward the restaurant.

Your mother took the pins out of a shirt and I stepped behind the curtain and tried it on. It was tight around the neck but I figured that was okay, because any guy I'd ever seen dressed to the nines had looked like he was choking to death.

"We ought to have a tailor take in the jacket." Your mother looked around with her hands on her hips. "Of course there aren't any."

"I'll be all right with this."

"*Suit* yourself," you said.

You had a smile across your whole face.

"What a wit," said your mother.

We looked down at the parking lot through the hole in the wall. A bunch of soldiers in short pants were piling into a Morris Minor. They gunned the engine, bounced off a black sedan and kept going. Circus clowns.

"Doesn't it smell of gin?" your mother asked. "I think the whole place smells of gin."

"We should get you home, Mum."

"Let me write a chit for these."

"I've got money," I said.

"Nonsense. Take the trousers as well, those will suit you. Where did we leave the driver, Lily?"

"We walked, Mum, Christ on a bike! You said you needed fresh air."

"Good Lord, I'd forgotten we were at Raffles. I do feel odd."

I pulled the brown trousers on over my old ones, then you held your mother's arm as you went downstairs. Her hips were exactly twice as wide as yours.

"Mind the step. I've got you."

"Our driver's run off," your mother said over her shoulder. "Told Cook he was going *pergi ulu*. Into the jungle."

"Mum, you've muddled it. Mr. Kwan is still at home, and Cook has taken her children and gone *pergi ulu*."

"I would think Mr. Kwan could have gone *pergi ulu* with his wife."

"But they have no children so they said they'd prefer to stay here."

"Did they?" asked your mother. "They have such a sweet little house, it is a shame they don't have children. I'll ask you to ring him, dear, and have him bring the car."

"We've lost the car, don't you remember?"

I watched your ankles as you turned on the landing.

"*Pergi ulu*," said your mother. "I do like the sound of that."

"I can run over and get your radio," I said. "Which one did you have your eye on?"

"What did we have, Mum, was it a Philco?"

"Goodness, I'm not writing any more chits today! The colonel would have my head on a platter."

"Mum!"

"You know very well he would."

We walked past the sign explaining about the café, then out the front door. A soldier sat throwing cards into his helmet in front of a window display full of tuxedos. He looked up at us. Had a bottle of crème de menthe between his legs.

"An absolute shame."

Your mother seemed to be talking to the air above his head.

The booze smell was stronger all the time, until we finally came to an open gate behind the store — a bunch of Chinese guys were carrying crates of booze across the yard and white guys were taking the bottles out and throwing them at a brick wall. The pile of broken glass was a foot high, and flies landed on our hands and faces. My first thought was that they'd all taken the pledge at once. A Limey in a soaking wet white suit came over to us, carrying a bottle of Scotch by the neck.

"Mrs. Brown, hello." A smell like turpentine wafted off him. "I heard you'd moved out of Holland Park. Things getting a trifle bleak. Hello, Lily."

"We're in Raffles now," you said.

"What's this in aid of?" asked your mother.

Glass kept smashing behind him.

"Shenton ordered it. Suppose you heard how the Japs ran riot in Hong Kong? Every ounce to be destroyed. So even *he* must find things a trifle bleak. Say, those rags look like ours." Pointed his bottle at me. "You just get ahold of those?"

"I've written a chit for them. You've left all your doors open, Warren."

He was staring at you from under his eyebrows, his chin lowered, but then he stood up straight all of a sudden and brushed some green glass off his arm.

"There's an oversight," he said.

"This is Lieutenant Winslow." You touched the sleeve of my new brown jacket. "They bombed out his ship."

He twisted the cap off the bottle, but then he must've remembered it was a work day and pushed it back in.

"Is that all that smoke over the water?" he said. "Whereabouts you from?"

"Canada."

"And for what possible reason are you two hanging about? You ought to have gone weeks ago."

"We're waiting on Colonel Brown," your mother said. "*You* could go yourself."

"See if we surrender first. Every man'll do his duty, won't he?" He gave me a look and slid his jaw back and forth. "Any rate. Best of luck."

"And you," sang your mother.

"We must find a taxi," you said. "Marching across the *padang* took it out of you, Mum."

"It's this liquor in the air." Your mother took my hand and squeezed it — she had a grip like a prizefighter's. "You'll have a wash when we get to the hotel, won't you, Lieutenant?"

We found a taxi but it was up to its wipers in a crater. It was hot as a gas furnace out there and we each held one of your mother's arms. I kept looking across the back of her neck at you and you kept grinning back.

"Imagine if I'd had to do this on my own," you said.

We ran into a crowd of people lined up to cross a skinny bridge that was jammed up with Chinese dragging their houses behind them, and white guys in a green car, and Limey soldiers with their elbows in everyone's faces. Gordon Sinclair had once told me that Chinese babies never cried but on that particular day it must've slipped their minds. We crept along the rail, your mother hardly moving her feet, and I glanced down and saw Mikey the Irishman underneath us, rowing a boat with a crate of Milkmaid condensed milk up in the bow. Headed to sea. Slicks of burning oil floated around him so we had to hold our breath every minute or so. There were a hundred boats clogging the river further upstream, all long and skinny with a little tent in the stern. A chicken got away from a Chinese gal and we waited while she caught him jumping over the rail.

Then the drawn-out first note of the air-raid siren started on either bank, and dogs started to yap and that crowd on the bridge finally found its feet, pushing their buggies like it was a race. Of course your mother didn't run, and after a minute we could walk right up the middle, the metal grates ringing under our feet — that siren was the best thing that had happened all day.

"Quick march!" You talked in sing-song too. "Double time!"

We got to the other side.

"Get me that rickshaw, will you?" your mother said. "I do need a rest."

A rickshaw with a mattress strapped across the top sat in the middle of the street, and as you and your mother stepped over the shafts I spotted a Chinese guy in a bowler hat peeking at us from under the bridge. You managed to squeeze your mother in beside the junk heaped all over the seat, then I picked up the shafts and started it rolling. It was a lot harder work than those scrawny rickshaw guys made it seem. My wrists were burning right from the start and if it hadn't been for all of my rust-scraping muscles I would've had to quit, but even so it was easier than hauling the old girl around by the armpit. We rolled past some grey buildings then out beside a row of sycamore trees with a field behind them, a park or something, though the whole field was stuck full of metal poles. The smoke had cleared and you were trotting alongside us and it all seemed very pleasant, but then an old Chinese lady in pyjamas ran up beside us, shrieking like a seagull, and dug her fingers into the back of my hand.

"Never mind her!" said your mother. "Never mind!"

The Chinese gal kept boring into my hand but I kept my feet moving and held onto those shafts like my life depended on it — I was sweating like I'd just climbed out of a bathtub. She might've been saying something in those shrieks but I would have to have been Pat Ryan himself to have made out one word.

"Take this, here!" You shook a pound note at her, your black-and-white shoes clapping along the pavement. "Just take this!"

Your mother lobbed a picture in a frame at her and I tried to zigzag like hell so the wheels might run over her feet, but she was too far ahead for that, then I had to swerve around a guy with a pole over his shoulder who was coming along the pavement. He said one word to her and the old gal turned around, then let go a second later. I turned around too, to see what it was.

The guy in the bowler hat was standing at the foot of the bridge now, hollering his head off and pointing at a formation of planes coming over Robinson & Co. The sky was as blue as in a painting.

Two little kids were jumping up and down at Bowler Hat's feet and my old gal was running back towards them as fast as her legs would carry her.

"Kindly carry on," your mother said. She couldn't see what was coming but it was good advice. I got us rolling, but where in hell could we go?

"Under the trees!" you said, and yanked one of the shafts so we veered to the left. Which may have been more good advice, but we were so top-heavy from the mattress that the rickshaw started to tip over and all I could do was to jump out of the goddamn way. I saw you duck under a shaft as it tilted in the air, then the rickshaw crashed over and skidded across the pavement until the mattress ran up against a tree. Your mother rolled out into the road. You'd fallen on your face in the grass.

If I'd set out to woo you I was doing one hell of a job. But I can't say that it had crossed my mind in as many words — all that I wanted was for us to not end up like those women with their handbags floating off their fingers. Your mother was lying on her back, dazed, I guess, though her hat was still clamped onto her head, so I took hold of her wrists and dragged her up between the mattress and the tree trunk, even though I wasn't quite sure if her wrists could take the weight of the rest of her. Then I got you to your feet at the edge of the road. You had grass-stains up the front of your blue dress.

"Stupid," you said.

Then we turned around to see fence posts dropping out of the planes, and a second later a lot of water jumped up out of the river. Then they were flying over our side of the river, and where the bombs hit the road everything flashed orange and gravel flew into the air. We ducked behind the mattress and I pulled you down into my lap. The mattress smelled like my cabin on *Asia*, and there was a stain next to our heads the shape of a big fish. Your mother wrapped her arms around us.

"I love you both!" you hollered.

"Don't be a nitwit!" yelled your mother.

A wind whipped up and your mother's hat flew away across the field. Clods of dirt fell on us and I could hear rocks hitting the other side of the mattress, but then the roar became too loud to even hear that, it was like two trains crashing into each other. I felt your weight in my lap, and your head was under my chin so I smelled your hair, I rubbed my nose against the top of your head, and I knew chances were good that any second I was going to wake up in the bunk above Jimmy's. But a rock was digging into my tailbone and the back of my hand felt like it had been hit with a hammer, so then I wasn't too sure.

It went quiet. A piece of fern was stuck in my hair, falling down over my eyes. Your mother had your lipstick smeared across her cheek. She patted the top of her head.

"Oh, our cricket pitch," she said.

You pushed against my shoulder to get up. I hauled myself up by the trunk of the tree — the bark was hot on our side and cool on the back. There was a smell in the air like cap guns and digging in the garden, and more of that stink like burning tires.

"It *was* our cricket pitch," your mother was saying.

The nearest craters were thirty feet on either side of us. The rickshaw was covered in dust and there were broken bricks thrown over the bottom wheel but otherwise it looked all right. The two of you were still studying the craters out in the field.

"Why's it stuck full of poles?" I asked.

"A precaution," your mother said. "We couldn't have them landing in gliders."

We abandoned our friend the mattress and got the rickshaw back on its wheels. Your mother sat in the back, still patting her head like she thought she'd lost it, while I trotted like a carthorse again, steering around the craters like Red Grange going around linebackers, though I was hauling the only linebacker who could've given me trouble. We took turns looking back over our shoulders. That first batch of planes was long gone, but for all I knew they went around in circles.

"Lily, ride back here with me."

"I wouldn't give Harry any more to drag about."

You were breathing hard. You weren't the athletic type. But all the athletic girls in Vernon had ever competed in was broad jump, and I figured you could broad jump all right if you had to. The Chinese were crawling up out of the ditches. An old guy carrying a turtle under his arm and a chicken up to its neck in a sack stared at us as we went by, though he was quite a sight himself.

"Where these Chinks all heading?" I said.

"I beg your pardon?" your mother asked.

It wasn't as though my folks had taught me to say "Chinks." That had been Ray.

"They're going out to Changi." You pulled your hair back for a second. "They've their *kampongs* out there."

"Their who?"

"Their old villages."

"They figure the Japs won't look for them?"

"The Japanese want the *city*," your mother said. "But those little men shall never take the causeway, much less the town."

"We've blown up the causeway, Mum."

"Precisely."

"So why are you two sticking around? I mean, I'm all for having you …"

An old white guy with a moustache peered at us from a parked Rolls-Royce, then he looked away. There was another strip of grass to our right, and beyond that the big wide harbour with a lot of little islands on the opposite side, and smoke from my records still billowing up behind them. The water looked very green.

"Father is a colonel in the Malay Volunteers," you said. "They're defending Kuala Lumpur, and we're waiting for him."

I remembered that the pressed-shirt Aussie had mentioned Kuala Lumpur, but I couldn't remember what else. The International Date Line? A bunch of monkeys ran across the cricket field and one clambered up onto an anti-glider fortification — I'd seen little ones on leashes back in Bombay but nothing the size of these boys. Neither of you seemed bothered. The hill above the field was all jungle, with smoke billowing off it. What next, I wondered, tigers?

"*Pergi ulu*," your mother said.

Everyone we passed was walking, and I could only think that I was still running because I figured that a naval lieutenant wouldn't have stopped and walked. A swarm of blue birds flew over our heads and all of a sudden I wondered why I was there at all — I wasn't hunting down a boat to get myself out of there, no, I was pulling a goddamn rickshaw for two British ladies! I could still feel that Chinese gal's fingers in the back of my hand and the muscles between my shoulder blades felt like I'd been kicked. But then I looked at you chewing the side of your finger as the sweat ran out of your hair and forgot whatever it was I'd been thinking.

We passed a church on our left, with ambulances parked in front of it and stretchers on the lawn, and you stopped flat, looking through the fence as they hauled guys out of the ambulances. As far as I could tell they were all guys in uniform. Or pieces of uniforms. You stood up on the balls of your feet, leaning back and forth like you were looking for someone in particular. I didn't care for that. But all I could do was stop and stand there with the sweat seeping through my new brown suit.

"It's nearly tea time now, Lily," said your mother. "They will let us know if something has happened."

A little white kid stood on the back of a truck as it trundled along, waving at everybody like it was the last day of school. Maybe it was. We were back in the mob of people carrying stoves and baskets of eggs, and the street was so crowded that I had to make an annoyed face and slow to a walk. A guy in knee socks rode by on a bicycle with handlebars four feet across. After another block a big wide building came up on our left, with every column and shutter and corner of wall painted white. A sign up near the roof said RAFFLES HOTEL.

"Here we are," said your mother.

"Seek home for rest," you said, "for home is best."

I rolled the rickshaw under the palm trees and around the driveway and dropped the shafts on the white gravel. Blisters were grumbling on my palms. I couldn't even stand up straight. A big guy in a turban came out from under the awning and helped your mother out of the back.

"Come inside, *Leftenant*," you said.

"This is a hazard." Turban scowled at our rickshaw. "We cannot leave this here."

Your mother had her arm around his white sleeve.

"Mr. Singh, why shouldn't you keep it? My present to you."

My brand new pants had a rip from the cuff to the knee so my old pair showed through. You smoothed down your dress. I fastened my top button, which caved in my windpipe, then I followed you up the steps.

"You in the services, lad? I know you." A squat little Limey with a big moustache stood up from a chair beside the door. He wore the same sort of hat as Captain Smith only the band on his was red. "What you done with your uniform? You'll be up on a charge like a — what's your regiment?"

"Does the army *have* to be horrible?" you asked. You took my hand. "Mr. Winslow is our guest and no concern of yours."

"Is that right? Dreadfully sorry. You well know the other ranks can't just wander in. That wouldn't help anyone."

"We have no interest in the other ranks," your mother said.

She started in past the potted plants. The Limey sat down again.

"Anyhow," I told him, "I'm merchant navy."

"Oh? Then we won't look to you when the fight starts."

I had something else on the tip of my tongue but you tugged me inside, which was just as well since it was probably something a lieutenant wouldn't have said. Half a dozen Chinese boys in white shirts waited inside the front door with their hands folded, and a Chinese guy in a tuxedo was playing a baby grand piano. It might've been Beethoven. It sure wasn't Waller. I liked those high notes, though. You let go of my hand and went over to a little table where a girl handed you a glass of water. Your mother waddled over to the desk.

"Any messages for Brown in thirty-eight?"

The whole place could probably hear her. The lobby was three storeys high. There were balconies above us with tables and chairs perched on them. An army guy sat up there with a drink in his hand and a lady sat beside him knitting, and in the meantime I couldn't see anything out the front door except a mass of Chinese people who'd decided the best idea was to hoof it out to the jungle. Seemed like somebody had the scuttlebutt and somebody didn't.

"What about *Miss* Brown in thirty-*nine*?"

"Sorry, Mrs. Brown."

"Well, patience is a virtue," she said.

Someone was pounding with a hammer up above our heads — it would've been all right if he'd only kept time with the piano. I saw that I had half-moons of sweat under the armpits of my jacket. Ever since Robinson's I'd been wearing two sets of clothes.

"Lovely music, isn't it? Wonderful." You watched a couple of army officers going out the door. "It would be lovely to have more of this and less hiding under the beds."

I pointed with my chin up at the ceiling — it seemed a very naval-lieutenant thing to do.

"I wish they'd cut out the racket."

"Last night a bomb hit the roof, so they must have work to do. Oh, and later there'll be dancing!"

A sign at the back of the lobby said DAN HOPKINS AND HIS BAND — STILL SWINGING, BELIEVE IT OR NOT!

"Can you come dancing tonight? Before your ship goes?"

"I don't have a ship anymore."

"Don't you?" You bit your lip. "None at all?"

I didn't know what to make of that. Your mother hobbled over and handed you a couple of keys with wooden tags.

"He would have to buy a tuxedo." She leaned hard against you and I saw you square up your feet to keep from toppling over. "Though I suppose he could find a bargain in the shops. Let's go to the rooms, Lily, and the lieutenant can have a wash and decide what he would like to do next. It is a shame that you lost hold of your friend," she told me. "He seemed very nice."

We went up the staircase, each of us holding a big thick elbow. Your mother had to rest at the landing.

"They say they can send up a radio." She was breathing hard. "Which I suppose will do. But they won't be inclined to let us take it home, will they? When will Ah Lin have mended the wall, do you suppose?"

"I imagine he's gone by now, Mum."

"*Pergi ulu.*" She got a kick out of saying that. "Well, perhaps he mended it before he went. Lieutenant Winslow, you are very kind. They told us we were mad to go out walking with the Japanese about, but I did need fresh air."

We got to the top and went down a hallway that was open on one side so that we could look down on a courtyard full of palm trees and flowers. There was a breeze up there, which didn't make your mother any lighter but at least it cooled the back of my neck.

"Much as I would like to charge after your father, I suppose he would prefer if we stayed put," she said. "Lily, you *are* very brave."

Every door had a six-inch gap down at the floor, for air circulation, I figured, like my old ventilation grate. The guys would have robbed each other blind if we'd had gaps like that at the Dunsmuir Hotel. We came to room thirty-eight and I held onto your mother's wrist instead of her elbow while you opened the door. The blackout curtains made the room pretty gloomy. You went in and pulled the mosquito net back from around the bed, then led her over. I watched from the door. You pulled off her shoes. Everything was quiet except for a *boom* off somewhere.

"What have I done with that hat?" She touched her hair. "Ask the lieutenant to look for it." She sounded very wispy.

"I'll do that," I said.

"There you are. So many promotions in wartime. I know you will do very well."

You kissed her on the cheek. "I'll show him where to wash and then look in on you. I'll have them send up your tea."

"Just a little broth."

You pulled the mosquito net back across then you came out and shut the door.

"Come along to my room."

Of course number thirty-nine was neat as a pin so I couldn't learn anything about you from that, though I don't know what I'd been hoping to see — stacks of records, maybe. You had a canopy bed with mosquito netting over it, just the same as your mother, and a picture on the wall called *The Fox Hunt*, and beside that was the door to the bathroom.

"Bother. I forgot there's only one bath a day. The water mains are shattered so the boy has to bring it in. You'll save enough for me, won't you? Towels are just there. Oh, I am sorry, you scoop the water from the jar and douse yourself, the native style — funny, isn't it?"

You let the door swing shut and I peeled off my layers of clothes, which took a couple of minutes. They stank, I stank, and when I looked in the mirror there was an Irish stoker staring back at me, black right down his neck. During our afternoon together I'd imagined myself looking much more dashing, so I took it as a good sign that you were at least being polite. One consolation was that my pimples had disappeared under all that muck. I heard you shutting drawers out in the room, maybe you even had your dress off, and there I was with my mister looking down at the tiles.

Gotta get my old tuxedo pressed, gotta sew a button on my vest
'Cause tonight I've gotta look my best

I poured the water over my head. It was cold as hell. I hollered.

"Doesn't it feel wonderful?" you asked.

The water ran black down the drain. I tried to splash water up into all my corners and probably used too much of it. I scrubbed my neck with a bar of soap that smelled like flowers. I looked in the mirror again. I'd had a good sunburn under all of that muck so the pimples still didn't look so bad. I put my new clothes with the rips in them back on and left the old ones in a pile beside the ceramic garbage pail. There were little gaps up in the top of the wall, probably for more ventilation, and I'd seen blue sky through them when you'd led me in but by the time I'd finished it was dark outside. I mussed my hair in the mirror so it stood up in the front.

You were sitting on a stool holding a glass of water. You'd pulled all the netting back from your bed and laid a white gown out on it and a pair of those gloves that girls wear right up to their armpits.

"Who's this strange man?" you asked. "Goodness."

Your hair was frizzier than when I'd first seen you, and you'd taken your shoes and your pearl earrings off and you had streaks of dirt down your face that I hadn't noticed before. You looked like you might need some entertaining.

"Seaman Winslow, Cap'n." I clicked my heels together. "Here to swab the poop, Cap'n."

You put the glass of water on the desk. I would have liked some.

"It's a shame you haven't anything else to wear, Harry, it would have been wonderful to have had a dance downstairs but they're terribly stuffy about their ballroom, even at a time like this. Silly, isn't it? Still, people will tell you that that's what they're fighting for. That's why they signed up."

You opened the wardrobe and took a white bathrobe off a hanger.

"You'll excuse me while I have a bathe? I'll meet you in the foyer. It might tickle Mum if we were to eat supper in her room."

You crossed to the hallway door and held it open.

"Then you can decide where you'd like to go."

"I can get my hands on a tuxedo. My friend's got one."

"I thought your things were all burnt up."

"He kept his with him."

"What was his name again? Something funny."

"Bunny."

"I knew it was funny."

Our faces were a foot apart as I went out the door and I looked for a sign in your eyes but all they said was that you were tired as hell. I shuffled out into the dark corridor and you shut the door behind me. I shoved my hands into my pockets and carried on towards the stairs but my new pockets were much deeper than my old ones, which came as a hell of a shock. The door opened again and you stuck your head out.

"Mind you stay by the ditches. They might be dropping bombs the whole night."

"But Japs can't see at night."

"What rubbish!"

Down in the lobby three girls were crying their eyes out while two guys in uniform and one in a white suit rubbed their girls' arms and muttered into the top of their heads. I wondered what plans each couple had made before the Japs had come along, if any of them were married, or engaged, or neither but they'd still slept together that afternoon as a parting gesture. One girl with a flower in her hair kept throwing her arms around the guy, then resisting, putting her hands back in her lap, then throwing her arms around him again. It wasn't easy to watch, but I did. I felt terrible for the whole lot of them. Of course I wasn't usually so charitable to other people, especially not young lovers like that, but ever since I'd washed with your bar of soap I'd found my perspective had changed. A dad and mom sat on a chesterfield, two little kids in his lap, one of them wearing their dad's jacket with a lot of braid hanging off the shoulder. The mom kept blowing her nose. I nodded to the Chinese piano player and he threw in a couple notes from the death march song.

Outside the bugs were fiddling away under the trees and there was a hum in the air — maybe the breeze, I couldn't tell. Bushy Moustache was sitting beside the front door, his legs stretched out, a pipe in his mouth.

"Here, lad," he said.

I still couldn't figure out what that whining was — an airplane?

"What's the trouble?" I asked.

"Oh, no fear. It's no trouble." When he wasn't shouting he had a bit of a Liverpool accent. "I'm only curious why you're still around if you're not in the service." He pointed out at the water with his pipe. "If not for the stripes, if I were a civilian, let me tell you, I'd be gone in a canoe if I had one. I'm not the type to give a cause up for lost, but this *is* a lost cause. If a lady keeps you, a lady keeps you, but this Singapore's had it."

A ship exploded out in harbour — I must've been listening to the shell fly over the island! Chunks of burning boat flew up in the air then took their time fluttering back down to the water.

"I didn't plan that, lad. Just excellent timing. Here, keep that door shut." He glared up at Turban. "There's a blackout."

I walked along the cricket field, listening to the *boom boom* out beyond the city someplace. I couldn't figure out why the blackout was still on since half the houses were on fire and the glow from the docks reflected on the underside of the smoke. I looked back at Raffles but I only saw a couple of windows where the curtains weren't quite pulled across. I couldn't have guessed which window was yours. Somebody passed me on a bicycle. Just whirred by without saying anything.

The cricket pitch sounded like it was full of birds. I found our mattress right where we'd left it and I figured I might drag it back to you as a souvenir but somebody was lying on it. He jumped to his feet.

"Who goes?"

He sounded like an Aussie.

"Civilian," I said.

He rattled something in his hands. "Got anything to eat?"

"No, sir."

"All they give at the bloody Y is a bun and a cup of bloody tea." He lay down on the mattress again. "Come here to find our unit."

I could heard him drinking. *Dook-dook-dook.* A shell whined somewhere.

"Well, I have to be someplace," I said.

"No, you don't."

The birds in the field stopped chirping. He was tapping his bottle against something metal.

"Where you fighting?" I asked.

"McRitchie Reservoir? Name like that. I've no idea. Where you from?"

"Canada."

"Aw, we've got one of them!"

Somebody fired a gun out on the field and the noise rang off the trees. I could see shapes coming towards us, talking in loud voices, then from the sound of it one of them ran into an anti-glider fortification.

"That's my mates!" The Aussie got up. "Oy!" Eight or ten of them were coming at us, not one walking steady. "Which one's that Canadian bugger?"

"Here, Miss." It sounded like Ray. "Present."

"I've caught another one! What's your name, mate?"

"Winslow," I said.

"It's Winslow!" My Aussie fell back on the mattress. "Bloody Winslow!"

"Harry? From Vernon, B.C.?" Ray came and put his arm around me and poked me in the stomach with the end of a bottle. He had a helmet on. "What in hell you think you're doing?" he asked.

"I've got a date tonight."

He ran the wine bottle up my chest.

"We haven't found any whores," he said. "We haven't. Gentlemen! We are *not* going to bash him up. Look elsewhere. Harry. These are Australians. I know, we've had trouble with them. I know."

He stunk like a backed-up john. I held him up under the armpit. His beard went across my cheek. Somebody fired a machine gun twenty feet away, and a branch fell out of the tree. It rang in my ears for a second.

"We are confident!" one of them hollered.

"Our defences strong!" They started to go back across the field. "Wahoo!"

"Efficient," Ray muttered.

"What in hell you doing?" I said.

"All seriousness. Shh. These Australians know other Australians."

"Sure."

"Got a boat." He slid down onto one knee, then up again. "You, I'll vouch for. Good sailor. You don't want to be the goat, do you? Not us, boy, we're on an upward ..."

He held up his arm, showing me how we were on our way up, but it looked like an Adolph Hitler salute — pointing out the mustard on his face. That had been our old joke. Ray had been a lot funnier back then.

"Where's this boat?" I asked.

"The pier. Clifford Pier. That's twelve-thirty in the afternoon."

"Twelve-thirty in the afternoon. How many they got room for?"

"Half-twelve they call it. Ha! All right, Harry? All right."

He got up and held his helmet down on his head and ran out into the field. Their guns fired and a bullet rang off something right next to me. I ran out into the road but I fell in a hole and scraped the heel of my hand on something. A broken brick. In all your years in Singapore I don't know if you ever tried running around it in the dark when the roads were full of craters. They weren't shooting their guns anymore but I could hear Ray giggling. I picked up that piece of brick and put it in one of my deep trouser pockets — of course by then I'd decided where I was headed. That was clear in my mind. But every time I heard a shell go *boom* away in the distance I'd think, is this Halloween? Then back to picking my way along the road. Then *boom boom* away in the distance. Is this Halloween? No, it's not. Even then, with the possibility of kissing a girl right in front of me, a definite mission, I couldn't keep my mind right where I was.

The light improved as I got to the river. A lot of houses had fire flickering in the windows, and I could see guys carrying buckets down to the water. I walked back over the same bridge. The oil was still burning on the river. Three old Chinese guys dangled fishing rods over the side, laughing away about something.

I followed the smell of gin around dark corners to Robinson & Co., but when I crept to the front the only smell was burning rubber. The shells that I'd been hearing all afternoon must've been falling on that parking lot, because half of the cars were upside-down, their upholstery still crackling and popping. It looked pretty, like fires for a corn roast, but now I can't help but think what all of those cars would be worth if they were still in one piece today. There ought to have been a clause in the Geneva Convention against destroying quality automobiles, which of course would only have given the Japanese more paper to wipe their bottoms with.

At any rate I wasn't looking where I was going — trying to see which was the chassis of a Hillman — and slid three feet into a crater. It was wet at the bottom and my boot got stuck under something. I tried to work the toe loose and suddenly realized that more shells might still be on their way. Then I heard somebody whistling from the side of the store — "Danny Boy," it sounded like, which was better than a Jap shell splattering out my brains but not by much. A watchman? An escaped nut? I got my fingers on the grille of the nearest car and hauled myself up, then ran across the sidewalk and under the stone arches. The windows were dark but I figured I had the right one. The whistler had reached that middle part of "Danny Boy" that no one knows the words to.

I took the brick out of my pocket and threw it at the middle of the glass, and the whole sheet came crashing down. I kept my arm over my face. Somebody started to blow a whistle, *shree-shree-shree*. I'd committed one crime and was about to commit another, but keep in mind that I also faced the possibility of kissing a girl. I clattered over the splinters of glass and reached through the shards that were still hanging there — I felt the dummy under my hands and hoped like hell it was still wearing its tuxedo. I didn't want a lady's bathing costume. Yeah, there was the bow tie.

The *shree-shree-shree* was coming straight for me by then, feet were running up the colonnade so I got the dummy under my arm like a six-foot-long football and skittered back out to the parking lot, a hinged leg hitting the back of my knee with every step. I ran between the cars and hopped into a hole that turned out to be even deeper than the first one. I sat at the bottom with my dummy in my lap.

It was hot in that hole and everything smelled of gasoline. I could hear the Whistler walk back and forth through the broken glass but as far as I could tell he never once came down into the parking lot. He might've thought that I was Ray's whole gang and in his shoes I wouldn't have chanced it either. A piece of upholstery flared up behind me and I saw that the dummy's eyes were painted blue.

After the whistler didn't make a sound for five minutes I lay the dummy out across the top of hole and started to undress him. His outfit had all kinds of hooks and clasps so it took some time, and I hoped like hell that you hadn't picked up and gone dancing already. I pulled my brown suit off then climbed out of the hole in my stocking feet, but there was broken glass everywhere so I had to jump onto a car door. The metal was still hot as a stove so I had to hop back into the glass. All for Lily, I kept telling myself, and I tried to remember what you looked like exactly.

Turban was still at the door of the Raffles, trimming the wick on a little oil lamp, but Bushy Moustache had buggered off — instead there was a clean-shaven Limey officer who kept scratching the side of his neck.

"Good night for mosquitoes," he said. "What's this? Going dancing?"

"Here for Miss Brown." The tuxedo was meant for a guy with a much bigger neck, so I tried to look broad-shouldered. "Room thirty-nine."

"No business of mine." He had this lopsided grin. "That's not Colonel Brown's daughter?"

"She," said Turban. Though to tell you the truth it could have been a different guy in a turban and I would never have known.

"I see. That's how she's playing it." The officer stretched his arms above his head. "You'll have an auspicious night."

I knocked on thirty-nine but thirty-eight opened up.

"I thought it might be you," you said.

Not *hoping* that it might be. You had your white gown on but not your gloves-to-your-armpits. You took a step back so the light went in my eyes.

"Christ on a bike," you said. "Don't *you* look smashing."

The skin on your shoulders was the same colour as your dress. You'd put on the pearl earrings and your hair looked shiny. Your breasts were good-sized, as I'm sure you remember, their pre-internment size, but I had to quit staring as you led me in. Your mother was sneering at a ginger fizz on her nightstand.

"I cannot *stand* that, Lily. 'Christ on a bike.' Why would you go out of your way to sound common? Have you not found your crew yet, Lieutenant Winslow?"

She meant me. The *leftenant*. You went over and stirred her bowl of soup.

"I think it would be wonderful to see Christ Jesus riding a bicycle." You brought the spoon up to your mother's face. "Maybe he rings a little bell."

"Please go away. Go dancing or whatever it is that you're doing."

"Mum! You're frightful."

"And ask why there's no radio. He may have made a broadcast. The nerve of the *amah* to ask why we hadn't gone! You do look radiant, the both of you."

Then she made a noise like a sob and sat staring at the jug and basin. You touched her face but she batted your hand away.

"He won't be long," you said. "Have faith."

"Frightful," your mother said. "I'll muddle through."

You picked up a white handbag, then kissed your mother on the cheek. We went out into the hall and you shut the door. The light shone under the gap so I could see you well enough, and I decided that I'd try putting my hand on your cheek, then see if you'd let me kiss you.

"You're bleeding."

You took my hand and kissed the back of it, then you held it down in front of you so we could see it in the light — it was stuck full of gravel from when I'd fallen in the road. I wanted to turn it over to see the lipstick on the back — a kiss! The tuxedo seemed to be working. It seemed like a long time since we'd been stuck on the bridge with the sirens and the chickens.

"Let's run along to the Long Bar," you said. "Wash this up in the loo."

You took my arm and steered me away from the stairs, in a direction I'd never been before. Your ear was right beside my shoulder. Bugs whistled down in the courtyard under those coconut palms.

"Balmy night," you said.

"One of the craziest."

Then we heard a band starting up, clarinets and that, but far away, maybe even at another hotel, and the song they played was slower than molasses in January. Ray and I had nearly seen a dance band in Liverpool but he'd knocked over the ticket girl on our way in the door.

"We'll start with gin slings. They are *delicious.*" You squeezed my arm. "Pair of Singapore Slings." You reached up and tapped one of the dark lamps hanging over our heads. "Have you ever had one?"

"Heard of it," I said. "Never had it."

Which was true regarding more than just the drink.

We came up to a pair of frosted glass doors with light shining through them just as another couple came out — she was a hefty one with her hair stuck up over her ears and he was a little guy in a short white jacket and a pair of pants with big red stripes down the sides. He could've led a parade.

"Helen and Duncan," you said. "How wonderful. Your last night out?"

"Looks that way," said Duncan. "Bloody looks that way."

"Duncan," said Helen.

"Never mind."

"Duncan says that he must get some *makan*, so we're going for a walk in the Hastings Road."

"Good curry like coolies have," said Duncan.

"I'm sorry," you said, "this is Harold Winslow. Lieutenant Winslow. Helen Paisley and Duncan Henderson. He's in the Royal Engineers."

He put out his hand to shake.

"My hand's mucked up," I said.

"Never mind. Lucky to have our heads! You must have been in banking before this, Winslow, you'll always see a banker in a nice tuxedo like that."

"He *was* in banking," you said. "Just straightened the last of his affairs."

"Thrilling time for banking," said Duncan.

"Now this looks exactly like the tuxedo at Robinson's I was telling you about, Duncan, you see how they've brought the lapels out?" Helen ran her hand down my lapel. I tried to stand up straight. "But aren't you and your mother away yet, Lily? I'm away tomorrow, the P & O say they've something for us."

"We're waiting on Dad."

"Better for him now if you're away," said Duncan. "He shouldn't be too pleased to come across you in a bloody prisoner-of-war camp."

"Go and wash your poor hands." You rubbed my shoulder, and I could feel the knot from pulling that rickshaw all day. "I'll order you a *pahit*."

"You *must* write to me, Lily," said Helen. "I'll be throwing fits to see how this turns out."

I went around the corner and found the Gents on my left. They had electric lights turned on in there and everything was made of brass or crystal. I didn't have to go particularly, since all I'd eaten since breakfast was one sandwich, but I sat on the toilet anyway. It was the fanciest one I'd ever sat on that I wasn't going to end up cleaning. It was the fanciest toilet I'd ever sat on, period, and it croaked like a frog when I flushed. I figured that must be what good plumbing sounded like.

I tugged and tugged at a piece of gravel in my palm until I finally realized it was actually a piece of my hand. I caught a glimpse of myself in the mirror, elegant as hell of course, gritting my teeth with a tear in the corner of my eye. The faucets said *Vernon Tutbury England*, which was probably a much more refined place than the Vernon I knew, but for all that no water came out of them. I had to put the plug in the sink and fill it from a bucket. The rest of the gravel washed off all right but I was careful not to scrub your lipstick off the back of my hand.

The Long Bar was full of Chinese waiters in white shirts and bow ties. There were green hurricane lamps set all along the bar so that when I spotted you your face looked kind of yellow. Your handbag sat beside the bowl of peanuts. Two guys with cards in their hands sat at a table looking you over but they went back to playing when I sat down.

"Let's see the sorry hand." You inspected the palm, then turned it over. "You could have washed the lipstick off!"

"Figured I should keep it."

You smiled and put your elbows on the bar. You already had a big red drink with pineapple stuck in the top, and there was one in front of me too. We drank through straws. It tasted like fruit punch.

"There," you said. "Now you can say you've had one."

I kept sucking until it was gone. There were mirrors behind the bar so I could watch the bartender collect our glasses. His neck was shaved halfway up the back of his head.

"Now a pina colada," you said. "I adore coconut! In the right part of the world for it, aren't we? You fancy her?"

There was a painting above the bar of a girl lying on a tiger-skin rug; she was naked except for a little cloth over her privates. Her breasts were pure white, and she tugged on the tiger's ear like she was going to say something to him. Her hair looked just like Helen's.

"I don't like her hair," I said.

"She does look awfully romantic."

I picked up your hand and kissed the back of it.

"Thank you," you said.

I turned it over and kissed the inside. Tasted warm. You pulled it back.

"Mum doesn't like it. Says it's terribly gauche."

You were still looking at the painting. I was figuring out the limits of what the tuxedo could accomplish. The pina colada was too sweet. Overend had never drunk pina coladas as far as I knew but it made me think of him for some reason. The girl on the tiger kept watching us.

"At least she looks comfortable," I said.

"Well she isn't, that head's like a great rock. A girl I knew at school had one. Any rate, drink up. We've things to discuss." You touched your hair behind your ear. "Shall we dance after this?"

"I hope those shoes are sturdy," I said. "Grandma never finished teaching me."

"Your grandmother taught you? Honestly?"

"I'm just kidding you," I said. "My sister taught me."

The bartender slid me a slip of paper that said *Raffles Long Bar* at the top and *3 s. 6 d.* at the bottom. The way you Limeys wrote your money didn't make a lick of sense. You took the slip out of my hand and signed your name on it.

"Mum will treat. Now, I have a question to put to you — no, I'll wait until we're dancing. Whisper it in your ear."

You spun around on your stool then reached back around to take your handbag off the bar, and your chest looked just terrific — I'd seen movies with girls wearing gowns like yours but their chests just hadn't been up to it. Twenty guys in there, and twenty peanuts sat half-cracked in their fingers the instant you turned around. I slid off my stool but then I had to hold the leather seat to keep steady. I never was a big drinker.

You took the hand without the gravel and led me out of the bar and down a spiral staircase. Your heels clacked across the tiles of the courtyard. Crickets sang in the trees, though of course we were in the Orient so maybe they weren't crickets at all, and I could hear the clarinets again but they still sounded far away, like when the Vernon & District Show Band played the band-shell on a Saturday afternoon and I was stuck at home chopping wood. Of course they'd been terrible but the injustice of being kept home had made them sound a lot better. You walked us between rows of big potted flowers; I could smell them more than I could see them.

"That band sounds a hundred miles away," I said.

"I will really be annoyed if the dancing is off."

As soon as you said that I got the feeling that there was something behind us in the dark. I didn't know what. I pictured Japs on their hands and knees. I didn't want to turn around so I kept my eyes on the outline of the door ahead of us, the light creeping through the slats, and when we got to it I turned around and of course there was nothing back there, just grey light down the trunks of the palm trees.

You looked up at me and straightened my bow tie.

The ballroom was gloomy except for little candles on the tables, there were no bright lights, no couples, no band — the dance floor looked as bleak as a winter night. Guys with perfect combed heads eating steaks at the tables around the door. A couple of them laughed like ninnies. You gave my hand a little squeeze — I guess that meant you were really annoyed. But those steaks they all had smelled like honest, juicy meat, not the smell of congealed grease like we'd had on *Asia*, and I realized that I was starved half to death. My legs sometimes gave out when I got hungry like that. I was no good at being hungry. A waiter in a white jacket lit a candle on a table, then he blew out the match and waved us over. "Order what you like! It's on Mrs. Brown!" But instead you led me through all the tables and out across the dance floor to the front of the stage. The music stands and chairs were still up there and somebody had left behind an accordion with a handwritten sign propped against it, saying *We'll Be Back!* The sign was in your shadow so at first I didn't see it. You turned to face me and put one arm around my waist and your fingers through the fingers of my gravelly hand. I leaned down to kiss you but my jackass lips hit the side of your nose.

"We're *dancing* now," you said.

You pulled my arm straight out to the side, and I recognized the dance so I put my left foot forward, then my right leg between your legs and started moving you backwards. I did it quickly so you'd have no doubt that I knew what I was doing.

"What's this?"

"It's the foxtrot," I said.

I smelled your forehead as we went along and decided that that was your exact smell; a person's forehead couldn't smell like anything but themselves. We were getting closer to the tables so I did those complicated little turning steps. You had your fingers in the small of my back and the middle of your body pressed against the middle of mine. It was different from dancing with Roberta, who I hadn't touched at all if I'd been able to help it. I counted four. Then I counted four.

"Shouldn't we dance properly?" you asked.

I just kept counting four.

"*Stop*, Harry."

We stopped. I could feel your shoulder blades beneath my hand. One of those officer types scraped a knife across his plate.

"Is that how you foxtrot in Canada? Do you have to rush back out to cut timber?"

"My sister was usually in a hurry in case her beau came over."

"Her beau. What song would you dance to, the 'William Tell'?"

"'Tain't No Sin,' by Lee Morse And Her Bluegrass Boys."

You looked up at me with your lips in a little knot. Your eyebrows were very symmetrical. You took a step backwards and pulled me with you, then did the sideways step, then the backwards step. We went so slowly that I could feel the side of your knee against the side of my knee. We glided right across the floor.

"So there was no cutting of timber?"

"In fact, Roberta told me to stay off dry land."

"Why was that?"

"Because the ocean is a lot safer."

You leaned into me so I started to go backwards in the other direction — we didn't have to make the complicated little turns at all! You started singing under your breath and your accent made the words sound very serious. Of course Lee Morse was a woman too, so you didn't sound far off.

When the lazy sync-o-pation

Step.

Of the music softly moans

Step–step.

You leaned closer into me and we did some of the turn steps out in the middle of the floor. I'd never figured that two people could foxtrot so close together.

"Benny Goodman was a Bluegrass Boy but they weren't that bad even so."

"Concentrate," you said.

A couple of the officer types whistled. You started humming the chorus so it sounded like a different song altogether. We did a lot of

spins out there. Then you backed against the stage and pulled me
into you. I put my arms around you.

"Have to ask you something," you said.

"All right." I kissed you on the cheek. Twice.

"It's for me and Mum."

"Okay."

"Do you have a boat to get away on?"

I looked at your nose. It had about six freckles.

"I do. Yeah."

"Can you get us out on it?"

"I thought you had to stay here."

"Yes, but *could* you get us out?"

You put your head back and gave me a look that said you didn't
want to hear any jokes. My mister had stayed calm through all that dancing, which was a real miracle, but as of that moment he was ready to
try something.

"I don't see why not," I said. "They told me half-twelve tomorrow."

The grim look evaporated from your face. You put your forehead on
my shoulder. It really was warm in that ballroom. You held the back of my
jacket and pulled me closer so I knew you could feel my mister then. But
I didn't jump away. I figured I'd let you be in charge and see where I ended
up. My mister didn't want to go anyway. Your hands moved up my back.

"There's something I'd like us to do." You were speaking into my
chest. "Before we go away together."

"What's that?" I asked.

I imagine that my voice cracked but maybe it didn't, maybe I ought
to give myself more credit. Of course I had an inkling what it might be
but I thought I'd better play dumb for a minute in case all you wanted
was to go for an egg cream.

"You *know*," you whispered.

I didn't know if I knew! But if it was something other than what
I thought, wouldn't you be able to come out and say it? As far as I knew
there was just the one thing that people didn't talk about even when
that was exactly what they were discussing, or that's what I'd been led
to believe.

"Do you think it's a rotten idea?" you asked.

"No!"

I waited to see what would happen next. I wondered how quickly I could unhitch those pants if I had to. But you didn't say anything for a while. And my mister was becoming less giddy by the second even though there was a distinct possibility that this was going to be the biggest day of his life. The top of your head smelled a bit like salad dressing. I started to think that I might have imagined the whole conversation. You kept your hands tight around my back. *We'll Be Back!* said the accordion.

"It's been like a film." Your voice was a bit muffled by my armpit. "Ever since I came back from school I knew they were coming. My friends from school knew they were coming. I have their letters that say, 'Get your mum and dad out of there.' I knew they were right, I knew the Japanese were coming, and they just want the town, don't they? They've no use for us. They'll kill us all, and why shouldn't they? What possible use could they have for us?"

I kept looking at that sign. For all I knew the guy who'd written it had already had his head blown off.

"But no one here's done anything about it and I knew that no one would. It's been like watching a film that says that we're English and we're absolutely wonderful, and elsewhere in the cinema there are these other people with knives waiting to chop us to bits. And I knew it would be like that, I knew when it was the beginning of the film and then the middle and now it's the end." You looked up at me. I thought your face would be all crinkled, your nose running, but instead you just looked a little sleepy. "But I didn't know that you were coming, Harry. I honestly had no idea."

I thought that maybe after we went to bed you were going to ask me to pick up a gun and chase the Japs back into the ocean, and for all I knew after I'd been to bed with you I'd be able to. I had no idea what I'd be able to do, though just then I couldn't picture what a Jap even looked like. Ted Yakamura? He'd have kicked me jackass to breakfast. I smoothed back the hair on the side of your head with my fingertips.

"They have always told me not to say certain things," you said.

"Not to go certain places, not to talk to certain people. And I have been as good as gold. If they were travelling second class I would walk right past. And look how useful that's been. Wasting one another's time. But *you* know exactly what's going on, you've arrived to see the place as it really is. You could never have wasted as much time as I have. I've never been to bed with anyone before tonight. Not entirely."

You kept looking at me. I was waiting for you to say something else.

"Okay," I said.

You leaned up and we kissed on the lips. At first the kiss didn't feel quite right but then it started to go really well, and after half a minute it felt like we could each make an honest living by kissing the other one. It was like we were just lips and mouths with our arms and legs floating out behind us. That really was the picture I had in my head. But then you quit.

"I've always thought that I would be married," you said. "When I was little I decided that I would have to be married before I went to bed with someone."

"We can get married," I said.

You put your hand flat over my lips and I kissed your palm. You didn't say it was gauche, you just took my hand and walked me back across the dance floor. You were looking at the ground. Did you know where we were going? We've talked about that night a hundred times but we've only ever talked about Ricky, never about the things that happened before. Just then I couldn't help thinking that the whole evening might be a joke that you'd planned while I was in the Gents, that was why you'd been grinning when I came into the bar, and once you got me up to your room Duncan and Helen were going to jump out of the wardrobe and throw blue paint over me. No one had ever talked about going to bed with me before so I couldn't convince myself entirely that I wasn't being taken in. A steak-eater with a flower in his buttonhole pushed his chair back and got to his feet. He leaned his knuckles on the table, he was tipsy as hell.

"Dash it," he said. "My handshake is my promise."

We left the ballroom and went up a corridor that was completely dark. Glasses tinkled on shelves as we walked by and you kept changing your grip on my hand. The night smelled like flowers and that made me nervous again. We came out into the back of the lobby. The only light was a candle on the piano; a dozen guys were asleep in the chairs and another dozen sat staring off into space with cigarettes between their fingers. I felt pretty damn good to have a place to go and someone to go there with. I steered us towards the stairs and room thirty-nine but you stopped dead beside the piano, with those dozen guys all watching us.

"Outside," you said.

You led me to the front door and I tried to keep my chin up as we crossed the lobby like this was all part of a plan. We stepped out into the night with the chattering bugs, and there wasn't a light to be seen, just that glow in the sky — Head-Scratcher and Turban had buggered off, thank Christ — and you turned on the top step and started kissing me again. You had your hands on either side of my face but I could still hear the *booms* up the hill. The inside of your mouth was warm. You gave sharp little kisses and then long ones; my mister paid very close attention. The front of my brain was kissing and the back was wondering how long it would be before we were up in your room even though your mother would be asleep next door. You kept your hands over my ears. I could feel the zipper of those new pants pressing against my mister — it didn't feel good but I figured I could live with it under the circumstances. Somebody in the lobby sat on the piano keyboard, it sounded like, then you looked up at me.

"Maybe we *can* get married."

I hope the surprise didn't show in my face. Because I must've figured that once we'd said we would get married that would be the end of it.

"See the light across? That line in the trees. They've got their curtains down but that's St Andrew's. We know the bishop there. Mr. Wilson. Mum knows him well. Shall we go and see if he won't do it?"

You'd already gone down a step, so what could I do? I shrugged and went down with you. So you made a serious proposal of marriage and I answered with a shrug. I didn't see any reason to *not* get married, especially after everything that had happened that day. I didn't have my articles after three and a half years of trying to keep the paper from getting wrinkled, and it felt like walking around with one shoe. I had no affiliation. I wanted to go up to room thirty-nine and pull your dress off over your head, but even if it didn't get that far I still wanted that evening to keep going the way it was, and I figured that if I just said, "Are you dead sure about this?" you might drop my hand and wander away under the trees. And where would I go then? Look for Bunny? For Ray? It would be better to hold your hand come what may.

As we crossed the road a lot of motors came roaring at us out of the dark so we had to dash across, then held hands by the ditch and peered at the line of trucks going past with their lights off and canvas flapping. Then motorcycles with their lights out too. One rider looked like he had a bandage around his head. We stood in the quiet after they'd gone.

"Look at the moon," you said. It sat right above the hill. "There's no man in the moon, do you see it? Because it's sideways here. Can you see it's a rabbit?"

It was only a half-moon so I couldn't make out any rabbits.

St Andrew's turned out to be the church where we'd seen the guys on stretchers — I saw the ambulances as we got closer. Twigs snapped under our feet.

"I've never come quite this way before," you said.

"Or for this reason."

You bumped your shoulder against mine.

"Nor for this reason," you said.

It was a nice big church, lit up on the inside with all kinds of candles. There was a guy under a blanket on every pew, and nurses were handing out gauze and pouring glasses of water under the altar. I realized how thirsty I was from all that dancing in my monkey suit. It was stuffy in there and smelled like an outhouse as we walked down the aisle, so some guys must have lost control of themselves. They were singing a hymn. At first I'd thought it was just chatter but no, some guys with their arms in slings were sitting up, belting it out, and other guys lay stark naked except for the bandages around their chests, whispering away as best they could.

Praise my soul, the King of Heaven
To His feet thy tribute bring

One guy in uniform hopped up from a pew and grabbed your bare arm. He had mud all over his boots.

"How's about a dance?" he asked.

"You'd best sit down," I said.

And he sat down! Just as you'd said, the whole thing was like a movie. Except that we were in colour instead of black and white. We got to the front and stepped over three or four guys on stretchers who were staring up at the ceiling.

"Yes?" asked a nurse.

"Is the bishop here?"

"I don't believe so." She had a syringe in her hand. "Haven't seen him all day."

"Ricky would know," the other nurse said.

"Of course," you said. "We'll just find Ricky."

We walked up some wide steps beside the altar. More guys lay on cots up there. A black guy with his arms full of hymnals walked between the choir stalls.

"Oh, Ricky!" You nails bit into the side of my finger. "Is the bishop here?"

He straightened up and peered at us. A black guy with glasses and a moustache.

"Who's that?" he asked. "Looking for Mr. Wilson?"

"That's it." You swung our two hands back and forth. "We want to get married."

"Miss Brown! I didn't see you. You mean the Hawkings wedding. That was two-thirty yesterday afternoon. Perfectly beautiful."

"I know *that*, Ricky, I was there, can't you remember? Now *I* want to get married to Mr. Winslow here."

"Mr. Wilson's not here."

"Is he not? What a shame. When will he be back?"

"He's not here." Ricky shifted his stack of books. "And what's more he's married to Mrs. Wilson already."

A real comedian, old Ricky. A regular Gracie Allen.

"I've no intention of marrying *him*," you said. "I'm marrying Mr. Winslow."

You looked at me out of the corner of your eye. I realized that I still hadn't introduced myself so I stuck my hand out.

"Mr. Winslow," I said.

I felt very sophisticated with my tuxedo on. He put his books down on the pew so he could shake hands. He looked me up and down.

"Ah, *this* is Mr. Winslow. A pleasure, sir."

"Ricky is one of the assistant vergers," you said.

"Keeps me from the tin mines." He grinned. "Though having said that, it might get me into worse trouble yet because Mr. Wilson will not evacuate. He tells me that the worse it becomes the more people need their bishop. Mr. Stenton gave him a berth, but no."

"But surely *you* can go, Ricky?"

He put his hands on the railing. "I am assistant verger."

"What about Reverend Bennit? He could marry us."

"Today he has been everywhere." He gave a deep nod. "He has just gone to the Adelphi for a wash. Oh — candle!"

A nurse picked up a candle that had fallen over. Ricky gave a little grimace.

"But must it be tonight?" he asked.

You looked at me for a second. You still looked good, with that dress and the pearls, but you looked tired around the eyes. You squeezed my hand again. Our hands were sticky from holding each other, the way fingers get after peeling oranges.

"Yes," you told him. "Tonight."

"I am qualified to perform the wedding service," he said.

"Are you really?"

"Yes, of course. I have just written the examination. Who will be the witnesses?"

"My mother, I suppose." You looked at me again. "But she's not herself, Ricky, she won't make the trip. Could we not go to the Raffles?"

"I will fetch my papers and meet you outside."

The two nurses didn't look too impressed as we picked our way past in our evening wear. You walked me back up the aisle with candles flickering on either side. The soldiers all sang *Praise Him, praise Him, Hallelujah*. I saw a guy pee into a bottle.

We kissed again outside the church. The trees were full of squawking birds. I started to get a taste in my mouth like I'd drank a lot of milk, maybe that was a side effect of too much kissing. Then you moved away from my mouth and kissed me on the neck and this tingle went straight down my leg and into the ground.

"Did you ever imagine it?" you asked. "Not a priest but a Tamil assistant verger?"

"What's a Tamil?"

"From the south of India. Don't you think he's lovely?"

"I don't have a ring for your finger."

"I don't mind about that."

"I could cobble something together."

"We are ready?" Ricky stood in the open doorway with the candles flickering behind him. Those doors had to be ten feet tall.

We kept holding hands even though the sweat ran off our fingers. Ricky followed five feet behind us, under the trees, back into the Raffles, and all along he was humming something, *hm hm HM HM hm hm hm*, and it wasn't until we were passing the piano in the lobby that I recognized it as "Ode to Joy." Roberta had been learning it on piano just as I quit practising, which made me think of how my folks had talked about what would happen when Roberta got married, what kind of cake Ma would bake, the dress she'd sew, who was going to come, but they had never once talked about me. I felt better when I realized that, that we weren't going to be breaking their hearts back home. We led Ricky up the stairs. The world can change that quickly, as quick as you snap your fingers. That's how I'll explain it to the folks, I thought, when the time comes.

You knocked on thirty-eight and went right in.

"Mum?"

The lamp was lit beside her bed and she sat there with her hairnet on. She looked like Frankenstein's monster.

"I didn't ring for a boy," she said. "I didn't ring."

"Christ on a bike, Mum, don't you recognise Ricky? You've only seen him every day. That's fine there, Ricky, everything on the table. Prepare yourself, Mum, I have an announcement. Are you prepared?"

"Oh, well then." She settled the pillow behind her. "I imagine I am."

"Harry and I are getting married, in this room, at this very minute." She gave one long blink.

"There will need to be another," said Ricky. "There must be two witnesses."

"Does it matter who?" you asked.

Ricky opened a fat book and ran his finger down the page. He moved his lips a bit. "I suppose not," he said. "But they must be able to comprehend English."

"Back in two shakes."

You let go of my hand and went to the door but then you came back and kissed me on the lips, and I was glad as hell that you did because as soon as you'd let got of my hand it crossed my mind that Helen and Duncan might come charging in with their paint can after all. Ricky waited in the middle of the room with his Bible pressed against his chest, looking like he was either trying to remember something or to not pass gas.

"Lieutenant Winslow," your mother said. "Do take a seat."

I sat down on the chair beside the bed and held the armrests for dear life. The quilt was folded over her knees and she kept smoothing it from the middle out to the sides. She wasn't looking at me. I kept glancing at her to make sure she wasn't.

"We once had a Tamil gardener," she said.

Ricky rocked back on his heels.

"In this part of the world it is possible to have a really beautiful garden. Like Eden, if you could manage it. Eve and Adam. We used to have a Tamil gardener named Malaravan. It took me six weeks to memorize that. Malaravan. Colonel Brown said we ought to call him Milo but I could never come around to that. I called him my lion among gardeners. The lawn was spotless. The beds revitalized. Then one day he asked leave to go to Melaka for his brother's wedding, which we allowed him to do, and of course he never came back. After Malaravan had gone the only ones we could engage were Chinese, and let me make this crystal clear — the Chinese have minds of their own. We had a long line of them because they refused to speak English to me, though at the time they were engaged every one of them insisted he could, so only Colonel Brown could instruct them as he speaks fluent Chinese. He would instruct them to trim the hedge and they would go off and plant marigolds in the middle of the lawn and never mind. Now right as you came in I was sitting here thinking how wonderful it must have been to have been upset by such a thing as marigolds. Wouldn't it be lovely to be worried about marigolds? And then I wondered how Malaravan was getting on, because I often think of him, and you came in, Ricky, the only other Tamil I know by name, at the very moment that I thought of Malaravan. As though it were foreordained."

I half-expected Ricky to throw on a coolie hat and say, "But Mum, it is me, your Malaravan, come back to your arms!" Because in a movie they would have wound up being the same guy. But Ricky didn't even blink.

"Those Chinese," your mother said. "All the way to this country to plant a lot of marigolds. If you ask me they're the ones who need repotting."

Then you came back in looking frazzled, but I got to my feet and you smiled like seeing me really did make you feel better. I'd never made that impression on anyone who wasn't my mother. A hotel boy in a white jacket came in behind you — he was rubbing his eyes and the hair stood up on the back of his head. He looked about thirty.

"I found a boy," you said. "Will he do?"

"Quite all right," said Ricky. "Stand just here, please."

I took your hand and we stood in front of Ricky and his Bible. Your mother stayed in bed and the boy stood beside her.

Ricky talked but I can't remember what he said. We said some things back to him. He took a ring off his finger, dropped it into my hand and I slid it onto your finger. Everything was strange and quiet like the room was full of water.

Then you had your arms around my neck and we were kissing, your tongue moving under mine, and I knew exactly what was happening.

Ricky put the Bible under his arm, went to the table, put down the Bible, opened another book, dipped his pen and looked over his shoulder at the hotel boy.

"What is your name, please?"

"Wee-Wee, sir," said the boy.

You had to clap your hand over your mouth. Ricky made Wee-Wee sign his name, then Ricky carried the book over to your mother and Wee-Wee picked up your mother's empty soup bowl and left the room. Wee-Wee, the witness to history. Ricky put the book back on the table and we signed our names. I remember that moment better than anything — you had a beautiful signature while I almost forgot to dot my *i*.

"What time is it, please?" asked Ricky.

Your mother found her watch on the nightstand. "Nearly half-one."

"I must empty the toilets," he said.

"We'll come and see you tomorrow," you said.

"Thank you, Miss Brown."

"Winslow," you said.

Mrs. Winslow — that was you. I hadn't made that jump yet.

"Miss Winslow," he said.

And out he went. You'd moved the wedding ring to your thumb; it was copper-coloured except for a black plate across the top with a letter R carved into it. We probably should've given it back.

"Kisses." Your mother held up her arms. "Mother of the bride."

We went to the bed and each got a peck on the mouth. She wasn't as gruff about it as I would've thought. She almost seemed happy.

"Your father will applaud your thrift, dear, since you always said you wanted salmon and champagne at Café Wien. And an officer — you did get that. Do you know Café Wien, Lieutenant?"

"Call him Harry, Mum."

"I don't know it," I said.

"It is prohibitively expensive. You'll make Colonel Brown's acquaintance soon enough, Mr. Wilson. Perhaps when the four of us are elsewhere we can do this again. He'll find it very interesting."

"*Winslow*, Mum."

She sank back on the pillows and closed her eyes.

"Winslow," she said.

You smiled down at her, rubbing your hand up and down my sleeve. My mister mentioned that he hadn't forgotten about pulling your dress off over your head. You stopped rubbing my arm and gave me a sour face.

"Look at this! I'm bleeding!"

We held your hand next to the lamp. There was a spot of blood on the meaty part of your palm.

"Sliver?" I said.

"Bit of glass. In this hand too! This is nasty, I've heaps of them. But this light isn't any good."

We went next door to your room and switched on the overhead light. I threw my jacket in the corner as though I'd been living there for years. My shirt was soaked through the armpits.

"Check the curtains, will you? I'll find a tweezers."

There was a strong light over the bathroom mirror so we stood under that. I held your hand in mine and used the tweezers to pick out the shards of glass and drop them down the drain.

"Ow," you said. "Christ."

Two drops of blood sat in the palm of your hand. I wiped them away with a damp towel that had some of your hair stuck to it.

"A sailor from Canada." You held up your other hand for inspection. "You must have married lots of girls."

I held the towel under the faucet and turned the tap. Of course, no water came out.

"You're the first," I said. "No matter which way you look at it, you're the first."

"There's no sense in teasing me."

I saw a bead of sweat sitting between your collarbones. I dipped the towel into the bucket of water and tried to think of something funny to say, something snappy. I felt unsteady on my feet.

"I've got no reason to tease you," I said.

I wiped your fingers. You pulled on my arm and put your tongue in my ear. Your tongue was hot. You kissed down my neck and my mister stood up like it had been struck by lightning. I pushed it against you and put my hands around your behind and you rubbed your body against my leg. You held the back of my head and licked up and down my neck. Then you pulled away and looked at me. You looked drowsy. I leaned in and ran my tongue down the back of your ear, and it tasted like medicine.

"Oh," you said. "Christ."

I pictured Christ on his bicycle, ringing his little bell. You were licking the roof of my mouth. I was still moving my mister up and down against your middle.

"Ah," you said.

I tried to get lower while I kept kissing you on the mouth, I tried to get lower and all of a sudden my boots slid on the wet tiles. My legs went out from under me and I fell back and hit my head on the tiles. I remember you bending over to try to pull me up, biting your lip to keep from laughing. I saw those slats up in the wall until a light or something seemed to pass over them.

Then apparently you said, "That was the funniest thing I have ever seen."

That was our wedding night.

I woke up sweating and my head pounded like there was a big empty room inside it. I was lying in your bed in the Raffles Hotel. The shutters stood open but it was too grey outside to know if it was morning or afternoon. The door banged open and in you came.

"Oh, hello! Mum didn't believe me you'd taken ill, said it was one of my *ploys*. She claims to not remember Ricky or any of it. I *am* pleased you didn't break your head. Thought I might have killed you. Is it broken?"

I sat up. I heard an air-raid siren going.

"Air raid," I said.

"Don't fret, it's away across the *padang*. See the smoke?"

A yellow alligator-hide suitcase lay open on the table. It was full of clothes. I slid my legs over and my head swam around like an emptying drain. My mister was ready to pick up where it had left off. I was just wearing a pair of underwear that were a long way from being clean.

"I had to find a boy to get you into bed."

You opened the wardrobe. My jacket and shirt were on hangers.

"I have to see a man about a horse."

"I'm sorry?"

I walked across to the bathroom. I kept my hands in front of my underwear, and once I got inside I had to wait for my mister to calm down before I could pee.

"Did you sleep all right?" you said through the door. "You never got your dinner, did you? I had steak and mashed potatoes, they were lovely. Would you like something? We'll need to leave for the boat in an hour."

"Steak and mashed potatoes."

"I'll just go and tell them. I'll see that Mum is ready. Don't forget that loo doesn't work properly."

I poured water down the toilet and went out and put on my new tuxedo pants and old boots and undershirt. Just as the air-raid siren quit I heard the tail-end whine of a shell coming down and the *bang* a couple of blocks away. Your wristwatch on the dresser said it was ten o'clock. It was a little lady's watch but I put it on anyway.

Then I heard what sounded like a gunshot down on the ground floor — *The Fox Hunt* rattled on the wall. I went to the window and saw a guy in a white suit running down the road. The house across from the hotel was missing its front half, so I could see all the pictures on the dining room wall. Billboards still stood over the shops — MORLEY'S PURE SILK STOCKINGS FOR THRIFTY LOVELINESS, Ovaltine, Tiger Beer, Tiger Balm.

Hold that tiger, hm! Where's that tiger?

Here's that tiger! No no no!

The Mills Brothers sang that song. In a single day I'd lost a record player and gained a wife. If as much happened on February 6th as had happened on the 5th there was going to be nothing left of me. I probably should have gone next door to see your mother but I felt a lot safer just leaning on the windowsill. So many rooms in so many hotels — how could the Japs ever find me if I just stayed put?

A brick flew in the window. It clocked me on the side of the head and I fell down on one knee. The brick rolled under the bed. I held my hand to my head then took it away and saw blood on my palm. I felt like

an emptying sink all over again. All kinds of hoots and hollers came up
from the street.

"Get under cover, Grandpa!" Sounded like Aussies. "It's dangerous!"

The air-raid siren started up again — music to get hit in the head
by. I stayed where I was, looking at the bottom of the windowsill. A
spider scuttled along upside-down. I was much less adaptable. You came
in with a hotel boy who carried a tray.

"What is it?"

You knelt down and pulled my hand away. You smelled like lilac.

"That brick came in the window."

You took out a hankie and touched it to your tongue. At first I was
a bit annoyed that you weren't making more of a fuss about it, screaming and swooning, but then I figured that if you weren't going to faint
then I wouldn't either. And I have to say that you were a lot gentler
swabbing the side of my head than Ma would've been.

"They just shot a tiger downstairs! It had been under the billiards
table all night. How long did they say it was, boy?"

It started to sting like vinegar.

"Seven feet, eight inches, Miss." He dusted off the chair with a
napkin and opened the beer bottle. "They call him Stripes!"

"Crept in like he owned the place! That's all, boy, off you go.
Terrifying, isn't it? You're sure you're all right? I must go and tell Mum
not to look out of the window."

You went out again. My head still felt like someone had left a screw-
driver in it. You'd been all business with me but then your mother
needed looking after so off you went. Of course, if my ma had been sick
in bed with bombs dropping around her I couldn't have pretended she
wasn't there either.

Where were we meeting Ray? Clifford Pier. Someone downstairs
would know where that was. I climbed up into the chair and touched
the linen napkin to my head. It left a blotch that looked like a snake
coming out of a bucket. I cut into that steak and it was the juiciest,
reddest, most beautiful thing, then I ran the piece through the mashed
potatoes and crammed the whole thing into my mouth. Jesus. Then
I took a long pull at the beer. A hit on the head does wonders for a

guy's appetite, especially if he's been starved half to death in the first place. You came back in, picking at something in your front teeth, and I pushed my chair back so you could sit on my lap. But your mother came in after you; she didn't look nearly as infirm as the night before.

"We can ask *him*," your mother said. "Don't get up, Lieutenant, not during your meal. What about Penang? Could he not have taken a ship from there?"

"Mum, they evacuated Penang *before* he left for K.L. Don't you remember? The Smythes came down from Penang."

Your mother sat on the bed and wiped her chin with the back of her arm. You gave her my bloody napkin and she blew her nose on it. I kept chewing.

"Dad can only get to us now if he got onto a ship." You came over and took a pull of my beer. "I've told you that we've blown up the causeway from Johore. That's as bad for Dad as it is for the Japs. You've known for a week now."

"Who has? We have?"

"*We* have."

She flopped back on the bed. It wasn't her most flattering angle.

"Unless he boarded a ship," she said.

You grabbed my wrist to read your watch, as though we'd always been married and I'd always been the one who wore the watch.

"It sails in two hours. We need a cab."

I came to the last piece of that steak. I wanted to savour it for a year but it went down just as quickly as the rest.

"Then, I suppose," said your mother to the ceiling, "there is little sense in waiting any longer. I've made up my mind that fate will deliver him to us wherever we are. Let me lie here a moment longer. I've made up my mind. Go and ask Mr. Winslow when it will be time."

"I'm right here."

She lifted her head.

"Didn't you find my hat?"

"Last night? It was pitch-black out there."

"You certainly are brave."

Turban piled us into a taxi and we drove past the cricket field at about two miles an hour because of the crowds. Your mother sat in the front seat, pointing out the different races for my benefit.

"See this little one? Malay. They're not as Chinese as the Chinese are. And this entire family will be Indian. No, no. Sikhs, doubtless — the beards."

"I told you Clifford Pier, right?"

"Yes, sir," said the driver.

Was he Malay? He looked like Wee-Wee but younger.

The crowd got tighter and people put their hands against the windows. I saw mouths without teeth. Two old women knelt at the side of the road with their heads thrown back, mouths hanging open, and three or four little bodies lined up on the ground, tangled in clothes and dirt and chunks of pavement. You sat right up to the window but your mother picked at her stockings. As we got into the open again a flock of birds flew against the windshield.

"Oh, driver! You must stop," said your mother.

One of her hands darted toward the steering wheel. He caught my eye in the mirror and I shook my head. You bit your lip. Your mother flopped her hands into her lap.

"They were Java sparrows."

"We can stay with the Hepburns," you said. "You remember the photgraphs Anne showed us of her garden? There's no lack of sparrows in Australia."

I put my hand on the seat between us and you lay your hand on top of it. We resumed sweating.

"Which pier was it, sir?"

"Clifford Pier!"

"Could he not have given you a marriage licence?" your mother asked. "Something to show them?"

"I'm satisfied." You gave a little smile with your lips together. "Harry?"

"Peaches and cream."

My head had stopped throbbing. I always felt better being on the go. The bridge from the day before was deserted, then we made a sharp left and the driver stomped on the brakes — cars were parked up the middle of the street and over all the sidewalks. No people anywhere. He shut off the engine.

"Is this the place?" I asked.

"Only another few minutes. But I cannot go. One pound seventy, sir."

He left us on the pavement and backed all the way around the corner with two skinny dogs yipping at his front tires. We didn't stand there for a powwow, either, we picked up the bags and marched. I carried your mother's; her cases matched yours. I didn't even have an overcoat to tie around my head but I had you, Lily Winslow, shuffling along behind me with sweat on your upper lip. I'd completely forgotten to go to 81 Orchard Road to collect that woman's record player.

There were big offices on our left and warehouses on our right, and whenever we saw the water between them it was grey and choppy. One warehouse was still smouldering and the smoke blew in our faces; there was no point getting cleaned up in Singapore because a guy'd be grimy again two seconds later. Half of the car doors were hanging open, blocking our path, so I was always setting the bags down, pushing that particular door shut, picking the bags up and carrying on. One car had opera playing on its radio. If it hadn't been for the clouds of smoke and open doors, that street would've looked like a used car lot — maybe that planted a seed in my brain.

I heard that whine again and crouched behind a car door with a suitcase over my head. You crouched beside me but your mother just stood there like she was window shopping. You hauled her down on top of you just as the shell hit a building behind us. Chunks of masonry dropped onto the roofs of the cars like hail, and we sat waiting while a cloud of dust drifted down.

"Mum, you have got to find cover! You'd have been killed!"

"Wouldn't have mattered."

If she had been my mother I would've given her a good shake at that point. We came to an intersection with another street full of cars, and two soldiers with their shirts off stood at the junction. They slid their rifles down off their shoulders and each of them had a white stripe across his chest, that was how badly sunburnt they were.

"What boat you making for?" they said. "Let's see the ticket."

"Haven't got a ticket, have you?"

You set down your cases and rubbed the back of your neck.

"We don't need tickets," I said.

"What about you, deserting? Turn around, mate. Back to your company."

"Back to your company."

"I'm a seaman. These ladies are passengers. The captain's waiting for us."

"That's all right then, isn't it?"

"Got any vittles? Anything?"

They climbed on top of a car and bounced it up and down.

Another siren sounded from the end of the block, and after a minute of coercing your mother grimaced and crouched down next to us. A Jap plane flew right over our heads but I'd already seen that it was only dropping pamphlets.

Pack up your troubles in your old kit bag and co-operate with the Nippon Army.

"If he was wounded in K.L.," your mother said, "he might have seen Dr. Thorton."

The next warehouse had its sliding doors open at both ends so we could see the guys inside throwing strongboxes into the water. A sign over the door read *Property of Hong Kong & Shanghai Bank.*

"Even Honkers and Shankers are in a panic," you said. "Time to withdraw."

You grinned at me. It took me a minute to see the joke. We hadn't known each other for an entire day yet so I didn't always know what to expect from you, and I was also busy wondering whether or not we'd be able to sleep together on the boat or if we'd be sharing a bed with your mother and Ray and a couple of lizards. Your lady's watch said that it was already one o'clock.

"Should've sailed a half-hour ago."

"Mum!" you hollered.

We found her seven cars back, sitting sideways in the front seat. Her feet were cock-eyed on the pavement like a little kid's.

"He might be at the Raffles now."

"He is *not*," you said. "Christ, Mum, *please*."

I heard gunshots from the direction we'd come, and those two Limey kids were standing on the roof of the car one second and gone the next. The rear-view mirror next to us shattered into pieces.

"Mum, we have to run now."

We hustled down a row of trucks and I dragged those suitcases along the ground, but then I heard hoots and hollers in back of us, guys laughing like hell, and I realized it wasn't Japs shooting at us after all. I recognized the laughing.

We came around the end of a warehouse and there were boats pulled into slips for about a mile, twenty or thirty of them, some just little towboats and some as big as *Asia*. It was the same dock I'd stepped onto the day before — the same women in floppy hats were probably standing in queues and the same Chinese women standing on boxes to wave them goodbye. Everything looked different from that angle. *Felix Roussel* from our Bombay convoy had smoke rising from her funnels, soldiers around her gangplank, busting to pull away.

"Is that ours?" you asked.

"I don't know yet. I've got to find my buddy."

All down the line, guys in suits were sitting at desks, surrounded by women and screaming kids and flying bits of paper. I couldn't have burrowed into those crowds if I'd been a shoehorn. But there was a big tug tied up in front of us with one sailor in white pants guarding the gangplank, a rifle in the crook of his arm. The front of the boat said *Bowral* in green paint.

"You taking on passengers?" I asked. "I'm trying to get these ladies the hell out of here."

"That depends who you're with." He was another Aussie. "We're waiting on a couple of soldiers, then we're slipping berth. Ought to have left an hour ago. How are ya."

Two seamen carrying paper sacks full of oranges went past him up the gangplank.

"Where you headed?" I asked.

"Perth."

"Couldn't these ladies —"

"You best move along," he said.

"Goddamn it, there's only three of us!"

A tall old guy with liver spots on his head appeared on the bow.

"They've still not come along, Victor?"

"I want to get these ladies aboard," I called to him.

"I've chased off half of Singapore, Skipper, and this one marches up like he's Robert bloody Menzies."

Then, either by accident or design, your mother sat on her suitcase and it tipped over so she fell on the pavement, and you tried to pull her up by the armpits but she was too heavy and you banged your shin on another case and straightened up with your hat on the ground and your hair falling over one eye as you looked up at the captain on the bow. You could have been Garbo in one of those movies where the guys fall over themselves to take pity on her.

"You," said the captain.

"Yessir?" I said.

"Get their bags on. See to it."

You brushed the hair from your face and said something to your mother. I heard more gunfire down the way but for all I knew it was really a firecracker factory catching fire. Victor twisted his fingers around the stock of his rifle. I got a suitcase under each arm and started up that wobbly gangplank.

"What bloody sort of trousers are those?" he asked.

"Doak'll show you where to go," said the captain.

When I got to the top a hunched-over seaman with a stubbly white beard grabbed a case and took me astern, through their flapping laundry, then down a ladder into the hold. It was lit by one bulb. He took me into a cabin with a Bible on the table and we dropped the cases there. A bunch of guys were smoking cigarettes in the cabin across the hall. Doak turned around and looked at me.

"You staying here or coming away?"

He had a tic that pulled the side of his mouth up and down.

"I'm coming away."

"You'd best come away," he said.

We went back up the ladder.

"We take printing presses and the like back to Perth but we arrived last arvo to find it all blown to blazes so Skipper says we'll take any Aussies want to go." We ducked under that laundry. "Bloody hell, what's this?"

You were tugging your mother up the gangplank as it twisted like a jump rope and Ray was coming around the corner of the warehouse holding a barking little dog over his head while his Aussies pushed carts full of booze and fired their rifles in the air. Half of them were in their underwear. We pulled your mother up onto the deck.

"This the one?" hollered Ray. "Windsock?"

A buddy of his fell flat on the pavement and came up with a bloody nose. You were fussing with your mother but then you straightened up and gave me a look which I understood to mean you were done with Singapore and the *Bowral* could leave forever with your blessing.

"We'll be out in a second," I said.

"True enough," said Doak. "Only a moment."

"Is one of you Graham?" the captain hollered. "I'm MacIntyre. Which of you is Graham?"

A seagull flew across the dock and Ray's gang took shots at it. The seagull fell in the water. The folks waiting for other boats all ducked down, not knowing where the guns were, and the men at the tables put on their white hats and tried to get through the crowd but they were hemmed in. Not that I spent that long studying them. The Aussies were taking gin off the cart and shuffling towards the gangplank but old Victor just held his rifle up like they were little kids he was going to scare away. Why wasn't the captain taking the Winslows and Mrs. Brown out to open water? His offer couldn't have applied to Aussies who were stark raving nuts.

"Get these two down the cabin," said Doak.

I turned around to take you aft just as the air-raid siren started from shore, working itself up to speed. A bottle smashed on the dock. I got the two of you through the laundry and we got your mother turned around with her foot on the top rung of the ladder. The sweat was beading through her makeup.

"The luggage," she said.

And you glanced up at me like you weren't sure who I was.

I hustled back to the bow, but then I looked up and saw a formation of planes hanging there above our heads. I jumped into the wheelhouse and flattened out on the floor with my arms over my head. Everything started to rattle. I could only hope that you two were down the ladder. I looked out the door as the roof of the nearest warehouse slid onto the pavement. Then there was a thud in front of us like somebody had dropped a bowling ball and the whole boat heaved to starboard. The window above me blew out and the wheelhouse filled with hot air. I could feel the sweat dry up on the back of my neck. What were you doing during all of that? I've never found out.

"That was the fella next to us," the captain said. He was only five feet away, lying under the chart table. "That was right next door." He got to his feet though we still were pitching like hell. "Get the engines up, shall we? And going."

I pulled myself up in time to see Ray knock Victor across the face with a rifle. He fell down with his head over the edge of the dock and the underwear guys started to kick him with their bare feet. He tried to get up but two of them held him down.

I ran down the gangplank and put my shoulder into Ray and an elbow into another one. It was like elbowing a sack of potatoes and somehow I bit my tongue. Victor was on his feet in two seconds, his eye swollen shut.

"Cast off!" He ran straight up the gangplank. "Cast bloody off!"

I picked up the last two suitcases. A boat on our port side was on fire and its smoke sat over everything like a ceiling. Some of the underwear guys tried to dance with the women by the desks. Ray sat there on the cement. The fire made his face look orange, like we were at a Halloween bonfire, and his beard looked sticky. Doak appeared beside me, pulling ropes out of their cleats, dancing over the lines, then I saw you and your mother coming down the gangplank, which was the very last thing I'd wanted to see. She stepped off and walked right by me into the crowd.

"She won't go," you shouted. "We'll have to stay."

"Stay where?"

"It doesn't matter." Your face was dirty. "She loves him and says she won't go."

I held up the suitcases. You just looked towards your mother — she'd walked twenty feet and stopped.

"You're coming," I said. "Make her come back here."

Doak hurried past us up the plank. "We're away!" he yelled.

"She's not going to come," you said.

"We'll carry her! Wait right here."

I ran up and dropped the bags on deck, then the boat shifted and the top of the gangplank slid away and dropped fifteen feet to the dock. I saw you hurrying off after your mother.

"Harry!" hollered Ray. He was on his feet. "Jesus Christ!"

The *Bowral* kept backing out.

"Make them stop!" he said.

I was losing sight of you in the crowd. I looked around for a rope I could swing down on but couldn't see one anywhere. I had my hair in my fists.

Ray jumped into the water and started to swim. I kept looking for you through all the ash blowing off the other ship — there you were! Looking over your shoulder for just a second. Your mother had jostled her way to a desk. You turned and went after her. Ray was banging the side of the boat with the flat of his hand, paddling through the eddies around our bow. The captain hurried up behind me, wiping his face with a rag.

"Everyone below," he said.

I woke up soaking wet, all the bedsprings digging into me at once instead of waiting their turn. I groped around for your little watch, but even after I'd found it I couldn't say if I'd been asleep for two hours or sixteen because I didn't know what time I'd gone to bed.

I stumbled into the passage where the light bulb swung back and forth, and on into *Bowral*'s hold. Five Aussies in their underwear stood in a circle. One guy held a two-by-four, another a rag tied in a knot, and the other three waited on either side with their hands on their knees, swaying with the boat, the light falling across their skinny shoulders. I hustled between them but right then the rag was tossed in the air and the guy swung the two-by-four and I had to drop to the floor and crawl the rest of the way while one of the guys flung himself into the corner and caught the rag. I reached the barrel and wrapped my arms around it like it was Ma herself.

I drained a tin cup. The water tasted like diesel.

Doak hopped up from the bench and drove his elbow into the side of my arm. You remember Popeye's voice on the movie cartoons, so gruff and garbled — didn't he sound Australian? Doak even had the tic in his cheek and the corncob pipe, and he liked to lead with his elbows.

"Here's Sleepy Pete!" he said. "You have a lie back down and I'll fix you a bite."

"I can go up."

"Afraid not. It's my turn coming."

"What's this powwow in here about?"

They all straightened up and looked at me like I was the original bohunk.

"It's cricket," said Doak.

I went back to bed but didn't fall asleep right away so I got annoyed with the *Bowral*'s engine that always sounded like a tractor falling downstairs and felt homesick for the sound of the big screws on *Asia* that had sounded like friendly distant thunder on a summer afternoon. Then I missed you like someone had sat down on my chest, and one of Ray's Ink Spots songs came into my head:

If I didn't care
Would it be the same
Would my ev'ry prayer begin and end
With just your name?

And I wondered how it was that the Ink Spots and I had been mulling over the same idea but their thoughts were so succinct while mine were all over the map. A wave picked the boat up and threw it down and I hardly noticed, I was too busy worrying how I could be so much stupider than the Ink Spots. Nearly twenty-two and my life wasted!

Had you got onto a boat? Maybe you'd found a seaplane to lower you onto the *Bowral*'s deck and had crept into my cabin and were sitting there right at that moment with your hand over your mouth to keep from laughing. The longer I lay there with my eyes shut the more I became convinced that if I stuck my arm straight out into the middle of the room my fingers would brush against you. Which was something I wanted. But I also didn't want to stick my arm out and have my fingers *not* brush against you, so I lay there wondering if I should do it or not until Doak came in with a plate of diesel-flavoured toast smothered with raspberry jam.

"There's oranges too," he said. "See if I can't get my hands on some."

Captain MacIntyre stepped into the doorway wearing a big Chinaman's hat that blocked out half the light.

"Oh, hello," he said. "Wide awake, are we?"

I got to my feet, of course. He was the captain.

"Why not come for a turn on deck? Victor's coming down now, so there's a spot. Just three at a time. Maintain our wondrous disguise."

I followed him into the passage.

"I've got a question, sir."

"Fire away."

"Have you got a record player onboard?"

He put his hand up and stopped the swinging bulb. It almost made me seasick to see it keep still.

"I've got one."

"With records?"

"I've got Buddy Williams."

"Is that jazz?" Maybe it would be stride piano!

"You haven't heard of Buddy? The Yodelling Jackaroo?"

"The what?"

Victor came down the ladder and with great ceremony took his Chinese hat off and placed it on my head.

"Wear the bloody thing in good health."

I followed MacIntyre up the ladder and through the hatch, and the world was so bright that I nearly dropped back down into the dark.

"Heaps of flying fish," MacIntyre said. "You just missed them."

The sky was white and the water blue, and dark green Borneo was off the port which meant we were south of it, heading east, and I'd studied the map at the back of *Cannibal Quest* enough times to know that Australia was further south from Borneo than it was east. So where exactly were we headed?

"How many knots?" I asked.

"Four. It wouldn't do to *look* like we were running, would it? Though I must say we seem to be going nowhere in the meantime."

Asia could have made twenty knots standing on her head, but on a little boat like *Bowral* four knots felt pretty quick. We had to hold our hats down. He folded his arm around a rung of the ladder on the side of the wheelhouse though the rungs were solid with guano.

"Every other trip I've jogged right across the Java Sea," he said. "Straight across the middle, Lombok Strait, down to Carnarvon and home. Just now I want to keep land in sight should anything happen. Before this I never saw more of Borneo than the point off Ketapang. Never ran with the hold empty either."

He was only letting three on deck at any one time because he didn't want any Japs to fly over and see a lot of white guys sunning themselves on the hatches — three was the number of wicker hats he'd bought for his kids. The flag snapped against the wind; he'd taken the Australian flag down and tied an old shirt to the pole.

He patted one of the rafts lashed above the rail.

"These here are self-inflating," he said, "if that gives you any peace of mind."

I spent an hour picking raspberry seeds out of my teeth until Doak leaned out of the wheelhouse, which still didn't have a window. He looked a scream in his giant hat.

"Time's up then. How you at splicing?"

We climbed down to the hold and I passed my hat to Tony, who always wore a *Jesus, what now* expression. Apparently it was his first time off Australia.

"Stout heart there, Tony," said Doak.

He lit an oil lamp and a gang of us sat in the hold pulling ropes apart.

"So what's *Bowral* mean?" I asked. "Is that what Bovril's called in Australia?"

"We've got Bovril. No, Bowral's the town Bradman's from." He squinted and put a pinch of Log Cabin in his pipe. "Dare say there's not much else to recommend it. Reckon the owners are keen on cricket, hey?"

"Yea." The other guys nodded.

I was in the middle of a very neat back-splice.

"Sorry," I said. "I don't have the foggiest what you're talking about."

"Don Bradman? Hit for 452 against England — don't you see any newsreels?"

"They don't put cricket on our newsreels."

Doak whistled through his pipe as he rolled up the pouch.

"What's doing when we hit Perth?" I asked.

"Seaman work. Lot of that."

"Rail yards," said Humphrey. "My old man's in there. He'll sign you on."

Humphrey was a sailor with a long skinny head and an overbite, so I imagined his old man was some kind of hairless animal. He had the sort of Aussie accent that could open a tin can.

"Hell," I said, "I wouldn't mind dry land for a change."

"Stone a crow! Look at you splice," said Humphrey. "You are bloody clever."

The swells picked up. Every four or five seconds we thumped onto another wave like we'd dropped from the sky. I could hear Tony puking in the WC.

"Scheduled for dry dock when we get in." Doak white-knuckled the doorframe. "See if we're not too crook to make it!"

At 1600 it was my turn to put the Chinese hat back on, and some-body could've made a circus act of me climbing that ladder. I came up through the hatch and the wind tried to push me back down. The sky was blue with wisps of cloud but the water had been lashed white. I climbed up towards the bow, then ran down towards the bow, then up again. MacIntyre was in front of the wheelhouse holding his hat down.

"Strait of Makassar!" he hollered. "Four currents at once!"

"Didn't you cut across the Java Sea?"

"We'll keep past Timor! I don't trust the Java Sea!" He wiped the spray off his chin. "But you've brought us luck!"

I watched Humphrey bend against the wheel with water streaming down his face.

"How's that?" I hollered.

MacIntyre smiled so he was all gums.

"Humphrey, he reckons having a crew of thirteen'll be the end of us!"

Then our stern kicked in the air like a mule and MacIntyre and I tumbled through the wheelhouse doorway. We knocked Humphrey's legs out from under him. I got pinned in the corner with MacIntyre's arm over my chest, and seawater poured in the cabin door and sloshed over us. I had to wipe at my face before I could see anything.

"The engine," Humphrey sputtered. "They let the bloody pressure top out!"

"Like hell!" said MacIntyre. "That's a torpedo."

I pulled him to his feet just as we lurched back again and all the water ran out of the cabin — the stern must've been taking on water like a bucket down a well. I ran the twenty feet to the hatch and grabbed the first pair of hands to appear — Tony's. Jesus, he was white as a sheet. Maybe I was too. I kept pulling them up — Victor, Doak, Shepherd the donkeyman. Each a little wetter than the last.

"Self-inflatables," said MacIntyre. "Humphrey!"

The cleats on the stern were already under water, their ropes bobbing on the swells.

"I'll give you a hand," I said.

"You go to hell," said Humphrey.

I got up on the tilting rail anyway and we unscrewed the clips for the life boats. They both said *Bowral* in black letters.

"Pretty damn small!" I hollered.

"Big enough for twelve!"

It felt like we were riding a downward elevator, and even from up on the rail the only things on the horizon were white peaks of water. I saw how Humphrey opened the nozzles and I did the same, then we let both of the rafts drop over the side. By then they only had six feet to fall.

We hopped down from the rail and a wave broke over the side and soaked us through, but I didn't feel too anxious because I knew we had those rafts to jump onto and I figured they wouldn't smash our teeth together the way *Bowral* had. A couple of the Aussies whooped like Red Indians and jumped out to the lifeboats. We hadn't tied them on so they'd already drifted thirty feet.

"That's it!" MacIntyre had a little canvas bag over his shoulder. "We're off!"

Victor helped him up onto the rail and they both jumped. Tony grabbed my arm as a wave broke over us — we were up to our knees in water anyway so that didn't make too much difference. He wiped the salt water out of his eyes with one hand and held my shirt with the other. His nose was running like a river.

"You'll be all right!" I said.

I held his shoulders steady as he got up on the rail, then I hiked up my tuxedo pants and jumped out into the waves too. Green water closed over my head. Half the ocean went up my nose.

When I came up the sun was hitting the swells at every angle, trying to blind me, and the seawater tasted like tar. My boots slid off as I started kicking but I didn't care provided I got closer to the rafts. I hauled myself onto the nearest one and Doak gave my shoulder a squeeze that almost put my arm to sleep. He was just being friendly. His tic was going crazy all the way down the side of his neck. I had to wipe a lot of muck out of my eyes because the seawater was full of diesel.

The bow of the *Bowral* had gone under and we could still see the flagpole and the funnel and the roof of the wheelhouse. Bubbles kept farting up out of every nook and cranny and steam fizzed off the funnel as it met the water. A seagull landed on the top of the flagpole, that shirt still whipping in the wind, but his ride dropped out from under him, a foot at a time, until he was sitting on the water. Then he beat his wings and went to find some dry land. I'd never known a boat could drop so quickly. If I had known I would never have gone to sea.

We all held on. The rubber squeaked under our fingers. Neither of the rafts had inflated properly so they looked just like a couple of tea saucers, and when MacIntyre tried to stand up his side dunked under water.

"Nah," said Humphrey. "Torpedo leaves a wake. You see a wake?"

The swells were still five or six feet high but Doak sat up and tried to peer over them. Shepherd was on the other raft, fifty feet away already, so we couldn't ask him if it really had been the engine.

"He looks like he's in one piece, though," I said.

"He went in the WC after me," said Tony. "That would've kept him clear of it."

"What'll you say to the owners, Skipper?" asked Doak. "Flip a coin?"

"May as well say U-boat, Skipper," said Humphrey. "That'd beat telling them the boat was crook."

"My boat," MacIntyre said, "was not crook."

Everybody kept chatting away like we weren't all a hundred miles from Borneo, half of us hanging in the water with the waves washing over our backs. It kept off the panic.

"Who are these owners?" I asked. "They decent guys?"

"Square," said Doak. "We'll get berths again, no problem."

It was like we were coming into harbour under full steam but with a bent propeller, a bit of a worry for the captain but otherwise all was well.

Then Tony started in.

"A shark ate up my Uncle Charlie's leg at quarter past six in the morning."

"Christ almighty," said Doak.

Everybody pulled their legs out of the water. I slid right up to the middle where Tony already was. I realized that your little watch was stopped at quarter past five. That must've been when I hit the water.

"Pass the biscuits around," said MacIntyre.

"No biscuits. Not a tin."

The wind dropped to nothing. The water was flat, but if a guy looked in every direction all he would see was one other raft a hundred feet away.

"Which way do we head, Skipper?" asked Humphrey.

MacIntyre pulled his compass out of his pocket but his hands shook and it fell in the sea. Then he sat there with his feet over the side, not looking at any of us. Not that we could've headed anywhere anyway — there weren't even oarlocks, much less oars. I wondered if the rafts weren't upside-down. The sky just had one long thin cloud. Doak started singing.

Our Don Bradman

Now I ask you is he any gooood

They all joined in. Humphrey was all smiles, and with his mug it wasn't pretty.

Our Don Bradman

As a batsman he can sure lay on the wooood

The rafts drifted further apart. We paddled, everybody with one arm in the water.

"Java Sea, hey, Skipper?" Humphrey said. "Didn't trust it."

"We're none of us drowned yet," said MacIntyre. "I'll have a doze."

We all made room for him to lie down. Even with the sun going down I could see how pale he was.

That night it got so cold that we all pulled into the middle and lay with our heads on the next guy's shoulder. We were like a nest of mice. I got Doak's shoulder and he smelled as though he'd never washed his shirt in his life and I missed the clatter of *Bowral*'s diesel, so I couldn't sleep. I thought of all the boats I'd been on that hadn't sunk, but there'd only been *Skidegate* and *Harbour Lion*, which meant that I was batting exactly .500. Seamen with that average had to end up on the bottom eventually. My bare feet felt like they'd been fished out of a jar of herring and my clothes were wet and almost frozen and I had that hollow feeling in my chest that I get when I'm ridiculously tired, but at least I was on top of the water.

Tony was shaking my arm.

"Something's down there."

It was black out and the rest of the guys still had their heads down. Jesus, my chest felt hollow. He pointed out these lights below the surface that kept coming together and then breaking apart. They didn't seem to be very big.

"It's the U-boat." He kept wiping his face. "What in blazes is it?"

His face looked yellow from the lights and his teeth chattered. That part of the world doesn't feel too tropical when a guy is in the middle of the ocean in the middle of the night.

"Might be jellyfish," I said.

Somebody shushed at us, like we were violating life-raft curfew. Tony kept staring.

"How old are you anyway?" I asked.

"Nineteen at Christmas."

I was a few months short of twenty-two, but even so it felt like a hundred years since I'd been nineteen. I lay back down and imagined having a kid and pointing jellyfish out to him. I was a married man so there was no reason not to contemplate it.

I woke up with everybody chattering because it was too foggy to see the other raft and we didn't even know if it was morning or afternoon because everybody's watch had stopped at quarter past five. Salt had dried in the corners of my eyes. MacIntyre sat up on his knees, craning his old turkey neck.

"All clear over there?" he hollered.

That fog made us colder than we'd been at night. It settled on a guy's skin.

"It ought to be fresh water," said Doak.

So we started to lick our arms but mine tasted awful they were so salty. The hair on my head was stiff as a broom.

"It's a fever of the palate is all," said MacIntyre. "The palate needs water more than your stomach does. Tell the stomach that."

They all looked sick and green. I felt sick and green. In the back of my mind I'd been figuring that we might drift toward land overnight, but it was the next day and as far as I could tell we hadn't moved ten feet. What did that leave for us to do? Just get sicker and sicker. The rubber squeaked under my fingers. I didn't feel so bad then that I'd left you on Clifford Pier.

"I reckon we must be near land to get a fog like this," said Doak.

That got us looking around again. The wind blew the fog off and put grey swells under us, and as we rode to the top of each one we flicked our heads around like a bunch of prairie dogs, looking for the other raft or a sliver of land. We saw grey waves.

A rain started and we put back our heads and let the swells wash over our legs. I couldn't taste any water at first because my tongue was wrinkled up like a piece of leather. MacIntyre took out the plate of his dentures and let the water collect in that, and with his eyes shut he looked a guy from Bombay begging for pennies.

"Well, lad," he said after a while, "I'd say you picked the wrong boat."

I kept my head back. For five full minutes I couldn't think of anything to say. I finally collected enough water in my mouth to swallow.

"Not dead yet," I told him.

By noon it was hot again and as far as my fever of the palate was concerned it had never rained a drop. The sea went as still as a bowl of soup. I lay with my lower half in the water and my arm thrown over my eyes to block the sun. The bottom of my arm started to burn. After a while I peered out at the horizon and saw a ship. It looked entirely black, and seemed to stand above the water like a grain elevator. Was it coming any closer?

"Ship ahoy," I said.

I couldn't holler it out with my neck bent like that, and at the same time it crossed my mind that if I hollered I might scare it away. But none of the Aussies said a word, they must not have bothered to even look. The ship was still there. I wasn't imagining it.

"Oh, yea!" said Doak.

Then they all sat up and started waving and splashing and I saw grins all around, and as soon as I figured that I might get fed before long I was a hundred times hungrier than I'd been ten seconds before. I was so hungry I could've thrown up.

"Going to be the Nips," MacIntyre said. "Nobody else."

He was still flat on his back, his arms folded under his head. They looked at him like he'd taken away their mutton pies.

"But it is somebody," he said.

After a while I could make out the guns, and it was bigger than any gunboat I'd ever seen. It just kept coming.

"Which one's bigger, a battleship or destroyer?"

I must've figured that all the doom and gloom was behind us if I was worrying about things like that.

"Doesn't matter."

"Aw, battleship."

"Don't matter — they've got to feed us, haven't they?"

"All they eat's rice."

"I'll eat rice every day for a week."

We kept paddling towards it even when the bow was up above our heads like we were standing in front of the Dominion Building. There were a hundred Japanese letters written up the bow and a line of heads like pinpricks looking down at us from the deck. We watched a rope ladder unspool down the side, and just then a flying fish jumped out of the water right by my toes and skittered thirty feet, its long fins catching the sun, then slid back into the water and didn't come up again. It was strange to see just one of them because in the Indian Ocean we'd always seen them in packs.

MacIntyre clambered to his feet and we held him steady as he stretched his hand out for the ladder. The water was up to his knees.

"Beard the rascal in his lair," he said.

Then he waited about a minute before he lifted his foot out of the water and put it on the rung. We all held onto the end of the raft that was still above water. Once he started up he looked steady, though. I thought about waiting at the bottom so I could fish him out in case he fainted, but after every other guy had started climbing I said forget it, because I was still hungry enough to throw up. The rope felt smooth as steel, and when I had both feet on the ladder the whole raft bobbed up to the surface. I kicked it away so it might do somebody else some good, and it left a little wake behind it.

It was a long climb, and my arms got the shakes because I'd been holding the raft for so long. There was no land in sight no matter how high I climbed, and our little raft looked more and more ridiculous on that expanse of water. I decided that the Japanese Navy was a friend to all mankind.

I nearly ran my head into Doak's back end. The side of the ship was hot as a stove-top, and as each of us reached the top we tumbled over the rail like one sausage link after another. A hundred Jap sailors in blue outfits stood around us in a circle or hung off the steel stairwells. They all wore peaked caps with anchors on them and white puttees wrapped around their legs, and not one of them said one word.

We all stood up at attention, looking just as bedraggled as the *Asia* guys in line at the hospital. A Jap went to the ladder and looked over the side.

"*Imay-ma!*" he called out.

A couple more of them ran over and hooked the ladder to a winch and started pulling it up, then the sailors around us jumped back as an officer stepped over the ledge from the companionway. He wore a uniform with gold braid all over the shoulder and a sword in a scabbard on his hip. I'd never seen anybody wear a sword before. There were guns the size of grain silos right above our heads, and here he was with a big knife.

MacIntyre saluted. "Appreciate it," he said.

The Jap captain stood looking at us. He kept changing his grip on the handle of his sword, tight or loose, further up or further down. His lower lip was folded over his upper one. He seemed to be looking over our shoulders and not quite at us. What kind of food was it going to be? That was the only thing I wanted to know.

"Wel-come," said the captain.

He let go of the sword and bowed with his hands down at his sides.

We watched to see what MacIntyre would do. He wiped his forehead with the back of his hand, then bowed about an inch, so we all did the same.

The Japs muttered about that a little bit and the captain barked something over his shoulder and two sailors, one short and one tall, walked out of the crowd with rifles over their shoulders and waved us toward the companionway and down one steep set of stairs after another. Tony held onto MacIntyre's wrist. The short Jap was always waiting at the bottom with a grin across his face.

"*Goch-ewy,*" he said.

The ceilings were low. We trooped past little white doors with porcelain handles and Jap words written in red. It was hot inside that boat — hot like leaning over boiling water. They took us along another passage, then we had to wait while they decided which door they were supposed to open.

"Prisoners of the Jap warlords," Doak whispered.

It surprised me that I hadn't thought to say that myself — I'd been too busy worrying about sausages and fried potatoes. They put us in a little cabin that was half full of canvas sacks. MacIntyre went straight in and lay down next to a water pipe. Tony blew his nose on his shirt. The tall Jap came in and fiddled with the light bulb.

"Christ, get me to the loo," said MacIntyre.

The tall one looked back at the short one in the doorway. MacIntyre got to his feet and hobbled back out, and the short Jap looked worried. I couldn't hear what MacIntyre said to him but all of a sudden the Jap gave a big nod and they hurried off somewhere. There were a dozen or so other sailors out in the passage by then, jostling to look in at the white guys with the purple sunburns and sinuses full of muck, but they backed out of the way after a minute because a skinny guy in white cap was pushing a steel cart over the lip and into the cabin. The cart had three shelves and each shelf had three bowls of soup. I thought that meant there'd be extra for us but after he'd handed six to us he gave the seventh to the tall guard and that meant the last two were for the short one and MacIntyre. Then we all got a pair of chopsticks, and of course I'd heard of them but never used them, and it looked like the Aussies were in the same boat, so to speak. We tried to lift up the noodles but they slid right off again and they were too hot to eat with our fingers, so we blew on the broth and drank that. It tasted like chicken soup, only saltier. There were pieces of white fish at the bottom of the bowl and I tried to spear one with a chopstick but all I did was lose the fish in the noodles, so I dropped the chopsticks and reached in for it. Jesus, that smarted, and once I'd got it into my mouth the fish was too hot to eat and I had to hold it out at the end of my tongue. The Japs around the door were laughing like it was a Harold Lloyd movie but I wasn't bothered about that, the worst of it was that I had to keep leaving off what I was doing to slide my hand down the front of my pants and scratch all around my crotch, like I had ringworm or something.

"Aw, feeling bodgy?" asked Doak. He was squatting on the balls of his feet with soup dripping off his elbows. "You know what you shouldn't have done? Shouldn't have spent so long in the ruddy water."

After four days we docked at a little port that could've been anywhere, though it must've had a harbour of some depth considering the draft of a boat that size. The seven of us were marched up out of the storage room and across the deck and Jap sailors stood in a line on either side of us and gave a bow as we went by. It didn't seem like a very big deal right then, the bowing, though in hindsight I can see that those sailors must've been the most straight-dealing guys in the Japanese nation. Maybe it had crossed their minds that they too might find themselves floating around the ocean one day, in which case they'd want the same treatment. The golden rule, right? And if they really thought that then they were the only guys in the history of the Japanese military to do so.

From the deck we could see two white buildings, and a brown woman in a shiny green dress carrying a sewing machine between them. There were just a lot of trees beyond the buildings, and brown hilltops covered with clouds.

MacIntyre was still feeling a bit crook so Tony helped him along, while the raw skin between my legs chafed every time I walked a step.

The captain with the gold braid waited by the rope ladder.

"Whereabouts is this?" Humphrey asked.

The captain cocked his head.

"Whereabouts are we?" said Humphrey.

The captain smiled and shook his head.

"Aw, you don't have Buckley's hope," said Doak. "This'll be Borneo now. There's parts of Borneo looks like this."

And I figured that if they *had* taken us back to Borneo, especially the west of Borneo, then it was just a dinghy ride back to Singapore. I just had to wiggle away from the Japs and find a dinghy. It never entered my mind that they could have shipped you away from Singapore already, that you might've been on your way to a coal mine in Japan, which did happen to some people. I just figured that if I got back to Singapore there you'd be.

The wharf smelled like creosote, and a couple of short native guys in those sarong skirts leaned against a piling. They were trying to grow moustaches but weren't getting very far.

"Australeee," they said.

"G'day, gents!" said MacIntyre. He smiled at them but, Jesus, he looked like he was going to pass out.

"Nippon number one," they said.

At the end of the wharf our escort gave another bow and I didn't see anyone else around, no customs office, nobody from the Manning Pool, so I really thought that they were going to leave us alone and in spite of my scheming I wasn't sure I liked the idea because the Japanese Navy had been feeding us three times a day, and who'd feed us if we had to shift for ourselves? It's a scientific fact that the stomach has more clout than the brain.

So I wasn't unhappy to see two Jap soldiers in tan uniforms trudge up the steps onto the pier. They had dust wafting off them and black muck in their noses and grubby-looking stubble on their cheeks, but we all needed shaves too. That was the fashion that year. One soldier was thin as a rail with cheekbones like he'd been lost in the desert, and the other one had a head like a bulldog and no neck to speak of. Right away I thought of them as Skinny and Elephant. They waved at us to follow them, then went back down the steps. I watched their rifles knock against their backs. I preferred those guns to the steel bayonet stuck to their barrels, because it's easier to imagine what a knife is going to do to a guy. Anybody who's ever carved a turkey can picture it. The knot in my stomach was the same I used to get when I went looking for a job; the things I got worked up over had changed completely in just a couple of years.

We trailed down the steps after Skinny and Elephant. Only once did Elephant look back over his shoulder. Skinny never did. One white building had a red, white and blue flag on its wall, but the flag had been whitewashed over.

"Dutch East Indies," said Doak. "Covers a thousand bloody miles."

We came around the corner and Skinny and Elephant were waiting behind a truck, holding the flaps back on the canvas tarp. Each of us stepped up onto the bumper and into the back. What was our option? We sat on the benches along either side and the tarp was pulled down again. I scratched my crotch with the side of my hand. Doak got MacIntyre settled in the corner. The engine roared to life and it sounded healthy.

Two guys to collect seven of us. They hadn't expected trouble and we hadn't given them any.

By peering under the flap I could see palm trees and a couple of yellow houses going by. After a while I saw a post as we went through a crossroads but there weren't any road signs attached to it — maybe the Dutch had hauled them down on their way out of there. The only thing I knew about the Dutch East Indies was that it was about a thousand different islands.

"Is Borneo part of it?" I hollered — the road was getting bumpy.

"It is," hollered Doak.

Then a signboard went by full of Japanese letters, and I realized that for all I knew we were *in* Japan. After that I sat up straight for a while to rest my back, then went back to looking under the flap. Some kid stood beside the road in his underwear. With a water buffalo! Before that I'd only ever seen a photograph of one in *Cannibal Quest*. Meantime we sat there sweating and I was so thirsty I nearly licked my arms again.

"I *asked* if it was bloody Borneo, didn't I?" said Humphrey.

In the afternoon it started to rain. They drove through puddles that threw water in under the canvas and we had to lean into each other because whichever Jap was driving took his corners a thousand times too fast.

"Laurel and Hardy, hey?" said Tony.

"Remember." MacIntyre was propped in the corner with his chin on his chest. "Keep your mouths shut. Keep your mouths shut and we might get through."

The driver geared down once, then again. A little squeal of brakes, nothing to bruise us, then we stopped and sat there with the engine idling, *chug-a, chug-a, chug-a*. I heard something metal moving in front of us, maybe hinges or machinery of some kind. MacIntyre got to his feet, hanky clapped to the top of his head, so we all got up too. The truck lurched forward and we all had to catch ourselves and I twisted to see if MacIntyre was okay and the other guys were all doing the same, everybody with a hand on him.

"She's all right, boys," he said.

I heard the wheels splash through a puddle, then we stopped again.

The engine shuddered and one door in the cab slammed shut, then the other. We heard footsteps on gravel. Then the sound of the hinges or machinery, only now it was behind us.

"What I'd like," said Humphrey, "is a lot of girls."

"*Tadaima*," said a voice outside.

Was that Japanese? Fingers appeared in the gap, and some brown cuff. Four hands untying the flaps. The canvas was jerked away and I had to shade my eyes — the clouds were low and grey with orange across the bottoms, as though the sun was going down somewhere behind us. We'd parked beside a high fence that looked like a lot of little tree trunks tied together, and there was a gate twenty feet behind us that two other Japs were tying shut with a rope. The rest of the place was just a lot of one-storey houses with roofs made of leaves, except for a couple that looked like tin. There might've been twenty-five or thirty houses — about the size of downtown Vernon. The fence circled the whole place, and a lot of scrubby-looking trees stood outside it.

"*Mushi mushi*," said Elephant. They were waving at me to jump down.

A hundred or so white guys in wide hats and blue shirts stood at the edge of the huts — they had to be Dutchmen if these were the Dutch East Indies. I jumped down. The ground was soft. A dozen more Japs were marching over the muddy ground, holding the stocks of their rifles against their chests.

"Where you from?" called one of the white guys.

"Canada," I called back.

Skinny and Elephant were waving the others down so I walked a few feet out of the way but the two Japs from the gate hustled over and started hissing at me. They looked older than me but also a lot shorter. I held up my hands to try to show them I was harmless but they didn't like that, they took their rifles off their shoulders and pointed them at me. One bayonet had a spot of rust on the side. I backed up toward the truck again. It felt like a shot put hit me on the head and I dropped to the ground with something on top of me. I saw a bare foot splash into the puddle next to me and from its black toenail I knew it was Tony.

Skinny and Elephant screamed down at us, screaming, screaming —

veins sticking out of their necks! — and the two from the gate aimed their rifles. They were all of three feet away. I didn't know what they wanted me to do next.

"*Kura,*" Skinny was shouting. "*Kura!*"

I felt Tony's fingers push off my back, but the very next thing he was back in the mud with a red gash in his cheek. I rolled over and saw Elephant standing above him with a length of wood about a foot long, swinging it back and forth like he was waiting for a serve in tennis. Skinny said something to him and Elephant smiled and said something back. Another honest day's work for them. Skinny wiped his nose on his sleeve and waved at Humphrey to jump down.

"Jesus Christ." Tony kept dabbing at his bloody cheek. His legs were still on top of mine. "Aw, Christ."

I made sure that one of the gate Japs had his eyes on me before I got up. I didn't want to surprise him. There was grass under my hands, and every blade felt as wide and stiff as a wood chip. Not one thing was the same as I was used to. I got to my feet, head throbbing, and I put a hand down to help Tony but somebody else was already doing it, a tall white guy in a yellow nightshirt. He was as bald as the end of your thumb. He held Tony's arm and asked him something, and Tony wiped at his cut cheek and nodded. Doak jumped down out of the truck and stood beside us. The new Japs were still blinking at me, one rifle pointed right at my belly. What were they afraid I'd do? Get in the truck and drive away?

"*I'm* not bloody Canadian," Humphrey was saying. "He's the only one."

"Is that so?" the bald guy asked. He had an accent. "What are the rest of you?"

"Us? We're Australian!"

"Sorry about dropping on you," said Tony.

The way my head throbbed made me think of the Raffles Hotel.

MacIntyre was the last out. We all helped him down — Nightshirt was the tallest so he took the skipper's hand. By then there were ten Japs in a circle around us. Nightshirt shuffled into the middle of our little cluster and I realized that he looked like that button Bunny had given

Jimmy, the Yellow Kid himself, the bald guy in a yellow nightshirt!

"Thank you anyway," he said to Humphrey. Then he looked over Humphrey's head and asked me something. "*Quoi* —"

That was French. There'd been enough Québécois guys at the packing house for me to recognize it but that was as far as I went.

"Sorry," I said. "I don't speak French."

"Not you either?" He raised his eyebrows. "What a pity!"

But he didn't seem that bothered — not by my language skills, the Japanese, the rifles, any of it. Elephant was herding us away from the truck, and MacIntyre licked his lips and stumbled along. Skinny gave Doak a shove so he knocked against me and I stepped into a puddle. Yellow mud came up between my toes.

"Hello," Doak said to him. "How do you do as well."

A trickle of blood ran down Tony's neck. Nightshirt wandered along with us, gazing around like we were on a field trip to the town creamery. I wondered why they had to move us in a circle like that. Why couldn't we go stand with the guys by the huts who were shading their eyes?

"*Yas-umay*," said Skinny. He had a voice like a bullfrog.

We stopped in the middle of the yard. The Jap in front of me slid back the bolt on his rifle, pulled the bullet out, blew in the chamber like it was dusty or something then put the bullet back and slid the bolt shut. Then he looked at me like he was ready to go to work.

Were they going to kill us? Maybe those hundred guys in hats were just the survivors of other scenes. I couldn't help but think that. And therefore what fraction of them had been killed already? Seven-tenths?

Doak kept rubbing his corncob pipe against his leg until one of the Japs knocked it out of his hand and stomped on it until the bowl broke off.

"Bless you," said Doak. "I'm sure that was necessary."

Skinny came around and pulled our wristwatches off, even though they'd all stopped. As long as he only needed to tell the time at quarter past five exactly he wouldn't have any problems. He took yours too, but it was so tight on my wrist that he had to use his fingernails on the clasp. I just stared into space like I was getting a vaccination. Once he'd yanked it off he tossed it up in front of my face and caught it. Then he walked past Nightshirt without even looking at him. Maybe they were buddies.

The mark of your watchband stayed in my skin, so deep at first that I hoped it might not fade at all. But of course it disappeared even as I stood there.

Tony kept moving his tongue inside his cheek.

Nightshirt wandered between me and the rifle without paying it any attention. He gazed down at me with his hand on his hip.

"You see, I thought that if *all* of you were Canadian, then at least *one* would be from Quebec. I thought that someone would speak French."

Just like chatting at a tea party.

"Your English sounds all right," I muttered.

"Oh, yes." He shrugged, palms up. "I think I do okay."

"What's your name?" I asked him.

"Ney. Michel Ney." He gave a little smirk and wiped his forehead. "Yes, exactly. The same as the hero Michel Ney."

Which meant about as much to me as a dress pattern.

"*Su-kan!*" Elephant said, followed by a lot of other things in Japanese, and whatever he said made the other guards face the huts and stand up straight. Another Jap was walking across from the huts. He wore a tan jacket with buttons down the front that glittered as he came toward the setting sun. He walked carefully around the edge of one puddle, then carefully around the next.

"You do not know Marshal Ney?"

Michel was giving me a very intent look.

"From the last war?" I said.

"No! He was Marshal of Napoleon, he —"

"Marshal Ney." MacIntyre stood up straight as a pole, all of his weight on Humphrey's shoulder so that Humphrey was bent in half. "Hero of the retreat from Moscow."

"Exactly," said Michel. "Thank you, my friend, yes. The last Frenchman to quit Russian soil. The escape from Moscow."

They nodded vigorously at each other, as though there were no mud or bayonets.

"Kept his men going to the last," said MacIntyre.

The glittery Jap rounded the last puddle, and the guards around us stepped back with just a wave of his hand. He wore white gloves and had a little moustache like Ronald Colman's.

"Okay," he said. "It's fine. *Tenko,* now, okay? Line up. *Mushi mushi.* Lines of five men for *tenko.* Okay, *keto*?"

Lines of five? That was just jake with me — an order to do something specific! Mitchell had drilled us enough back on *Asia* that I was as quick as MacIntyre's boys and in two seconds we had five men across the front and Tony and Michel and I at the back. Michel went straight to attention — his Adam's apple stuck out like a doorknob — so we more or less lined up around him.

"Welcome to Pelayaran Camp," said the glittery Jap.

Did that mean Borneo? He didn't elaborate — he held onto the sides of his pants and gave a bow. Lining up must have made the Japs seem less crazy, because I'd already quit worrying about them and gone back to wondering what we'd have for dinner.

"You will bow, *keto*," he said.

MacIntyre took a little bow, so we all bowed. I looked at the mud between my toes. It was almost evening so it didn't look nearly so yellow.

"I am *Chui* Tsuji," the officer said. "Lieutenant Tsuji. I am the English interpreter. *Tsukan.* I'm good friends with all the prisoners. Are there Americans?"

Nobody said anything.

"The commander of the camp is Colonel Kobayashi. The old man, I call him." Tsuji looked over at MacIntyre and smiled. "At *tenko* this morning the colonel addressed all the men. About the food supply. He might want to tell you this himself, but I like you guys, so maybe it's better to hear it now, okay? The Imperial Japanese Army has seized all of Asia. Half of the world. Isn't that good?"

Of course I knew that wasn't on the level — all of Asia? They'd only been pulling into Singapore the week before, they couldn't have taken the entire East Indies in that time, Java and Sumatra and all the rest. Unless he just meant mainland Asia; that was a possibility. He walked up and down the line but then stopped in front of MacIntyre.

"What regiment, sir?"

MacIntyre gave a lurch.

"No regiment." He had a bubble in his throat. "A little merchant ship."

"Ah," said Tsuji. "Businessmen. Men of business. You'll understand the problem." He strolled down the line towards Humphrey. "To tell the truth, we built this camp very quickly. Don't worry, there is plenty of room for everyone. But it is such that at this time there is only food for the Emperor's troops. We have been on Celebes now for one month, and the food that came with us is nearly gone. You will have to make do with the food you brought yourselves. That is the truth. I will not keep anything from you. We must work together to be successful."

"Beg pardon, sir," said MacIntyre. "We haven't brought any food at all."

Tsuji turned and smiled at him. It was like he'd heard his favourite song.

"Then it will be very hard for you," he said.

The guys in the front row looked at each other and shuffled their feet, but I wasn't bothered — with his moustache and lapel pins it seemed like he was all show. And I'd always been low man on any totem pole so it had always been somebody else's worry that I get fed. If I did my job, the food took care of itself. I didn't see why that should change even with a Jap for a boss.

"You should say hello to the colonel," Tsuji said.

Two Japs took MacIntyre by the arms and he stumbled along between them — it looked like his grandsons were taking him off to a party. They went past the crowd of guys in wide hats and around the side of the huts. Before they disappeared around the corner he looked back at us over his shoulder.

"Remember this proverb," Tsuji said, then he rattled off a lot of Japanese — I thought I heard *shit* a couple of times! "Okay? I'll tell you what this means: Follow the customs of the village you enter. I mean *this* village, okay? After *wakare* you can go to meet the others. The others will show you the place where you sleep."

"Excuse me," said Michel.

All of the guards looked at him. Elephant stepped out of the group and came down the line, spinning his piece of wood in his hand. Tony stood between Michel and I, and he shifted a bit closer to me.

"It's all right, *tomadachi*, it's okay," said Tsuji. "What is your concern, my friend?"

"Sir, before you begin *ichi ni san*," Michel said, "I should tell you that I have been counted once today already."

"I don't understand this."

"I was counted at *tenko* this afternoon, and if you count me again you will expect two of me to be at *tenko* tomorrow, but when you find there is only one of me you will not think well of the other one."

"We have told you that if a man attempts to escape the local people will turn him in again. Everyone understands this."

"Yes, sir."

"There is no problem, it is very clear. If one man escapes we will make an example of the other men. To tell the truth we have no choice about it. How many men will we need to make a good example?"

"Six," said Michel.

"How many?"

"Six."

"That's right. Okay."

"Yes. Excuse me, sir. I have been here three days and I have been counted many times. I only went to the gate today to say hello to these Australians."

"You are also an Australian?"

"I am from France." His accent got stronger. "I am Michel Ney."

"From France? Okay. I remember. Okay, *keto*, you may go. I will watch for you tomorrow. The rest will wait."

Michel walked past Elephant and over to the crowd of guys by the huts. There were fewer of them by then. The sky had turned a dark blue and little bats were flapping around everywhere.

"To tell the truth," said Tsuji. "We meant to have *shushun*. Name tags. Then there will not be as many problems. They will arrive in a few days. Do you know what the colonel says? He says you will very likely eat them. Okay, *mushi mushi*, and afterward you can go to bed."

He turned around and stepped in a puddle.

We stayed at attention for another twenty minutes so that Skinny could count us. There were only the six of us and it took him ten minutes,

"*Ichi, ni, san,*" over and over, he'd always get confused and have to start again when he came to Tony and me in the back row. I read in a book a while ago that Japanese schoolchildren have to learn so many characters that they don't have the brainpower left to learn to count. That was the author's theory. I never mentioned it to you because I knew you'd say it was hogwash.

"*Wak-ar-ay!*" said Skinny.

He wandered away, and the other guards all yawned and stretched before they marched off too, their guns knocking against their backs. The sky was black by then. It was still hot out — the sweat ran down my back even with the sun gone. But a breeze had come up, that made some difference. The bugs in the trees were kicking up a lot of chirps and fiddle tunes out there in the dark, and from the way the bats were looping the bugs must've been all around us too. I realized that if the air was full of bugs then the ground probably was too, hookworms and that from the biology textbook, and that standing in bare feet in the mud for hours and hours had been a bad idea. Something behind the fence kept saying *gronk*. A lizard?

All of a sudden the guys in the hats were all around us — a damp warm hand was shaking mine. I could smell rice! God bless those Dutchmen.

"How are ya, boy?" my handshaker said. "Bloody *tenko*, eh?"

They were all Australians too.

"Bloody Nips," whispered another. "We'll see the outside of that fence inside a week."

"See the outside inside."

"Too right," said Humphrey.

"Saw you had a bit of a nick there, lad."

"No worries." Tony was already eating something — they'd put a pan into his hands. "She'll be good as new."

"A tin fish did us," said Doak. "Bloody torpedo."

A lot of nodding heads, a lot of shaking hands. My handshaker let go and a bigger guy loomed over me, then I was holding a little square pan too. I brought it up to my face. It smelled of rice but I couldn't see a single grain. I ran my finger around the inside. Nothing.

"Inside a week," the big guy was saying. He sounded like his nose was broken.

"How long you blokes been in here?" Humphrey asked.

"What, five days? Feels like a bloody year, doesn't it? You the Canadian?"

"That's me," I said.

"My brother-in-law's Canadian. Came from Canada. Plays rugger like you wouldn't believe but says he doesn't *enjoy* it. Unbelievable. Where's he from now — Hamilton? That's it. Hamilton. Here, here!" he called to somebody. "He'll bunk with us in Seventeen. Nah, it's just the one." He took the tin out of my hands. "Not bothered if we drag you off from your mates? Not many beds to go around."

"Good enough," I said.

"Yeah, he'll come in ours!"

I followed him between the huts. Dry leaves from somebody's roof brushed the top of my head.

"I'm Sergeant Falkiner. We're 29th Brigade, 8th Division."

"Able Seaman Harold Winslow."

"What outfit's this? You was torpedoed, that it?"

"Just the merchant navy."

"Ah."

I didn't feel steady. I was thirsty as a pail of ashes.

"We were making tracks out of Singapore," I said, "when this —"

"Should've run *to* Singapore, mate, that was your bloody mistake."

"Not likely," I told him. "The Japs burnt it to the ground."

I was exaggerating, of course — I hoped to hell it hadn't burnt to the ground — but sometimes I did that with guys who were bigger than me.

"Aw, you're joking." He stopped walking. I could only make out his silhouette — he'd put the square tin on top of his head. "That's a bloody ill tiding, mate. I hadn't heard of that. Be inside a year before they get us out, then, won't it? Have to scramble up from Darwin."

I knew Darwin was in Australia.

"Where are we now?" I said.

"This is Celebes," said Falkiner.

He swung around another hut and we bumped into more guys in hats. As far as I could tell the roofs of the sheds were just palm leaves tied together, the walls too.

"Out east of Borneo. Did you not know that all this time?"

Celebes? Gordon Sinclair hadn't mentioned that one. *East* of Borneo. Farther from Singapore.

"Did they make you build this place?"

"Chook houses, aren't they? Some bloody natives did it while we stood around. One of the little buggers started mouthing off the Nips — wouldn't work, hey? So what do you reckon our Kobayashi did to that little wog?"

"Gave him a right thumping," I said.

"Stuck him through the gut with a bloody bayonet," said Falkiner. "That's what he did. I told our diggers, hey, you're not doing your bloody duty by the empire to get one of them stuck through your guts, so let's keep the cards close to the chest."

A generator started up somewhere ahead of us. It sounded like a two-stroke chainsaw, but muffled like it was shut inside a trunk. A big light came on in our faces. I stood there blinking with my hands over my eyes, Falkiner's lanky outline painted over my eyeballs. I heard the big filament humming even over the generator.

"Is it that late?" he asked.

Moths swarmed around the light. We were in another muddy yard, beside a long shed that didn't have a wall across the front. A long row of guys were stretched out on their beds, each of them with a hand up to block the light; it was mounted on a clapboard shack out in the yard. I thought maybe the Japs were going to show us a movie. The bats breezed through, too, tiny ones.

"Right opposite the *kebetai*," said Falkiner. "Prime spot isn't it?"

"The what?"

"Guardhouse — the *kebetai*. The Nips' guardhouse. They pop out of there to put us on parade. *Tenko*. Practice counting us. *Tenko*. Myself, I love it out there. I could stand out there all day long and not a whimper. I'm joking of course, don't look at me that way."

"You a Japanese expert or something?" I said.

"How's that? No, but I believe we have to stay on top of this situation. Now you flop down here, mate, and I'll quit bashing your ear. Bobby, where in hell's that old bed gone? Shipwreck wants to take a load off."

A skinny blond guy lay at the near end of the shed, stretched out on a bunk with sheets and a pillow and everything. I figured this was Bobby. He wore shorts and a pair of wool socks with mud ground into the soles, one foot crossed over the other.

"Them Dutchmen out of six nicked it, Chief," he said.

"What bloody Dutchmen?"

"Vooren and them, gave us this lot for it. What I thought was, maybe we'd build something."

A pair of sawhorses with a door propped across them stood between us and him.

"What in Christ we going to build?"

"Box for the canary?" Bobby said. "But hell, he could sleep on *that*. Where you from, mate? It'd beat sleeping on the ground."

There was yellow paint flaking off the door and a bunch of brown lizards chased moths across it in the bright light, little *chi-chack* lizards.

"Bugger," said Falkiner. "Here they are. Causing mayhem."

"Who's the what?" I asked.

He grabbed my shoulders — he had some grip — and sat me down on the door so it went *clack* against the sawhorses. Those *chi-chacks* evaporated. Falkiner went striding away down the shed.

"Heads down. All heads down."

I watched his big shadow go along the back wall, then he flopped onto the bunk at the far end and started flipping through a big brown Bible. Right then there were three whistles like somebody calling a dog team, and fifteen Japs with rifles hanging off their shoulders — Tsuji and Elephant and a bunch more — piled into the yard from all directions, lining up sideways, bumping shoulders as they figured out who was standing where. That proved just how fresh and new Pelayaran Camp was, because guys in most outfits can do parade in their sleep.

"You'll like this." Bobby leaned on one elbow and plumped up his pillow. "They're as big a bunch of bash artists with each other as they are on you or I."

In that light every Aussie's face was white down one side and black down the other, so it seemed a bit like a gangster movie.

"Nothing on how they knocked the boongs around that time," said the next guy along. He had a blue singlet and a face like a round of cheese.

"That's true enough, Pete."

"Can't hold a candle to that."

"Tell you what." Bobby propped one foot on top of the other and squinted over at me. "After we find you a decent bed we'll knock together something real swank out of that old door. Birdhouse? Heaps of birds fly through here during the day."

"No meat on them," said Pete.

I sat on the door, picking off flakes of paint and piling them next to my leg. My feet didn't quite reach the ground so they were clear of worms for the moment. I watched the *chi-chacks* poke their heads around from the underside of the door. Of course I hadn't meant them any harm but maybe that's what the guy who has the upper hand is always going to say. I watched Skinny out there and figured he was just about as far from home as I was. His mother was probably worrying if he was getting enough to eat too, though he probably *was*, and when it came down to it I didn't give a fig what his mother was going through.

"How's the rice look for tomorrow?" said Pete.

"Chief said that might've been it."

"Listen, these Nips have *got* rice, they're just holding their bloody aerodrome over our heads as ransom —"

"I'm not lifting a finger for this lot. Not for anything."

"Any of you guys got a girl?" I asked.

"You having us on?" said Pete. "We're not bloody queers, all right?"

"Or a wife, I mean, is anybody —"

"Mine wanted to get married before I shipped out. Wanted to be my bloody cook," said Bobby. "Remember that, Ect? Bloody farce that would've been."

"But she's still your girl?" I asked.

"Oh, absolutely," said Bobby. "Her dad's got cattle."

"But when do you figure you'll see her? What if we sit here years and years?"

"Not bloody likely."

"We'll bide our time," said Pete. "Chief told us that from the first, bide our time. No good having too much sand."

"Hunker down, Frogs' Legs," Bobby said. "Or the chief will have words for you."

Michel Ney stood smoking a cigarette at the end of my door.

"Oy." Pete snapped his fingers. "Hit the rack!"

The bald guy next to Pete sat up like a dog smelling beefsteak. He wore a green T-shirt soaked through the armpits.

"Byrnell, what you after?" asked Pete.

"Where'd you get that baccie?" said Byrnell. "Hawkes smoked the last yesterday."

"It was this one's shipmate." Michel poked me in the shoulder and my shirt stuck right to my skin. I was that sweaty. "They broke his pipe so he said he had no use for tobacco."

Old Doak's corncob pipe. That already seemed like ages before. Byrnell stretched his arm across Pete's legs, reaching for the cigarette.

"What'd you trade?" he said.

"I asked him, please could I smoke the tobacco. He apologised for it being wet. That was your shipmate," he said to me.

"Hand it over now, mate," said Pete. "Or we'll rescind your adoption."

Michel turned the cigarette in his fingers and passed it to Byrnell. I got a whiff of hot mud — it was Doak's Log Cabin all right.

"You buggers," Falkiner hissed. He was still away at the other end of the shed, waving his hand at us to get down.

"Oy," said Pete. "Kobayashi."

Byrnell took a long pull on Michel's cigarette and passed it back across Pete. Michel sat down next to me and stretched out his arm to take it. A bug with long feelers landed on his wrist, then flitted away. Michel stuck the cigarette back in his mouth, stood up, straightened out his nightshirt, then flopped on the door again so it went *clack* against the sawhorses.

"They do not like us to watch them," he said. "They want to find another place where they will be away from the Australians."

"They've got the whole island, don't they? They could walk out the gate."

"You are right. That is exactly right." Michel looked at me over his shoulder. "When we arrived this Kobayashi was doing terrible things to the native people. It is only a matter of time."

"For what?" I said.

"That *was* a sight when they cut up them boongs," Bobby said. "Nearly chundered, didn't I? And Ectacles, he did, eh? Ect turned the bloody faucet on."

Another Jap came down the steps of the *kebetai*, bump, bump, bump — I figured that this had to be Kobayashi.

"*Ki-ot-ski!*" He barked like a dog tied to a tree.

As he walked out into the light I saw he wore a sword like our naval captain, except that his looked to be longer than his legs. That was what had bumped down the steps. He walked behind his men, right past our shed, and his sword cut a trench through the mud as he went along. Tape was peeling off the handle.

He barked again — *Hadarimaki? Hadaronaki?* — and the Jap soldiers all spun to the left. Moths fluttered all over them. Elephant was sucking in his belly. Kobayashi started talking, holding the handle of his sword, trudging around in front of them. Tsuji let his chest sag every time the old man looked away, then he'd straighten up when Kobayashi turned around. I couldn't help watching. I'd spent a lot of time in the bottoms of ships so I got my entertainment where I could.

Kobayashi quit growling at them and a second later I heard this *awhooo* from way out past the fence. He went back to talking, pointing at one of his guys, pointing at the guardhouse.

"What the heck was that?" I said.

"I reckoned I was the only one heard that!" said Bobby. "Must be a bloody monkey."

"That's the call to prayer down in the town, Bob." Ect sat up. "The *muezzin*, right? We heard that five times a day on Ambon."

Bobby blocked the light with his arm.

"I had no idea what anything was on Ambon."

"Bloody Laha," said Pete.

He watched the Japs while he scratched his armpit.

"What's Laha?" I asked.

"That's the town on Ambon," said Bobby. "Gave us some strife."

Michel was picking the mud out from between his toes and wiping the gunk on the side of my door. The leaf still smoked away in the corner of his mouth.

"Ambon was indefensible in its entirety," said Ect. "And it didn't much help that they forgot the artillery in Darwin."

"Nothing comes good with no artillery," Bobby said.

Byrnell shifted on his bed, squeezing his jaw muscles, still watching Michel.

"If it's bloody indefensible," said Pete, "how come we never shuffled along to take it back?" He scratched the top of his head and a moth flew out of his hair. "Then we could — could put this lot out on *tenko* all bloody day if we wanted."

"Can't forget how he drank that stuff," said Bobby.

Drank what? They'd been on Ambon, I'd got that much, wherever Ambon was.

"All bloody *day*," said Pete.

The Japs were still lined up not forty feet away but Aussies were muttering right down the length of the shed. A pack of cards came out. And there was Falkiner down the end, blowing through his teeth and waving his hands.

"That's still going there," Byrnell said. "Let's have a look."

Michel pulled the cigarette off his lip and peered at it.

"It is only the leaf now."

"I'll have a look."

Michel passed the thing — the size of a fingernail trimming — to Bobby, who passed it on to Byrnell. A thread of smoke wafted off it and Byrnell tried to suck that in. Then he licked his lips.

"Christ Almighty, there's no taste in that."

Michel had gone back to picking his toes.

"Aw, this is murder." Byrnell kept sucking at it. "Not a shred. Am I the only gink going mad without a durry?"

"I *could* have a durry," said Bobby. "But I'd sooner have a pie."

"Same," said Ect. "Mutton. Quite a few."

"Oy!" whispered Pete.

That made us all look up. The Japs were still in their line, except for Tsuji, who was standing down at Falkiner's end of the shed. A bug picked that moment to flap around inside my ear.

"*Kura,*" said Kobayashi. Or that's what it sounded like. "*Tadai-ma.*"

Today, Ma.

"What's that mean?" I whispered.

But Michel held his big toe between his fingers and just kept watching. Tsuji bowed at the edge of the shed, and Falkiner was already standing beside his bunk. He kept his arms straight at his sides and bowed back. Jesus, he was slick enough to pass for a Jap even with his big broken nose.

"*Sukan,*" Falkiner said. Then a pause. "*Ari-gato.*"

"What's that mean, '*sukan*'?"

"Maybe 'translator,'" said Michel.

The guy beside Falkiner got up and bowed too, then there was a scramble right down the line and before I'd thought about it I had my feet down in the dirt. Michel and I stood on either side of the door — his bow looked bad and mine couldn't have been any better. When I looked up again Kobayashi was walking around, swinging each leg out while he figured out where to put it down, and talking quietly like he wanted every one of his guys to take particular note of whatever wisdom he was imparting. After listening to him for about a minute I couldn't help but go back to fretting over how empty my stomach was because it was worse standing up, and I realized that my Aussies hadn't exactly had their forks out for the evening meal, either, they'd all been going to bed.

Kobayashi stopped talking and stood with his hands behind his back.

"*Hai,*" said Tsuji. "The colonel is in charge here, and he wishes you would have respect for him. You are prisoners, okay? You know this."

Pete shuffled his feet. Another guy cleared his throat.

"You must have respect for all Japanese people." Tsuji sniffed up his nose. "So you must say sorry."

Kobayashi barked about three words more.

"*Hai,*" said Tsuji. "He wants each prisoner to say sorry to him."

"Beg your pardon, sir," said Falkiner. "How do we say that?"

"*Sumimasen.*"

I watched Falkiner's profile. His head bobbed like a chicken's.

"*Suni-basen,*" he said.

"*Su-mi-ma-sen,*" said Tsuji.

"*Sumi-masen.*"

"Go say this to the colonel."

Falkiner ducked under the thatch roof and out past Tsuji. A guy might've thought Falkiner was just playing some game with his kid brother if not for the way he was clenching and unclenching his fists. He walked out to the middle of the yard, around those Japs on *tenko*, and stopped in front of Kobayashi. The filament in the light was still buzzing. Kobayashi kept his hands behind his back.

Falkiner bowed, smooth as ever. The moths scrambled to stay on his shoulders. Then he straightened up.

"*Su-mi-ma-sen,*" he said.

The brim of Kobayashi's hat gave a twitch — a nod, I figured, *dismissed* — so Falkiner bowed again, and as he stood up Kobayashi slapped him hard across the face.

Pete brought a hand up to his chest. Our line of guys shifted.

Falkiner stared down at the old man and Kobayashi stared right back at him. I felt like I was watching a drama production. Were they giving MacIntyre as good a show wherever he was? One of Falkiner's eyebrows raised a little. Of course I didn't know Falkiner well enough to know what that meant, but from the way Bobby was standing there I knew they all figured he was going to do *something*.

Kobayashi muttered a few words.

"That's all for now," said Tsuji. "Come back."

Falkiner turned and walked back to the shed. From the look on his face he might've just been figuring out a crossword. He went around Tsuji and ducked under the thatch again. Pete and Bobby craned their necks to get a look at him.

Michel scratched his neck with his index finger.

"The next man," said Tsuji. "Okay? You."

The guy next to Falkiner went out. He was only wearing a pair of green trousers and had arms like broom handles. He stopped in front of Kobayashi and I could see his lips working, *Suni? Sumi?* After a second Kobayashi turned and walked away from him, looking right and left at his guys on parade. His boots made a noise in the dirt.

"*Wakare.*"

Elephant and Skinny and the rest of them gave a bow, then spun around and walked out of the yard, two going one way and three another.

"'Dismissed,'" whispered Michel.

Of course what I knew about the military you could've fit on a postage stamp, but I figured that that made sense. It was going to take a long time for Kobayashi to slap us all so his boys could do other things in the meantime. Like cook my dinner. I really didn't mind that I was going to get slapped — Grace had slapped me on the head when I'd fouled a line in the prop and that hadn't bothered me much, so what was the harm? I was just worried that there was nothing to eat. Kobayashi put his thumbs in his belt and wandered back over to Broom Handle.

"Say sorry," Tsuji called out. "*Sumi-masen.*"

"*Sumimasen*," said Broom Handle.

He bowed, and as he straightened up Kobayashi slapped him. Broom Handle's face came into the light.

"Okay," said Tsuji. "Now hurry back."

One by one the Aussies went out and came back in, and because Bobby had mentioned a meat pie I started thinking about the one my ma always made in a big casserole dish; I'd break through the crust and it'd be full of gravy.

Kobayashi was out there on his own again, muttering something to Tsuji.

"*Hai*," said Tsuji. "One more thing the colonel wishes to say. We worry what is happening to the women in Australia. These are your girlfriends — they think you are all dead, okay? So they are everybody's girlfriend now." He wiped his moustache. "Okay, the next man."

The next man had hair growing out of his shoulders.

"*Su-mi-ma-sen*," he said.

It just went on and on, Ect, Byrnell, Pete and then Bobby, across the yard, *sumimasen*, bow, slap, back across the yard, like Kobayashi was teaching us to square dance. He had to shake out his arm after each guy so it must've been getting sore.

Bobby ambled back in with his arms folded in front of him and then it was my turn. I walked out across the dirt and wondered if I was supposed to be feeling terrified. Because I wasn't. In fact it was all I could do to not bust out laughing.

I stopped in front of him. Jesus, it was bright out there! A bug tried to fly up my nose. Kobayashi was peering at me from under the brim of his cap. He had hardly any eyelashes, and scars under the corners of his mouth like he'd bit himself. Maybe he wasn't that loony after all. We were his prisoners. We'd been talking when we shouldn't have been. How different was that from Grace giving me a whack? It was discipline. This Jap was just trying to run his outfit.

"*Sumi-masen*," I said.

I held the sides of my pants and bowed. I saw the end of his sword on the ground between his feet. I heard him make a noise in his chest as I straightened up, then his hand caught me just above the temple. It didn't hurt very much — mostly he just hit my hair — but it came sooner than I'd expected so I nearly lost my balance, I had to kick out my right foot and it came down on a chunk of gravel. Was I supposed to bow again?

"That's all now," Tsuji called out. "Come back."

I limped a bit as I walked back, and before I was under the thatch Michel was already on his way out, with a spring in his step! I was back at our door in time to see him bow to Kobayashi, say *sumimasen*, bow again, and Kobayashi reached right back and belted him. It had a hell of a lot more torque than any of the slaps before it — he must've figured it was his last so he could use up his reserves. But Michel stood there like it hadn't even happened. He looked down at Kobayashi and asked him something — it sounded like French.

"That's all," said Tsuji. "Come back."

So Michel gave a big nod like he'd had a wonderful time and came springing back to the hut. In the meantime Tsuji went out to the colonel.

"Okay," he said. "You will have respect for Japanese people. *Wakare*, okay?"

He bowed to Kobayashi, Kobayashi bowed to him, and the two of them walked to the guardhouse and went up the steps. The Aussies sat on their beds and of course I jumped onto the door and got my feet up as fast as I could.

"Crikey," said Pete. "We tossed it in well and good, didn't we?"

The generator shut off. Everything went quiet, and a second later the big light clicked off. That left us sitting in blackness. I wondered if that meant it was time to eat. The first thing my eyes made out was Michel's white head.

"No, I asked if he could speak French," he was saying.

"*Parlez-vous français*," said Ect.

The Aussies were squawking down the length of the shed, and a couple of them had voices like nails on a blackboard.

"She'll be right," I could hear Falkiner saying. "She'll come good."

"Name's Ect, by-the-by."

"Harry Winslow," I said.

I could make out his glasses and a grey forehead.

"Odd way to spend an evening," he said. "You need to go *benjo*?"

"That mean take a leak?"

"Yeah, the dunny," he said. "My concern when I went to get bashed was that I might not be able to hold it. How about you, Michel, want to come *benjo*?"

"We need to make a plan," said Michel. "I will go to my bed."

He had his own bed! Jesus, I'd thought I'd be spending the night with him.

"Here." Ect touched my arm. "I'll get the torch."

"Oy, Ect," said Pete. "Don't be tardy for the bloody cards."

I waited for a minute. I could see most of them by then.

"*Non*," Michel said. Who was he talking to? "*Non, mais —*"

"Even a spud," somebody was saying. "A spud at every meal."

"Here we are," said Ect. He switched on a flashlight and my feet appeared below me. "Hate to fall into it, wouldn't we?"

I don't know how my bladder could have wanted to pee since

I'd been sweating like a watering can all day and I hadn't had a thing to drink since the tea they'd given us on the battleship. We went across the yard and between more huts in the opposite direction from the way I'd come with Falkiner. Ect kept the light in front of our feet.

"Now, remember to say 'benjo,' all right? We're not meant to walk about at night except for that. Tell them benjo. We reckoned the Nips wouldn't let us bring the torch in so I handed a piece out to each of the lads, they tucked it away in their packs, then after the search we put it back together. Nothing more simple. I've heard tell of a radio they've got in pieces in shed eleven as well, I might volunteer to patch that together."

He held the light on a bug hurrying ahead of us: the biggest cockroach I'd ever seen. It hustled underneath a piece of burnt-out stump.

"He'll last longer than you or I," said Ect.

"At this rate."

"That's it. Even if we weren't famished."

We took a right around one shed and a left a minute later. I heard pots clanking and voices, though I couldn't see anybody. The blackness was all the blacker for staring at the flashlight. I could smell something burning.

"We're no longer among Australians," said Ect. "This is our Little Amsterdam. Dutch militia and that. These blokes stayed behind, sent the families on."

"Where'd they send them?"

"Oh, they reckon Java will hold out."

Some thick-necked guys stood in a doorway blowing on mugs of something.

"Here's Willie — played footie for us the other day. How's that tea, Willie?"

Willie was a tall one with a long upper lip. He didn't say anything for a minute.

"This is the last we have," he told us.

We kept going.

"He sent his kids off from Makassar not a week ago," Ect whispered, "so it'd be best not to mention how you were torpedoed and that.

Right, after much preamble here at last is our *benjo*. It may not look like much but we're going to empty it onto the garden."

We seemed to be at the edge of a field. He waved the flashlight around and I caught flashes of a dozen guys crouched over trenches with their pants around their ankles.

"Shut off that bloody light," somebody said.

Ect turned the light on the fence behind them. It looked tight as a drum.

"Some boongs from town were up here last night."

"What, taking a leak?"

"Nah! Trading through the fence. Diggers from shed eleven got a chicken and a pound of tea, and all they had to give up was a wristwatch. Had themselves quite a banquet. I suppose if we loitered about with hands full of cash the Nips would soon catch on."

A chicken and a pound of tea. I couldn't imagine anything better.

"Needless to say, the sergeant's already had words with us about it."

A bug or something bounced against the side of my head. Ect went over to a bucket of water and took out a scoop. Then he walked off to the right, set the flashlight on the ground and dropped his drawers. The place didn't smell half as bad as some of those toilets on the *Empress*, a breeze blew across it, but I didn't much want to stand there in bare feet either.

"I said shut that bloody light off," somebody said.

Ect reached over and shut it off. That gave me a chance to let my pants down and have a feel around my crotch, which I'd been wondering about. The raw skin didn't seem to have spread anywhere, not to my mister or my nuts, it was still just the groin itself, which I suppose technically was just the top of my leg. That was a relief, as you can imagine, even though Ray used to tell me that a guy wasn't a real man until his short arm had been through the ringer. Of course, Ray had had syphilis.

I shuffled ahead a couple of feet and peed in as near the direction of the trench as I could guess — it sounded like it was going in, anyway. Jesus, the noises coming out of some of those other guys would've broken your heart.

"What's the story on grub?" I asked Ect on the way back.

"Well, it looks as though we've had the last of our rice. But there'll be tea in the morning after *tenko*."

"Tea means dinner, right?"

"Means tea. As much as you want, though! And it's one of ours who makes it, he was telling us how he boils all hell out of it to kill the microbacteria and that. So that's something. Have as much of that as you like."

The night was cooling down by then. My shirt was coming unglued from my body. The bugs kept humming right along and I could hear branches snapping out behind the fence somewhere. I kept my eyes on the pool of light in front of us because I didn't want to step on that cockroach.

"I reckon the Nips'll have to come good though. They hauled us up here to build this airstrip, right, so they can't expect us to get far on empty tanks."

"What's this?"

"Clearing land for an airfield. I haven't been out to see it myself. So far they've just taken Dutchmen."

"And the Dutchmen get something to eat?"

"They get tea in the evening as well."

I have to confess that I was pining away for you less and less the emptier my poor belly got. Some soup, some noodles on the battleship, that was all I'd had that day, and by the next day it was going to seem like Christmas dinner. How's a guy supposed to rescue his girl without at least a sandwich and a glass of milk? Cap'n Blaze always gave Pat Ryan and Terry something to eat no matter what else was going on — it might sound inane to compare real life to that, but how many times had I been held captive? How often had you? It takes some getting used to. Somebody came toward us in the dark.

"Who's that?" said Ect.

Nobody else had a yellow nightshirt, and a second later the light was hitting Michel under the chin so he looked like Boris Karloff.

"Harry," he said. "If we see Tsuji we can work tomorrow."

"I can work," said Ect.

"Ah, yes. When was the last time you had a big meal?"

"That was before surrender. Ten days ago."

"This is why he asked for Harry. We must hurry."

"Fair enough." Ect flicked the light on and off — there'd be a wall of leaves then no wall of leaves. "Put a word in for me all the same, won't you?"

Michel spun around and strode off into the dark. For twice as much tea I figured it was worth my while to keep my eyes on his nightshirt and run after him. What did it matter if I stepped on a cockroach? I was bigger than it was.

"Two more Hollanders have taken ill," said Michel. "With some luck we will be the first who ask to take their place."

"What do we get fed when we go to work?"

He stopped and peered around a corner, then spoke quietly. As far as I could tell he was looking right at me.

"We will be fed nothing at all. But we will be outside the camp. You understand? None of these men have balls. Not any more. It is not their fault. Only you and I have a chance, before they take our balls too."

Take our balls?

"A chance for what?" I whispered.

"To go. To keep fighting. In my family we have always fought," he said. "Grandfather, so on, back, back, back. Do you feel ready? Here is the *kebetai*."

We were behind the guardhouse — I could see a light burning in the back window. After all our sneaking around I figured that he was going make a birdcall and throw some pebbles, but we just marched around to the yard and stopped at the front steps. It was too dark to see the guys in our shed but I could hear Falkiner lecturing some poor sap about *shearing*, it sounded like. Michel went down on one knee in the dirt. I did too.

"*Su-kan*," he called out. "*Arigato, su-kan*."

We heard a chair slide back inside the shack, then footsteps across the floor.

"What is it?" Tsuji stood halfway in the doorway, holding a lamp. He didn't have his glittery jacket on, just a white undershirt and suspenders.

"Sir, we want to be on the work party."

"Have you come to say sorry?" asked Tsuji.

Jesus, it was going to be a square dance all over again!

"I'm only making fun," he said. "It's okay. Come inside. Come inside."

Michel didn't move, though — I saw he had his head bowed, so I did it too.

"Yes, that's good," said Tsuji. "Okay. *Yasume*. Come in now."

We went up the three steps and followed him inside. There was one table and one chair and two steel cages in the corner, each about the size of a hay bale. On the table there was an ashtray, close to full, with a lit cigarette propped on the edge, and an open book showing rows and rows of tiny Japanese letters. There was also a teacup without a handle and a lot of grit in the bottom.

"We are good workers," Michel said. "We will be the strongest ones."

"Vows and eggs," said Tsuji. "Easily broken."

We both stood there with our hands folded in front of us.

"That's a proverb. Okay. Sit down, *keto*."

He dragged the steel cages over for us to sit.

"I must tell you that we don't have tools. When we have tools every man will work. We are waiting now. Only men who know the area well can work now."

"But when my friend and I join them, we —"

"Wait, okay? Wait. *Tor-anu* —" He rattled off a lot more Japanese, then looked at me. "It means, 'Don't value the skin before you've caught the badger.'"

"Harry ate a big meal this morning. He was on a navy boat this morning."

"Sure, a great big breakfast," I said. "I'm strong as an ox."

"What food did they give you on that boat?" said Tsuji. He flicked his cigarette butt out the window. I'd have to tell Byrnell about that.

"Oh, noodles, sir. And we had fish in soup. Great stuff."

"Who was the commanding officer?"

"Who, on the boat? I'm afraid I don't know that. I wish I did. He was sure good to us." I tried to smile endearingly but I had an idea my face wasn't made for that. "I could ask the other guys, maybe one of them caught his name."

He gave me a weird smile back, his lips pressed together. I tried to keep looking friendly. His eyebrows looked exactly the same as his moustache. His moustache was like a third eyebrow!

"My brother," he said.

His jacket hung from a peg on the wall and he leaned over and took a pack of Lucky Strikes out of the pocket. Which was a normal thing to do, but I knew that if Byrnell had been there with us he would have suffered a cardiac arrest.

"Yes, sir." Michel had his elbows on his knees, his hands clasped together. "Your brother."

"Okay, yes," said Tsuji. "My older brother." He reached in his pants pocket and took out a lighter. "He is a captain in the navy. *Shoko! Naore!* I cannot be like him, can I? Okay. I cannot."

He lit a Lucky Strike, puffed, puffed, then exhaled slowly so the smoke hung under the brim of his cap. He set the lighter on the table. It had a silver ukulele on the side.

"The army gives us tobacco from Formosa. It's really shit, you know? They can grow it in this country but nobody picks it. I hear it is very good."

He leaned back and crossed one leg over the other. His trousers looked like they were made of sailcloth.

"It's the same as any army, but it's soft for me, okay? Because I can speak English. I wrote the tests so that I could be an officer like this. Do you know which was the worst one?"

"The arithmetic," said Michel.

"Proverbs. That was a bad exam."

Tsuji pulled a bit of tobacco off the end of his tongue.

"You are good guys, aren't you?"

We nodded — we really were. Michel stuck out his bottom lip to emphasize it.

"But you are too new in the camp." Tsuji pointed at me. "It is not fair for the other men who came at the start. I have to keep our men, your men, the old man, keep them all happy. It is very … *tight*. It is very tight."

He tilted the chair sideways with his feet, then set it down again. He smiled at us with the cigarette between his teeth like he'd just told us the best joke he'd ever heard.

"Yes," we said.

"You will not work tomorrow." He pointed at me. "It is very tight. But *you* may go. You are the big guy."

"Thank you, sir," said Michel.

Tsuji crushed out his cigarette, then sat there with his fists on his hips.

"Why do you want to go work?"

"For exercise," said Michel. No hesitation. "To work is better than not."

"Most men would not say this."

"I say it, sir."

It wasn't really an argument — all three of us knew that Michel would get to leave camp tomorrow, and he and I both knew it might be for good. And there I'd be with Falkiner and the rest, digesting our stomachs, lying awake wondering how far he'd managed to get. Then I realized that if Michel went for good, Kobayashi would fix it so that no one ever went again.

"Please reconsider, sir," I said.

"It is tight, I said. I told you. You, big guy — after tea in the morning you wait by the truck. Okay. *Heso* —" Then a load of Japanese. "You know that one? 'It's no good trying to bite off your navel.'"

"My friend is very strong," Michel said. "He ate fish this morning."

Tsuji hopped off the table. We stood up too. The blood rushed from my head.

"This work is hard," Tsuji said.

Michel and I went down the steps. I could see the flashlight beam playing across the bunks in our shed.

"Do not be discouraged," Michel was saying. "More Hollanders will be sick. Everything is very contagious."

Half a dozen Aussies sat playing cards around a bed, each with a little pile of matches in front of him. Ect held the flashlight in the air. Pete was collecting the cards.

"You sit in this next one, Shipwreck," said Ect. "I can't do the both at once."

I sat down across from Falkiner and two other guys. A few dozen matches lay on the grey sheet in front of me. Ect stood up on the bed with his flashlight against the ceiling, the moths flapping against his nose and landing on his glasses. He didn't seem concerned that I'd taken over his matches — they couldn't have had much use for them with nothing to smoke. I looked around for Michel but didn't see him, and for all I knew he was already long gone, leaving me right up to my neck in my new life. Maybe in a few days we'd be eating the matches. Maybe our stomachs would be happy with that. Pete dealt the cards. The back of each one showed a nude girl with a big pearl in her hand kneeling beside a pond, and over the picture of the pearl it said *Pearls*. And it was the same in her reflection in the pond. I looked at the backs of my cards spread out on the bed for a while. Even at a time like that, when all hope seems to have deserted him, a guy will stare at a pair of boobs.

"Blind Tiger," Pete said. "Ante in. Your bet, Chief."

We each threw a match into the middle; they looked like a little pile of kindling. A girl with curly hair sat on the inside of each card with her breasts pointing up in the air, right there with the hearts and spades. The cards felt as thick as plywood. They sucked the sweat out of a guy's fingers.

"Your women do wait for you." Michel sat on the next bed behind me. "It is the Colonel's trick and only his trick."

"You can't know that," said Bobby. "What I'm saying is nobody can. All this time our girls reckon we've bought it, so what else they going to do? Sit home? We was only engaged."

"That's two to you," said Falkiner. "Get the bloody lead out."

"Two to stay in, Shipwreck."

I threw two matches in. I was still trying to make sense of my hand.

"Let me tell you," said Michel, "there was once a soldier called Odysseus who went away to fight and he was gone from home for twenty years. He fought in a war for ten years and was a prisoner for ten years after that."

"We only fought two weeks," Bobby said. "Christ Almighty."

"But his wife, her name was Penelope, she was a very fine woman. For the twenty years, one hundred men sat outside Penelope's house, waiting, you know, to fuck her. Every day they asked her, but she never would."

"Yeah, but that was ancient times." Ect batted the bugs away, his legs spread to keep balanced. "She'd have been stoned for adultery. Nowadays the neighbours'd just say, 'Oh, no problem, a girl's got to have some fun.'"

"No, the whole world believed that Odysseus was dead, and the people told Penelope to find another man. It was only her heart that made her true."

"Well, that's pretty," said Ect. "That is."

"And what is more is that Odysseus was not true to her. For nine years he lived with Calypso and with Circe for another. Like man and wife with each of them."

"Fucking?" said Bobby.

"Yes, fucking them."

"What exactly they look like?" Falkiner sniffed up his nose. "Those last two."

"Them? Goddesses."

We sat there staring at our cards. I wasn't even sure whose turn it was.

"And our girls will reckon just the same as his wife, is that the theory?" said Bobby. "Except as it happens we're like a lot of choirboys. No bloody jiggy-jig at all."

"For two years after that Odysseus was fighting against sea monsters or swimming in the ocean, for weeks at a time. All to be back with his true love."

"That's twenty-three years," said Ect.

"How did this lovely miss disport herself in the interval?"

"Sewing. She never stopped sewing."

"Is that all."

"Aglaé Ney, as well," said Michel. "She would often wait months for the Marshal to return home."

"I'll fold," said Falkiner.

I'd been raising it by two or three matches at a time because I had two tens, and with nothing wild that might've been something.

They all folded so I had to show my hand. It crossed my mind that if every match in camp came into my possession I might be able to cut some deals. Maybe this would be the start of an empire, one humble hand of cards after another.

"You need a pair of jakes to win." Falkiner shook his head. "Deal it again."

Pete swept up all the cards.

"What game is this?" I asked.

"Blind Tiger," said Pete. "Like I bloody told you."

They left the pot piled in the middle of the bed; it was possible I'd win a lot of matches with the next hand. Pete straightened the cards into a stack then pulled off his singlet and mopped out his armpits. His little belly was white as a ghost, the moths liked the look of it, but I figured that even he would just be ribs after a couple of weeks of playing cards and eating nothing. All ribs, like the inside of a rowboat.

"Anybody ever seen that Human Skeleton?" I took a little bug off the end of my tongue. "Maybe at the carnival or something?"

"Keep bloody talking," said Falkiner.

He must've taken it as a criticism.

"Oy, Ect! What's this?"

The light flickered as Pete dealt. Ect made a face and tapped the end of it with his finger. We reached for our cards. The light went out.

"Ect," said Falkiner.

"Afraid it's carked it, Chief. Batteries."

"Who's got a light?" asked Pete. "That's a straight flush. Feel that card. That's a king. Strike that match, Swampy."

"A match is currency. I can't just *strike* the thing."

"It's a straight bloody flush!"

"We've got all of tomorrow to sort this out," said Falkiner.

Ect leaned on the back of my neck and hopped down to the ground.

"Byrnell, you'll shout me a bloody match," said Pete. "Where you gone?"

"He wanted durries," said Bobby.

Everybody quit talking.

"Don't tell me he's gone up there," Falkiner said.

"Nah, what's he got that the boongs would want?" asked Pete. "Nothing."

"Gold filling," said Ect.

"Here, pack this up," said Falkiner. "They'll be coming by."

"I'll just leave the straight flush here then," said Pete.

"Keep the bloody deck together," said Falkiner.

We all felt our way back to our bunks, and within a minute it sounded like half the Aussies were snoring. Of course I had to curl up on that door, and I wished like hell I had a blanket even though I was sweating out of the backs of my legs. But at least I'd traded being hungry for being cold; the little dog in my gut had quit his whining. If everything worked out for Michel maybe I could have his bed the next night.

The odd shard of light flickered through the wall above my head, then Elephant came around the corner carrying a lantern with a cloud of bugs around it. I opened my eye a slit to watch him. His was sticking out his lips and he stumbled a couple of times as he went past. When he'd gone around the next corner I figured that that was the last of the excitement for the evening, so I started to flex my feet, the old standby, and counting each time I did it. Never in my life had I reached one hundred.

When I was at fifty-three, fifty-four, fifty-five a hollering started out in the direction of the *benjo*, three or four voices, and I couldn't tell if they were Japanese or English or some other thing. Maybe that was how the natives let us know they were ready for business. I opened my eyes and saw a lot of Aussies sitting up in the dark. I stayed on my side with my hands folded under my chin but of course I was listening too.

After a minute we heard somebody run across the wet ground in our yard, then boots thumping inside the *kebetai*. I imagined Tsuji crushing out his cigarette. What was the time, anyway? Midnight? Three? Maybe it was quarter-past nine. A couple of voices spoke in the yard, then the generator started. Falkiner said something down at the end of the shed. The big light came on. All of the Aussies were sitting up, one leg out of bed.

"Shit," said Pete.

Kobayashi barked in front of the *kebetai* as his men ran past him. Something moved in front of the light. It was Byrnell in his green T-shirt. He craned his neck to look over at us. He said something but I couldn't make it out. Elephant and another one had him by the arms, and they dragged him into the middle of the yard and threw him on the ground. Elephant put the sole of his boot against his face. Ten or fifteen Japs stood around them.

Why didn't I get up to help? Bobby and the others were on their feet but none of them moved.

Kobayashi pushed through the middle of them with his sword out of the scabbard so the blade really caught the light. He stood over Byrnell with a foot on either side of him, held the sword so it pointed down at the ground, then he lifted it up with both hands. He held it like that for one second, then he brought it down. Byrnell's legs jerked.

The Aussies started out of the shed. I can't remember if they were screaming or what they were doing.

"Here!" said Falkiner. "At ease!"

Elephant lifted his rifle to his shoulder and something went through the roof above our heads — dust floated down through the light. Then every Jap had his rifle up.

The Aussies backed into the shed again. Bobby sat down.

Kobayashi wiped his sword with a handkerchief. Byrnell still lay on the ground.

"Nothing," Falkiner hissed. "You do *nothing*. That's our *duty*."

Eight rifles still pointed at us. The old man went up the steps of the guardhouse, past Tsuji, who stood in the doorway with his hat off. Elephant picked Byrnell's arm up by the wrist and gave it a shake.

I lay down on my side. I shut my eyes again. I could still see the bright light through my eyelids, though, and hear Bobby's bed frame creaking next to me and the Japs walking around and talking. They were dragging something across the yard and they had to keep stopping and starting from the sound of it. Byrnell hadn't been a little guy.

"That didn't just happen," muttered Pete. "That didn't bloody happen."

The light shut off and we lay in the dark. I could hear the Aussies swallowing, rolling over, coughing, but nobody said anything else. Not for a long time.

A guy can make up all the cockamamie excuses he wants to for why he does *something*, quitting his job, throwing a punch, and maybe one of them will stick. What's done is done, that's what a guy will usually say. But if he *doesn't* do something, he knows why not. I couldn't have saved Byrnell any more than I could have survived a jump from the *Bowral* onto that cement pier. I would have been dead in either case, and what help would I have been to you then? But would every single one of us have died if we had rushed out to Byrnell? Not likely. We had superior numbers. We might have wrestled the guns away from them.

I'd hardly known Byrnell to see him. It was the way his legs had jerked that bothered me.

The itch came back into my crotch like a switch had been flipped — more like a sting than an itch. All I could do was clamp my hand between my pantlegs and grit my teeth because I knew that if I started scratching I'd be at it the whole night. Jesus, a blanket would have been nice! Somebody cleared their throat and I concentrated on that. Maybe they were going to say something interesting. Anything but my crotch.

"Shipwreck," said Ect. "Empty bunk for you now."

I wasn't sure if I'd heard him. Maybe I'd fallen asleep in that minute and I'd dreamt it. I lay there listening in case he said it again and the bugs just seemed to get louder and louder, like a plane flying over.

"Yeah, Shipwreck," said Pete. "Go on."

I woke up the next morning with my nostrils full of wood smoke, and since for once I wasn't smelling iron filings at the bottom of a ship my brain figured I was still in Vernon and it was time to get down the stairs for my oatmeal. But then my crotch started itching, then my arms and legs, and I realized how many birds were singing, which reminded me that I was in Byrnell's bed and there would be no oatmeal or sugar or heavy cream.

Byrnell's mattress must've been chock-full of lice; I felt like the

crotch itch had spread all over me. I ran my hands along the backs of
my legs and felt the bugs move between my fingers. I went to work
crushing them between my nails and Christ, they really popped.
The Aussies were still fast asleep, they all had a fire under them, boy —
just brimming with life. There was already some light in the sky.
Michel at least was sitting up staring at the ceiling. Planning the first
thing he was going to do once he was out, that's what I would've been
doing. Roast chicken sandwich, cup of coffee, slice of fruit pie. The lice
had a kerosene smell when they burst, though I couldn't be sure if that
was them or my blood inside them.

Yeah a bedbug sure is evil, they don't mean me no good
And
Wish they'd cut their own doggone throats

That was a Bessie Smith song I'd heard when Ray and I had splurged
on a hotel in Liverpool — someone had played it in the next room
while I'd been heaving into the basin. I wasn't going to scratch my bites.
That was the one thing I could do to keep my situation from sliding any
farther into the toilet. I didn't want to be lying in Byrnell's bed in six
months time with my eyes rolled back in my head, wishing to God I'd
never scratched those bites. But, Jesus, I wanted to! I pulled up my shirt
and saw the spots of blood down the side of my ribs.

"Christ," I said. "Bela Lugosi."

"Aw, yeah," said Pete. He sat up slowly, like he had a bum shoulder.
"The bities." He blinked at me a couple of times. "I couldn't reckon how
you'd ended up here. Old Byrnie." He twisted the bad shoulder around.
"He's a box under the bed there. Let's see if he's any bloody matches."

It was a shallow box like we used to pack cherries in. I took things
out one at a time: a crucifix whittled out of wood, a photo of an old gal
in a nurse's cap, a collared shirt full of moth holes — his shore leave shirt.
I noticed dried blood under my nails.

"Thing is, Chief, it's within our power to lodge a complaint."
Ect was crouched down next to Falkiner's bunk. "Worst thing Byrnie
should've got was thirty days. Geneva Convention, right? Remember
that captain told us?"

"No, the thing *is*," said Falkiner, "he should've been bloody clever enough to tell you that we're not the blokes in charge here, and I'm not about to tell another bloody mum how her lad had *too much sand*."

Pete unrolled Byrnell's sewing kit and poked through all the buttons. He shook it and a cigarette tumbled out, all wrinkled and sat-on. It lay there on the sheet.

"Stone a crow," said Pete. "Don't tell me."

"We forget him and carry on," Falkiner was saying. "I'll not lose one lad more."

"Ask what their policy is," said Bobby.

"Yea, to clarify," said Ect.

A bell rang as the sun rose above the trees, and I followed the Aussies out into the yard. For *tenko*, I figured. They formed their lines beautifully, all in their uniforms: blue shirt, brown pants, the big hat. That left Michel and I in our civvies, such as they were. Falkiner gave me a puddle to stand in.

"Nothing personal, Shipwreck," he said over his shoulder. "It's the lines."

A swarm of flies buzzed over a patch of dirt in front of us. I looked at Michel and he was staring at me already.

"The blood," he said. "You see what our chances are."

The Jap who counted us was like a cartoon Jap with great big buck teeth, so that made him Donkey as far as I was concerned. He was real slick with the *ichi, ni, san*, but then he started in giving us commands that of course I didn't understand, so I studied Ect — if anybody was going to have it figured out I knew it'd be him.

"*Migi mak-ay migi!*" said Donkey.

Ect turned right, then I turned right, then everybody else turned right. *Migi mak-ay*. Did I want to learn Japanese? No, I did not. Was I going to have to? Yes. For all I knew every person in the world was.

"*Hadar-ay* —" And a couple of other words.

We turned straight again.

"*Na-oray! Wak-aray!*"

"Breakfast," said Michel.

They hustled back into the shed and ran back out with their mess tins. I didn't even own a tin, though I could've drunk my own weight in tea — if a guy drank enough could it constitute a meal?

"Go beg one off Willie," said Ect. "He's good as gold."

"He'll have a spare?"

"Him? A ruddy kitchen."

They must've been finishing *tenko* all over camp, because it was like swimming upstream to find my way back to the Dutch neighbourhood, through all the guys clutching cigarette tins and canteens and china teacups. I couldn't remember which was Willie's shed so I poked my head into one and there he was sitting on a bunk, the only guy still at home. He had a blue bedspread with white flowers, all tucked in and straight, and blonde stubble across his cheeks. I stood there swaying but he went on studying his boots. Was that just how he was, or had five days in camp done it to him? The camp was never going to do that to me, I knew that much.

"I'm over with the 29th Brigade," I said. "Australians. They told me that maybe you'd have something I could drink tea out of. I'd appreciate anything you could spare."

He reached under the bed and slid a crate out between his feet. He had a whole set of enamel dishes — white with green rims. He handed me a nice soup bowl. He still hadn't looked up.

"So it's chow time now, huh?" I said.

He picked out a bowl the same as mine then finally straightened up and looked me over. He had wrinkles around his eyes like spiderwebs.

"Time," he said.

The cook shed sat beside that big yard with the gate and the puddles. We stood in line behind Falkiner and them. Guys were already crouched against the shed in the mud, blowing on their steaming tea. I could see Tony and Doak waiting with upturned helmets in front of them. I didn't feel as gnawing-hungry as I had the day before, just jittery. Michel squatted beside us in his nightshirt and nodded up at me. His balls were hanging an inch above the ground. Not a pretty picture, as my dad would've said. His tea was steaming like a geyser but he poured it back in one go.

He wiped his mouth. "It is not good," he said.

Tony came down the line, tea slopping out of his helmet, and he was watching it so carefully that he stumbled on a rock and almost crashed into me. I caught him by the shoulder and he managed to keep most of it from sloshing over us.

"Winslow!" he said. "Haven't seen the skipper anywheres, have you?"

One of his upper teeth was gone. I figured if a guy lost an arm or a leg he might still look all right, still be handsome enough when he got home, but Jesus, without his teeth he'd always look like a moron. Like a moron who walks around in three sweaters.

"Haven't seen hide or hair of him," I said. "Say, did you hear about this airfield they're building? Maybe if a guy could —"

"The man is *ill* — you don't reckon they'd make him work? You saw he was ill. You hear one of these fellas was tortured last night?" he whispered. "Tortured!"

"I don't think they'd drag the captain out to work," I said.

"No?"

"You know why he is sick?" Michel was still crouched there. "He has given up. These all have given up."

Nobody paid him any attention. Tony tilted the helmet back to drink his tea and half of it went down his chin.

"I'm not giving up," I said. "I have to get back to the wife."

"Jesus Christ!" Tony made a face like he'd eaten soap. "What do you suppose the Nips get to eat?"

"Rice," said Michel. "And fish. The same as we eat on Java."

"You been on Java? These camps there too?" Tony asked. "Talking garbage to you all day long?"

"I never saw a camp."

"So how'd you end up here?" I asked.

"I came by boat, but I have only sailed as the cook before. I was never a sailor."

He smiled. I figured it might be his last conversation with white men for a while so he was trying to enjoy it.

"What'd you have to eat in that boat?" asked Tony.

"I took fruit with me, a big basket of *rambutan*. But on the first day I ate too many, I had diarrhea. You know?"

Tony and I both nodded.

"*Rambutan* is good, but you must eat something else, for the stomach." He rubbed the top of his head. "You know, that is what they call me in Jakarta — *Rambutan*. It means 'hairy.'"

"Cause you're bald like that?" asked Tony.

Michel pushed himself up and walked off. I knew he was on his way to meet the truck or whatever it was, but he didn't even give me a wink. We were already miles apart from him. The cook was changing the kettles so the line stood still. Willie swung around and glared down at me. Then it was like he remembered something else and turned around again.

"It's all bloody *men*, isn't it?" Tony muttered.

"What's this?"

"Not like we had many girls on the boat." He probed the hole where his tooth had been with his tongue and swirled the bit of tea around in his helmet. It was murky as ditch water. "But a *boat* is on its way somewheres, hey? And there's going to be the odd female when they get there, no matter where it is!"

"Who's this now?" Doak knocked me with his knobby elbow. "Nearly rid of you, weren't we?"

The line moved — a short guy was getting his tea, then it would be Willie, then me. The stuff Tony was drinking may have looked like hell, but with steam billowing out of the pot, that cool white bowl in my hand, I convinced myself that a dose would cure my ills. The Aussie working the ladle reached for Willie's bowl but Willie held it against his leg.

"I won't bloody bite you," said the Aussie.

Willie turned and walked away from the line, his eyes on the ground. His boots rippled through the puddles in the yard. After he'd gone fifty feet he brought his arm back and threw his bowl towards the gate, but it missed and hit the fence. It went *bong*, then rolled along on its rim until it settled upside-down. He stopped walking and stood watching his bowl. A guard came out of the little shack beside the gate and blew a whistle. Willie heaved his shoulders up, maybe took a deep breath, then he started to run towards the gate. It was shut and barred and there was a man with a rifle in front of it, but if any of those things had occurred to him Willie didn't seem bothered. He ran through the puddles, one big leg in front of the other, yellow mud spraying up his back. The guard at the gate aimed his rifle.

And what was I thinking? As soon as this is over I'll get tea.

The guard fired a shot — *pop*, like a cork gun — and Willie dropped onto his back. For an instant his legs stayed in the air, then they flopped down too. He lay still. But after a second he lifted his head and looked at the gate again.

Japs ran into the yard from all directions, so I took a step backwards. Of course they weren't coming anywhere near us. They went out and stood in a circle around Willie. The Aussie with the ladle had his bottom lip between his teeth.

"*Yasu-may!*" somebody hollered. The Japs all looked up from poor Willie, and here came Tsuji, walking around the puddles and wiping the corner of his mouth with a goddamn napkin. He stopped and talked to the soldiers, they bowed, then hauled Willie up by the armpits with his legs dragging behind him. They were taking him towards the gate and it crossed my mind that they were going to leave him outside for the tigers, but the guard came out of his shack with a spool of wire and they lifted Willie up and tied him to the fence. They stepped back and admired their handiwork. He hung there like a bag of laundry. Then they walked off, most of them striding along like they were racing. Maybe they'd been in the middle of breakfast too.

I rang my bowl against the edge of the pot. The bowl Willie had given me.

"Let's go," I said. "I'm dying of thirst."

The cook didn't ladle very carefully. The tea sloshed out of the bowl and over my fingers, and I had to tiptoe back down the line trying like hell to keep it level. I ignored the feet the Aussies kept stretching out in front of me, their slick talk, I just held my bowl out on my fingertips. Then just beyond the edge of the bowl I noticed Tsuji standing in my way.

"Hello," he said. "You are having a good morning?"

A fly landed on his cheek and he batted it away, then stood there looking at me — he really expected me to answer! The whole line watched us. All I could think was that my tea smelled like motor oil.

"You will build our airstrip for us today," he said.

Did he mean outside the fence?

"Okay," I said.

"Okay, but the *keicho* is not ready so first you must do another job. The *keicho* must collect the tools, then you will meet the other volunteers. At the truck."

I tried to remember all of that, but I also couldn't help but think that I was about to be taught an important lesson involving a bayonet or an axle handle or a rifle butt. He had that line of guys watching! That bowl felt very heavy.

"Oh, but you see," he said, "there is a problem. This one worked with the doctor at the hospital." His eyes flicked towards the gate, so he must've meant Willie. "You must visit the hospital to help the doctor, okay, then come back for the truck. But the *keicho* must collect the tools so you have ten minutes like this. The hospital, you know it? Go to the *benjo*, you will see the hospital. You know the *benjo*?"

"Yes."

"Okay, you will have a good morning."

Michel stood behind him, but I couldn't read his expression one bit.

"Okay," I said.

"*Mushi mushi.*" Tsuji showed me his canines. "Go fast."

I turned around to go look for the *benjo* and tea splashed over my hands. An Aussie cackled. The ladle resumed its clanging against the side of the pot.

I had to walk past Willie to get around to the *benjo*, but I could only bring myself to look at him from the corner of my eye. I couldn't see where the bullet had gone in and I couldn't tell if he was still breathing. Was he better off alive or dead? Alive, of course. A guy didn't have any options once he was dead. In Willie's situation 93 percent of people would want to stay alive. Maybe as high as 97 percent. Who knows how I came up with that but it distracted me while I had to walk by him, and if Willie did make a sound I never heard it because there were so many birds singing on the other side of the fence.

Once I was out of sight of the cook shed I gulped down all the tea I had left, then dropped the bowl on the ground and kept walking. That was what Anthony Adverse would've done in his slave camp in Africa — whatever it took to survive. But then I felt dizzy as a turbine. All that liquid hitting my guts. I wished I'd given Willie some tea while I still had it.

The morning was still and hot so I could hear the flies at the *benjo* already enjoying themselves, and the smell of the place wrapped itself around my head like a wet towel. The hospital was a shed with two red shirts tied together on the front wall to make a cross. A guy with a black beard was sleeping in a chair outside the door. I stood there wondering how to wake him up — all that tea felt like a watermelon in my belly — but then he jumped to his feet so his chair fell over.

"I'm Vooren." He sounded like a Dutchman. "I'm the doctor. I think you look like my nephew. Not my nephew, but my nephew's friend."

"They told me to do what Willie did, then I have to be someplace else."

"Where is Willie?"

I stood there with my mouth open. Three flies tried to glide in at once.

"I can ask somebody else," he said. "You got to empty the pans. Where the hell you from?"

"Canada."

"Oh yes? Japs get you next. Canada. Jump, jump, jump." He hopped his fingers along his arm. "I'll go for a sleep now. You get all the pans, empty them out in the *benjo* here, or maybe you get a kick in the backside. The bedpans. Hey, no joke! We'll both be one of these guys one day, do not make a joke about it."

I thought I'd escape the smell of the trench when I went inside but it was a lot worse. The close quarters. It's funny how much a guy can learn just from a smell — as soon as I stepped in I knew that every prisoner in Pelayaran Camp who started to shit himself was sent to hospital.

"That's not Willie," somebody said.

"Hello to you, anyway, Not-Willie."

It was gloomy in there. There were a dozen bamboo beds down either side and most guys just lay there naked next to a tin plate, except that some of them hadn't quite hit the plate. There was a little guy lying on his stomach just inside the door who had one eyebrow that went straight across.

"You must've done something bloody horrendous," he said.

I turned and went back outside.

"He beats a retreat," somebody said.

I kept walking, away from the hospital, the *benjo*. I walked along the fence until I found a leaf on the ground. Then I went back inside the hospital and fought the urge to vomit and picked up the plate from beside the guy with the eyebrow. I kept the leaf between the plate and my hand. I wasn't going to spoil my chances of getting on that truck. A swarm of tiny flies took off from the plate and landed up and down my arm.

"That's the spirit," Eyebrow said.

I went back outside and shook it out into the trench. The sound of that stuff hitting the bottom made those toilets on *Asia* seem like a lot of ice cream sundaes. I realized on the way back that there wasn't a Jap to be seen anywhere.

"Sorry, mate." The next guy had something in his throat. "Sorry about this."

"You guys all come down with something?" I tried like hell not to gag.

"Dysentery, the doc says. He says I might've had it since Darwin, but I might come good yet, you watch."

I took his plate outside. I was a waiter in the most buggered-up restaurant in the history of forever.

One guy lay on his side with the stuff all dried across the backs of his legs. I used the rim of the plate to try to scrape it off. That made him lift his head.

"My mate'll be by to give us a wash," he said. "Don't bother."

That time when I went outside something started to twitch down in the bottom of my gut and I had to run to the trench like I was in a three-legged race. I dropped the plate then ran a little further so I wouldn't have to hunker over right next to it. I managed to get my pants down before it was too late.

That ate up valuable time. I wondered how long Michel would be able to stall the truck, or if he would even bother. More than once a noise came out of me like a kettle wailing — was that what dysentery sounded like? Could I have caught it just like that? No, it was all that tea. My guts were playing tricks on me.

I took in the scenery. Two beautiful palm trees stood over the camp.

The next guy had a long white moustache, and sat up on the bamboo slats with a big smile on his face. His plate was empty.

"It's no good work for a young man," he said. "These Nipponese must do this work. *Smiecht!*"

I still wasn't steady on my feet and had to take deep breaths in spite of the smell.

"Is that what you call the Japs?"

"No, no!" He pushed himself up the wall a little. "We say *apenaaier.*"

"What's that, *arpen* —"

"*Apenaaier.* Monkey-fucker!"

He laughed, but then he started to cough and spat a hunk of blood onto his plate. He smeared it around with his thumb.

"*Apenaaier,*" he said.

How long would it take to get a truck ready to build an airstrip? There were a lot of guys and plates. If I missed the truck I'd be doing Willie's job forever and it wouldn't be long before I needed a plate of my own. I hustled — I really did. That leaf of mine fell to pieces, so after that I didn't worry about it and carried two plates at once.

I came to the last guy at the end of the second row. He was on his side, wheezing in and out like a bad valve, and seemed to have some kind of tremor in his legs. The stuff on his plate steamed even in that heat.

"Hold on for just a minute," I said. "I'll bring this back nice and empty."

His eye rolled back towards me but he didn't say anything. He looked a bit like MacIntyre. It *was* MacIntyre. A scarecrow with liver spots across his forehead.

I hustled to the *benjo* and as usual the flies went bonkers around my arm, I was the bringer of glad tidings as far as they were concerned. I'd never seen anyone as sick as that in my whole life, and just the day before he'd stood up there on *tenko* and told Tsuji we were merchant navy. I shook out his bedpan. I really shook the hell out of it. I found a clump of dry grass and wiped it on that.

I set the plate down beside him.

"I'm leaving camp right now," I said. "I'll be gone in five minutes." He still faced the wall.

"Skipper?" I said. "I want you to know, I appreciate the —"

All of a sudden he propped himself up on one elbow. He could barely hold his eyes open. Of course he didn't have his dentures in.

"Take Tony along," he said. "He's the youngest, you see."

"I'll see if I can find him."

His eyes shut, and after a second he lay back down. The bamboo creaked. I turned around and hustled for the door. The guy with the eyebrow lifted his head.

"See you back here shortly then, mate."

Just like Clifford Pier, I ran even though I was an hour late. I ran between the sheds, jumping over buckets, around men sitting there reading, Dutchmen sweeping off their doorsteps with corn brooms, but I must've taken a wrong turn because I came around a corner and there was the *kebetai* and shed seventeen and all the Aussies playing cricket in the yard. They had wickets with the leaves still on them.

Bobby stood against the shed with his hands on his knees.

"You much good as a fielder?"

"I'm late!" I took the corner like I was rounding third.

"Be home for tea!" said Ect.

"It's wog's work, isn't it?" Falkiner was saying.

Between the next two sheds I nearly ran into Donkey, fastening the button on his breast pocket. Could I have gone past him? I could have, but then chances were good that he would have slid the rifle off his shoulder and shot me just for looking panicked. Two escapes foiled in one morning! Lucky Strikes for everyone! So I dug my heels into the gravel and pulled up two feet in front of him. I felt a toenail bend back. He looked behind me up the alley, maybe to see who was chasing me.

I remembered to bow. I saw that bent toenail, the second-smallest on my right foot — a little pink mouth gaped at me.

He said something that didn't sound encouraging.

"Work," I said. I pointed behind him. "Airstrip."

He frowned with one corner of his mouth. This is a waste of precious Japanese time, the corner of his mouth said.

I said it louder: "Work."

I play-acted that I was shovelling dirt over my shoulder.

"*Imaima?*" he said. His eyes went wide.

I raised my eyebrows and shovelled again.

He fished a wristwatch out of the same breast pocket, held it up, couldn't read it, turned it the other way around. He sucked in a breath, looked from the watch to me.

"*Mushi mushi!*"

He spun around and started running, and when he reached the corner he looked back and waved me towards him like a traffic cop, so I started to run too. I went around two guys carrying a washtub and caught up to him. He ran with his rifle in one hand. We ran into the big yard, alongside the cookhouse, and there were Tsuji and Kobayashi themselves, studying a piece of paper. Tsuji stood up straight and snapped his heels together and we were probably supposed to stop but Donkey just barked something at him and we ran right on by. Then I saw that the big gate was open and the truck was still there, driving out, a rear wheel splashing through a puddle. Donkey looked to make sure I was still with him.

"*Ter-yu!*" he yelled at the gate. "*Ter-yu!*"

The truck kept rolling, canvas flapping. Three guards by the fence quit chatting to look up at us. Another guard stood next to the gate with a rope in his hands, and the other three started to yell at him but he went on watching the truck drive out.

Donkey put his hand on my shoulder as we ran along.

"*Ter-yu!*" he shouted.

The truck was out, gone, but then the guard with the rope looked back and saw us. He realized what the other guards were shouting and stood there like a moron for one second, then he dropped the rope and ran out after the truck. It hadn't picked up any speed — I could hear the driver trying to find second gear. The guard started pounding on the tailgate, running along behind it, and of course Donkey and I kept running too. We were almost to the gate ourselves. The other three waved us on, and as we went through the gate the truck was right there in front of us and our friend was holding the canvas back. He and Donkey lowered the tailgate and I threw a foot up but couldn't pull myself the rest of the way. A dozen big Dutch faces looked down from the benches. They must have imagined I was just throwing myself around for the exercise. Then Michel's white head reared up out of the gloom and his big hand came down and caught mine and he hauled me up like I was ten pounds of flour. Already the Japs were lifting the tailgate and the canvas was coming down, putting us in the dark, then somebody slapped the side of the truck and we started rolling. The benches were full so I stayed on the floor, and through the gap I watched the guard from the shack slap Donkey on the back as Donkey pulled his cap off — he was just about bald — and waved it in front of his face. He was laughing so hard that he was bent over double.

The wooden floor felt cool underneath me so I leaned back and rested even as the truck crashed and banged like a third rate roller coaster. I lay my head down gently on the boards. I saw that scratch of light where the two flaps came together.

"Harry," Michel was saying. "Wake up now."

Those Dutch knees jutted out over my head like rafters in a barn. My mouth was dry and my arms felt so hollow that I had to wiggle my fingers to make sure they were still there. That's what a day without food will do to a guy, so imagine if we'd waited a month before endeavouring to run away. As usual my crotch was asking for a scratch, but with all those guys staring at me all I could do was poke at it through my pants with the side of my hand. The truck was grinding along in a low gear.

The Dutchmen all swayed to their feet so I rolled onto my side so I'd take up as little room as possible. The canvas folded back and they started jumping out. I could see the grey sky. I slid my bottom along the wood until my legs were over the edge of the tailgate, then I dropped down too.

We stood in a clearing with a pile of branches and uprooted trees in the middle and clouds of tiny bugs everywhere, but they must not have been biters because the Dutchmen didn't even wave them away. There was a heap of jagged-looking rocks beside the woodpile and a banged-up blue wheelbarrow beside that. None of the trees in the forest were much taller than we were and there was a bird parked in one of them that sounded annoyed as hell. There were puddles, too, but not as many as in camp. Michel looked across at me from the other side of the crowd, nodding, then he touched the side of his nose with his thumb. I didn't see any Japs around — was he saying it was time to go already? What had your mother called it? *Pergi ulu*? But, no, he didn't budge. Maybe he'd just had a bug up his nose.

One Dutchman was muttering to another, pointing out some gnarled stumps at the edge of the clearing. The wood was still green where they'd been cut. Skinny came around from the front of the truck with an oilcloth bundle, tottering like he had the blind staggers, then he dropped the whole thing in front of us and the cloth fell away. Shovels and pickaxes. Skinny straightened the bottom of his tunic and said something to us, then Elephant handed him a rifle. Elephant had his wooden club from the day before.

A little silver-haired Dutchman took charge, handing out tools and pointing the direction each guy was supposed to go. I couldn't have guessed how old he was, because he didn't have a wrinkle. He seemed pretty excited about the whole operation. The others were already digging under the stumps, dirt flying around them, and all of a sudden I just wanted to do what I was told too. An airstrip out there in boon-docks! Part of my brain really did want to see the project through even if it meant starving to death, just to see exactly what a bunch of white men were capable of — months in the future, as we watched the first plane circling to land, I could stand there and do the arithmetic in my head, man-hours per cleared acre, that kind of thing. That was what I was thinking as the silver-haired Dutchman put a shovel in my hands.

An airstrip! But then a bug started chewing on my temple, right at the
end of my eyebrow, and when my first thought was whack it with the
shovel I knew my thinking had gone a little off-kilter.

"*Jij bent niet*," he said, that's what it sounded like, and then a couple
of other things. He squinted at me — he seemed concerned.

"Come this way." Michel had a shovel too. "We will dig rocks."

We found a hole in the ground where they must've pulled out a
stump the day before. Two big Dutchmen were levering rocks out of
the wet dirt, and they must've been brothers because they had the same
double chins and blond eyelashes and moustaches. I stood there watching for a useful spot to dig my shovel in. Michel picked up a baseball-
sized rock in one hand and walked back to the middle of the clearing to
set it on the pile. He came back and said something to the Dutchmen so
they blew little chuckles out their moustaches. One of them looked at
me and nodded. They'd found the bottom edge of a rock, so I slid my
shovel underneath and we wiggled it out into the open, then Michel
jumped down into the hole and lifted it out with his bare hands. I felt
something bump against the back of my leg. I figured it was some
smartass making free with his shovel, but I spun around and found
Elephant standing there. He'd pushed the wheelbarrow up behind me.

"*Arigato!*" Michel called out.

He lifted the rock to his chest and threw it in, and of course it made
that sand-between-your-teeth wheelbarrow sound. Elephant folded
his arms. His club was looped over his belt like an English bobby's, and
he had his lower lip folded over the upper one so he looked even more
like a bulldog. Maybe he practised that in the mirror.

"*Arigato*," the fat guys muttered.

Any plan that Michel might have had probably hadn't involved
Elephant watching us like a mother hen. Michel tugged at a root with his
bare hands and I dug in with my rusty shovel with the ball of my foot,
because I figured that would be the toughest skin. The two Dutchmen
both wore leather shoes with white laces, and Michel had bare feet too
but he'd managed to keep busy without his shovel. My work must've
looked pretty tentative. I flicked up the odd pebble and waited for
Elephant to knock me across the back of the head. I scratched away

enough dirt to show the top of a rock, then I dropped the shovel and got down on my knees and started digging with my fingers. The bugs decided they liked me down low and that they'd hold a powwow in my ears, and because of Elephant I didn't bother to wave them away. I looked at Michel for some kind of sign. Why were we killing ourselves to build an airstrip when we could've been learning cricket-fielding from Bobby and Ect?

"*Van-on-der-en!*" somebody hollered and at the same time there was the sound of leaves and branches tearing from across the clearing. The top of the tallest tree tilted out of sight behind the others, then there was a crash. I peered between the trees and the silver-haired Dutchman was already on top of the trunk, stripping branches off with his axe. Elephant must've figured that that was a more thrilling show than ours because he walked off past the rock pile, one brown boot ahead of the other. The skinnier Dutchman licked his lips as he stepped onto his shovel. Michel stayed crouched against a tree. He had mud up to his wrists.

"When you drop the rock into it," he said, "make a big noise."

"They'll look over here."

The Dutchmen didn't even glance at us. They must not have known English.

"They will only see that we are working, and after that they will not look for a while."

I got my fingers around either end of the rock and pushed it out from my chest. It really sailed. One of the wheelbarrow legs lifted off the ground and I thought it would tip, but then the rock rolled to the middle and the leg went down again.

Skinny looked over his shoulder at us. He'd been lighting a cigarette.

"We keep working now," said Michel.

Skinny shouted something, angry, and I looked up because I assumed we were in trouble up to our neckties, but he was marching across the clearing to where the skid road came in. Two Dutchmen were loading rocks into a basket — where'd they get a basket? Skinny hollered again and they ran back down, the basket slung between them. The road was the only way out of there and Skinny didn't like us wandering in that direction.

The fatter Dutchman slapped something on the back of his red neck. It left a white handprint. Michel stepped down on his shovel. I wished like hell I knew what was going on in his head, if he was still working on a plan, or if this was all part of his plan, or if he was just trying to imagine what his long-lost wife looked like with her shirt off.

After two hours of bugs crawling out my ears I'd lost all ambition to finish the airstrip. I listened to the grunts and groans as a gang of Dutchmen tried to kill themselves hauling a stump out of the ground — then hacking at the roots, then trying again — and wondered why we didn't just set the trees on fire. Because it was the rainy season? They'd burn all right if we doused them with gasoline. I stared at Michel's square toes squishing in the mud while we tried to uproot a rock the size of a fire hydrant. Weren't there bulldozers in Celebes? I thought what a bundle a guy could make once the war was over exporting bulldozers to Celebes.

Skinny strolled between the woodpile and their truck, singing in a nice deep voice. The more we tugged on that rock the slipperier it got, and I remember that at the worst point, right before our two Dutchmen hustled over with their shovels, he was singing a real bouncy number that went *ano-waki, ano-waki, ano-waki*. It sounded like a Louis Armstrong tune. We rolled the wheelbarrow right down into the hole and managed to flop the rock into it, then two of us held the barrow straight and the other two pushed, and just as we got it up to level ground the sun broke out through the clouds, showing us the bugs in all their millions.

"Maybe now we can start that fire," I said between my teeth.

"Yes," Michel said, "you see." The sun was right behind his head so he was hard to look at. "They light one now."

The Dutchmen groaned and kept pushing. Those two could really work. We rolled the wheelbarrow to the rock pile and, sure enough, the little silver-haired Dutchman was bent over a little mound of smoking tinder. We all straightened our backs and Michel asked our white-laced cronies something.

Oh yeah, they nodded, oh yes, definitely. Whatever it was, they were sure of it. We went back to our shovels.

"They give us rice for dinner," Michel said.

"You mean 'dinner' as in right now?"

"In a few minutes."

The two Dutchmen nodded at me too. Vigorously.

"What if we can't get rid of these two?" I asked. "Do they come with us?"

Michel started walking away through the brush and I followed him, twigs crackling under us. I figured maybe this was it, the moment, but he stopped in front of a cluster of rocks at the base of a dead tree. That put two trees between us and the hole we'd been working in, and beyond our dead tree the ground dropped away five feet into thick bush. Despite the bugs in my ears, I heard water trickling down there. The fatter Dutchman came through the underbrush after us, using his shovel like a walking stick as his brother called out behind him. That would've been the end of it — four could never escape the way two might. The fatter one said something back to his brother, pointed his handle at us, but then still another Dutchman, this one with mud smeared on his forehead, hollered something across the clearing that made both brothers trot over there on the double. Nobody seemed to be calling us.

"We keep working," said Michel.

The cluster of rocks looked like one big rock that had splintered apart. Was it igneous rock? That was something I should've learned in high school. Michel started hacking at a shrub with his shovel. A bird above our heads went *ack-ack-ack-ack-ack*. I chopped a bush into the ground then dropped to my knees to pull up the roots.

"Everyone is too interested in food," he said.

"But we're not?"

"No."

"We've got priorities," I said.

I threw down one bush and started on the next. I could see the truck and both of the Japs and most of the Dutchmen. Nobody seemed concerned that we were so far away. The silver-haired Dutchman held a pot over the fire, and Skinny must've been telling jokes because every now and then Elephant would whinny like a goddamn horse. The sunlight bounced off Skinny's bayonet.

"It will take ten minutes to boil rice," Michel said.

"That's not much of a fire he's got."

"Fifteen minutes."

The roots were crawling with little silver grubs, and I started to brush them out of my way until I realized that they might be edible, or then again they might be poisonous as strychnine and I shouldn't even be touching them.

"So how'd you learn English?" I asked.

Michel wiped his forehead with his sleeve and raised his shovel again. I figured we were both nervous — I was trying to make conversation and he was slaving harder than ever. The fourteen minutes, or however long it was, seemed to take two weeks. We worked away, pulling and hacking, and I tried to keep the creepy-crawlies from going up my pant leg and told myself that I wasn't hungry, I didn't even want a grain of rice though I could smell it cooking. Was it getting close? There's a certain thing that a guy's stomach does when he's about to do something boneheaded, a tightening like he might have to poop or be sick, which is also exactly how a guy feels when he hasn't had anything to eat in a while — nausea with something extra stacked on top of it.

"When the Japanese take their food we will go down the bank." Michel scooped dirt back into a hole. "Keep your shovel with you."

"Are we going —"

"Now."

He dropped down the bank.

Had they seen him go? I told myself not to look around, it didn't matter, forget it, if I wanted to see you again I just would have to be boneheaded. So I was down the bank one second after him, and he was already hightailing it up the ditch with his behind in the air. The ground was mostly mud so we hardly made a sound, but then we started sinking up to our knees and if we hadn't had those shovels we would've gone in to our waists. I had to use mine like a handrail. We frightened a couple of black-and-red birds out of a tree and their wings went *thud-thud-thud-thud* like Ma beating a rug. Michel looked back at me and sat right down in the mud.

"Wait," he whispered.

"What the hell for?" I was breathing pretty hard. "We've got to move!"

"I want to wait until they know we have gone."

"I don't want that!"

"Then they will come for us in this direction."

"Christ, no! Look, get up and —"

"Then we steal the truck."

There was a sweet smell around us like somebody had dropped a pot of jam, and my heart beat up in my throat. By then I didn't care how long we had to sit in the jungle, I did not want their bayonets coming at me; if Skinny or Elephant found us they would tear up our bellies. Something ran down my nose.

"What's this about the truck?"

"I told you yesterday."

There was no point in arguing with him, and to give him his due, he'd already got us as far as that ditch full of mud. I heard a noise from the clearing like two dogs barking, one high and one low. That was Skinny and Elephant. It was the same noise they'd made when they found Byrnell the night before. Jesus, that was not something my stomach wanted to remember.

"*Chik-u-shoo!*" called Elephant. He was somewhere behind us.

The nausea spread out into my arms and legs. We were still just sitting there.

"Now," I said.

"Wait."

The mosquitoes encouraged us to stay.

"Throw the shovel. There." He got to his feet and pointed out to our left. "I will throw mine too. Ready?"

I stood up and threw the shovel but it hit a vine and flipped over so Michel's went sailing miles above it, but wherever they landed they made a hell of a noise.

We waited again. I heard the low barking, that was Skinny out to my left, just like we wanted, and a second later Michel was climbing the bank. I pulled myself up by the branches; I kept my head low and my eyes on his nightshirt skittering through the bushes ahead of me. Everything snapped under my feet — I must've been easier to follow than a parade. Where in hell were we going? I would've bet any money that the truck was to our right. He bobbed up and down, around trees and behind them, and it was all I could do to keep within fifty feet of him.

He stopped when the woods got brighter. We were at the edge of the skid road. He wiped his nose. His head looked like it had been dipped in mud. We were ten steps from the clearing, looking down at the side of the truck and half a dozen Dutchmen sitting on the ground behind it. Elephant stood over them with a rifle, looking away from us. Where were the rest of the Dutchmen? Maybe on the other side of the truck. My heart beat against my ribs and for once food and drink were not a priority. Just seeing the back of Elephant's head made me nauseous.

"You must drive," whispered Michel. "Keep with me."

He tiptoed out into the road so that we were in plain sight to any-one facing that way, but after ten steps we'd cut the angle so that the truck was between us and Elephant. I stepped around any loose rocks. We came up to the truck's passenger side and for a second I thought that it might be like our taxi in Singapore and have the steering on the near side, but no, there it was across. The Dutchmen didn't make a sound and neither did Elephant. It was like we were the only ones out there. We crouched beside the front wheel. Michel looked me in the face, just listening, I guess, then he stretched up his arm and lifted the door handle.

"Go a-*round*," he whispered.

I bent low and ran around the front. I left a handprint on the dusty bumper. The chrome was shiny underneath. Somehow my brain noticed that. The only place to go from there was the other side of the truck, so I carried on, and I did not run smack into Elephant and his bayonet. In fact I did not see anyone — they must've still been on the other side of the woodpile. I swung the door open and climbed up to the cab, thinking that in the next second I'd be saying to myself, well, that's it, Harry, they've put a bullet through your ribs. I pictured Byrnell's jerking legs. The leather on the seat felt damp. Michel was already in, leaning out his window to look behind us. Had I forgotten something? I couldn't think of what. Was there a key in the ignition? Yes, there was. I put my foot down on the clutch and turned it. The battery was dead.

No, it started. I looked through the windshield and there was Skinny coming through the trees straight ahead of us, running like he was on punt return, and even over the engine I could hear him holler. Elephant appeared in my side mirror. Skinny raised his rifle to his shoulder.

I found reverse and stepped on the gas, then it looked as though Skinny were flying backwards away from us. I turned the wheel and all the trees swung past us. My stomach didn't like that. Black birds flew by. Were Skinny and Elephant shooting? I couldn't tell. They must have been. My ears may have quit working. When we were pointed at the skid road I put the clutch back in and found first gear. It worked just like a regular gearshift. The last thing I'd driven had been Ray's mother's little grey Austin Seven when I'd taken her sister to the bus station on Seymour. I'd been wearing shoes. Wearing shoes had been all the rage back then. I gave the truck a lot of gas and was careful not to stall it. We went up the road and branches knocked against the sides of the cab and I kept looking in the side mirror to see Elephant hanging off the canvas but he simply was not there so I was ready to hoot and holler, let me tell you, because, Jesus, it sure looked like we'd made it! But Michel still leaned out his window, looking back. Then he had to start looking forward, because of the branches coming at us. It was a narrow road. It really did seem like we'd made it.

We drove out of the forest and joined a straight stretch of road with a big rice field on the left. I put the gas as far down as it would go but everything vibrated and my crotch didn't like that. The canvas shook in my side mirrors. There were a lot of gauges in front of me and one of them said *benzine*, that might've been the gas, with *leeg* and *vol* on either side of it. The needle was a lot closer to *leeg* than *vol*.

"They could have built an airfield here!"

Michel pointed out at the rice field, his hand between my face and the steering wheel.

"What?"

I figured that I'd heard him right but I wanted to make sure in case it was crucial information.

"They could drain away the water and build the airport there!" He was still pointing. "It has no trees!"

"But how deep's the water?"

"Not deep!"

Maybe he'd been an engineer as well as a cook on his Chinese boats; even so it seemed like a hell of a thing to start talking about. He climbed up onto his knees and looked behind us out his window for a long time. Finally he sat down and rolled the window up. Then he rolled it halfway down again.

"What's the scoop?" I said.

He looked at me like he'd forgotten I was there.

"Oh," he said. "Everything is fine."

We passed two water buffalo in a field. Each of them had a big white bird standing on its back, and when I looked farther up the road I saw a whitewashed shed approaching on the left. There was someone standing in front of it, and from the colour of the uniform it looked like a Jap soldier. Could he stop us? Pull a gate across? Maybe he had a telephone? There were no telephone poles. Once we got within fifty yards I saw that he was holding a long stick — he was drawing in the dirt! I put on the gas, because what would the point have been in slowing down? He only looked up right as we went by, and when I looked in the side mirror he was still bowing.

"When Ney led the Third Corps across the Dnieper," said Michel.

A brown guy walked in the long grass at the side of the road. His hat looked like a Mexican sombrero.

"What's this?"

"Across the frozen river!"

"What's this?"

We were coming to a hill so I dropped it into third.

"When the marshal led them across the Dnieper."

I glanced over and he was smiling at me. The mud had cracked on his cheeks so he looked like the Mummy.

"For them it was the middle of the *night*. It is so much easier for us!"

From the top of the hill we looked down over the rocks and black bushes at the sea disappearing into the distance, and a minute later a lot of tin rooftops rose in front of us. A town. And it didn't look to be on fire like Singapore had been, but of course it would be full of Japs. The road twisted like a rattlesnake, switchbacking down the hill, but I craned my neck one way then the other to see where else we could go.

"We need to find local people," said Michel.

It was sunny and hot as hell, it must've been two in the afternoon, and thorn bushes leaned out over the road. I felt thirsty as the Sahara but I figured that if we ended up somewhere that didn't have water then we could drink out of the radiator. The road straightened and I looked down the slope to our left. There were trees at the bottom. It looked dark and out-of-the-way. I spun the wheel as far to the left as it would go and dropped it into second and we bumped over the edge of the road.

"Good," Michel said. He had his hands against the dash.

Little trees snapped against our bumper and their leaves flew up over the windshield. Jesus, it was getting steep. I felt a rock thump against the floorboards. Then another. The trees at the bottom came closer. We went over a ledge and felt the loudest thump yet — I lifted my feet off the pedals. I glanced at Michel and saw grinning teeth. Steam wafted in front of the windshield and I tried to keep steering but the wheel wouldn't budge, we kept rolling like in the song about Ezekiel. I figured I'd stalled it so I found the clutch pedal and tried the ignition. The ground was level again but we didn't slow down. Green branches slapped the glass, I figured it might be a willow tree, then we ran into a tree trunk six feet wide and stopped dead. The steering wheel rammed into my chest so the air went out of my lungs and Michel knocked against the dash and fell onto the floor. His door swung open. A black water buffalo stood looking at us.

I pushed myself away from the wheel and tried to get some air — all I had to do was breathe in, I knew that. A bug with antlers sat washing its hands on the hood.

"Harry," Michel said. He was back up in his seat. "We must go."

I opened my door and slid down to the ground. Steam billowed up from under the wheel wells. I looked underneath and saw three pipes snapped in half. The truck was probably leaking gas all over the forest floor.

"Harry," Michel said.

He was on the other side of the truck so I had to hustle around the tree. I wasn't steady on my feet. It was shady under there but we weren't anywhere near the bottom of the valley, the hill kept going down and down. The hood had bit into the tree so we wouldn't be able to get water out of the radiator. When I came around to the passenger side that buffalo swung her head around and blinked at me a few times. She had green spit all over her lips and a ring through her nostrils. I reached up and scratched her forehead and felt a whole lot better. My head quit spinning. The thick part of her horn was ridged like a cold-air grate, and little bugs like mosquitoes flitted around her eyes.

"Harry," said Michel.

He was looking at something behind me, so I turned to look. A wooden cart pulled by another buffalo was bumping towards us, with an old native guy up in the seat. The tongue of his cart had two yokes but only one buffalo, so I figured that my friend was an escaped prisoner just like us. The old guy was smiling but for all I knew that was because he was the Japs' best pal. My buffalo leaned in and put a lot of snot on my neck.

"*Goe-de-middag*," said the old guy.

Michel stood up and said the same thing. The old guy wore a patterned sarong dress and a yellow shirt with about a hundred pockets down the front. The back of the cart was piled with tin buckets. He kept smiling. He didn't have many teeth. He drove into the shade under our tree so that his buffalo was right next to mine. The new one leaned her nose into me too, and I made sure she got my shoulder instead of the middle of my chest where the steering wheel had hit me.

The old guy pulled a big glass jar out from under the seat. It looked like it had been filled from a puddle. He unscrewed the top and passed it down to Michel, who took a swig and then handed it to me.

"What is it?" I asked.

"He says it is tea."

Tea again! It tasted like dirt, but at least it was wet. I drank half of it, then stood there panting like a little kid who's been drinking Kik in July.

"Tell him thanks."

The old guy screwed the lid down again while he and Michel went on talking. From the tones of their voices they might have been talking about sports — they weren't mad at each another but they were mad about something. After a minute the old guy reached down by his feet and brought up a great big long rifle and set it across his knees, then brought up a piece of buffalo horn with a metal cap like they always show Daniel Boone carrying. He stood up on his seat, still talking, and poured powder down the barrel. By then both of the buffalo were tugging grass into their mouths, ignoring me, so I sat at the base of the tree and thought about going to sleep. The bark looked woven. I figured that if the time came to run for cover Michel would let me know. He and the old guy kept saying *Nederlands*, back and forth, *Nederlands*, then the old guy made a face like he'd tasted medicine. He stopped talking and stood there looking down the hill. The end of the rifle came up to his chin.

"*De grot*," he said.

"*Grot?*" asked Michel.

The old guy lifted a metal rod from the bench and slid it up and down the barrel, concentrating so he got a crease between his eyes.

"He wants to hide us in a cave," Michel said.

"Ask him if he's got anything to eat."

"We cannot ask him that."

"Why not? What language is that?"

"Dutch. They learn Dutch when they are children."

"You said you were French."

"On Java I learned Dutch."

The old guy took a little grey ball out of one of his shirt pockets and dropped it down the barrel. Michel asked him a long-winded question, but by way of an answer the old guy just sat down and started cocking his rifle. It looked like he was winding a clock. Then he aimed it at a tree.

"*Voor do japanners*," he said.

Then he started laughing so lines went all down his face, and Michel started laughing and he looked at me. I couldn't even guess what they thought was so funny. I was going to vomit the tea back up if I didn't get something solid in my stomach.

The old guy tied the runaway buffalo back into her yoke, then the three of us climbed onto the bench. The old guy brought out a red whip and knocked it against the wooden tongue between the buffalo. That was enough to start them down the hill.

"Pelayaran," the old guy said.

"The town," said Michel. "Not the camp."

I must have looked panicked. I could see the silhouettes of the buildings miles below us at the bottom of the hill. The cart went over bushes and cactus so it listed like a boat, over to one side and then the other, and we had to hold the bench with the backs of our knees. Even sitting down Michel was a foot taller than the old guy, who clicked his tongue and knocked his whip against the wood.

"Ask him if he has food," I said.

"We must be invited."

"Whose side are you on?"

But I knew that I would've been completely lost if it weren't for Michel, regardless of his escape plan and his Dutch — people just found him charming. He and the old guy chatted and after a while the sun dropped down toward the sea, so that meant we were travelling west. That made me think of those two Limeys off of Bombay who'd been so muddled with their directions, and of course that led me to thinking about you and where in hell Singapore was in relation to where we were and how exactly I was going to get there, but I didn't get too worked up about it because at least we were moving. My time on *Asia* had taught me patience if nothing else. Be patient and everything will turn out peaches and cream — of course Falkiner was teaching his boys that too. The old guy started laughing.

"He says that we do not want to get away from the tiger just to fall into the crocodile's mouth."

"No, I guess we don't."

"No!"

We came out of the bush onto a dirt road and I figured that was a step in the right direction, a road would lead eventually to food, but then the old guy made us lay in the back under all his buckets. They smelled like old lard, sort of a rancid smell, and that took me back to old *Asia* too — our dirty underwear. As we rolled along the buckets shifted over me so I could see bits of the sky between them, and I got drowsy as hell.

The bottoms of the clouds turned red. I thought, how *did* we escape, anyway? All I could picture was Michel lifting us in a giant hand.

The bucket lifted away from my face and there was his white head and the night sky full of stars up above it.

"We eat," he said. "I thought that you would want to know."

Chicken was cooking somewhere; it smelled like the pan had been put down in front of me. And what would they be eating in Pelayaran Camp that night? They'd be sucking their fingers.

The air was cool and I heard water splashing. I pulled myself up by the back of the seat and the cart rolled a bit — our buffalo were gone.

"By the wheel," he said. "Come here."

Treetops were silhouetted against the sky but they seemed to be miles up, maybe on top of a cliff. My foot found a spoke and I climbed down. Bugs clicked all around us.

"We will do well with these men. They do not follow those in power. They follow their beliefs."

"That sounds dandy."

All I wanted was their chicken. He led me through wet bushes. They could've had thorns so I tried to step where he had stepped.

"When the Bourbons sent the marshal to arrest Bonaparte, do you remember? 'Bring him back in an iron cage,' they said — what could be more clear? But when he reached Cannes the marshal joined with Bonaparte rather than arrest him. The marshal followed his beliefs instead of those in power. Maybe I have told you already, but Cannes is not far from where I come from."

"I never heard that story."

We went around a log the size of a boxcar and I could see a new old guy sitting next to a fire inside a cave, with the light dancing across the ceiling. As far as I could make out the place was a ravine of some kind, with a waterfall away to our left and that cave tucked into the bottom of a rock wall. We crossed cold stones, then something moved in the bushes next to me and I tried to turn around but slipped on a rock and fell right down on my backside. It was some native kid shaking the old guy's gun over my head. The light flickered across his face.

"*Maputi!*" he said. *Maputi-maputi* something-something!

He had a little moustache under his nose exactly like Hitler's, but even as he hollered I thought, hell, he's probably never even heard of Hitler way out here.

"Loé," the old guy called.

Michel saw me on the ground and a big sputter like a cod laughing burst out of him.

"Loé," the old guy called again.

The young guy put his gun down and stepped back into the bush. He disappeared completely. The old guy pulled me up — he had fingers like a pair of pliers.

"*Kom, kom,*" he said.

Michel was already bent over the fire, pulling strips of meat off the spit and stuffing them into his mouth. Juice dripped off his chin. There was still dirt caked around his eyes so he looked like the Mummy eating chicken.

"We must be careful." He took a bone out of his mouth. "We cannot eat too much."

I tore some off the spit and stuffed it in my mouth with the juice running down my arm. It was full of bones and tasted like smoke but it was still meat. There were a lot of rocks inside the cave so I sat on one that looked flat. Michel pulled more chicken off the stick. The old guy pulled packets made of leaves out of a basket and started unwrapping them. Rice! They were neat little packages of rice. He passed one to me and I wolfed that back too. It was cold and sticky and I thought, honest to God, this is the perfect food. The old guy sat on his haunches, watching me. He wore a black hat that looked like a lunch pail and gold bracelets that jangled as he rocked back and forth.

"Rice," I said. "Jesus."

"This man is called Kasa," said Michel.

The lunch pail guy put his hands together in front of his face and bobbed his head. His bracelets jangled. The kid wandered out of the bushes to have a smoke. Michel pointed at him with a hunk of chicken.

"That is Loé."

Michel and old Kasa talked in some language I didn't understand, which meant it could have been anything other than English. Kasa moved a log with his bare foot. I pulled some skin off the meat. The skin had fur that stank like cat pee. Whatever kind of chickens they had in the Indies they weren't going to win any 4H prizes.

"Where's *our* old guy?" I asked.

"Monto?" said Michel. "Here he comes."

The old guy with the pockets came in from the trees, leading one of his buffalo on a rope. He handed the rope to Loé, who spit. Monto had two blankets over his shoulder that he dropped beside the fire, then he turned the meat on the stick and said something.

"He says the two of them will keep each other awake."

Loé scratched the buffalo's forehead and she leaned into him. I admit I felt a little jealous. I threw the furry bit of skin out into the bushes. Kasa waved the smoke away from his face and wrapped his arms around his knees. He looked at me and asked something.

"They want to know how you like the meat," said Michel.

"Greatest I ever had."

Wherever the fur had come from, the meat didn't taste that bad. They watched me go on eating. Loé held his cigarette between his teeth.

"*Vleer-muis-vlees*," said Monto.

"Oh!" said Michel. "It is a bat. A big bat."

Kasa put his thumbs together and flapped his hands. I must have quit chewing for a second because they all burst out laughing. Bat meat. Was there something the matter with bats? Not that I'd ever heard of. I pulled another hunk from the spit and stuffed it in my mouth. They chuckled for a while and Kasa said *mupati* again. He said that a lot.

"What are they saying?" I asked.

"I do not know." Michel pulled a blanket over his shoulder. "It is their own language."

"Did they say we're going to sleep here?"

"We must wait for someone."

"*Aya!*" said Monto. "Loé!"

The buffalo had a lit cigarette stuck between her lips. It would've

made a nice ad for Sweet Caps, on the front of a magazine or something
— no women would've smoked them after that. Loé scratched his belly
and grinned away. Monto lobbed a pebble that hit him in the shoulder.
Loé made a face like that had hurt his feelings, then he scratched
the buffalo between the ears and took the cigarette and stuck it back
in his mouth.

They talked for a while longer. I passed gas as quietly as I could,
then I lay down with a rock under my head and pulled a blanket over
me. The taste of bat kept rising up in my throat.

"*Maputi omani,*" said Kasa.

I liked hearing languages that I didn't understand. I liked that
there was more to the world than the two or three dozen things I knew
already.

When I woke up inside the cave it sounded like two of the birds out in
the woods were having a bout and the rest were betting on it, screaming
and hopping up and down, clutching dollar bills in their feet. I still had
that rock under my head and I'd rolled onto my side so I had a sore ear,
and when I opened my eyes I was looking at Michel's leg sticking out of
the bottom of his nightshirt. The hair on his calf was crusted with mud
and a beetle was crawling up his ankle. Nobody else was around. The
ashes from the fire had been kicked all over the floor. They hadn't left us
any jars of tea to drink — not that they owed us a jar of tea. For that
matter, why had they helped us at all? I pulled up my shirt and saw the
bruise that the steering wheel had given me.

I stood up and stretched, and my knuckles came down from the
ceiling black with soot. I reached down my pants and scratched away
for a while; the skin couldn't have been more raw if I'd ripped off a
scab. I knew I shouldn't have been scratching at all, but Jesus, once I'd
started there was no stopping. Maybe that's how a dog feels when a guy
rubs its belly.

"Here they are."

Michel was on his feet beside me. I withdrew my hand. Monto and another guy picked their way over the rocks at the entrance. Monto raised a hand to us to say hello; he held a red umbrella and the new guy was all in white, with a cloth around his head.

"*Goedemorgen*," called Michel.

Good morning? Half the time Dutch sounded like pig Latin. The guy in white walked up and stood smiling between us. One of his front teeth was chipped in half.

"*Ik heet Muzakkar*," he said.

Was that Dutch? He and Michel shook hands, which seemed to involve grabbing the other guy's elbow. I thought they were going to foxtrot. But then the new guy turned to me and we did the same thing, and I think I did it right — the bones in his elbow felt frail as a chicken's. I nodded my head a lot and so did he. He smelled like wet tobacco.

"His name is Muzakkar," said Michel.

Muzakkar said a few more things to us while Monto fiddled with his umbrella, then we followed the two of them out of the cave and into the woods. I only saw a couple of green birds flying in and out of the trees but it still sounded like every single bug and bird and Tarzan-monkey out there was arguing over who had won the bout.

Then I heard the splashing water that I'd heard the night before and we were walking through tall grass with mist blowing all around. A waterfall poured off the cliff into a pool in front of us. Butterflies fluttered through the mist or rose out of the grass; a black-and-white one with yellow spots landed on my shoulder. The grass was so wet that Michel's nightshirt looked like he'd waded across a river, but the spray and sun both felt pretty good. We clambered down some rocks to the pool, and I stretched flat on my belly and scooped water into my mouth. I drank one handful after another. Dragonflies skittered over the water. I wiped my mouth on my undershirt.

"What happened to Monto?" I asked.

"He has gone on ahead."

"How come?"

"To see that we do not meet anyone."

I felt like I was on an outing with my folks, which isn't a feeling that most grown men savour, but I was clearly in better shape than if I'd been out there on my own. Before long I couldn't hear the waterfall anymore. We emerged on a hillside with another grove of trees at the bottom, and a valley of wet fields beyond that stretching out to the blue horizon. The palm leaves brushing against each other sounded like someone shuffling cards.

Muzakkar lay down on the grass so we did too. It was sandy soil and little brown ants ran everywhere. I figured that we were waiting for Monto to shoot up a flare before we went any farther. It wasn't nearly so wet there as where we'd been building the airstrip. The breeze smelled sweet as a hay barn. The odd buffalo stood out in the rice fields, and somebody who was either brown or wearing brown walked under some trees.

Muzakkar pulled down his headcloth so it went right over his face, then he started to talk. Michel leaned on one elbow and listened.

"What's he want?" I asked.

Muzakkar lay his arm over his face and went on talking.

"What's he want?"

"He says that Java is the safest place."

Muzakkar tugged these little square papers out of his headcloth and handed one to each of us. It was flimsy paper showing a red star and a hammer and sickle, which as far as I knew meant it had something to do with Russia. He flashed his own paper at us, held neatly in his palm.

"*Als de japanners —*" he said, then he pretended to put it in his mouth. He gave a big gulp. Then he tucked it back into his headcloth and put the cigarette back in his mouth. He picked some tobacco off his chipped tooth.

"Like hell I'm going to eat this."

"These tell people that we are his friends." Michel studied the paper an inch from his nose. "If we show it to his friends, they will be our friends too."

"*Japanners,*" said Muzakkar.

"And if the Japanese try to see your paper, yes, you must swallow it."

"But are the friends going to give us anything to eat? I mean, *besides* this?"

Michel asked.

Muzakkar nodded, with his cigarette against his knee.

"*Perserikatan Kommunist Indonesia*," he said.

"They are the Communists." Michel leaned forward, pulled his nightshirt over his bottom and sat down on it. "The Communists in France are good men. They made a law for a fair wage and my father does not like that."

"But they fight the Japs?"

He asked and Muzakkar had to give a hell of a long answer. Of course I'd heard of the Communists from Dad's newspapers and my days with Grace, they'd been agitators, rabble-rousers, bad seeds, the lot, but of course that had been in Canada where to the best of my knowledge the Japanese were not killing people off one by one. As long as they weren't Japs, I wasn't going to sit in judgment on anybody. That bat meat had still been food, hadn't it?

Muzakkar kept showing the shape of a ball in the air then he'd quit talking for a second, then he'd start up again. Michel sat there nodding and pulling the bark off a stick.

"He says that the native people here want to have their own country. They want the Japanese to go and they want the Dutch to go. When he heard that the Japanese were coming he and his friends took the Dutch from around here and put them into jail."

"That's great news. Dandy."

"He will not do that to us. He says that his colleagues in Java must be told what conditions are like under the Japanese, because they are not what he had hoped for. He does not mind white men if they work for him."

"Did he say that?"

"No," said Michel. "But it is clear."

"Did he say who's taking us to Java?"

"No."

Muzakkar looked up at the sun for a minute, then he got to his feet and turned to face the hillside. He started talking to himself, then he fell to his knees and put his face in the grass. We saw his trousers' blue-checked backside. Then he sat up again, still talking.

"He prays," said Michel. "It must be one o'clock."

"They do that on Java too? The natives?"

"Five times each day."

'Natives' — that was what Gordon Sinclair always called them. Of course Falkiner called them wogs, but I got the feeling that Michel might not like that. What had you called them back then? Probably called the Chinese "Chinese," Indians "Indians," and so on, that was really the sensible way to do it. I admit that I wasn't taking old Muzakkar's Java suggestion too seriously at that point since it seemed to me that we had enough resources to travel about a half-mile. Java! But then like a rocket being lit the idea came to me that you had been evacuated to Java. There wasn't any question. I knew it was a fact. Your mother had changed her mind or your dad had shown up after all and they'd evacuated you to Java where the communist agitators were sending us for a reunion.

I love coffee, I love tea. I love the Java Jive and it loves me.

Muzakkar sang some of the time too, he sounded a bit like Jack Teagarden with that little hum in his voice, the way Teagarden sang on "You Rascal You" with Waller. That was a terrific song. And that was a funny comparison to have made since Teagarden was white while Muzakkar seemed darker than Waller himself, though it was hard to say exactly from the photos of Waller that I'd seen.

"Why does he have to face uphill?"

"To face Mecca." Michel picked his toes again. "I think we must wear disguises to go into the town. Like Odysseus when he entered Troy as a leper."

"I'm not going into town. There'll be a million Japs."

He seemed to have found something really breathtaking under his toenail.

"The marshal went into Mannheim dressed as a beggar," he said.

Muzakkar looked at us and straightened out his headcloth. Then he showed me that paper in his hand, the hammer and sickle, so I pulled mine out of my pants pocket and showed it to him. What would Dad have said about all the cloak and dagger?

"Monto has been gone too long," Michel said. "It is time to leave."

Muzakkar cinched up his trousers, nodded to us once, then ran straight down the hill with clods of dirt flying over his shoulders.

I ran after him; it felt like jumping off a cliff, but I kept my arms out beside me and let gravity take my feet. Thorns scratched my ankles but I wasn't bothered. It was good to be going. Muzakkar still hadn't reached the bottom. I realized that so long as we were away from the Japanese nothing else was really a worry — food or shelter or the war in general. I watched him run between the trees, then over a log that crossed a creek, then into some bushes, and when I came to the creek myself he was gone. I jumped in it and drank a handful of water, bouncing my feet against the sandy bottom, but the current was stronger than I'd expected so I put a hand out to Michel.

"He will not wait."

We caught up to Muzakkar on a dirt path at the edge of the rice field, talking to a guy who was up to his knees in mud, with a cigarette tucked under his big walrus moustache. His chest was so bony that it looked like a washboard. He held a water buffalo by a rope attached to the ring through its nose, and the buffalo was white with a few brown patches and a pink nose, which was the kind of coat I would've expected on a housecat. The guy didn't notice us when we walked up; he went on talking to Muzakkar, but then he looked over at us and the cigarette fell out of his mouth into the mud. He didn't say another word, just tugged on the buffalo's nose and headed off across the field.

"You figure he hasn't seen a white man before?"

"Perhaps he has not seen them so dirty."

Muzakkar led us along the path between the fields, across the valley toward what looked like grass huts. The hills were reflected in the water. Michel was stooped over so I did the same, thinking that if a Jap roared over in a plane or looked down the valley with a pair of field glasses we wouldn't give ourselves away by our ridiculous height; all he would see would be a native guy taking his two hunchbacks for a walk. Not that I could see anything that resembled a Jap — just a couple of birds floating way up in the blue and a cockroach buzzing past us a foot above the water. As we came closer to the houses I heard little kids shrieking — the happy kind — and a yapping dog. We came into a coconut grove, the skinny trees a long way apart from each other and big green husks lying all over the ground. A black dog with a bald back ran up to us, barked twice and ran away again. The kids were still shrieking. We came up to a half-dozen wooden houses built on stilts so they stood a few feet above the ground, and three kids ran out at us from under a tree: a little boy who only wore a shirt, a girl who only wore a brown skirt and an even smaller boy who just had a red string tied around his middle. Muzakkar put out his arms to pick them up but they all stopped dead in their tracks, eyes very wide, then the littlest kid shrieked — the unhappy kind — and jumped behind the bigger boy, who said, "*Bombo.*" The girl wiped her nose. Then they turned and ran up a ladder into one of the houses. I really wished that we hadn't scared those kids. We walked towards a different house and I heard Muzakkar say *spoken* to Michel.

"They think we are ghosts," said Michel.

The houses had the same palm-leaf roofs as in Pelayaran Camp — maybe these had been the guys that built it. A yellow dog was curled up in a ball under one of them, his ear twitching from the flies. I climbed a rickety ladder behind Muzakkar, so I got to study his blue-checked backside again. An old man in a yellow sarong was laying on a mat on the floor of the house, but he sat up right away and gave Muzakkar and me a lot of little nods and bows and motioned for us to sit down too. He didn't seem frightened by a white man, thank God, and he had the craziest earlobes, without exaggeration, on the face of the earth! Gordon Sinclair could've done a chapter on them; he'd pierced the lobes through the middle, as far as I could tell, then stretched them over what looked like tin can rims so that each of them was three inches around and of course I could look right through the circle of each earlobe at the wall behind him. It smelled like woodsmoke and chicken poop in there and sunlight slanted through the wall between the strips of wood. I dug into my pocket for my Communist voucher and showed it to him just as quick as a wink. He furrowed his brow. Cripes, wasn't he a Communist?

Michel clambered up the ladder and the old guy's jaw dropped just as far as mine had. Maybe he'd figured that I was as big and white as a guy could get and had been wrong on both counts. He had Michel sit down, though, then hollered through the doorway behind him and a woman's voice called back — they sounded like two goats bleating at each other.

Muzakkar took the makings of a cigarette out of his shirt pocket. He rolled one and passed it to the old man, who stuck the whole thing in his mouth, then pulled it out and left it hanging there soaking wet. A line of ants went up the wall and across the ceiling, but where they came from or where they were going I couldn't tell, and there didn't seem to be any end to them. Through the gaps in the floor I watched chickens pecking the ground underneath us — there was a little grey one that the other ones kept trying to scare off. I looked at Michel but he was just staring at his feet again. Was this really the quickest way to Java?

Then I heard a sizzle and crackle as something went into a frying pan in the back room — there's no sound quite like food going into a pan — and I had to swallow back a mouthful of spit. I could smell oil and steak and coconut, and my gut wanted to get up and see what they were making but from the way the old guy kept staring us down I could tell he'd rather we stayed where we were. He sat there like he hadn't even noticed that two enormous earlobes were dangling on either side of his face.

The frying stopped. Everything was quiet except for the chickens underneath us. I watched one peck its own foot. The old guy bleated over his shoulder but there was no response. He sat there holding his ankle, listening.

I looked at Michel and he raised his eyebrows.

One old woman and two young women hurried in with big plates of food. The old woman had grey hair and little silver earrings and one big tooth that stuck out over her bottom lip. Both of the younger ones wore what looked like nightgowns, white with purple stripes running down them, and silver bracelets on their wrists and necklaces made of orange beads. The taller one had a purple cloth piled on her head but the other one just had her hair in a bun, and she had such a sad expression that I couldn't take my eyes off her. Why did she look so sad? Maybe she had a boyfriend who was far away. Maybe she'd just woken up. Girls! That day was getting better and better. The food smells were more than I could take in. The old guy poured tea from a pot with a picture of a rabbit on the side.

Once they'd put down all of the plates and bowls, Bucktooth

clucked her tongue and herded the girls out again. They didn't even look
back at us. With the distractions gone, all that was left was to tackle the
feast: a pyramid of rice on a wooden plate, cubes of squash or something
like it, hunks of meat sitting in a brown sauce that smelled like coconut
and three or four more other dishes like it, the meat chopped into
different sizes — whether they were from different animals I couldn't
tell. Noodles in a red sauce, noodles by themselves, chopped green vegetables, peanuts, a hot yellow sauce with nothing in it, and a white fish
covered in crushed tomatoes. We each had a clay bowl to put our food
in. We ate with our fingers. The cubes of squash were dry so I dipped
them in a different sauce every time. I tried to go as slowly as I could,
swallowing one mouthful before I started the next — I knew that that
would be better for my guts — but seeing how quickly Muzakkar was
putting away the stuff I thought that maybe I was being rude rather than
sensible. The old guy seemed to be enjoying his lunch too much to be
offended anyway. I was worried about offending him! That had to be
Michel's influence. But for all I knew Bucktooth could put the word out
and have the Japs there in ten minutes, so what was the harm in watching my p's and q's? Only that Michel might empty every platter before
I'd had my fill. He had brown sauce smeared on his neck.

Then a belch thundered up out of me like I'd swallowed the
Hindenberg and I took that as a sign to stop. The others were finished
too; Michel sat there panting. Muzakkar got up and went into the back
of the house, holding his sticky hands out in front of him. The old guy
started coughing and I thought he might've got a fish bone caught in his
throat so I got up to club him on the back, but then he just leaned over
and spat through a gap in the floor. I sat down again. The spit hung off
his lip for about a minute and he had to lean back and forth, steering it
through. Muzakkar stood in the kitchen doorway and said something to
Michel, who got up and went out with him. Back to see the girls. The
old guy said something to me then lay down on his mat and shut his
eyes. So I did the same. The Japs could have been right outside the door,
but until I knew they were, why not catch forty winks? I'd eaten just the
right amount of food to be sleepy as hell.

"Harry."

Michel stood in the doorway wearing a pair of houndstooth trousers, with a piece of blue chiffon over his head and a piece of fabric with gold roosters all over it hanging from his shoulders to his knees. He batted his eyes at me. The chiffon looked tight around his throat. The old guy started chuckling. Not for one second did Michel look like a native woman, if that was what he'd been trying for. He looked exactly like a six-foot white man dressed up as a woman.

"We dress like this," he said, "because the Japanese do not bother the women."

"I don't mind if we spend the night here."

"The Japanese will kill these people if we are here."

The old guy clapped his hands and kept laughing. Bucktooth hustled in from the kitchen with some fabric folded over her arm, weaved around the stacks of dirty dishes and stopped in front of me. She had a white piece and an orange piece. She held up the white piece. It was a dress. A design in the fabric looked like barbed wire.

"Listen," I said. "You've got us this far, I'll give you that, but this —"

"When Michel Ney had insufficient troops to take Mannheim —"

"Goddamn it, okay — what did he do?"

"He dressed as a peasant selling vegetables, and my friend, believe me, you and I resemble this lady in front of us more than Marshal Ney ever could a peasant selling vegetables. Yet Mannheim fell before dawn."

"But his costume must've covered his goddamn knees! Look at your pants."

"The Austrians carried the very same bayonets as these Japanese, and yet, and yet ..." Michel held his hands in front of him like he couldn't quite move his arms. "He showed no fear."

There it was! He was saying that I'd be a coward if I didn't go along with his plan. Bucktooth held the dress in the air and gave me any number of encouraging looks. I was putting a gun to my own head, that's what I was doing, walking myself right back into the *kebetai*. But I admit that I'd already been swayed by the fact that any guy who can argue so heatedly while dressed as a woman must really believe that his scheme is going to play out. The old man quit laughing and held his hand to his chest. Spent.

I put my arms above my head and she pulled the dress down over them until the collar stuck around my temples. She tugged until some of the stitches snapped. As my head popped through I saw Muzakkar tuck a long slip of paper into the front of Michel's houndstooth pants. Then she wrapped the orange scarf over my head and under my chin — the material was so gauzy that I kept sucking it against my lips. It smelled of cinnamon.

I peered outside the door of the hut to get an idea of the crowds before I made my debut, and the three kids scattered just like marbles. If a Jap was watching through his field glasses he was really going to have a good giggle. I swung my behind around and put my feet on the ladder and started down but the goddamn gown was so tight around the knees that I couldn't lower my foot to the next rung without ripping the hem. I put my hands flat against the floorboards and hopped down with both feet at once. I found the ground and started across the yard, the hem around my knees making me more pigeon-toed than any pigeon that came before. It was ripping the hairs out of my legs and the fabric under my armpits was so tight that my arms had gone to pins and needles. I turned around to watch Michel sit at the top of the ladder and slide down with his feet in the air. It only took him two seconds. Even coming down a ladder he had to be the hero.

The old man led a brown pony and blue cart from the back of the house. Bells jangled around the roof of the cart and the pony had a red plume attached to the halter across his forehead, which was too bad because if I'd been able to scratch his forehead I might've been able to relax, though I could barely raise my arms anyway. The old man showed us the bench across the back of the cart where Michel and I would have to sit facing backwards. I climbed on and felt the front end lift up as the rear sank under my weight. That pony would have had a lot less trouble if we'd jumped on before lunch. Michel pulled himself up by the corner post and the nails all shrieked and the bells rang an all-stations alarm, and I'd swear the pony's back legs lifted in the air. I won't try to fool you — that cart was not built for us. The old guy muttered to the pony as we sat there looking back at the hut, hands folded in our laps, the axle groaning. My crotch demanded some attention. I told it that I would be ignoring it, because every time I scratched I had to go farther down the insides of my legs and I couldn't help thinking that before long there was going to be nothing left of me. I imagined Ma telling me to put slices of cucumber on it. Michel frowned at me over his blue scarf.

"I know Java better than this," he said. "I will have confidence there."

Muzakkar threw the end of his cigarette at a chicken and ambled across the yard with his arms swinging. Just then the bugs in the trees all went dead quiet like they'd remembered something — thousands of them, all at once. Then they started in again.

He climbed into the driver's seat and started us out of the yard, jingle, jingle, farther away from the waterfall and the cave, and I could only think that that was good, it was better to not be going in circles. The old guy just stood there looking after us with his arms at his sides. None of the women came out of the house. The two boys and the little girl jumped out from behind a stump and ran up the road after us, laughing and snorting, brave as hell now that we were leaving.

"*Bombo!*" they said, and slapped at our feet.

The boy with the string around his middle fell on his face and the other two stopped to help him up. The girl shook her fist after us but she was still grinning from ear to ear, like chasing away white guys was the best new game since basketball.

We creaked alongside another rice field and I saw us reflected in the water — gold and blue, orange and white, and the sky above us without a cloud.

"What happened to the rainy season?"

"It has ended too soon," Michel said. "Nothing is the same this year."

I peered over my shoulder. So many flies covered the pony that he had to swish his tail like a windmill. The reins dragged on the ground. Muzakkar sat with one leg folded under him, waving a hand at the flies. He started singing.

Da mu-tu-ny kan-dooooo

We creaked past the guy with the walrus moustache, pushing a plow behind his cat-coloured buffalo. They were up to their knees in water. He glanced at us, Muzakkar said three words to him, he said two words back, then looked at his buffalo's rear end again like dressing white men up as native women was something that happened every day in those parts. Michel kept rearranging his rooster cloth and I glared at my crotch to see if that would help. The sweat was soaking through the front of my dress.

Kan-do-oo-oo-oo

The bells jangled as we rode along. The rice fields had ended; it was green meadows on either side. We passed a bent-over old woman with a stack of bricks on her back suspended from a strap across her forehead.

The road started up a long hill so The World's Smallest Horse decided that rather than pull us he'd prefer to walk into the ditch. Muzakkar slid to the ground and said something to Michel. After the pony had been unhitched Michel started pulling the cart up the hill while I pushed from the back. Muzakkar led the horse behind us. That cart didn't weigh much but the blue paint kept flaking off on my hands, and of course I could only walk eight inches at a time, so I stopped for a second and rolled up the hem of the dress and stuffed it in the front of my trousers.

Muzakkar said something.

"The disguise is ruined that way," Michel called back. "He says there is a reward for us. We cannot let anyone see."

This from the girl whose feet looked like pontoons. I rolled my dress back down and took tiny steps and keep my head down like a good native girl would do. The ground was grainy and yellow, and there were spatters of red every ten feet like somebody had been spitting blood. I looked up to make sure it wasn't Michel. We overtook three twelve-year-old boys, climbing the hill with their arms full of leafy vegetables. I kept my head down. Out of the corner of my eye I watched them kicking each other and not paying us any attention. I had other reasons to sweat anyway. The heat seemed to be rising right out of the ground. Was Java going to be any cooler? *Asia* had steamed us through Sunda Strait, hadn't it, between Java and Sumatra? That hadn't been any cooler.

We stopped pushing when we reached the scrubby trees at the top. Pelayaran lay at the bottom of the hill, with all its tin roofs and green harbour. By the time we'd hitched the pony up again the brick lady had caught up to us but I didn't bother trying to look ladylike because I knew that if she straightened up to look at us the bricks would have pulled her back down the hill.

"Some guy's bleeding," I whispered, and nodded at the red marks.

"*Sireh.* They chew it like tobacco." Chiffon covered Michel's mouth and chin, and sweat dripped off his nose. "Look."

The brick lady spat half a cup of blood onto the ground.

"You sure she's all right?"

"Oh, she could not be happier."

More people filled the road ahead of us so Muzakkar stopped the cart and came back and draped his shirt over our feet, then pulled the cloths down over our foreheads and across our noses so we just had slits to look out. We stuffed our hands in our armpits.

A side road joined ours and the kids with leafy vegetables ran past. Other kids carried baskets full of those neat little packages — I could smell the rice inside. I was hungry even though every time we went over a bump I'd get a taste of whatever that yellow sauce had been. Muzakkar got the pony trotting and we passed all kinds of people travelling the same way as we were, carrying sticks of bamboo over their shoulders or big yellow pots or chickens tied up in leaves and carried like handbags. One chicken seemed to be eyeballing us, and honest to God, for a second I thought it would raise the alarm. A guy in a purple sarong had a hundred MacIntyre hats stacked on his head, he kept weaving back and forth to keep them from toppling over, and I realized that I must be accustomed to the Orient by then because if I'd seen that guy walking along Price Street in Vernon I would have wet my pants with excitement.

"Your nose shows."

I pulled the end of the scarf across my nose and tucked the end behind my ear then stuffed my hands back into my armpits.

"When do we sell our vegetables?" I whispered.

"It is working."

As far as I could tell he was right. Everybody was just walking into Pelayaran, happy as pigs in muck, carrying their scrawny chickens, chattering away, saying hello to Muzakkar now and then but not giving two cents who was in the back of his cart. Maybe a naked lady was walking ahead of us and she had everybody's attention. Maybe Michel and I had been treated with Dr. Zorka's invisibility ray.

"There are so many because of the afternoon market. They go to mosque because it is Friday."

We passed a cart loaded with bananas of all colours and sizes. I'd seen lots of different kinds in Africa but never piled all together like that. Its driver leaned over and said something to Michel and me.

"*Bawine*," Muzakkar told him.

The two of them carried on talking. I watched the ground pass under our feet.

"Muzakkar tells him we are good women."

"That was Dutch?"

"It is their own talk. It is not difficult to learn."

Grown-ups hustled their children along like they were late to see a ball game. Kids touched our wheels as we rolled by. A woman with a baby on her hip stared at us. We were covered from head to toe — what was she looking at? My blue eyes! I shut them and pretended I was asleep.

Then no one around us was saying a word, though their belongings still creaked in their arms and the chickens clucked the odd time. The bells above our heads went *jingle jangle*, announcing us to the world. *Jingle jangle. Jingle jangle.* Sweat ran into the corners of my eyes and stung like vinegar, and from there it ran down into my mouth.

I felt Michel's elbow in my ribs. The people around us were making noise again. Some guys started singing in unison just like the Mills Brothers.

"Look," said Michel.

I opened my eyes a crack. The singers were those same boys with the leafy vegetables striding along behind us, and fifty feet behind them three Japanese soldiers stood on the porch of a little house, smoking cigarettes and watching the crowd go by. The stupid disguises had worked. The bells kept jangling like it was Christmas.

Michel's eyes crinkled up. He must've been grinning at me.

"'I have had infinite trouble both by land and sea already,'" he whispered. "'So let this go with the rest.'"

"What's that?"

"Odysseus."

"Listen," I whispered, "'They have proud red mouths and firm, tawny breasts.'"

"What does it mean?"

"It's *Cannibal Quest* by Gordon Sinclair."

We passed a beat-up looking building made of red corrugated tin with a dome shaped like an onion on top. A lot of native guys wearing lunchpail hats like Kasa's stood in front in groups of three and four, chatting, using their hands a lot. They might have been playing *Bowral*-style cricket but they didn't have any tied-up rags or planks of wood.

"The *mesjid*," said Michel. "The mosque."

"What's that, the movie house?"

"The church. They will have a bigger one in town. Yes, you see it? The tower."

I peered over my shoulder and there one switchback below us was the town. The streets looked wide and the buildings were only a storey or two high, made out of more corrugated tin, it looked like, except for some wooden ones painted yellow or white with balconies up on the second floor and some Italian-looking places with red tile roofs. Any places with shutters had them clamped down tight, and I didn't blame them because if that wasn't the hottest time of day I was dying of fever. In the middle of everything stood a skinny white tower five storeys tall, with filigree around its windows and an onion on the top. A silver onion.

I peered through my eyelashes as we rolled into Pelayaran. There were people hustling everywhere: women wrapped up like Michel and me, little kids holding hands, men wearing white shirts that hung down to their knees or short-sleeved shirts like a banker might wear in July, or bare-chested but wearing a lunchpail hat or a headcloth like Muzakkar's. I was happy to see them all. I figured that the thicker the crowd, the less likely we'd be caught, because there'd be that many more people to pick us out of, though of course if the crowd got so thick that we couldn't budge then we'd be hard up too. Michel leaned against me.

"It was a *pregnant* woman," he said, "who helped him to enter Mannheim."

Clop, clop, clop went The World's Smallest Horse. I tucked one foot behind the other and dozed. I heard people laughing and blowing whistles, a few guys in the middle of arguments, a bicycle that clattered past us, a truck or something that must've had a V-8 at least. Then I heard singing above our heads — that humming sort of singing, like Jack Teagarden. From up in the mosque tower? From a PA? I couldn't tell.

Allahuuuuuu Ak-bar

Each time it sounded less like Jack Teagarden and more like Pee Wee Russell on the clarinet, though it was still a guy singing.

Ash-hadu Aaaallah

It started to fade after a while — maybe we'd moved too far away.

I heard seagulls instead. I opened my eyes. We were out in the sun, rolling along a cobble-stoned promenade with the blue sky stretching over hundreds of masts — a dozen jetties lay below us with a blue-and-green sailboat in every slip. The sunlight reflected off the water just as bright as that light on the *kebetai*. The *kebetai*. I didn't see a single freighter, only sailboats. There were men at the other end of the promenade: guys with nets, one on a bicycle.

We came up to an old man spreading a net over a drying rack. The pony slowed down then stopped altogether, and the cart lurched as Muzakkar jumped down. I craned my neck to see him shake hands with the old man, each with a hearty grip on the other's elbows. The pony shook his red plume. A fly knocked right into my forehead, then droned off over the water.

Muzakkar gestured to us; Michel slid down from the cart. I pried myself off the bench and as soon as my feet hit the cobblestones my dress split right up the back so that it hung from either shoulder. Like shelling a peanut! The air felt cool up my back.

Muzakkar's mouth fell open, showing off his broken tooth. The old man watched us through his net; he wore what looked like a diaper. Muzakkar pushed us between the drying rack and a circle of barrels piled with rope.

"Why did you do that?" Michel whispered. "We are not on the boat yet!"

"Did it look like I did it on purpose?"

"But *why* did you do it?"

Obviously they hadn't given me their newest dress.

It was like a bunker behind those barrels; we could see out but a guy would have to be right on top of us before he could see in. Jesus, did that fishing net stink! Muzakkar stretched until his back cracked then said something to the old man, who smiled down at us. He flashed us a paper showing the hammer and sickle. I twisted around to dig mine out of my pocket — the poor thing was crumpled into a ball but by then the old man wasn't even paying attention. Muzakkar went to the edge of the retaining wall. A guy in a blue headcloth stood up in the bow of a sailboat and waved. The boat was shaped like the kind of cradle you always see the Baby Moses in: half a barrel on its side with a little roof for his head. Was that our boat to Java? More likely it would take us to a bigger one offshore.

The pony knocked a hoof against the pavement, *clop*, *clop*, until Muzakkar hopped back into the cart and started it rolling.

"He will not come back," Michel said. "He says he will stock the boat with supplies."

"What kind of supplies?"

"He did not say."

"They'll be a surprise."

Michel wiped sweat off his forehead. I thought it was funny, anyhow; he was just mad that I'd ripped my dress. He pulled down a length of rope and sniffed it.

"Why'd you leave Java in the first place?" I asked.

"What do you ask?"

"Did you leave Java because there were Japs there already?"

"There may have been some. I do not know."

"What's that mean? Should we go or not?"

"Oh, yes!"

"Well, did you *see* any Japs?"

"Not on Java."

"You promise me?"

He sat up straight.

"I promise."

"Then what'd you come here for?"

He picked a splinter off the side of the barrel.

"I had a bad fright."

"A bad *fright*?"

The guy in the blue headcloth was Loé's brother; he came and sat behind the barrels with us and brought along a gallon bottle of water that we passed back and forth.

"So," I asked, "that's Loé's boat?"

"No, no. This is Loé's brother. The boat is his wife's brother's."

Loé's brother had the same holes through his earlobes as the old guy from the hut, except that his were smaller and he had a cigarette stuck through one of them.

"Loé's brother's brother-in-law."

"Yes."

Was the brother-in-law who owned the boat a Communist?

Loé's brother didn't think so. He must've been asthmatic — every time he said two words he had to suck his breath back in through his teeth, but we didn't mind because that gave Michel time to translate what they were talking about. Michel kept asking him if any Japs were coming up the jetty and every time he would jump up to look. There never were any Japs on the jetty, apparently, but a big grey boat did steam into the mouth of the bay. Did he think it was a *japanner* boat? Yes, he did think so. The poor guy was just about having kittens, so Michel started telling him how the Japs had already had us and lost us, he kept pointing his thumb at me and talking about someone called *Harold*, and about five minutes into the story he demonstrated how *Harold* could handle a steering wheel like a demon.

"Oh ho!" said Loé's brother.

After an hour a lot of shirtless guys in headcloths went bounding down to their boats, pulled up their sails and put out to sea. The sun was going down and that must've been when Pelayaran went fishing. Hundreds of sailboats steered straight for that grey ship as the sun dropped into the sea behind it.

I was still wearing my blue headcloth and Michel was still draped in roosters, so after half the town had run down to the docks we stood up

in plain sight and lifted the net off its rack with Loé's brother. The sun
had sizzled behind the horizon by then and they didn't seem to have
any street lights in that town — maybe they had the blackout too — so
we tiptoed down the steps to the jetty in the dark. The net was heavier
than it looked. I glimpsed the silhouette of somebody crouched by our
boat and imagined him blowing a whistle and spotlights pinning us to
the dock, but when I made out the shape of his diaper I knew it was
our old man. He folded the net over his shoulders and slouched back in
towards shore. He never said a word. My hands smelled like cod-liver
oil after that.

Loé's brother made Michel and me lie shoulder-to-shoulder in the
bow, and a lot of things shaped like softballs rolled under our legs as we
squeezed ourselves in.

"Coconuts," Michel whispered.

Loé's brother untied the painter and we sailed out in the midst of
the last boats, all with lanterns in their bows. I'd never been aboard anything as quiet as that before — no engine, no coal, no screws, no petty
officer. Just water rippling under our heads. Somewhere in the dark we
must've passed the big grey ship but Loé's brother wouldn't even let
me sit up to see if it was Japanese.

"Eat this please," said Michel. "It is in my way."

He dropped a banana into my hand. Jesus, that tasted all right!
The banana really is a marvel.

Loé's brother finally brought the sail down and called us to sit under
the mast with him. The stars came out one by one, sparkling on the
water so that it looked as bright as Granville Street. We rocked back and
forth on our little piece of ocean.

"What now?"

"He says that we must be patient."

Five minutes later I saw a light coming closer. It was a boat flashing its
lantern. Loé's brother put a foot up on the rail.

"*Goed geluk*," he said.

Then he jumped overboard. We scrambled to our feet. Every now and then we saw his arm come up out of the dark water, farther and farther away, then we heard the water pour off him as they hauled him into the other boat. The lantern flickered out.

"Where's the other ship?" I asked.

"What ship is this?"

"The big one! To take us the rest of the way!"

"There is no other ship." The boat lurched as Michel sat down again. "Make sure we are pointed toward Java."

"You *show* me how," I said, "and I'll do it."

"I do not want to fight," he said.

I crawled back into the bow. It was already cold and I was only wearing my undershirt and Robinson's tuxedo pants.

It was bright and hot when I woke up. Michel lay under the little roof, surrounded by coconuts and bananas and a big purple fish that looked like Mackenzie King, it had the same lower lip — if you'd ever seen Mackenzie King you would've thought the same thing. Coconuts rolled fore and aft with the waves. I scratched myself using the sharp part of the inseam of my pants. I must've been raw halfway down my leg.

"Put up the sail," Michel said from the stern.

The roof was barely big enough to cover him. The carved tiller beside his head looked like a cross-breed between a crocodile and a chicken.

The mast stood in the middle of the boat, just off the end of my feet. I tugged the rope that hung from the bottom spar and the sail slid up like a venetian blind. It was a mat woven out of bamboo like we'd sat on back at Bucktooth's house, with knotted ropes across the top and bottom to keep it taut. I tied down the free end and the sail filled with wind.

More coconuts rolled off Michel as he went up on one knee and looked ahead. Loé's brother's brother-in-law's boat had to have the worst set-up that I'd ever seen — the guy who was steering couldn't see where he was going. Michel could only keep a fingertip on the tiller. Or maybe we were just doing it wrong.

"Now," he said. "Where do you wish that we were going?"

"Java!"

"No. If you could go to *any* place, where would it be? Home to Canada?"

"Singapore. Java. Either one is good."

"You should say why. It gives me something to think about."

"All right, where do *you* wish we were going?"

"Soerabaja. That is on Java. I will tell you why." He pulled the rooster cloth out of the back of his pants — that was one hell of an ensemble he had on. "The first reason is to listen to a record that I have heard only once before."

Jesus, that was better than Napoleon! I could sink my teeth into that!

"Which record?"

"It was by Django Reinhardt. Do you know him? He plays the hot jazz. And the song was called 'Naguiné.' It is a very simple song, very beautiful."

"What's he play, piano?"

"No, no, no. Guitar. He has only two fingers!"

He pretended to strum a guitar, and it looked like the hand making the chords might be the one with the two fingers. The bow rose and fell behind him, *slush, slush.*

"He lost the other fingers in a fire. Imagine it. I can think of nothing worse."

"Losing your teeth would be worse."

"You cannot lose your teeth in a fire. I know this. My cousin, Camille Girand, once his house burnt down, the walls, the roof, everything was ashes. We had to ride in a cart from the village and we arrived too late. All we found were some bones near the chimney, and no skull but an *entire* set of teeth. We laid them out on the ground, thirty-two teeth, and I said wait a moment, gentlemen, Camille Girand had only eleven teeth. And he came back the next day. He had been hunting pigs."

"So who was in the house?" I asked.

"In which house?"

"Whose teeth were they?"

"Oh, we never knew. It was too bad. It would have made a better story."

The wind picked up and the mast started to squeak like a set of rusty brakes. The bow rode up so I could look back over the roof and see the waves all riding up and down, regular as clockwork, with nothing on the horizon. We dropped into the next trough and all I could see above the roof was blue sky and a couple of seagulls. The plank over the bow would only have covered Baby Moses' toes; it kept my head and chest in the shade.

"Which way you steering?" I asked.

"Java lies in the southwest."

"How did you figure which way that was?"

"By the sun."

The sun was straight over us.

"When the sun begins to set we will know where to go."

So he knew as much about navigation as I did. He smacked a coconut against the side until the shell broke open and the juice splashed onto his arm. He held it out to me so it wouldn't spill, and I drank the juice with a hunk of shell poking me in the nose. Jesus, it was even better than the banana the night before.

"Eat the fish." He pulled a hunk of cream-coloured meat off the ribs and threw it to me. "They told me it was smoked, but I do not think it will keep."

It tasted like smoked trout, which right then I realized had to be the most delicious food in the world. I'd fantasized about ham sandwiches and hot dogs and apple pie with ice cream but never smoked trout, which was an insult to smoked trout.

A seagull settled on top of the mast, eight feet above our deck. The feathers in his chest looked as white as sugar. Boy, he was a clean bird.

"If this seagull up here was your pet seagull," I said, "what would you call him?"

Michel dragged himself out for a look. The whole boat seemed to tip forward.

"Garuda," he said, and lay back again. "In Hindu stories, Garuda is a magic bird who devours snakes and carries —"

"We don't have any snakes."

"But Vishnu — the king — Vishnu rides on him. He is Vishnu's companion. And look at you and I." He balanced a bunch of bananas on his shoulder. "We are kings."

"I'd call him Connie," I said, "and he would be our houseboy. He'd wash our undershorts and bring us gin fizzes. Oh — and answer the door when we had visitors."

"I do not have undershorts."

"I know it."

After a while I needed a stretch, my back could only thump against the ocean for so long. I slid out from under the bow and got to my feet, and the seagull stretched out his wings and floated away. I didn't like to see him go. And I didn't like that it was so easy for him *to* go.

"Pass me some fish," I said.

I held a hunk up in the air. Connie floated down again, beat his wings two times and grabbed the fish. His beak brushed my thumb and it felt as smooth as a teacup. He landed on the spar again and swallowed his mouthful.

"That a boy, Connie," I said. "Now go steam my ascot."

He spread his wings — maybe he was drying them. The sky behind him was bright grey. He tilted his wings up and down.

"It looks like he's carrying us."

Michel lay back in the gloom.

"In that case he is the Roc. There is a story where Sinbad is trapped on an island. Do you know Sinbad?"

"Sure."

"Then you know it. He has nothing to eat, and the Roc lands near him. It is an enormous bird, so Sinbad ties himself to its leg and they fly away to an island of plenty."

"I saw that. Douglas Fairbanks."

"Do you still have your paper?"

It was wet, but I could still make out the hammer and sickle. The sun was going down ahead of us. I stretched my hands out so the wind poured through my fingers. I liked the ocean right then. We weren't hiding from anyone. We just happened to be out where nobody else was. It was a very little boat for a trip to Java, sure, but after what had happened to a boat the size of *Asia* I could only think that that was in our favour.

"Come and see this," he said.

I crawled under the sail. He was leaning on the roof, looking astern with the rooster cloth over his shoulders. I followed his finger and there was one long wave sliding diagonally across the others, going from eleven o'clock behind us to three o'clock beside us. Where did it think it was going? I held onto the mast with one hand and scratched myself with the other.

"A submarine," he said. "It was the same when they captured me."

"What, they caught you with a submarine?"

"Yes."

The wave rolled under us and went off to starboard. We watched it go. Then it was gone and the regular waves kept up what they'd been doing.

"Okay." He turned around, scratching his jaw. "I suppose it was nothing."

I cracked open another coconut and climbed back under the bow. Connie made a noise like a needle scratching a record — maybe that was what his burps sounded like. Michel lifted his behind and slid out of his pants. We were just a happy family, and there was no time like the present to set my mind at ease.

"Do you think the guys took any knocks because we left Pelayaran?"

"Yes," he said. "Of course."

I got a hollow feeling under my ribs.

"How do you mean?"

"You know."

"I promise you," I said, "that I don't know."

"Do you wish me to tell you?"

I didn't.

"Yeah," I said.

"We were told that six men would be killed for every one that escaped. I heard him tell you. I did not trick you. I was also on *tenko* when he told you."

"So you think they did it?"

"We saw men killed for much less."

"But that was because of stuff they did themselves!"

"They do not mind. These Japanese." His face had disappeared in the gloom. "I did not make the decision lightly. You saw the place they called the hospital?"

"Yeah."

"You saw that all of them were dying?"

"Yeah."

"Every man in the camp was walking toward that place."

Connie brought one wing in and left the other stretched out. There I was, watching a seagull, and most likely there were six guys up-island who weren't watching anything. I wondered who they'd picked. Ect and Falkiner and — or maybe guys I didn't know! Goddamn it, if I didn't know them then all was well. Guys I didn't know were so much easier.

"Months from now," said Michel, "when they are starving to death, their bellies swollen, they will look back on those killed as being the fortunate."

"I want you to stop talking," I said.

"I believed that you knew about this."

"Please shut up for a minute."

"We have spirit," he said. "And that is always rewarded."

"Okay."

And I decided right then that we didn't know if anybody had been punished. Maybe the Japs had only cut back their tea ration, but we didn't know, so what was the point in getting tied in knots over it?

Michel gave a big sigh. Even over the wind I could hear it. Connie tilted his head.

In the morning the water rolled along like an empty field moving under us. The sun rose over the stern, so we were going west, though for all I knew we'd been going east all night. Connie still sat up on the mast. Michel was asleep.

I whacked a coconut open against the side and that didn't bother either one of them. A guy could bash coconuts in that neighbourhood morning and night and none of the neighbours would ever say boo about it. I settled down in the bow, sucked the blood from where I'd bashed my knuckle, then took a long drink of juice. Connie lifted one leg and balanced there on the other. Jesus, we had a lot going on that morning. The sky was a shade of purple like a lady's hat.

I crawled aft and tore off a sliver of Mackenzie King, then lay back in the bow holding it in the air, and I only had to wait ten seconds before Connie flapped down and took it. He gave my thumb a peck in the process. I thought about docking his wages.

I was about to throw some squished bananas overboard until I realized that Connie might want those too, so I reached up and put one on that plank above my head. He waited four seconds, then glided down and stood there eating, taking his time, his tail feathers twitching right above me. That was all I could see of him. Then as he flapped back up to the mast he took a dump that hit the rail and splashed across my pant leg. Boy oh boy, we were having a riot on that boat of ours. I could've sold tickets.

"I saw you scratch yourself," said Michel.

"I don't have the foggiest what you're talking about."

"You must have the Java Balls. That was what Mills called it. You get it when you are new to the tropics. I had it at first. Has the skin peeled away?"

"It's not worms, is it?"

"Oh no. A fungus."

He was peeling a banana. I lay there all bowlegged, trying not to scratch. I'm not sure how a fungus is preferable to worms, but it was.

"Give it air," said Michel. "The sun will heal it. Lower your trousers."

I wasn't sure if there was any logic in that but it made more sense than lying there being miserable, so I got to my feet and turned back to the bow and dropped my pants. Of course sailors are not notoriously shy about their private parts — if we were in the middle of nowhere on the *Skidegate* we used to swab starkers — but with just the two of us I felt like that might've been strange. I sat down with my pants around my ankles, my feet in the bow and my back against the mast.

From my crotch to halfway down my thigh looked just like a steam burn. The sun wasn't high enough yet to fall right on it but I could already feel the breeze drying it out. Every time a wave picked us up I looked off at the horizon, but there was no land in sight. No boats.

"Do we have any shot at finding Java?"

"Java? Oh, yes. There is nowhere else that we could go."

"Today, you mean? Tomorrow?"

"Time will tell."

So I figured that meant it would be one or the other.

"Do not give any more food to that bird," he said.

It wasn't until then that I realized that there wasn't a nail in that whole boat — little pegs held it together. I reached for my coconut shell and scraped some meat off with my bottom teeth.

"You will enjoy Java."

"Yeah?"

"What have you heard about the place?"

"Not too much."

"My friend Mills, he would often tell stories to pass the time. Most of the men would not talk, you know, they would lie on their mats and say nothing, but I understand English thanks to Mills because he was always talking."

"Where was all this?"

"Oh, at Eu Chin's house, in Batavia. I learned Chinese when I worked on the ships, I told you this, a cook, and of course I spoke French, and Eu Chin believed that white men spoke only one language so that whether his customers came from China or America or any country in Europe I would be able to look after them with only Chinese and French. He had never run a smoking house before, his business was in sugar. He did not know that to look after someone in a smoking house you only tell them '*tiga rupee*' or '*sepulu rupee*' and nothing else. You take the money, you show them their mat and put the pellet in the pipe. And Mills always told me that a Frenchman could not say 'H' properly, so he had me practice by saying, 'One shouldn't talk of halters in the hanged man's house.'"

Was he talking about an opium den? I'd always pictured guys who looked like Ming the Merciless working in places like that. Obviously I didn't know the first thing about it so I tried to think of something to say that would make it sound like I did.

"And one day Eu Chin told me that the other customers wished Mills would stop talking, it disturbed them, but we could not ask him to leave because he paid for each week in advance. He brought his friends to talk to me as well, English friends who did not believe that there was such a thing as a white man who worked in an opium house and could speak English. Never before in all of the Orient, they said. I would tell them about Ney and they would ask to hear it again and again, the story of when Bonaparte said to him, 'Ney, you are covered in blood,' and Ney said, 'It is not mine, sire, except for where the bullet passed through my leg.'"

"And you smoked the stuff too," I said — this was the best I could come up with. "So you figured it was the job for you."

"Yes. At first every day. But the men look like skeletons, you know. I said to myself, 'What if one day I am asked to introduce myself to an educated person and I am lying on the ground like that, and I must look up and tell them that my name is Michel Ney, yes, the same as the Prince of Moscow.' So I stopped. And whenever I was paid I would take the money to the Sailors' Rest Home and write *Michel Ney* on the envelope."

"Why didn't you send it home?"

"In France it would have been worth nothing. Centimes."

For years the CPR had sent half of my packet to Ma, so I figured that I could tell Michel about that later if we got hung up for conversation — but that reminded me of my articles smouldering away at the bottom of the *Empress*, and whenever I remembered that it was like somebody had kicked me.

"A funny thing about my friend Mills, he only wanted to talk about grandfathers. If you could not talk about grandfathers he was not interested. But I saw him outside the house once and then he would only talk about export duties. His own grandfather was shot in the Boer War."

"In the where?"

"But this grandfather had always wanted to go to Java because *his* grandfather had been to Java, so to some degree my friend Mills came to Java to please *his* grandfather. He said religion is false, it is your grandfather's life that decides your fate."

"But everybody has two grandpas."

"My own grandfather Mallet, he joined the navy and sailed all the way to Shanghai. In Cotignac, everyone said that he was crazy, because people from there do not go away to sea, and they were right to think him crazy because he caught malaria in Shanghai and came home to die. His gravestone says so, it says, '*Décédé des suites des maladies contractées en Chine.*' I dreamt of going east after that because I knew it was the last place any of them would go."

He threw his banana peel over the side. Connie dove after it and brought it back up to the top of the mast so that seawater ran onto my head. Christ! But it was getting hot out there anyway. The sun was on my bare knees but not on my crotch yet. We rolled up a wave and I saw something on the horizon that looked like a cigar. Then the bow went up and I lost sight of it.

"This Grandfather Mills came to Java with Mr. Raffles in 1811 — did you know the English were in Java for five years? During Ney's time. Old Mills made many drawings and paintings and took them back to England but they were burnt in a fire before my friend Mills was born, and when he was a boy that was all anyone would talk about, what a great loss it was, so that when he was a man he came out to Java to make new ones. But he never left Batavia. He would lay on his mat and say that he could not paint his way out of a parasol, that was what he said. You should have met Mills."

"Where is he now?"

Connie sat up there with one wing stuck out again.

"He heard that the Japanese were coming, so he drowned himself in the canal outside our house. The canals smell horrible. I would never have done that."

"But did you see the Japanese?"

"Did I? No. They told us on the radio that the Japanese had bombed Soerabaja, away in the east, but Eu Chin told us to calm down, the government was dropping bombs as a test. But our customers went back to their ships, and business became bad. Mills still came to the house, he was the only one. Then they did bomb Batavia, but only the warehouses. They were not far away. We heard it — boom! boom!"

"That's the same as Singapore. But why are we —"

"I went out with Eu Chin the next morning and the first thing we saw was Mills in the canal. A seagull stood on his face, pulling things out. Eu Chin knocked the bird into the water with a brick. He told me to get my things, and then he put a padlock on the house because he was going to look at his sugar and then leave Java, he had an airplane, and I went to hide in the village where Eu Chin and I had gone fishing on Christmas Day. That was on the coast. The men there said that I could take a boat if I wanted to run away, that seemed a good idea, but instead I only looked at the sea for a long time. It was very peaceful. The water did not care if the Japanese were coming, and I did not like to run away, of course, but if they were burning up our means of survival what reason was there for me to stay? It was the same as 1812 when Ney and Bonaparte came into Moscow but the Russians set fire to it. What reason did Ney have to stay?"

There was the cigar on the horizon again — long and black. That was all I could say about it. No funnels or sails. No smoke up above it. Ray had told me once that if it wasn't spouting then it wasn't a whale, and it wasn't spouting so it couldn't have been a whale. Then our bow came up and I lost sight of it.

"But for all that I decided that I would stay on Java. Those waves, you know, they were very peaceful. They had bombed some of our warehouses and perhaps that was all they were going to do, so I turned back to the village, to ask the men for a place to sleep, and all of the huts were on fire like a lot of haystacks. The people had gone. I saw no one. Even today I cannot guess what happened. So I pushed my canoe into the water."

"And that was your bad fright?"

"No. The fright was seeing Mills in the canal."

"You promise me you never saw a Jap?"

"I have promised you already."

He put his feet out beside me, in the sun.

"That boat needed to be paddled, it was not like this one, and I see now that I should have left from the south coast of Java rather than the north, because if the Japanese had come it would have been from the north. I should have tried for Australia. Perhaps if we find that Java is not good we will continue there."

My crotch already felt better, drying out like that. I looked up to watch Connie spread his wings and float away. I was going to have to use the *benjo* before long.

"Maybe Mills was the same. He thought the Japanese would lock him up by himself, so in the end Eu Chin and I found him with that bird eating him."

"You'd never do that to us, would you, Connie?"

I looked up at him but he was gone. My back was sore anyway, so I got up and stepped out of my pants. He was flying right beside us, a couple of feet above the water, studying those waves like anything. What was he looking at — a school of fish? I clambered onto the plank above the bow and peered down into the water too. Something black went under us, the size of a boxcar. I jumped back down to the deck where I tripped over a lot of coconuts. My neck was tight as a fishing line.

Michel stood on the roof and threw the last coconut shell into the sea and that meant we couldn't even pee in the shell to have a drink any more, though I couldn't remember how long it had been since we'd had anything to pee. We'd been in the boat two or three weeks by then. And with no shells we'd have no way to bail out the brine if we got another storm.

We'd tried to eat the husk itself at one point, and Michel had got the runs worse than ever and a hunk had got caught on its way out, so that he'd had to pull it out with his fingers — you get the idea. Like something out of Edgar Allan Poe.

The shell didn't sink right away. It turned bottom up so it looked like the top of some guy's head as he floated away.

"Now we have nothing," Michel said. He lowered himself down carefully. "Now God will send us something."

Even Connie hadn't hung around after we'd finished Mackenzie King fifteen or twenty days before. I lay in the bow and tried to keep the little ring I'd been working on from falling apart. It just needed another thread of wood woven in. I'd been using my thumbnail to peel the strips off the edge of the rail because I wanted to have a ring on every finger, so that when I finally saw you I could wave both hands at you and say *hello* and it would be a very big deal. After two or three weeks in that boat, that seemed important. But I needed to sleep before I'd be able to peel another strip.

"We never stop moving forward," he said. "We must run into land. Today or tomorrow."

"Some currents go in circles."

We said the same thing every day. The glare off the water gave me a headache from dawn until dusk, even lying under the roof with my face pressed against the tiller, and in the morning when I woke up my only chore was to decide whether the pain was going to be in the front of my head or the back or one side or the other. Some days it sat around my eyes like a pair of glasses. I knew that one drink of water was not going to take the glare away but at the same time I was convinced it would.

"Look," said Michel. "Here he comes."

A couple of times a day he would tell me that he saw Connie. I figured that if it really was Connie he was only coming to see if we'd starved to death so he could peck away at us.

I'd realized that we might never get off the boat, that the last person I would ever see or talk to might be Michel, and that once we both had passed away there would be no record, no memory, of any of the things we'd seen or done. I found that very depressing, because even in the most dire straits a guy can say to himself, 'Hell, this will make a great story.' I'd said that a dozen times already. But what was the point of living through a great story if a guy never got to tell it? I wished that I could leave something permanent behind me, but is anything more temporary than a boat on water? I wanted you to know that I'd never stopped thinking about goddamn Clifford Pier and that your mother had had the keenest sense of survival of all of us for shying away from open water.

I decided that using my fingernail to carve my name in the wood would be too final, too grim. I'd wait a few more days. And I was too tired just then anyway.

"I think it *is* him. Look."

At first he looked like an eyelash, away up in the sky, but it sure seemed to be Connie as he got lower. He looked as white as he ever had. He was the first bird that we'd seen in a while. We had seen flying fish a hundred feet off the side, and I'd talked about swimming out to grab one but then Michel had seen the shark and I sure as hell wasn't going then. Then he had said that maybe it was a porpoise, and that porpoise steaks are truly delicious. Even if it had been a porpoise, I couldn't have killed it with my bare hands.

Connie landed on top of the mast and stuck his beak into his chest just as he'd done so many times before. He shuffled his yellow feet a couple of times, then he took a dump that poured straight onto Michel's shoulder, but Michel just rubbed it into his arm and kept watching Connie.

"How will we get him?"

"I fed him one time," I said, "and he came down."

Connie took his beak out of his chest and looked at the water.

"Perhaps you have an idea of what to feed him," said Michel.

"Magpies like things that are shiny."

"We have nothing shiny."

"Don't we?"

"No."

Then he jumped straight in the air, flinging his arms at Connie, but by the time his feet had left the deck Connie was already thirty feet in the air. He looked like an eyelash again. Michel ducked under the sail and lay down under the roof.

But after a while I looked up and Connie was on the mast with a fish sticking out of his mouth.

"Lulu's back in town," I said.

Connie tilted his head back and swallowed the fish. He sat there staring at the water. I slid my ring off and held it up, I swayed it back and forth, and his head followed the motion of that. Jesus, he was dumb. I hadn't realized.

I felt around on the plank over my head for the peg that the bowline had been tied to. I slid the ring over that.

Connie spread his wings and lifted up from the mast. I kept my head under the plank so that I wouldn't spook him. I'd have to be patient. I watched the sail gust in and out. His tail feathers stuck out just above me, and something went *tock tock* on the plank — pecking at the ring. I saw the corner of a yellow foot.

I reached my hands up and found his two legs. They felt like a couple of clothespins. He didn't like that, of course, he gnawed at the web of skin between my fingers and thumb and beat his wings like crazy, but even so I didn't let go of those legs. I pulled him into my lap. His wings beat against my arms and face but I sat up and held him down on the boards. I managed to get one hand over his chest and he slashed the back of it with his beak. I let go of the other leg, and I took hold of the back of his head and gave it a good twist, just like turning a doorknob. And that was it. I wiped my bloody hand off on his wing.

"*Dieu merci*," Michel said. It was one of the only times that I heard him speak French. He had the shape of the tiller pressed into the side of his face.

I popped my thumbnail under Connie's ribcage. His blood shot up my wrist and his guts fell right out, but of course there were feathers stuck to everything. His heart looked like a walnut. I pulled the stomach apart and that fish he'd eaten was gummy but still in one piece. I swallowed that and gave Michel what was left of the stomach. It was like a wet rag. He popped it in his mouth.

I put Connie under my foot and tugged on his leg with both hands. I wanted it to break off. But that was work — I got dizzy as hell. After a minute the foot came away with a few threads of meat hanging off of the bone. I sucked on those. Michel was eating the heart. I pulled at the skin where the foot had come away but he'd shit on himself so everything was slippery as hell. I scraped some meat away with my fingernails and started to chew on it but then I had to cough up all the feathers.

I leaned over the rail and watched them come out of my mouth.

There wasn't a lot of meat, even after all that.

"There'll be meat inside the bones," I said.

"The bones are hollow."

Which was right, of course. We piled the wings and the bones up on the plank and Michel climbed onto the roof to watch for more. I curled up beside the tiller and fell asleep instantly. But I was awake again after a minute. I almost didn't get my behind over the rail in time.

"I think we will do okay," said Michel.

"How's that?"

Four seagulls flew above us in a circle. I admit that it was tough to get excited about them in the position that I was in.

Michel went back by the tiller. I waited a minute to make sure that I was finished, then I spread Connie out on the bow so he'd look as appetizing as possible and hid myself under the plank, my legs pulled in and everything. But then I couldn't see the seagulls.

"Perhaps this one."

Michel was sitting cross-legged just behind the sail. He kept looking somewhere over the bow, flicking one finger back and forth.

"What's that?" I said. "Is that one of them?"

He nodded, kept moving his finger back and forth. And then down — he was pointing right at me. I looked up at the bottom of the plank and there was a little *thunk* and that *eck eck* they make in their beaks. It had taken the bait of Connie.

I started to bring my hands up but Michel waved his finger like I had to move them to my left. Then I must have moved them too far because he waved them back. Then he nodded. I threw my hands up and grabbed the legs and hauled him down, Connie Jr. or whoever he was, but some of Connie was in his mouth and the whole mess came down on top of me. I rolled him onto his back and tried to put my knee down on his head, but the end of his wing came up and got me in the eye and that stung like hell.

"Here," said Michel. "Look here."

The seagull looked too. Michel brought our whole tiller down and crushed Connie Jr.'s head like a plum. But his wings kept on beating so

Michel kept on thumping him until Connie and Connie Jr. lay there all tangled up together.

With Connie Jr. we took our time. It got dark but there were all kinds of stars, and we sat there pulling pieces off of him and thumping them with the tiller just for hell. Of course there wasn't much meat on him either, but Jesus, it *was* meat. I was so tired that I kept getting the shakes. All of those bones looked yellow.

"Connie is the prettier one," I said. "At least he had a head."

Michel had a good long burp.

"They have sacrificed everything for us."

"Like when the marshal fed his arms and legs to the troops."

"Yes," he agreed. "Yes."

My feet had tanned so dark that I couldn't even see them at the ends of my legs.

I opened my eyes when I smelled a cigarette. The light was grey and I was looking at Michel's arms. There was blood dried all over them. Was it really a cigarette? It smelled as acrid as burning tires. Something bumped against our side.

I rolled over. Somebody wearing a plaid sarong was hanging his brown legs over our rail, and on one knee there was a brown hand with a cigarette between its fingers. I knew from the bumping that there had to be another boat somewhere.

I sat up and saw him trying to lean below the roof to get a peek at me. He had a neat little movie-star moustache and hair falling in his eyes. He wore a white shirt with a starched collar. He said something. Half of his teeth were black.

Michel sat bolt upright beside me.

"*Pagi!*" he said.

I started to crawl out, but Michel was ahead of me. I didn't know who Smoker was but he hadn't killed us yet — that was the only thing going through my mind. I pulled myself up by the mast.

There wasn't any land in sight. The other boat was ten times the size of ours and had two big brown sails. Nets hung in the stern, and I could smell fish that had gone bad and cooked rice and cigarettes. I couldn't see a rope tying us to them, but Smoker seemed to be able to sit on their rail with his legs in our boat without crushing his balls between them. It was a lot for my brain to digest. Another guy stood behind him, eating out of a pot of rice with his fingers. He wore an old white undershirt just like Jimmy used to wear. An eleven- or twelve-year-old kid in blue short pants sat on top of their aft cabin, pushing the boom back and forth. The sky was grey, like I said, and there was hardly any swell. I watched that guy eat rice. Michel kept saying the word *kami*, and I figured that that meant "food," or "please," or "water."

The guy put rice in his mouth.

Smoker stretched out his leg and touched Connie's beak with his toe. He said something about *chamar*.

"*Chamar!*" Rice had a big smile.

Smoker was smiling too, but the kid in the short pants didn't seem to think much of anything was funny. He ducked his head behind the boom.

"*Kami*," Michel said again, then some other things, and Smoker turned around and took the pot of rice from the other guy and handed it across to us.

My arms felt like they were going to come out of their sockets, so it was just as well that Michel held the pot. I took a handful of rice but my mouth was so dry that at first all I could do was toss it around on my tongue, then when I wanted to swallow I had to coax my throat to open, like it was a rusty hinge.

Smoker flicked ash onto my foot as he said something to Rice, who got up and ducked into one of the cabins, then came out with a tin jug and handed that across to Michel too. Clear water sloshed out of the spout, and he probably only drank for ten seconds but it seemed like an hour. Then I got my hands around it in a hurry, and a lot of it went down the front of me but I didn't care, even after all those days of going without.

Do you remember when you and I used to wake up late on a Saturday or Sunday morning feeling dry-mouthed and awful, and how the first glass of orange juice used to feel as it poured down between your ribs? Well, I could feel that water trickle all the way down to my heels. I finally had to take a breath in.

"Jesus," I said.

Then I had to concentrate like hell to not be sick.

"You speak English?" asked Smoker.

Rice was holding his hand out — he wanted the pot back. Michel still had rice in his hand. He told Smoker something.

"France!" He crushed his cigarette on our rail. "So, actually, neither one is *Belanda*?"

"*Tidak*," said Michel.

"You speak English?" I asked.

Smoker looked at me.

"I have been to school in Holland. I told your friend," he said, "we look for our fish traps. Have you seen them?"

"I don't —"

Rice said something. He sat down and folded his arms.

"My friend wants to know," Smoker said, "where are your clothes?"

Michel set the pot down.

"Put on your trousers!" he said.

I crawled back to the tiller and untied them from the post. That had been my medical miracle, keeping them off — I hadn't had Java Balls in that whole time. I tugged Michel's houndstooth trousers out of the gap in the ceiling and crawled back out, but as we pulled our clothes on Short Pants was already tugging on all kinds of ropes, putting the boom into the wind. Rice had gone into one of the cabins, and Smoker lifted his feet and hopped back down into their boat. He and Michel had quit chatting.

"Farewell, then," said Smoker.

Michel just stood there fiddling with the fly of his trousers. Jesus, I felt dizzy — all that water in my gut!

"Hold on a minute," I said. "We want to get to Java."

"Oh," said Smoker. "We come from Java."

He had their jug in one hand and the other still on our rail. He looked down at Connie for a minute. Michel still wasn't saying anything.

Then Rice stuck his head out of the cabin and asked Smoker a question, and the two of them started to have some kind of argument, they kept saying *Ingriss* and *Belanda* back and forth. Michel leaned against our roof. I guess he was listening.

"I'm sorry, friends," said Smoker. "My friend says the English have an empire even larger than the Dutch."

"I'm not from England," I said. "I'm from Canada."

They looked at me like I'd said I was from Mars.

"*Pay-kah-ee*," said Michel.

Short Pants poked his head out from behind a sail.

Michel put his hands on his hips and said it again.

"Really?" said Smoker. "You are with PKI?"

"*Tidak.*" Rice was shaking his head. "*Tidak.*"

Michel held up one finger.

"Show them the paper," he said to me.

So that was it — he'd been trying to figure out whether or not to play our trump card. These fishermen didn't like white men but that didn't necessarily make them Communists. Was there ever a Communist fisherman with a starched collar like Smoker's? I felt in my pockets but found nothing in the first one.

Michel looked kind of sick.

Yes, there was a hunk of something down in the second one, I pulled up a little white lump and tried to unfold the thing without ripping it in half. Smoker was sitting back on our rail. I pulled back the edges and could see the hammer and sickle, blurry as mud. I held it out to him.

"Oh!" said Smoker. "Celebes!"

Rice gave a whoop and Short Pants spat in the water. Smoker and Rice kept smiling and chattering away, but they still hadn't invited us aboard. Had I got dressed up for nothing?

"We have brought information," said Michel.

Smoker swung his head around. He brushed his hair out of his eyes.

"The Japanese are in Celebes," said Michel.

"Oh, yes! This we know. They are in Java also," said Smoker. "Actually, we are in Soerabaja, and we are going to stop them."

Alip was Smoker's real name and Short Pants' was *Mohamad*, and Rice's was *Sudjangi* — old Alip even spelled them all out for me so that I'd remember. Sudjangi was their cook, it turned out, and he gave me a bunch of oranges that I peeled and ate one after another. Some had mould on them. It was funny to think that some people would be bothered by that. For a native guy he sure had broad shoulders — he could've played football. Or maybe I was just so scrawny that everyone else seemed bigger.

They claimed to not know anything about any English people taken as prisoners of war on Java. *Ingriss* people. There were Dutch soldiers, certainly, being held somewhere outside of Soerabaja, and they'd heard there might be civilians in a place called Tasikmalaja, but Alip wasn't sure where that was.

"Listen." I'd just spent five hours asleep under their galley table, so I was still pretty woozy. "I'd sure appreciate it if you could help me find her."

"I cannot say now. We must discuss it," said Alip. "Actually, Mohamad is the owner of this boat. It belonged to his father, but his father was killed because he was PKI. He was hanged."

"I've never heard of the Japs hanging anybody."

"Oh no, the Dutch. The hanging is by the Dutch. Mohamad, he does not like any Europeans. He wanted to kill you, actually, but we told him that you are PKI so he said okay."

"So you guys work for him or something?"

"That's what we say, yes. Actually, I came on this boat to get away from the Japanese. Even my parents, they don't understand why the PKI should be against the Japanese. They think that if we are against the Dutch that we are on the side of the Japanese, but both are Fascists, we have come to believe, because the Japanese do not consider the welfare of Indonesians. When they came we would do anything they said, to make a new country. But what do they tell us to do? Make warships for their emperor."

"*Kaum fasis*," said Sudjangi.

"I get it," I said.

Sudjangi put a plate of cold rice in front of me. Alip poured out the tea.

It was a floating cafeteria as far as I was concerned.

"Actually, Sudjangi is a PKI cell leader. Tomorrow we will meet at Ibu Pri's, then you can give your message to the cell."

My message? Michel must've spilled the beans about the paper Muzakkar had tucked into his pants.

"You know about PKI, right? We learned about it in our student society in Holland. We met some girls that way." Alip lit his cigarette with a piece of wood. "But I knew that I must study English so that I could get a good job, so I could not spend as much time with PKI as Sudjangi could. Now he is a cell leader for Soerabaja. I don't mind. *Baik baik*, right? But, oh, when the Japanese come to my house or to his house," he knocked on the floor — *tok, tok, tok.* "Then we must go out in the boat."

Sudjangi said something with *chamar chamar* at the end.

"That is right," smiled Alip. "We go to eat seagulls."

Sudjangi went out of the cabin and I watched him sit down under the sail. After a minute he started to sing.

Oh aku rinduuu

"What's he singing about?"

"Every song is the same," said Alip. "The boy misses his wife."

"Where is she?" I asked.

"His wife? We will see her at Ibu Pri's, she is there every time when we come back. She is always saying how she *misses* him. You know?"

He winked at me through the hair hanging in his face.

"*Misses* him, you know?"

I figured I understood pretty well.

Sudjangi was boiling coffee first thing in the morning, so I got that Ink Spots song in my head all over again.

I love Java, sweet and hot,

Whoops, Mister Moto, I'm a coffee pot

But I could smell something else too. I peered through the window and saw a line of palm trees off starboard. My heart beat like wild at the thought of dry land. Sudjangi made motions that we should stay put and went out on deck, and a minute later the boat bumped against something. I heard their feet thumping around, then that sound when a coil of rope hits a wharf. Then everything gave one good bounce — somebody had jumped off. But we didn't hear a splash, so it must've been onto a pier. I swirled the grounds around the bottom of my cup.

"Shush," said Michel.

I hadn't been saying anything.

Sudjangi stuck his head inside, laughing about something — of all of the Communists we knew he was having the best time. We followed him out on deck. I couldn't see a soul anywhere except for Mohamad and Alip walking away from us up the pier, and two goats lying in front of a white house on the shore. It had a pink roof and that onion-shaped dome.

"Where's everybody?" I asked.

Michel asked Sudjangi, who answered by pointing at the sun, the boats, the mosque, talking all the time.

"It is Friday," Michel said. "Everyone is at prayer."

He and I jumped across to the pier while Sudjangi threw back a hatch and disappeared into the hold. Mohamad drew up beside us with a handcart but didn't say a word. Sudjangi reappeared with a net full of dripping pink fish over his shoulder, swarming with black flies. He hoisted it out over the pier and dropped it onto the handcart with a slap like a load of wet towels. A fly went into my mouth and buzzed around in the top of my throat until I pried him out with my finger. He fell at my feet and I stepped on him. The part of me that still didn't believe that we really had been rescued from Loé's brother's brother-in-law's boat asked why I didn't swallow him.

Then a blanket was dropped over my head, and someone pushed my shoulder to get me moving down the pier. I watched the grey boards go by under my feet and sometimes I caught a glimpse of Michel's square toes beside me. I had to be careful as hell because mooring ropes cut across the pier at every possible angle.

Then I could hear the mosque, and instead of the one guy that they'd had in Pelayaran this sounded like six or eight, murmuring a ragged sort of chorus.

Allahuuuuuu Ak-bar

We walked off the pier onto a stretch of gravel that felt like tacks, then over tufts of dry yellow grass. Sudjangi lifted the corner of my blanket. We stood at the back of some kind of delivery van. The doors hung open. Michel hopped inside.

"Yes, we have this truck now," Alip said. "The Dutch left many things."

I kept my head low and climbed in. I was ready for a rest after our march down the pier, and it was hot as a crockpot in there. Alip leaned inside, holding out his hand.

"Give me the quilts," he said. "Lie down."

"Wouldn't this have been smarter at night?" I asked.

"At night there are roadblocks."

He got the blankets out of the way just as Mohamad pushed the handcart up against the bumper, and Sudjangi pushed the net in so all the fish sat just off the ends of our toes. There seemed to be some complication involving the knot that kept the net closed. The flies were much louder in there and fish juice was getting our toes wet. They didn't expect us to ride into town next to half a ton of fish, did they?

"Lay down," Alip said.

I slid my shoulders against the floor, then Sudjangi pulled the knot apart — I could see what he was doing but didn't quite believe it. He lifted the net and poured the pink fish over top of us. They were as hot as little furnaces from rot. I managed to keep my face above them. Communists!

"More than enough for both of us," whispered Michel.

Next he was going to say that Marshal Ney rode in a truckload of rotting fish to win the War of 1812, and then I was going to sock him in the nose until he cried and screamed and swore that he would never say it again. Jesus, the flies were crawling into my eyes, and my hands were too sticky to wipe them away. Like lying in a *benjo*.

"*Ikan*," said Mohamad.

He smiled for the first time. He threw a fish and it hit the wall and slid down against the back of my head. Then they shut the doors and we were in the dark. The two doors for the cab slammed ahead of us, then the engine started.

"It is a very good hiding place," said Michel. "Look there, a hole."

Light shone through a knothole beside my head. I rolled onto my belly to peer out, and tried not to inhale too many flies. I remembered somehow that the rotting process used up oxygen, and I hoped that air was coming through the knothole too.

I could see into the cab and right out the front windshield. The mosque must have just let out because the field was full of guys in black lunchpail caps and pink sarongs and yellow shirts, their Friday best, and women with scarves over their heads carrying kids. The van started to move between the groups of people. Sudjangi was driving. He was telling a story, waving his hands back and forth, and right in front of me I could see Mohamad laughing and thumping the dash. The three of them were passing a cigarette back and forth. The only thing I could hear was flies buzzing. I was wet to the skin and Jesus, my crotch did not like that. But I did have the knothole.

"Are there Japanese?"

"Not yet," I said.

I couldn't see much. There were leafy trees on either side of the road, and above them was a blue sky with some white clouds. Java. I got up on my elbows and saw Sudjangi's hand on the steering wheel and wet rice fields out his window. The clouds reflected in the water, and from where I was laying it was very disorienting. I hadn't seen still water in a long time.

"I see some rice fields."

"Only rice exists in this world," he said. "The world above and the world below are the same."

"What's this?"

"I learned this in Batavia. This why they are a calm people in Java, they believe the world above and the world below are the same. They will not upset the balance."

I peered at him — my eyes were adjusting. He had a fish on top of his head. I heard the engine drop down a gear. We were slowing down.

"See what it is," he whispered.

I could see the tops of two brown trucks that looked like they were parked sideways across the road. We were stopping. A hand in a tan sleeve came up in front of the windshield. Sudjangi shut off the engine. A roadblock.

"It's them," I whispered.

I slid down into the fish as best I could, and Michel must've been doing the same. It sounded like someone swimming in porridge. The fish were hot against the side of my face and I could only breathe out of the corner of my mouth, so that was where the flies tried to crawl inside.

Then there was a lot of talking outside Sudjangi's window. Maybe they weren't Japs after all because they weren't barking.

"*Ikan hanya*," said Sudjangi.

"*Ikan?*" asked the voice.

"Only fish," Michel whispered. I could barely hear him over all the flies.

There was a lot of fast Japanese talking — or Indonesian? One guy outside the window seemed to be asking and another seemed to be telling, without our guys saying anything. Then gravel crunched in back of us. I pushed away the fish from my beneath my face and pressed my cheek flat against the floor. I was waiting for the doors to open. They were going to see the back of my head no matter what I did.

"*Tidak, tidak*," Sudjangi was saying.

The cab's passenger door creaked open.

"*Tidak!*" Sudjangi said.

Mohamad started to holler to beat hell, and one of the Japs outside hollered too. We heard gravel getting kicked around — whoever had been behind us was running back to the front. The truck creaked on its springs.

Everyone quit shouting. Then the voices were farther away.

I put my eye to the hole. I could see the back of Alip's head out in front of the van, and a lot of guys wearing tan caps twenty or thirty feet ahead of us. They were watching something to our left.

A Jap stuck his head out of the back of one of the trucks parked across the road. He waved an arm in our direction then went back inside. A second later Mohamad's head followed the Jap into the back of the truck. They must've had steps behind it, because two Japs went up behind Mohamad and stood outside the canvas. The Japs had business

with little Mohamad, but not with the other two? I couldn't figure it
out. To the left Sudjangi started yelling in the Japs' faces. He was tugging at his hair. The steering wheel was in the way so I couldn't see the
looks on their faces. He finally turned around and I saw tears running
down his face, and he was yelling in our direction, at Alip. What did he
expect Alip to do? All Alip did was raise his hand and scratch the side
of his head.

Sudjangi had twisted the front of his shirt into a knot. Somebody
started a motorcycle, I couldn't see where it was but the noise drowned
out the yelling. Sudjangi turned back around, and a second later I couldn't
see the two Japs who had been standing in front of him. Had he knocked
them down? He must have. I could just see the white fleck of his undershirt as he ran away from us toward the trucks. One of the Japs on the
truck lifted his rifle and I saw it shift in his hands. I couldn't hear the shot
over all the other noise. But I couldn't see Sudjangi anymore.

"What has happened?" Michel whispered.

I must have made a noise in my throat. The light from the knothole
showed his white face.

"I think they got him," I said.

"Who has?"

I rolled out of the way and Michel put his eye to the hole. We were
still up to our neck in fish! After a minute the noise of the motorcycle
faded away, so then we could hear our flies as loud as ever.

"They have him," he said.

"Sudjangi?"

He slid back down into the fish. The doors on either side of the cab
squeaked open and slammed shut, and a second later the engine started.
Were the Japs driving? I glanced through — Alip was at the wheel.
No sign of Sudjangi.

We drove slowly for a little while, tires crunching over the gravel,
then we picked up speed. Changed gears. It seemed cooler back there
somehow, maybe a breeze was getting in from somewhere. I could hear
Mohamad crying, big wet sniffles, and a few times I heard Alip say,
"*O-rang gila.*" If that was supposed to calm the kid down it wasn't
helping any.

"What's *o-rang gila*?" I asked.

"A crazy person," said Michel. "A crazy man."

Alip kept muttering to Mohamad, and even in all that not-quite-*benjo* I managed to doze off. It's possible I passed out. Then I heard traffic around us, a horn honking and chickens squawking every now and then. I looked through the knothole and two-storey buildings were going by, and green-and-white awnings, and the roofs of black cars. Mohamad lay curled on his side on the seat in front of me. Alip rubbed his shoulder, then he put his hand back on the steering wheel. It crossed my mind that maybe they'd forgotten all about us, which would've been understandable.

Then we were driving on gravel again. I'd dozed off in the mean-time and ten thousand flies had settled on my face. We stopped, but the motor kept running. A door squeaked open and I heard feet running around. Everything was quiet — I didn't even look through to see if it was a roadblock. After a second the back doors opened up, and I had to shade my eyes to see Mohamad holding his nose.

"*I-yo*," he said.

I sat up with a noise like a rubber boot coming out of mud.

It looked like an alley, with high wooden fences down either side of it and a brown pony tethered in the long grass beside the shell of a car. We stood dripping onto the dirt under a tall tree with tiny leaves, and even then the fresh air had to fight to get up my nose. Flies still covered us. Two black dogs stood halfway down the alley with their noses in the air. Mohamad closed the doors and stepped back about four feet. He pulled a big white hankie out of his blue short pants and blew his nose. His eyes were red. Michel and I stood looking at him. The Japs really had shot Sudjangi, that was all there was to it. I wondered if the kid blamed us. He looked at his feet and sniffled, and I wanted to help him blow his nose again, at least give him a pat on the shoulder — isn't a grown man supposed to look out for little kids everywhere? I stepped towards him but he took a step back. I wanted to tell him not to take any wooden nickels but I only knew how to say *crazy, quiet, seagull* and *no*.

"*Hebat, hebat*," Michel said. "*Buruk*."

I didn't know those ones, and Mohamad didn't seem to be listening anyway. He bit his bottom lip and a tear dripped through the dirt on his cheek. Jesus, he didn't want to stand there with us! Why was he still standing there?

Alip came ambling around the corner of the van. He stopped beside Mohamad and ruffled his hair. He had a big smile on his face.

"He was crazy," he said. "It's okay. Here, this is Ibu Pri's house."

He walked over to the fence and pulled a latch and a big gate made out of bamboo swung open. Somebody's backyard — I saw a flat roof and some potted plants. Alip stood there motioning us in like we were a flock of ducks.

"Please now. It is dangerous for me."

I followed Michel — I tried to give Mohamad a smile but he'd already gone. We went through the gate. It clicked shut behind us and a second later we heard the van putter away.

The yard was concrete. The roof came out a long way past the back door, casting a long shadow. This was Java and there was no sign of you. Michel was watching a bird flit around the branches over our heads. I realized that if he had not been there I wouldn't have even considered knocking on the back door, I would have hidden behind the biggest plant pot and stayed there until I had starved to death.

"Whose place is this?" I asked.

A tiny woman in a black jacket and black dress came out of the shadows, her grey hair in a bun with a pencil through it. She smiled as she came toward us, her hands clasped together, chuckling even, looking at the ground rather than at either one of us. But once she was ten feet away she stopped shuffling and looked up. She put a hand to her throat. You probably would've realized she was gagging, but do you know what I thought? She was having some kind of stroke.

"*Ibu* —" said Michel.

"*Ting-gal,*" she said.

She hustled back into the house, her sandals snapping against her heels, her arms pumping like anything. She disappeared back into the darkness. The last I saw was her silver hair.

"She says to wait," said Michel.

His hand shot out at one of the flies. Then another. I couldn't be bothered.

A minute later she came back out dragging a five-gallon bucket of water behind her, spilling a pint on the ground with every tug, and nattering away to someone who must've still been back in the house. Her dress was soaking wet. She got within six feet of us that time, lifted the bucket as high as she could and threw the water over the both of us. I had to take a step back. It was colder than I'd expected. She was already dragging the bucket back inside.

There were fewer flies after just one bucket.

"It's good, isn't it?" Michel stepped out of his trousers and hung them on a nail. "The native bath."

"Shh, shh!" She hustled back out and pointed at the neighbours' fence. "*Diam*."

Quiet. That was one word I knew. She dropped two wooden brushes in front of us and went back inside as a young guy in a white T-shirt and green sarong came out dragging another bucket of water. He stopped in front of us, picked up the bucket and said something that sounded friendly.

Michel said something friendly back.

The water crashed over us. He hustled back in. I picked up a brush to scrub my forearm and honest to God, the muck rolled off of me like pencils. I scrubbed my chest, my back, then I undid my pants but I just scrubbed with my hand down there. That brush would've broken me open.

"I want to hear the Django Reinhardt record," said Michel.

"You told me. 'Nagging' or something."

"'Naguiné' sounds of Europe. You will hear it."

I stepped out of my pants and wrung them out on the concrete. The water was black. Michel was already striding towards the house, trousers over his arm. I hustled after him across the hot cement, and all of a sudden I remembered Sudjangi. Something awful had happened to him while our day had just carried on with even more laughs than usual. A yellow *chi-chack* lizard was curled in an *S* above the door.

The hallway was concrete too. It was cold in there. The young guy in the green sarong stood there propping another door open. He was holding his nose, despite all our scrubbing. Then we were in the bathroom, covered in blue and white tiles right up to the ceiling, with a big brown jar of water in the corner just like you'd had in room thirty-nine at the Raffles. There was probably one in every bathroom in the Dutch East Indies, but it still made me sad as hell to see it there.

"*Un-tuk ber-mandi,*" said the young guy.

"How do I ask them about Lily?"

Michel picked up the brass scoop for the water.

"Who do you mean to ask?" he said.

I glanced at the young guy but he stepped out into the hallway. Michel dumped the scoop over his back, and a lot of it splashed onto me.

"What do you mean 'who'? Aren't they all coming tonight for a powwow?"

"But what will you ask them?"

"If they can find her!"

"What for?"

I went out in the hallway too. Of course he had his secret scrap of paper to hand over to the PKI and didn't want anything like a guy's wife to get in the way of that. I sat against the wall and looked up at a picture of a silver bridge on the wall opposite. I itched in those wet pants but I didn't mind, and the fish smell wasn't so bad either. I lay down on my side and went to sleep.

I woke up when water sloshed my face, and I sat up without the faintest idea where I was. The young guy was mopping the floor. He backed up a step, saying a lot of things, he sounded apologetic as hell. The bathroom looked empty so I pulled myself up and went in. I was not steady on my feet.

My crotch kept itching even after I washed, so I opened a cupboard and found a jar of something that might have been baby powder. I sat on the edge of the water jar and dumped it on one side and then the other.

And presto, just like that, my crotch did not itch. Magic.

I looked for my clothes and found clean ones sitting on the lip of the doorway — a blue sarong and a blue jacket with short arms. It was like Ma laying out pyjamas after a bath. But the jacket was as bad as that white dress from Pelayaran, I couldn't button up the front or bring my arms down, and the only way that I could keep the sarong from dropping was to tie the top of it in a knot.

There was nobody in the hallway so I walked further into the house. It was dark, but there must've been a window open somewhere because I could hear wind chimes tinkling. I came into a big room that wasn't quite as dark — there were curtains in one corner with light peeking in around the edges. It was cool in there and smelled like doughnuts. There were four chesterfields and three coffee tables, plus more chairs along the wall. A guy could've taught school in there. Michel was in a big black armchair with his feet up, wearing a black jacket with gold whirligig designs sewn into it and a purple-and-white sarong, and they looked like they fit. There was an enamel coffee pot and glasses on the table beside him, and a plate of curvy brown things.

"Fried bananas." He nibbled on one. "*Pi-sang go-reng*."

"*Go-reng*."

"It means 'fried.'"

I picked one up and bit off half of it. It was heavier than a regular banana and tasted like it had been fried in caramel. I felt like I'd discovered electricity or something — how was it that I'd never heard of a fried banana? Ibu Pri came in from the opposite doorway, her sandals snapping against her heels. She set a gold box full of cigarettes down on the table. She and Michel whispered for a minute, then she turned to me.

"*Diam*," she said.

So far my impression of Java was that they liked things quiet. She hustled out again, sandals snapping louder than any noise we'd been making, but then I had no idea how near to the window her neighbours were and guys speaking English might've sparked their interest, whereas they'd probably been listening to her feet for a thousand years.

I sat and took one cigarette out of the box after another, smelling them, marvelling at how firmly packed each one was, what a perfect cylinder, with the word *Kudus* printed on the paper. How was it possible to print a word on a cigarette — I was like stone-age man with those things! I didn't even want to smoke one.

"Put those back. Everything must be neat."

I barely got the last one in the box before I was stretched out asleep on the floor.

When I opened my eyes I had a pink striped pillow under my head and Michel was sitting in his armchair smoking something that smelled like cloves and cinnamon. The light was different — not darker, but browner. All of the bananas were gone.

"What're you smiling about?" I whispered.

He poked himself in the cheek.

"I cannot stop it."

I dropped my head onto the pillow again. I felt better. I couldn't even remember what I'd ever felt bad about. Then things started to trickle back into my brain, and do you know which one made me feel the worst? No, not Sudjangi at all — it was your dad. Because I hadn't given him a single thought before that moment. Sent up north, knowing that his wife and daughter were down south expecting great things of him, and as the Japs mowed him over or clubbed him on the head he must've been pulling his hair out, knowing he had no way to tell them to quit waiting for him. How many guys in the course of history had lost their minds because they couldn't get word to somebody? But what would I have said if I could have sent word to you? "Japs have taken Java! Where the Christ have *you* ended up?" But I figured the PKI would track you down. They'd been in the first stinking fishing boat to come across us, so they had to be everywhere.

The young guy brought in two shiny dishes and Michel lifted the lids and steam went everywhere. There was rice in one and meat in gravy in the other.

"*Da-ging ren-dang*," said Michel.

"*Ren-dang*," I said.

"Beef lung."

Was I bothered? Lung? I would've been more upset if he'd told me the sandwiches still had crusts. He used the silver spoon to dish it onto our plates, then we just shovelled it in our mouths with our fingers. The lung sauce was delicious. Michel had it up on his forehead.

"Hadi says that they will come for the meeting in a few minutes."

"Is this guy Hadi?"

"The houseboy. Even Jusuf is coming. He is the head of PKI for Soerabaja."

"They told me Sudjangi was the head of it."

"He says it is Jusuf. Hadi told me that at every meeting Sudjangi would tell them to tie all of the Japanese together and shoot them with a machine gun. He wanted them to begin making the rope."

I could imagine his grin as he said it. Hadi came in and started to clear the table. He'd put on a long white shirt and a black lunchpail cap. He held up the gravy dish with our thumb-marks smeared inside it.

"*Ay-nak*?" he asked me.

He seemed happy. The rice was sitting like a wad of gum in my chest. He piled up the dishes and went out. Michel sat back, sipping coffee.

"He says that Sudjangi's wife will come." He dragged on his cigarette, looking just as smooth as Ronald Colman — here was the same guy who'd pulled coconut shell out of his behind. "After he went fishing with Alip she would always come here to take him home. But they have not been able to get word to her."

What had I just been saying!

When *Allahuuuuuu Ak-bar* started to wail from somewhere above our heads, I jumped before I realized what it was. The mosque must've been right across the street.

"What time does that mean?"

"It means five o'clock."

I could hear Hadi murmuring from around the corner even while they were still calling *Ash-hadu* out of the loudspeaker. Maybe he had to get his business done before the meeting started.

"So the citizens are at the mosque now?"

"On their way."

"And the PKI sneak in while that's going on."

He stuck out his lips and made a very grave-looking nod. He didn't like it that I'd figured out anything about the PKI. He wanted to be the expert. There were probably another hundred things they'd told him that he hadn't passed on.

"So what does that letter say?"

He put out his cigarette in the porcelain ashtray.

"Which letter?"

"What are you talking about? The one Muzakkar gave you."

"I have not read it."

"Still? Are you kidding me?"

"It is not addressed to me."

Ibu Pri bustled in wearing a shiny blue jacket and carrying a platter of food, and another old lady came in behind her with a tray full of little bowls, and they started to lay out all kinds of nuts and fruit and fish and hard-boiled eggs and chopped-up vegetables and red sauce and piles of meat on sticks. It smelled like Christmas dinner. I picked up half an egg.

"*Orah!*" said the old broad.

"Put it down," said Michel. "We should not sit here."

So I put it down and we got up and sat on two of the chairs against the wall, and a dozen guys immediately started filing in from the back hallway. Most of them looked a lot like Alip; his outfit must have been the height of Soerabaja fashion — white shirt, sarong, little moustache. They trooped in, glanced once at us, then sat down on the chesterfields. It seemed like being in the PKI meant that they could behave like jazzmen or something, and since we weren't part of the combo we were beneath them. Third-class passengers.

But two guys did say hello. The first was a tall guy in a white sarong with curly hair and thick black glasses. I hadn't seen a native guy with hair like that before, and he was almost as tall as Michel too. He came right over and we each held our elbows and shook hands with him, and he looked from one of us to the other and said a lot of things in a soft voice. He reminded me of the Anglican minister who'd come into the store and talk Dad's ear off about gardening.

"Harry," said Michel. "This is Jusuf."

Jusuf was in charge of PKI Soerabaja, and therefore was the guy who was going to find you. But I didn't know how to phrase that. I could only have said seagull. *Chamar.*

"Hello," I said. In English.

He smiled and let go of my hand, and as he turned towards the middle of the room the guys on the couches all leapt to their feet, hands holding elbows all around. He murmured a couple of things and they all laughed and looked at the ground like Jusuf was just too wonderful.

He would've made a good jazzman, too, I could see that. Saxophone player.

Hadi went around pouring tea into glasses, and Alip came in with his hair in his eyes, looking smug as hell. He said something to Michel from across the room but didn't come over. Maybe he didn't know we'd had baths.

The last arrival shook our hands too, though he tripped over a table on the way over. He was a long-necked guy with short hair except where it hung over his ears; he wore purple pinstripe trousers and carried a square canvas bag that he put down to shake our hands and then picked up again right away.

"*Tjokro*," he said. He said it a few times, very close to my ear. "*Tjokro*."

I figured that that had to be his name. Everyone else had sat down but Jusuf was still up, looking like he had something to say, so old Tjokro had to hurry off to the last seat over in the opposite corner. When he got there he looked across, caught my eye and gave me a thumbs-up, so I guessed I was all right in his books. But he hadn't mentioned knowing where Lily Winslow was either.

Ibu Pri sat on a stool and the housekeeper went back out to the kitchen. They were the only women there, so Sudjangi's wife must not have come, and I hoped she would stay away. Seeing Mohamad afterward had been bad enough.

Jusuf said *Perserikatan Kommunist Indonesia* a bunch of times, I caught that much, and he kept watching a guy who seemed to be writing it all down. Then he said Sudjangi's name, he said it over and over, so he must have been telling the whole story, but slowly, like the Anglican minister would have. Alip sat there nodding like it was a very big deal and the other guys shifted around in their chairs. A couple of times Jusuf looked towards Michel and me and said *Michal dan Arry* so he must've been telling them about us though he never once said *chamar*, bless his heart. He took off his glasses and wiped his eyes and then watched while the guy finished writing. He said Mohamad's name a few times, but he didn't act out any of the punching or screaming or hair-pulling on Sudjangi's part so I couldn't ever tell quite where we were in the story. But the guys were sitting up very straight, holding the arms of their chairs, eyes wide; then after a minute they sat back, shaking their heads, and one or two muttered *gila*. Jusuf stood with his head bowed for a second, then he started to talk again and the secretary started a new page. So that was it for Sudjangi.

Jusuf looked at us again and said *Pelayaran*, so I figured that our time had come, the thrilling climax to our journey, but old Michel just stayed put.

"*Pertama*," said Jusuf. "*Makanan*."

I had an idea that that meant *food*, and sure enough they all got to their feet. But instead of picking up plates they marched down the hall in the direction of the bathroom.

"We must wash our hands," said Michel.

Of course when it had just been the two of us he hadn't bothered. The PKI jazzmen lined up in the hallway, going in one at a time, so I leaned against the wall behind Michel. I glanced back into the meeting room and there was a girl standing beside the coffee table. She was staring at me. Her mouth dropped open. Her upper lip was much thicker than her lower, and the part in her hair showed a line of tawny skin right up the middle of her head. No one else seemed to have noticed her. She was pinching the fingertips on one hand, up and down to each finger, then switching hands. She had black triangles on her knuckles. I tried to smile at her. She kept moving her lips every few seconds like she was talking to herself. She had hardly any eyebrows but her eyes were big as saucers and the bags under them were so black that they looked like they'd been put on with shoe polish. I hadn't had a female look me in the eye in many months, certainly not Ibu Pri or her housekeeper or any of Bucktooth's girls back on Celebes, but none of them had had tattooed hands either.

"Sudjangi?" asked the girl.

Christ Almighty, this was his wife. Ibu Pri hustled in from the kitchen and Alip pushed past me from the bathroom and they tried to aim her toward the chesterfield, both talking low to her. She wouldn't sit.

"Sintha." Ibu Pri patted her hand. "Sintha …"

Her eyes never went off mine, but I don't think that was because I was a perfect physical specimen; she just had to look at something while they gave her the news.

The PKI guys had crowded around me, they didn't want to miss the show, but when she took one step in our direction they all jumped back. Alip took her arm and he and Ibu Pri sat down with her on the chesterfield and the housekeeper set a glass of tea in front of her. I heard Alip saying *Jepang* and *Mohamad* but she didn't react to any of it, she just kept staring across the room at us. I guess that was her reaction. After a couple of minutes Alip got up and pushed past us to get to the bathroom, and most of the PKI guys decided that they had better go in with him and watch him wash his hands. Jusuf stayed next to me with his arms folded, exhaling loudly out his nose. Tjokro tiptoed across to the chesterfield and crouched down. Sintha looked at him and listened to what he had to say.

Good old Tjokro, I thought, there's not many like him.

But then she jumped up and threw her glass into the hallway. It smashed against the wall above our heads and the biggest piece bounced off the back of my skull. Then she just stood there with her fists clenched, breathing *huff huff huff*. She looked from one of us to the other. Most of the glass brushed off my shoulders all right. I didn't hold it against her.

"*Gila*," the guys were saying. "*Gila, gila, gila.*"

But I wondered how many of them had lost their true love to the stupid Japanese. Hell, maybe all of them had for all I knew. Ibu Pri pulled us back into the room — Alip had reappeared by then — and the house-keeper took Sintha's arm and they went into the bathroom, crunching over the bits of glass. We heard water splashing.

The PKI guys filled up their plates and sat there chewing. Hadi started taking the platters away, and as soon as there was a free table Tjokro dumped a pile of little red books onto it from his canvas bag. Little paperbacks. He brought one over to me but of course I didn't understand the first word so I passed it to Michel. The guys were flipping through them and chatting back and forth — it looked like Tjokro had a hit! Alip pulled a piece of gristle out of his mouth. The housekeeper started to sweep up the broken glass, then Sintha crept past her and went through to the kitchen without looking at anybody.

"It is an advertisement for toothpaste," said Michel. "All for tooth-paste." He had to move his finger along each line to follow the words. "Oh! Look here."

The pages in the middle of the book were different — the writing was tiny and there were a lot of diagrams with circles and arrows.

"'Do you want to chase away the Fascists?' it says. See here, 'Orang Fasis.'"

Jusuf stood up and hollered something, thumping the book in his hand, and Ibu Pri hustled in saying *shh, shh, shh.*

Alip finally pointed at us and said something about Pelayaran, so Michel got to his feet and reached in his pocket for the letter. It looked brown and wrinkled as hell. Alip took it and passed it to Jusuf. I could smell the fish on it even from where I was.

Sintha came back in from the kitchen. She went straight to Alip and stared at him until he looked up, then she quietly asked him a question — I heard Sudjangi's name and *Jepang.* Alip looked at Jusuf for a second, then back at her.

"*Tidak,*" he said.

She said something else, maybe she thanked him, then she went back out to the kitchen. Alip asked Michel something.

"*Tidak,*" he answered. It was all anybody could say.

"Have you read this?" Alip asked me.

"*Tidak,*" I said.

"We have not," said Michel. "This message is for PKI Soerabaja. We have spent many weeks bringing it here."

Alip translated that for the other guys, and Jusuf looked over the letter again. Sintha came back in, carrying a frying pan this time, and Alip must have had an idea of what was on her mind because he was already on his feet, saying something to her, and she swung the pan and hit him in the side so he fell down on one knee and made a face. By then the other guys had wrestled the frying pan away from her. She stayed right where she was with her hands at her sides. Alip looked up at her, rubbing his shoulder. He murmured something to her.

"What did he say?" I whispered.

"She will have to behave at last or there will more trouble."

Ibu Pri took the pan and gave it to the housekeeper, then she steered Sintha over towards us. They stopped beside me and Sintha slid down the wall until she was on the floor.

"*Sur-at ini*," said Jusuf.

Everybody stopped what they were doing and he started to talk very quickly, waving our letter around, pointing at Alip, then at Michel, then at me. Jusuf said, "*Australee*," and "PKI," and "*tidak* PKI." Then he dropped the letter on the table.

Sintha was looking at me and moving her fingers, pinching four fingertips, then pinching the other four, so that the tattoos on her knuckles hopped up and down. They weren't just triangles, the tattoos, they were more like arrowheads pointing back at her wrists. I liked the way her top lip sat just above her teeth.

Alip was reading the letter while Jusuf talked in his ear. Muzakkar had wanted to warn them that Japs were overrunning the Indies, and as it happened they already knew that, but what was the big deal? Alip folded the paper in half and looked across at us.

"We will try to send you to Australia as he asks. At Lake Situaksan it was decided to cooperate better with other cells."

They told Ibu Pri a few things, pointed at us, and she just went *ya, ya, ya*. Sintha's skirt shifted so that I could see some of her knee.

"No, no," said Michel.

"You will stay here while we decide how to get you to Australia," said Alip. He brushed the hair out of his eyes. "Actually, you cannot leave this room for right now, because if any other cells find out there will be trouble. You have placed everyone in a very dangerous position."

Then Jusuf stood up and shook hands with Alip, everybody holding their elbows — was that the end of the meeting?

"Hold on a minute," I said.

"Yes?" asked Alip.

"I need to find my wife."

"I know this."

"So what did they say about it?"

He muttered to Jusuf and a couple of the other ones. I was already as sick of the PKI as I figured I could get.

"We must wait until we have contacts."

Then Jusuf asked him something and Alip muttered back, nodding in my direction, and whatever he said Jusuf looked surprised —

his eyebrows went up behind his glasses. He took a pencil and notebook out of his shirt pocket.

"Jusuf would like to know what is your wife's name," said Alip.

They passed me the pencil and notebook. I wrote LILY WINSLOW, UK, and then I was going to write your birthdate under it because I thought that would be pertinent but I realized that I didn't know what it was, so I wrote LILY BROWN just in case you were using that name instead. I passed it back.

"It is two women?" asked Alip.

"It's only one."

"But which name?"

"I don't know which. I'm sorry."

"But this is your wife?"

"Yes."

He gave the notebook to Jusuf, and Jusuf walked to the doorway and shook the bits of glass off his waiting sandals. Half of the guys got up and followed him, and the rest just sat there. Sintha stood up next to the chesterfield, her hands folded in front of her. Hadi cleared the rest of the plates and the housekeeper came in with the enamel coffee pot. I took a glass but it tasted bitter as hell.

After a couple of minutes Alip got up and smoothed out his sarong.

"You see, it is dangerous if everyone leaves at once. *Selamat ting-gal,*" he said. "*Ting-gal.*"

"*Jalan,*" said Ibu Pri.

The other guys all went with him, Tjokro included. Sintha stayed by the chesterfield, sucking on a piece of her hair, and a minute later she hurried out too. It was just sinking in — we weren't allowed to leave that room.

Michel threw himself onto the chesterfield and rubbed his eyes with the heels of his hands. His bald head looked funny as hell sticking out of that jacket.

"We help no one by staying here! All of that trouble, the boat they gave us, it was only for our sake. It is very frustrating. Now we will sit and eat Ibu's food."

I drank the last of my coffee and found a layer of sugar. It had been hidden away at the bottom of the glass, just like two guys I knew.

"Perhaps your wife is in Australia after all," he said.

"What are the chances of that?"

"Do not be discouraged."

My trouble was that I could only imagine you in one place at a time; my brain couldn't get around the idea that you might have been in any spot on the face of the earth. If I worried about you in more than one place at a time my mind was going to turn into mush, and I'd already decided that you were on Java.

"Where was I?" asked Michel.

"Not again."

"It begins slowly. But as it continues it becomes complicated, and his guitar, you know, it sounds as though it is flying. He plays the small notes, very small, and then the chords. And the small notes again." He lay there moving his hands like he was strumming a guitar or feeling for a hernia. "It will be so wonderful to hear it."

It would've been a treat to hear anything new. Sometimes if Hadi left the window open we heard the neighbours' wind chimes and the guys out in the street hollering that they had ice cream or melons or whatever it was. And there was that call to the mosque, the muezzin, we heard him at first but since he hollered just about all of the time it got to the point where we didn't hear him at all except on Fridays when he was louder. We'd spent two Fridays there since that first one. We heard our lizard too, a little yellow guy up in the corner who didn't say *chi-chack* at all, he said *click-clack* like he'd swallowed a bottlecap, and some-times he'd drop a black poop on one or the other of us so we could have an argument about whether or not that was good luck. What else did we have for entertainment? We smelled that clove from our cigarettes, the wet concrete smell from hallway outside the bathroom, and the kerosene a half-hour before lunch every day.

"What's the song called again?" I asked. "'Big Guinea?'"

"'Naguiné,'" said Michel.

It was also entertaining to hear the PKI's messages to Ibu Pri. Their biggest news was that Tasikmalaja was not a civilian prison camp at all, but an airfield that the Japs had captured from the Dutch. It had only taken the PKI three weeks to unearth that information. To their credit they didn't seem to have been trying very hard.

"And what's his name? Django Trachtenberg?"

"Go and find Hadi, please. I want to speak to him."

I crept down the hall and looked around the corner until I saw a sliver of the kitchen through the doorway. Hadi was pouring something out of the kettle.

"Fsst," I said.

I couldn't say anything louder than that or Ibu Pri would come out and give me her tired-out look, and that was more than I could take. She'd told us that she'd seen Japs watching from across the street.

I reached up to the top of the wall and crumbled off a little piece of cement, then I lined it up ever so carefully and threw it. It made a *bing* on the kettle so that Hadi dropped it and water went everywhere and he turned around and saw me peeking around the corner. I hurried back into our room and lay down on my chesterfield like nothing had happened, and a second later Hadi came in but he didn't even look mad. He just looked tired. Michel started to talk to him, and he talked for quite a while, Hadi nodding now and then, and of course I didn't understand much of it though I did catch *rumah teman saya* — my friend's house. At the end Hadi said a couple of things back.

"Wonderful!" Michel sat up and rubbed his hands. "He says he will *only* do it if it is dangerous."

"Do what?"

"He will tell Ibu he needs to buy tea for the house. No, do not worry. It will be a very nice surprise for you."

That night after fried bananas we heard a vehicle in the back yard, so we crawled down the hallway and looked out the slat in the window. Hadi was pulling up in a big Studebaker or something, the moonlight shining across its roof. The steering wheel was in the middle of the car!

"A Panhard," said Michel.

"What's that?"

"From France. I would know it anywhere."

Hadi hopped out of the car and climbed the tree that looked down into the neighbour's yard, then he ran across and did it on the other side. Then he hopped down again and opened the trunk. He lifted out two square cases. We stayed low and ran back to our chesterfields.

"Where the hell'd he get that car?"

"Ibu keeps it across town. She does not wish to attract attention to this house."

Hadi hurried in, grinning from ear to ear, leaning back under the weight of the cases. All of a sudden I got a lump in my throat like a ball of rice was climbing back up, because if there were two things in the world I could recognize they were a wind-up phonograph and a box of records. I was in the same room with a phonograph and a box of records. Hadi set them down in the corner then hustled off to the kitchen as Ibu Pri started saying something to him. Michel knelt over the cases so all I could see was his purple-and-white behind.

"These belong to Koon Eng," he said.

He opened the clips and lifted the top off the record player so I could smell the metal and the oil, and my heart went *thud thud thud thud* inside my ribs.

"I met him two years ago when Eu Chin sent me to Soerabaja. The Dutch had stopped one of our ships in the port."

I heard the *thack thack* of records being flipped through, a sound I hadn't heard since the morning my Wallers melted down. I could smell them. The dust and the lacquer.

"What's he got?" I asked.

"These are Chinese records. See the label? Chinese. Oh, God. Look at this." He held up a record: white print on a blue label. "Django."

He bent over the record player.

"Are you ready?" He gave me a long look. "This is from France."

He turned the handle, then put down the arm.

"'Naguiné.'"

At first I thought that it didn't even have its needle because there wasn't a whisper coming out of it. But then the flickering sound started.

We heard a couple of guitar notes. They sounded like someone tuning a banjo. The guitarist picked out a few more things, warming up or something, and every second I was ready for a band to come in behind him. Michel kept his fingers on the edge of the record player. The guy played a couple of chords, then he went back to picking out the stray notes. Those chords were all right but it still didn't sound like any kind of song — he sounded like Bob Fitzgerald who used to sit behind our high school with his guitar, he'd tell us that he could play any song, we just had to name one, so we'd say something familiar like "Whistle While You Work" and he'd plunk away for fifteen minutes before he gave up. That's what "Naguiné" sounded like. All of sudden he played five good chords in a row, then that was the end. Michel picked up the arm.

"Does he have anything else?" I asked.

"His others are all in Chinese."

"Don't kid me."

"Once more."

I enjoyed "Naguiné" a little bit more that time, because of course I wasn't expecting much. I liked the *sound* of the guitar, regardless of what it was playing, and I liked watching our lizard run across the ceiling from one beam to another. But, Jesus, that song was a godawful mess. It came to the end and Michel left it going around and around.

"Not as good as I remembered," he said.

We heard slippers shuffling. Ibu Pri stood in the hall, her hand to her throat.

"*Japanners!*" she hissed.

Hadi ran past from the kitchen, vaulting over Ibu Pri on his way toward the back door, and Michel disappeared after him like a shadow. I looked down at the record player and wondered if it would fit under my arm, but if there wasn't one decent record there was no reason to get killed for it. I hitched up my sarong and ran around the end of the coffee table.

I figured that Hadi was going to slam the trunk lid on my fingers so I kept them folded right under my chin. He loomed against the black sky, then the lid came down and everything was black. The trunk smelled like iron filings. It wasn't very easy to breathe. Then the Panhard's engine started up so that every nut and screw vibrated like a tambourine.

"Where's he taking us?"

We backed into the lane, that was gentle enough, but then Hadi took the first corner so quickly that the top of Michel's head hit me in the mouth and a tire jack or something fell across my back. Gravel rattled under the wheels.

"You must hold on," said Michel.

He was using up more air than I was. We kept our arms and legs braced against the sides of the trunk for the next half-hour because two or three times a minute Hadi would turn another corner at sixty miles an hour. I'd hurt one of my knees so I tried to keep it where nothing could happen to it. Michel hummed that idiot song.

I tasted dust and wondered if we were out in the country.

Then the car stopped, and a second later Hadi was standing over us with the lid up. But he didn't help us out. I heard his feet run away, *slap slap slap* across pavement, then it sounded like he was knocking on a door. I scratched my crotch while Michel climbed out, then I went too, trying to be careful with the knee. Houses were packed tight together on either side of the street, they all looked whitewashed, and there were dozens of doors and windows but not a light on anywhere. Hadi was waving at us — the door in front of him stood open but it was dark inside. Electrical lines hung so low over the street that I could've bit them. Hadi came running back, pointing at the ground again and again.

"*Di sini, di sini.*"

That meant "here." He closed the trunk very gently and slid back behind the wheel, and a second later the Panhard was down the block and around the corner. Michel had me by the arm. We went through the open door and it shut behind us so that we were in the pitch black. It was the mustiest room I'd ever been in.

"*Selamat malam.*"

A woman's voice, moving past us from the door.

"*Selamat malam,*" we said. Good evening.

"*Diam,*" she whispered.

I wondered if any person in Java had ever yelled at the top of their lungs. A tiny hand went around my wrist and pulled me through the room. I hoped the hand belonged to the same woman who'd talked, because it had been a nice voice; I hoped that it wasn't a slack-jawed little old man. I held my free hand in front of me so I didn't run into anything but I pushed against something that made a real bang, maybe a hat stand.

"*Diam!*" she whispered again.

We seemed to go through about ninety-eight rooms, and she always had to wait for Michel to close the door we'd just come through. The concrete floor felt smooth and cool. My wrist got sweaty where she held it. She smelled a bit like glue but all the same I thought she smelled good. In the ninety-ninth room I saw a yellow light coming under the door, and she tugged me into a room with a high ceiling and a candle on the table. It smelled like fish and onions and limes. A kitchen. All I could see of the woman was that she had a skinny neck and a cloth around her head. Her face was never in the light. She sat me down in front of an iron stove that was hotter than I would've liked, then she sat Michel down beside me and muttered to somebody we couldn't see. A little old lady shuffled out of the shadows. She was facing the candle so I could see her at least — she had about eighteen hairs on top of her head and one eye that seemed higher than the other. As she picked up a kettle and said something I saw she had no teeth to speak of.

"Oh, *Bu Sintha!*" Michel said. "*Selamat malam.*"

And the young woman *was* Sintha — the upper lip, the bags under her eyes. She didn't answer him but just kept spooning rice onto two plates while the old one hobbled around lighting more candles. From my wide experience it seemed that the majority of the people in the Indies were old broads but that was probably just because they were squirrelled away in the same hidey-holes as we were.

The old girl brought us glasses of coffee with the grounds floating on the top.

"*Apa nama?*" Michel asked her. What was her name?

She gave a big smile. "Kartinah," she said.

Sounded like a little girl's name to me.

"Kartinah!" said Sintha, and looked at the old girl with her eyes wide open, and holy cow, I just about went under the stove myself. Kartinah hustled around the table and started breaking green beans into a bowl.

Sintha put her head in her hands. I looked at Michel — should we do something? He gave a little shrug. I blew on my coffee and looked at those triangles on her hands. After a second she cleared her throat and brought the plates over to us, then she squatted down next to Kartinah. Her zigzag-patterned sarong stretched across her knees.

"*Cuci?*" asked Michel.

I knew that: "wash." Sintha stood up and pointed to the back of the kitchen. Kartinah picked up a candle and went with him. He was always washing his hands. Some of the food was even spicier than what Hadi gave us, but I was used to it by then. There was fish in a sauce hot enough to peel wallpaper.

"*Bahasa Indonesianya?*" Sintha asked me.

"*Apa?*" I said.

That meant "what?" I had my mouth stuffed full.

She didn't repeat it. She sat there holding her knees. She wasn't pinching her fingers the way she had before. She stood up to the table again and started to beat one of the vegetables with a stick. Kartinah brought Michel back and he sat down and went straight into talking and stuffing his face at the same time. He gave this big long speech that must've been our life stories. He said *PKI* and *Sudjangi* a couple times and *ada* and *apa* and *saya* and *Arry* about a hundred. I never heard him once say *chamar*. I picked every grain of rice off my plate until he finished with what had just happened to us.

"*Dan ahli musik nama* Django Reinhardt."

"*Apa nama?*" Sintha asked.

"Django Reinhardt."

She rolled her eyes up at the ceiling.

Then she went around the kitchen collecting knives and dropping them into the sink, and telling him a story too. For a second she dropped to her knees and it sounded like she was crying, then she hopped up and kept talking like it hadn't happened. I couldn't follow it — she might have said "Alip" once or twice. I did figure out that she didn't have much of a bosom, because she shook her fist in the air an awful lot and nothing ever budged.

After a while Michel sat back.

"Alip did not seek revenge for Sudjangi. She plans to go to Ibu Pri's and see what is the matter with them. She believes that *we* are men who do things."

She ran at us all of a sudden and I just about jumped out of my chair, but then she gave a little bow, picked up our empty glasses, tiptoed back to the sink and threw them in with a crash.

"And she says that we will be very happy here until we leave for Australia."

"Does she know about any camps besides Tasikmalaja?"

He shrugged, then asked her something. Kartinah just sat staring at us like we were the greatest thing since the Lambeth Walk.

Kartinah hadn't minded gawking at me when I hadn't had more than five words of *Indonesianya* but after three weeks I knew enough to have a conversation with her, and, oh boy, then she was falling over herself to not look me in the face. But that was normal; Ibu Pri and her house-keeper had been like that. Kartinah had decided that we could only talk over the wall while I was in the bathroom, the *mandi*. Most of the time she and Sintha talked in a Soerabaja language that I didn't understand at all, so who knows what language she was teaching me, it might've just been specific to the houses on our side of the street.

"*Mas Ari,*" she said — that was me. "*Dimana Michel?*"

So I told her how Michel had gotten sick of waiting around for Alip or somebody to float us a boat to Australia, so he'd somehow got Hadi to come and pick him up so that he could be at Ibu Pri's for the next meeting, and I had asked him to please mention Mrs. Winslow as well. It hadn't been a *Japanner* raid that night, we'd found out fourth-hand, only a man selling ashtrays. Now Michel had been gone three weeks and I tried to have a bath five times a day, so Kartinah had heard that story a hundred and five times. But all the same she'd sit outside the *mandi* stall and chew up her *sireh* and drool it red into her spittoon, rock on her stool so the legs clicked against the floor while I dumped water over the back of my neck with a scoop with three ducks on the side, and she'd ask me again where Michel had gone. That was life at Ibu Sintha's. I never mentioned my suspicion that he'd only gone back to hear his record again, because if the record had been Waller that was what I would've done ninety-nine times out of a hundred.

I scrubbed away down there, trying to be very careful, and all of a sudden my mister started to get ready for something, which hadn't happened, honest to God, since I woke up thinking about you on the poor old *Bowral*. I'd put the lapse down to poor nutrition.

"*Siap?*" asked Kartinah.

No, I was not ready, but she passed me Sudjangi's pale yellow shirt anyway. I still wore that blue sarong from Ibu Pri's — I figured Sintha wasn't ready to start lending her husband's out, in fact Kartinah had told me that Sintha slept on a stack of them up in her room. I stepped out into the kitchen and Kartinah skittered over to her stool in the corner like she'd been there all along and the spittoon in front of me wasn't even hers.

"*Mas Ari, Tjokro disini.*"

"*Tjokro?*" I said.

Old Tjokro from the PKI came to the house all the time to use Sudjangi's typewriter. Sintha had that line of five rooms between the front door and the kitchen — it had only seemed like a hundred — that were full of empty oil cans and end tables with rat bites up and down the legs, and she made Tjokro use the typewriter in the room that was three away from the kitchen so that was, what, three away from the front door, square in the middle of the house, and even then she made him stuff pillows inside the typewriter and he was only allowed to hit one key every thirty seconds. I went in and he sat there tapping his heels on the floor, counting off the seconds.

I peered over his shoulder. So far he'd written *Stop immigran dari Djepang* — he quit tapping for a second, brought up his finger. *Tink.* A period for the end of the sentence. He had on a green sarong instead of his pinstripe trousers.

"*Apa kabar?*" he asked.

His big grin. He kept counting out thirty, tapping his hands on his knees like he was the Gene Krupa of Soerabaja.

"*Baik, baik,*" I told him.

That was just courtesy, it meant that I was good, though I was not so, but before I could ask my question he started talking a blue streak. The gist seemed to be that the Japs had stopped Alip and found his little red copy of *Menara Merah* and arrested him. Tjokro held up his hands in front of him like he just couldn't figure out what to do next, he was at a loss, then he spun around and hit the space bar.

Alip arrested! I know, I should have been crying or clicking my heels or something, but to be honest I just heard it as more stupid PKI talk. It was never what I wanted to hear about.

"*Pay-kah-ee dapat istri saya?*" I asked.

There it was — had the PKI found my wife?

"Oh, *tidak.*" Tjokro tried to look surprised at the question even though that had to be the hundredth time I'd asked him. "*Tidak, Ari, ma'af.*"

"*Kamu lihat Hadi?*" I asked — had he seen Hadi? Because the Japs had pulled him over a few blocks after he'd dumped us out and they'd worked him over for being out after curfew, so apparently he had a limp and couldn't push down the clutch hard enough so the Panhard was always stalling.

"*Baik, dia baik.*"

Hadi was good. But I'd realized that a Javanese would say that even if the guy in question had been dismembered. He stopped the foot-tapping and typed a letter *T.* I asked him who he was writing to.

"*Untuk persetuan pekerjaan.*"

Labour unions — a guy had to figure out some strange words just to live in that house. Then he said that if the PKI wanted to make a trade for Alip they would have to contact the Japs by throwing a brick, *batu-batu,* into the police station and the Japs would post their reply on a *jabatan* — a lamppost? — where many people could read it so that the PKI members would not have to give themselves away. He was all in a lather like they were going to make *him* throw the brick. I asked him what the PKI could trade for Alip.

"*Diam, Tjokro!*" said Sintha. "*Orah!*"

Her hair was down on her shoulders and she wore a black shirt buttoned up to the neck. She was telling him to shut up. He jumped to his feet and his chair crashed over. Then she told him to quit coming over every day and making such a racket, she knew that people were watching the house, didn't he know that? Did he want them to raid her house? *Serangan?* And his pamphlets were wasting everyone's time — she pointed at me and said that they were wasting *my* time — and she hit the typewriter with her fist so his letter to the labour unions was wrecked, then she pulled out the page and held it out to him, and when he took it she stood the chair back up and sat down on it and stared at the wall. Kartinah came in to see what was going on. Sintha said that Tjokro was leaving by the front door, it didn't matter to her if all of Japan was watching. Kartinah put her hand to her throat. She didn't like the sound of that.

So Tjokro played his trump card — he held the paper against his belly and told Sintha what had happened to Alip. It was like watching one of those silent movies, watching their mouths and trying to follow what was going on. She whispered a few things and nodded.

"Alip," said Tjokro, real sad.

Then he shuffled out and said *Selamat tinggal* and Kartinah hollered *Selamat jalan.* She was already back in the kitchen. After a minute we heard the front door close.

"*Orang gila,*" said Sintha.

She got up and made me sit down, then told me that there were PKI who didn't know that I was there coming over for a game of cards, and there wasn't any reason for them to find out so when they came over I would have to hide.

"*Dimana?*" I asked her.

She said the kitchen was no good in case they had to use the *kamar kecil*, so I would have to hide upstairs in her room.

"*Kamar kamu?*"

I'd never seen the upstairs. I slept on the kitchen table. I was supposed to sleep down on the floor but as soon as a guy lay down the rats started to come up out of the drain, so I slept on the table and smelled like garlic in the morning. Kartinah slept on the floor, but she'd done it for years and was used to it.

Sintha crouched down and looked at my foot and asked me, did I know that Sudjangi had been a good husband?

"*Orang bagus*," I agreed. A beautiful man.

Then there was a knock at the front door. I got up from my chair but my sarong caught under one of the legs so it crashed over yet again. Kartinah hustled through from the kitchen, sandals whistling over the concrete. She had coins in her hand.

"Itih."

Sintha got up, apparently to say hello to Itih the egg-peddler woman, but more likely to kick Tjokro in the pants if he was still mooning around. In any case I had to go back and hide in the kitchen.

After a minute they came marching back in, Kartinah cradling two eggs in each hand and Sintha with her hands on her hips asking the old girl how long she'd been running around with a *mata-mata untuk Jepang*, a Jap spy, and not telling PKI about it. Kartinah wiped her nose and said that Itih was a friend of the family.

I asked what was going on.

Sintha rolled her eyes and said that Itih had sold the eggs and then she had asked the two of them if they had any *kabar untuk Jepang*, news for Japan, because the Japanese had raised their price to five rupiah, and Kartinah had been very polite and said sorry, no, not today. That was the part that really made Sintha mad.

Kartinah sniffled again and said that she was sorry, *ma'af*, then she started to crack eggs for our omelette. As a joke I asked her what she would buy with five rupiah, and Sintha jumped in and said that Kartinah would buy a hundred bottles of *temu lawak*, this godawful soda pop made out of potatoes, of all things, that apparently the old girl was crazy over.

I tried to make another joke, but then Sintha started to pinch her fingertips, and Kartinah noticed right away and lost her nerve — she slid the bolt back and ran out into the backyard. I figured that it was the backyard anyway. I'd never been out there.

I sat on the landing and looked down into the room where they were
setting up the poker game, lit by a lantern hanging from the ceiling.
I could see Sintha's little feet beneath her long skirt as she hustled
around. Kartinah scrubbed the table and leaned all of the brooms against
the wall, but Sintha told her to put them in the corners, they didn't look
right all in one spot. The brooms seemed important but they hadn't
said why. Then Sintha saw that I was sitting out in the open and gave
me a look that meant trouble. Kartinah called it the *Iban gila*. The crazy
Borneo look.

So I walked back across the mat that she slept on and climbed back
into her wardrobe behind all the clothes. They weren't on hangers, just
piled up, so I stepped over the first pile and pulled all of Sudjangi's
sarongs in front of me. His black caps for the mosque were on the shelf
above me, plus the white one that his dad had worn after he'd gone to
Mecca. She'd told me all about it. I stuck my finger under the door and
swung it shut.

Through the crack I could see a basket next to the mat with a couple of pencils in it and the drawings of boats that Sudjangi had made.
That was what was left of the guy, like your lampshades with dried
flowers in them. I'd asked Kartinah if Sintha had tried to get his body,
his *mayat*, back from the Japs — I don't know how Sintha would have
gone about it but it seemed like a sensible enough question while we
listened to the rats skitter around in the dark — and Kartinah had said
that if Sudjangi wasn't there to pick her up and carry her around
anymore then Sintha wasn't interested.

I heard one knock at the front door, then another. They sounded a
mile away. Then for a long time it sounded like dance lessons down
there, guys whispering, moving chairs, I kept hearing the word *kancing*,
then the cards shuffled and somebody had a big belly laugh. Tjokro.
Then a bunch of different people were talking loud and serious; I heard
Ibu Pri once or twice. An hour went by with no more knocks at the
door, and I'd shifted my tailbone fifty times by then so I figured that I
could at least step out of the thing and have a stretch. Though for all
I knew Sintha would stab me if she caught me. I walked along the wall
where the boards didn't squeak, then I stretched out across the floor so

that my head hung over the top step and I could just see through the gap. Eight guys and Ibu Pri sat around the table, throwing cards down like crazy. It must've been some kind of rummy. I didn't recognize a few guys. Kartinah squatted in the doorway and Sintha walked in a circle behind everybody so that they held their cards by their chests every time she went around. Jusuf set his cards down in a little pile in front of him, folded his arms and said *Alip?*

Then there was a knock at the door. I could hardly hear it since it was four rooms away but everybody sat up like it was a gunshot. Kartinah shuffled off to answer it while Sintha threw a cloth over all of the cards and Ibu Pri and all of the guys picked up brooms and started sweeping the floor. One guy went into the kitchen and came back with a bucket of water. Then they all stopped and listened to the voice at the front door:

"*Kancing?*" the guy was asking. "*Ada kancing?*"

Then the PKI guys let out a long breath and leaned on their brooms, smiling. *Kancing?* I didn't know it but of course it must've been better than the *orang Jepang* coming to make a *serangan* with bayonets. I had to roll onto my back because the blood was running into my head.

When I looked down again a guy was standing in the doorway holding up a sheet of cardboard covered in buttons, one of the many guys from Ibu Pri's who'd looked like Alip but was shorter than Alip. Sintha tucked some hair behind her ear.

"*Selamat malam,*" said Jusuf.

"*Ada kancing?*" said Tjokro, and held up his own sheet of buttons and Ibu Pri went off to the corner to get hers too, chuckling away. So *kancing* was "button." That must have been their cover for the night if anyone asked why they were in the neighbourhood. They were button salesmen. And the brooms and that? That way if the Japs burst in they'd see everybody scrubbing and cleaning, just a lot of decent citizens spending the evening keeping things neat as a pin for the Emperor. But then if they saw through that, if they saw that were eleven people and only three beds in the house, then they'd lift up the cloth and say, 'Ah-hah! A poker game!' And they'd kick them all out and go away feeling smart as hell and never guess in a million years that they'd been standing in the same room with PKI Soerabaja.

I lay on my back after that and listened to the cards shuffle, and after ten minutes minister-voiced Jusuf said about three words.

Then they all said a lot of things about Alip. I listened for news of *Mas Ari*, too, to hear about all of the work they'd done on behalf of *Mas Ari*, and I listened for your name too, *Lili* — *Lili Brown*, they'd say, and they'd roll out the *R* for half a minute. But they never talked about either one of us, not in a whole half-hour, and I came to the realization that PKI Soerabaja had no reason to stick their necks out for either of us. What did I have to do with smashing Fascism? Nothing. Their lives would've been a hundred times easier if I disappeared into thin air, so why should they want to bring you onboard as well?

"*Mas Mical?*" Tjokro said all of a sudden, just as clear as a bell. "*Mungkin Mical?*"

I went up on one elbow. Maybe Michel for what?

"*Dia penting*," said Beard.

Michel was big? Michel was important?

"*Kita perlu Alip*," Ibu Pri said. "*Kita perlu Alip.*"

They needed Alip. They needed Alip, but maybe Michel? For what? I knew for what — the trade Tjokro had talked about. Throwing a brick at the police department.

"*Kita ada lainnya*," said Jusuf.

They had another? Was he telling them about me?

"*Mas Ari*," said Ibu Pri.

Then there was a lot of fast talking — some guys sounded surprised. Jesus, was that it? Had they sold me out?

"*Ari* —" Jusuf said again.

Then there was a crash of something big hitting the floor, crockery smashing, raised voices. I looked through the gap and Sintha was standing beside the overturned table with her hands folded in front of her and the green and yellow sauces pooling around her feet. Everybody else stood around the edges of the room with their mouths open, except for Kartinah, who hadn't budged an inch. Sintha just stared at the floor.

They stood like that for a minute, everybody watching to see if she'd do anything else, then Jusuf said a few words and Sintha turned and walked into the kitchen leaving green footprints behind her and Tjokro and everybody went for their brooms and buckets and started to clean the place in earnest. Maybe I was wrong about the scrubbing being an act. Maybe the same thing happened every time. Jusuf was on his knees picking up broken bowls. Nobody even said *gila* that time.

There was another knock at the door and Kartinah shuffled past. I didn't hear anyone say *kancing*; it was just Hadi there to pick up Ibu Pri. He limped in and out and she went out after him saying *Rumah sayah, rumah sayah*, my house, like that was where they'd meet for their next friendly game of cards where they always had so much fun and no life-and-death decisions were ever made.

The PKI guys said *Selamat jalan* to her. Then they all stood around muttering about Alip and rubbing the backs of their heads. Tjokro seemed to be pretty upset but nobody was even looking at him. Hell, maybe there were hundreds of Indo words that sounded like 'Alip' and I was just confused. I had a kink in my neck. Most of the guys went out. That left two newer guys, maybe from a different cell, and instead of saying *Alip* and rubbing their heads they said *Ari* a couple of times, and shook hands.

I was halfway into the wardrobe by the time Kartinah got to the top of the stairs with a candle and told me not to bother, it was time to go down to the kitchen table and sleep. I was sitting by the stove when Sintha stepped out of the *mandi*.

"*Selamat tidur*," I told her. Good sleep. I tried to say it so that it'd also sound like *I know all about you people* but I don't know if that came across.

Her hair was wet. She didn't look at me.

Kartinah put the light out and got down on her mat and I asked her if she had heard that they were going turn me in to the Japs so that they could get Alip back.

"*Orah!*" she said. That meant that we shouldn't talk about it.

But she went on to say that in Sudjangi's day she had heard a hundred plans being made in that house, to slow down the shipyards, build *batik* factories, give everyone secret identities, steal the opium tax, and she didn't think it was possible that all of them could have been carried off — did I know that there were women at the market who refused to speak to her because Sintha was her *mem* and Sintha had not been observing the widow's *iddah*? If she wished to behave like she was still in Borneo then she ought to go back to Borneo, that was what the women said — the women who supposedly refused to speak to her — though Tjokro had told Kartinah that even in Borneo no one would dream of behaving as Sintha did. Kartinah was worried she would have to find another market. Did I know that Tjokro's mother was from the Kelabit tribe? They hang money in their ears.

As usual she didn't mind talking so long as she couldn't see me, but then a rat started to chew on the table leg so she had to hurry up and fall asleep or they would keep her up all night.

Sintha didn't say anything in the morning, either, but while we waited for our coffee grounds to settle she did brush her hair right in front of me. Kartinah went to answer the door — it was still hours before Itih came, so I got ready to hide in the *mandi* — and she came back in and said that it was a little boy who had told her to tell Sintha that Jusuf had found a new place on Jalan Ziekenhuis, but it was dirty, *kotor*, and he was going to be speaking to workers at the factory all day — or maybe it was the shipyard — so could Sintha go and clean it up for him.

She asked Kartinah which boy had brought the message and Kartinah said that it was one she'd never seen before.

Sintha asked her whether Jusuf knew that she, Sintha, was not a member of PKI, that it was her husband who had been a member, and it was thanks to the PKI her husband was dead and she, Sintha, was all alone now?

Kartinah said that she didn't know, and crushed a clove of garlic.

I asked Sintha if she was really going to leave the house for the day, and Kartinah jumped in and said yes they were, they had to, both of them. Sintha didn't say anything. She went up the stairs to her room. Kartinah mixed me a drink with red syrup even though it was the last in the bottle, and she dropped a big piece of coconut into it too.

I felt like Edward G. Robinson being served his last meal.

Sintha came down wearing her orange cloth around her head and asked me not to leave the kitchen, they were going to be gone all day. She put her arm through Kartinah's arm and they went out the back door, their sandals slapping. They slid the bolt across from outside. That left me with my glass of red syrup and my old tuxedo pants hanging scrubbed and pressed in the *mandi*. Ibu Pri had brought them over. Of course I could open the bolt from the inside. I could leave whenever I felt like it, but why didn't I? Because maybe the house *was* being watched, and because months before I'd seen Byrnell's legs jerk in the air. If I'd never seen those legs it's possible that I would have done everything differently. I could have been braver. And why not mention Willie in the same breath, poor Willie who was shot and hung up on a fence? Because he'd wanted those things to happen, I was sure of that much. Sometimes a guy just decides to bring it all crashing down on himself.

I was wearing a black shirt of Sudjangi's and I figured that that was as good a colour as any to wear back to prison camp because it wouldn't show the dirt like a white one. But by that logic my old tuxedo pants would be better than the purple-and-white sarong, so I went into the *mandi* and pulled them on. Then I wondered what exactly the Japs would do when they came in. I imagined a lot of guys like Tsuji walking in with their thumbs in their belts.

What had Alip ever done for the PKI? Lots. If they could trade me for him they had every right to. But what if Jusuf really did have a house that needed cleaning?

No, there was no way around it: every one of them had abandoned me and from then on I'd have to scramble up the pile myself, as Ray used to say.

I went upstairs and took one of Sudjangi's boat drawings and a pencil out of the basket and sat down in the kitchen again and wrote *94 Jalan Astana Anyar* on the back of the paper. That was Ibu Pri's address.

I found some cold fried fish and some peanut sauce and I took the cloth off of the bowl of rice. After I ate I moved my stool beside the back door and listened for the one o'clock muezzin. Itih was going to take the address to the Japanese and they would raid Ibu Pri's, and whoever was planning to trade me for Alip would not get the chance to do so. They would be arrested. I'd be all right then. Of course I wasn't sure of the timing of the various raids, that was where it got dicey, but so long as I was trapped in that house it was out of my hands, and I had to do *something*. Maybe I hadn't been Pat Ryan as far as the PKI was concerned but I didn't deserve prison and starvation either. I didn't deserve what Byrnell had got.

Of course Michel was staying at Ibu Pri's, and what would he have said about it if he'd been sitting there? Well, if he had been sitting there everything would have been different, it would've been another situation entirely, so he wouldn't have had anything to say about it. I heard the muezzin call from eight or ten blocks away.

Ash-hadu Aaaallah

I took the scrap of paper that had wrinkled in my hand and walked through the five rooms, one after the other, until I was at the front of the house. There was an old teak desk straight ahead of me, the front door was in the left-hand corner, and a line of little square windows ran along the top of the wall above the desk. There was a quarter-inch gap under the door where I was going to slide the paper through. But I wanted to be sure that Itih had picked it up, I didn't want it blowing off down the street, so instead of putting it through the gap I stood there staring at the back of the door. It was painted white, but there were chinks along the edge that showed it had been green at one time. Still no knock. She should've come by then. I'd made my decision so I expected her to be there.

I climbed on the desk and rubbed the dust off one of the window-panes. I could see the electric wires and the fronts of the houses across the street. An old woman went past leading a buffalo with a cart, and a kid ran by with a kite behind him. I didn't see anybody carrying eggs. The house right across had the same high-up windows as ours, but theirs had pink curtains. If somebody *was* watching our house, then where were they? The dust on those windows smelled like old underwear. It was hot in there, especially up high, and the sweat ran out of my hair.

There was a knock at the door. *Tok tok tok.* I stayed up on the desk. "*Itih disini,*" a voice said. "*Ada telur-telur.*"

Itih's here. Eggs for sale.

But what if there was no trade at all? What if I had imagined it? And what if the Japs rounded up everybody at Ibu Pri's and only then found out that PKI Soerabaja also worked out of our house, and that was it for all of us? I'd feel pretty rotten then. I didn't want them to get me or Kartinah or Sintha.

So I watched the end of the buffalo cart go past and rolled the paper into a ball. Five rupiah Itih wouldn't be getting. *Dia ada tidak lima rupiah.*

She knocked once more.

Tok.

I put my face against the window and watched her back moving away up the street. She wore a purple blouse and had her hair in a bun. I noticed that the pink curtains across the street had been pulled back. No, they were closed! No, maybe they hadn't moved at all.

I dropped onto the desk. My stomach did not feel good about those curtains. I wanted to look again but of course that was the worst possible idea.

I sat on my stool by the back door. Sweat ran down the backs of my legs but I didn't take a *mandi*. If someone came into the house I wanted to know it.

The bolt slid across in the back door. I jumped off the stool and waited beside the table. Sintha came in, a big smile, all whispers — she had food for my dinner and Kartinah was still at Jusuf's so Sintha was going to cook it herself. She put the bag on the table and a cone-shaped tomato rolled out.

She took the cloth off her head and left it on the stairs.

"*Itih datang disini?*"

I told her that I didn't know whether Itih had come.

She put the pan on the stove and started chopping. I told her I'd make tea but she put some hair behind her ear and told me no, it was all right. Then she unfolded the front of her sarong and pulled out the side to fold it again, and I saw the skin at the bottom of her back. She looked back at me looking at her. Then she walked around the table to get a different knife and started pinching her fingertips, one hand and then the other.

The stuff in the pan crackled away. The line of daylight faded around the back door and she asked me to light the lantern, then she leaned on the table and asked where I wanted to eat dinner.

"*Tidak apa-apa,*" I said. It didn't matter.

"*Kamar saya?*" In her room?

She stood up straight and looked right at me, then she walked around the table and put her little hands around my face. She kissed my mouth. Then I kissed her. Her whole head seemed so small. We got our mouths sideways and kissed like that for a while. I put my hands around her ribs. She wouldn't let go of my face, she had her fingertips in my ears and her thumbs dug into my cheeks. I put my hand up her shirt and a nipple pressed against my palm. She knocked her upper lip against mine, she kissed with her mouth open, then she kissed all over my face and stuck her tongue up my nose. I could smell her hair again, like glue, and I kept one hand on her back and moved the other across her nipples. Then she held my wrists and looked at me for a second in the yellow light. She took a long breath in. I just watched her upper lip. Then she put her hand down the front of my pants and squeezed my mister right at the bottom. I had to steady myself against the table. She knocked her lip against my nose.

"*Kamar saya.*" That meant her room. Then she whispered half a dozen other things that I didn't understand at all.

I kept one hand down the back of her sarong as we went up the stairs. It wasn't quite dark up there. The tuxedo pants were so big that I stepped right out of them, then she had both of her hands around my mister and next thing she was flat on her back and I was on my knees overtop of her. She ran her hands up my stomach.

"*Bagus,*" she said.

She put her hand around my mister again and it was inside her just like that. I looked at the top of her head, the tawny line of her part. I couldn't figure out what my bottom half was doing, it felt like my mister was floating in something. I didn't want to move it. But she wrapped her legs around my waist and started pulling me in and pushing me away, I heard her saying *huff huff* and lights floated inside my head. The mat scraped my knees. I opened my eyes and saw her front teeth and her eyes wide open. The word "fucking" went through my head, then the light flashed in front of my eyes. I was done. But she kept going, the corners of her heels in my back, she went *huff huff huff*. Then she stopped too.

I rolled off her. Her hair was stuck to her face. I put my shoulder down on the mat and she moved against me so that my leg was between her legs and I could feel her hairs down there. My mister was sticky as all hell. She reached into the wardrobe and I watched her breast stretch out, her nipple pointing at the corner of the ceiling. She unfolded a sarong and spread it over us.

It was hot in Sintha's room. The light was grey when I woke up and the sarong was down around my feet. She was sitting up on the mat with her hair hanging over her face, running her fingers across my chest. I wanted some coffee with the grounds floating on the top. Her nipples had gone flat — in fact her chest didn't look all that different from mine. I kissed a triangle on her hand.

"*Apa kamu mau tatu?*" she asked.

"*Mungkin.*"

Did I want a tattoo? Maybe.

She got up. I watched her bottom as she stepped into a sarong. She went downstairs. Kartinah must've been back because a second later I heard her howling at the lady of the house — there may have been words in the howl but I couldn't make out any of them. Maybe Kartinah thought that she and I couldn't be friends anymore, and she was probably worried what the neighbours would think, though if it weren't for the howling they wouldn't have had any idea that anything had happened. I realized she must have come home in time to take the pan off the stove, because the house hadn't burnt down. All of a sudden there was a *bang* like a chair hitting the wall, and the howling stopped.

I sat up. But then I could hear them both muttering, Sintha was saying *jarum* like she was looking for some, whatever it was. I ran my hand along the lines that mat had pressed into my back. My crotch was still stuck together. I heard somebody on the stairs so I pulled the sarong over me, but it was Sintha carrying a glass of coffee and a banana-leaf basket. She still wasn't wearing a shirt. That would've been enough to make Kartinah howl.

I leaned back on my elbow and drank the coffee while she unloaded her basket — a cold lantern, a mallet, a bowl, a chopstick, half a dozen needles, string. *Jarum*, that meant needle. She tied the needles to the chopstick so they stuck off the end at a right angle, then she opened the lantern and dumped the soot in the bowl. I wiped the coffee grounds off my lip.

She pushed me down on my back and pulled her sarong up between her knees and sat across my stomach. She spat in the bowl and mixed it into the soot with the end of her chopstick.

"*Dengarlah*," she said. Listen.

She asked if I knew that her mother was from the Iban tribe.

I told her I'd heard that. She held out her hand and I kissed it.

Her tattoos were *song irang*, she said. They show that a woman can take care of a man and have children.

She traced a circle over my chest with her finger — over my throat, down to one nipple, across to the other, up to my throat. The bones were sticking out of my chest like I was corduroy.

This will stand for the garing tree, she told me. You will be like that tree.

"*Mengapa?*"

How come?

"*Tidak pernah mati.*"

Because they never die.

I put my hand in the middle of her chest, between her breasts, but she lifted it off and set it on the mat. She pushed her needles around in the bowl of soot. I liked the weight of her sitting on top of me.

"*Diam*," she said.

She held the chopstick over my face, then touched the needles to the base of my throat. They were cold. She tapped the needles with the mallet — it felt like a bug bite. She ran the needles through the soot again and licked her lips.

"*Diam*," she told me again.

I kept waiting for the needles to come away dripping blood but they never did. She told me that when her mother lived in Borneo the Iban women still did the tattooing, but nowadays it was the men. I told her that was too bad. After a while she held up a mirror — I had a black line between my collar bones and the skin was puffed up like a spider had been biting it. That was the start of the circle that eventually was going to look like a garing tree that never died.

"*Apa kamu tidak pernah mati?*"

I was asking if *she* would never die. That was what I meant to ask, anyway.

"*Mungkin.*"

And maybe she wouldn't.

Of course to you my question must sound as though I were inviting her to go on living forever *with me*, just as we were, with our shirts off, and cast Mrs. Winslow to the four winds. Of course I didn't mean that. At any rate, we'll never know if I did.

I reached for one of her breasts but she caught my hand and put it on the mat again. Then there was another crash downstairs, it had to be Kartinah dropping something, though it sounded like it had come from the front of the house rather than the back. And after a second Kartinah hollered *apa?* up the stairs, so it hadn't been her at all.

Sintha sat up, listening. Her eyes flicked around.

Then it came again, once, twice, a pounding. That little mirror shook on the floor. She got up and put on a shirt and handed me my pants.

Two more times. *Bam. Bam*. At the front door. I couldn't sort out which leg went where. Who else could it be but the Japanese? And what could I do but run with my arms flapping? They hadn't yet caught me on dry land, though Ma herself had told me I'd have better luck at sea.

"*Mecahkan pintu*," said Sintha.

Breaking the door. She went down the stairs and I finally stepped into the right leg and went after her. She was waiting at the bottom and pushed me towards the back door. Every plate on the table was jumping. *Bam. Bam.* Kartinah slid back the bolts. Then there was a crash from the front of the house like a car going through a telephone pole, and the lamp swung like a pendulum. Kartinah pulled the door open and Sintha pushed me out.

"*Lari!*" they hollered.

Run. Of course, run. But it was so bright out there that it was like jumping into the sun, and after three steps I could only stand there and blink. It was a backyard after all, with cement tiles instead of grass and a clothesline running down the side with one black shirt hanging from it — Sudjangi's shirt that I'd been wearing the night before. When had Kartinah washed that?

I took two steps and fell on my face. Something had tripped me. I looked over my shoulder and saw a Japanese soldier in a tan uniform standing above me. I tried to get up but he hit me in the small of the back with something and I fell on my face again. I heard Sintha start to shriek. I looked over my shoulder again, just long enough to see him lift his rifle butt into the air, then I felt it come down on my left leg.

The Jap went *hmf.*

I didn't feel pain right then so much as the sensation that something wrong had happened — something had moved inside my leg that shouldn't have been moved.

Then I felt him do it again.

There was an anthill between the two tiles in front of me, and a little further on a plant that looked like a dandelion. I could still hear Sintha. She must've been standing right next to the *mandi.*

I remembered that I was supposed to be running so I pulled my good leg under me and tried to get to my feet, but then some more soldiers were there. They took hold of me under the armpits and carried me right out of the yard. We went through a gate into an alley full of long yellow grass. In all those weeks I'd never seen it. A cat ran along the roof of the house opposite.

A truck with the red sun on the door drove up. Its engine rattled like the seals needed oil and the long grass had to bend under its bumper. There were a lot of different Jap letters written on the bottom of the door and I wondered if they all meant *kill.*

The Jap pulled the pin out of the tailgate and let it drop. They carried me around and I looked into the back. Michel was sitting on the bench. He had a fat lip. I thought that it couldn't be him. I figured that it had been so long since I'd seen another white guy that they all looked the same.

The Japs helped me onto the tailgate, then I used my good leg to push myself backwards on my behind until they could close it again. I cooperated. What else was I going to do, run? They tied down the canvas, which took a minute. Then I heard them walking off, the grass whispering. One of them belched.

The guy who may or may not have been Michel peered down at me. He swallowed.

"Where is Alip?" he asked.

I just stared for a while. It was him. But I couldn't believe that they'd caught him. They'd caught me too, of course, but I was just a regular guy.

"I never saw Alip."

I didn't sound normal. My voice sounded like a record.

"Then there has been a mistake." He leaned back against the bench. "It was to have been *me* for Alip. You know nothing about it?"

I couldn't get my brain around that. I tried to prop myself up so that I'd be ready when the truck started moving. I could hear a woman calling somewhere in the neighbourhood and it might have been Sintha, I couldn't tell. I started to wonder where the truck would take us.

"Are they going to kill us?" I said.

"Oh," he said. "It is difficult to know." He scratched his forearm. "I wonder if you remember how they killed the marshal."

"Firing squad."

"Yes!" I could see his white teeth in the gloom. "Firing squad."

Of course we never got the firing squad. That worked out well for you and me, but for a long time I used to think that it was too bad for Michel, because he really would've enjoyed that.

It was Michel's last night in Changi Jail. He'd gone under the wire on one of his missions and I had told him I'd stay awake until he got back. I was having a hell of a time doing it, though, because limping around for sixteen hours a day was taking it out of me like never before. I lay on my mat in our little hut near the fence, and the moon was coming in the doorway bright enough that I could spot any ants who came in under the mosquito net and squash them with my thumb. They gave a very satisfying crunch, and even though in an earlier camp I wouldn't have wasted a second in popping them in my mouth, I didn't have to do that. In Changi things were good, and you would've thought the same if you'd been the places I had. The Japs had brought me back to Singapore of their own volition, after all my plans to come by dinghy.

Killing ants was my job in our hut, just as providing food and shelter was Michel's. Beri-beri had screwed up my eyesight, and Michel had tried like hell to get me a pair of glasses but apparently there was a market shortage. I didn't need them to see the ants anyway because they were coming in six inches from my head and in the moonlight they stood out plain as day.

But then I woke up and found a dozen of them running over my hand like it was a playground designed with them in mind. I shook them off and stuck my hands in my armpits, even though it was hot and awful under there, and I blinked my eyes and ground my teeth and I told myself I was staying awake, under no circumstances would I be asleep when Michel came back in. I owed him, for one thing, and I wanted to know, very badly, sweetheart, if he'd found out anything, and for a third thing I was going to have umpteen-dozen nights to sleep and doze and roll around and pick my nose without anybody to wait up for once he was gone and I was on my own.

He and I had arrived a month before, thrown into a tent with a lot more Aussies, and Michel had slipped under the wire on the very first night and on every night since. A sergeant named Smith had initially told us that if a guy ducked under near Selarang Barracks he'd end up right on the road, and from there he could go down to the fishing village or all the way into town and in either case there were always plenty of ditches to hide in. If my leg had been better, who knows — I might've walked into the Raffles myself and gone gliding around the dance floor. Even so, I never liked the idea of Michel going on his own.

"They cannot keep track of ten thousand men," he'd said. "Koon Eng and Eu Chin told me the names of many men here. Perhaps they can help a little."

Despite my best efforts I could never stay awake to find out where exactly he'd been on any given night, and in the morning he was always up and raring to go, having somebody to confer with away on the other side of camp, and I'd try to tag along but at the speed I travelled I always ended up meeting him as he was coming back, and more often than not he'd have a scrap of beef or something in his pocket which meant that lunch was taken care of. The first few times I'd asked where in hell it had come from. What had he said?

"It is only what we deserve."

After bad eyes, bad knee and the Java Sea I wasn't going to argue.

I'd dozed off. I rolled onto my belly, peered at the floorboards and resumed the slaughter. Then I heard somebody shuffling across the gravel outside, and Michel never shuffled so I figured it must be Glad Tidings.

A hand pulled up the mosquito net, then he hustled in and tugged the net down behind him. He was that rarest sort of Jap who really was good as gold, like that old naval captain off Celebes, and for some reason of his own he'd taken us under his wing, though don't think for one second that he'd made me forget about the one who'd tried to chop my leg in half in Soerabaja, because that one cast a very long shadow.

"*Bonsowa-ru*," I said.

The nighttime bugs and birds went right on whistling and croaking.

"Oh, lying here waiting for the Nips to bow and scrape for you," an Aussie voice said. "Just as I've been ruddy saying, the two of you haven't any cause to be in here with us."

His face loomed up so I could see its black outline against the mosquito netting: Don the moron, vice-chancellor of the Changi Hygiene Squad or some goddamn thing. We'd slept on the floor of his shed when we'd first arrived.

"Well, Don," I said, "the fact is that we're not in with you. We're over here on our own."

"Where's your mate?" he asked.

"Out and about. Did you know I'm tired, Don, and I want to go to sleep?"

"Where is he, then?"

"I'm not his mother, Don." There was something about his name that it sounded like an insult every time a guy said it. "Are *you* his mother? I'm not."

"I didn't expect he'd be in here. Did you know, it'll be the best ruddy thing that ever happened to you when he's gone? Even Holmes has taken notice, and you'll be dragged down with him. You want a trip to Outram Road? I wouldn't reckon you'd last an hour over there, the shape you're in."

The net swayed — he was shouting at me! But Don's buddy Chester was going under the wire on a regular basis as well, that was well known, so I couldn't figure why he had such a witch in his niche. Ah, but what was that smell? Liquor.

"I'm tired, Don. I want to go to sleep."

I figured that if I really did fall asleep he just might go away, so I put my head on my arm, squeezed my eyes shut and flexed both my feet for a ten count. My stomach gave a little flip when I realized that right at that moment Michel might already be on his way back with his news, though I was still wrestling with the idea that I might be better off not knowing.

"If you must know, I've come over just now to inform you that there is no chance of you being allowed to reside in here on your own, and should you come bowing and scraping to bunk in our place again the answer will be a flat ruddy 'no.' So you'd best hatch other plans. Your reputation precedes you."

"My gimpy leg?"

A big sigh. That swayed the net too.

"I don't envy you that. I don't. Honestly. We're just after a little breathing room in there. After this next lot goes you'll have no trouble bunking somewhere. But leave us some space, won't you? Bluey's not long for it."

"He isn't?"

Someone else was shuffling across the gravel — *this* had to be Glad Tidings.

"*Bonsowa-ru*," he whispered from the step.

"Oh, this is rich," said Don. "Holmes ought to be here for this. Hello, mate, I trust you're here on business of the Imperial Army?"

Glad Tidings stood looking down at Michel's empty mat.

"*Mikel-san?*" he asked.

"Sorry," I said. "He's not here."

"This … is … *rich!*" Don announced.

"Okay," said Glad Tidings.

He knelt over Michel's mat and made sure the netting was tucked in all around it. He came in and did that every night. He had a soft spot for Michel.

"Okay," he said again. He got up, bowed to me, and went out.

I listened to him walk off and waited for Don to chime in again. But it was quiet. Just the bugs and birds. One bird kept going *cheet cheet cheet* without changing, like it thought it was the second hand on a watch.

I sat up on my mat so that I wouldn't fall asleep again. Michel had been gone for a long time. In the morning he would be leaving Changi, the lucky stiff, with a few hundred other guys bound for who knows where. My stomach did another flip-flop when I thought that doing this favour for me might somehow keep him from going.

But then over the *cheet cheet cheet* I heard his feet on the gravel, he walked faster than anybody, and a second later he came under the netting and lay down on his mat. He was breathing hard, and there seemed to be something on the side of his head that he kept trying to wipe away. I stretched out on my mat too; it didn't seem like he'd found out anything encouraging. Finally his breathing slowed down and lay his hands flat on the floor.

"I saw her," he said. "She is there."

"She is?" I sat up again. I thought I might be sick. "Jesus Christ, I figured you'd had nothing but a runaround! How'd she look, did you talk to her? Is she all right?"

"She is fine." He was still just staring at the goddamn ceiling! "She looks … yes, she looks fine."

"And what else, is her mother in there too?"

"Oh, yes. Mrs. Brown. They were all in good spirits."

"And did she say anything to you? Jesus H. Christ, was it even *her*? How could you be sure? I mean —"

"I found the women's camp. It is not far away. Two miles. Perhaps three."

"Two or three *miles*?"

"Yes, on your leg I suppose that is too far."

"Just tell what happened."

He rolled on his side to face me.

"I went through the wire. That was not difficult. It was the same as here. I waited in the shadows, and when a group of women went by I called to them. I thought that if I called to one she might scream, but that a few women together would not. And I was right."

"Women! You saw a bunch of white women! And she was one of them?"

"No. I did as you said. I asked for two women, a mother and daughter, one named Winslow and the other named Brown, and that I had come on behalf of the husband who was ill."

"But you didn't make like I was dying, did you? Did you tell her that?"

"No. And the women said that they knew the two I mentioned very well, and if I would wait where I was they would bring them to me. They walked away rather slowly, so that if you had watched them you would not have known they were excited, but from the way they held each other's hands I think they were quite terrified."

"And?"

"After eight or nine minutes they came. Two of them, and they were holding hands as well. They looked to be very well."

"And you told Lily I'd sent you. You saw Lily!"

I was hopping up and down as I sat there, sweetheart, my bad knee didn't like it but I did it anyway, and I could feel a grin way out in my ears.

"Yes. There was some confusion at first." He put his hand out and crushed an ant. "The mother thought that — Marguerita, she is the mother?"

"That sounds right."

"Marguerita thought I had come from *her* husband. She was very disappointed. But your wife was pleased."

"That was *it*? What did she say?"

"She kissed me."

"She did? Where?"

"Here."

He pointed to his cheek, just in front of his ear. I leaned across and put my hand on the spot. He was sweaty. I wondered if you could feel that I was touching the spot.

"Good." I leaned back. "All right."

"And after that I had to leave them. They said, they said that the guards would be coming around, and I, you know, there was nothing more I could do for them."

"Why? What's the matter?"

"Nothing! Oh, no, nothing! I said that your leg was troubling you or you would have come yourself, and that we had been looking for her all across the Indies."

"And you gave her my love?"

"And I gave her your love. She said to give you her love. Then I had to go. Marguerita sent you her love as well."

"But how was Lily, what'd she look like?"

He lay there, with a speck of moonlight shining on his forehead. I watched the ants scurry in one after another.

"I have been running all night," he said. "I am tired."

"I thought you just went there and back."

"I have been running all night. We will talk more tomorrow."

What else could I do? He'd done me a favour. You weren't dead, you weren't in Java, you weren't in Sumatra, you weren't in Australia, you were just across the rice paddies in the women's camp. It was the best news I'd had in a year and a quarter. If something wasn't sitting right it was because I'd expected Michel and I to sit up all night, talking it over again and again. But the lucky stiff was tired, that was all right. He had places he had to go. And it was better I stayed in Singapore, knowing what I knew.

I woke up the next morning and remembered it was his last

morning in Changi, and it gave me that feeling I used to have as a kid when I'd wake up on a January morning and realize that Christmas had come and gone. Just a feeling in my chest. Michel stood up above me on his tiptoes. He'd stashed the netting away in the corner and was tucking dry leaves into some gaps in the thatch. I sat up and yawned and tried to stretch the knee without hurting it too much. He looked down at me. He did look tired. He'd seen you in the women's camp. How did you feel waking up that morning? For me it was still sinking in — half my brain immediately said not to believe it, Michel had only said those things so I'd be less miserable with him gone. But he'd learned your mother's name!

"There is still breakfast," he said.

There was a mess tin full of soup. I slid over and drank it all in one go — it had that bitter taste that meant he'd scrounged some honest-to-goodness vegetables from somewhere. Vitamins and minerals.

"*Siap?*" he asked.

"*Siap*," I said. I only had about four words of Indo left by then.

He put his bag over his shoulder and went out onto the path. I had to hustle like hell with my stick to keep up with him because once he decided he was on his way there was never any waiting around. I kept my eyes on the back of his brown Aussie shorts and tried not to trip over the roots that were always shooting up out of the ground.

"You're taking the wrong way," I said.

"I will stop to see Bluey."

Bluey lived further from the gate then we did. He was the Aussie sailor that we had shipped off of Java with, aboard the *Tohohashi Maru*, the three of us and five hundred other guys, all surrendered troops, and thanks to God-knows-what planning Michel and I got lumped in with them as usual. I'd asked around if anybody had seen any British women loitering around Java and none of the Aussies had been near a civilian camp. Bluey and I had both had the Onepenny Trots and Twopenny Trots aboard the *Tohohashi Maru* so we'd been chasing each other up and down the rusty ladder all night and every night, racing for the *benjo*, though his eyes had gone in the six months he'd been at Tasikmalaja so he had to squint like hell just to find the rungs. No cricket was played on that boat, and I never did figure out the difference between Onepenny and Twopenny. They were both bad.

Then in Changi my eyes had gone too. Beri-beri — maybe girls at your camp had it too. I'd gone to the hospital as soon as the palm trees started to blur together, and the doc had told me that I was doing not too badly, in fact, because my skin hadn't swelled with water. I asked him if that was worse than going blind and he said that certainly it was. He was a short Limey with a beard. He said that I couldn't just eat rice all the time, that I had beri-beri because of malnutrition. He put me on the scale and I weighed a hundred and three pounds; he'd told me to eat as many tapioca greens as I could, then he'd had to go because some guy was screaming. I'd been happy just to not have scurvy, that made a guy's teeth fall out, and once I told Michel I needed greens there was no shortage of them. They'd told us on the *Tohohashi* that we were healthy specimens who were going to be sent out on work parties once we got to Singapore, so Bluey and I figured that we were a pretty good joke on the Imperial Army because we were good for nothing. But Michel was going on a work party.

Bluey always sat propped on his bunk in one of the little Aussie huts, he said there was no point in his going to the hospital because he was "plain crook," and of course if he wasn't going on a truck he must've been. The top of my foot was scraped bare from dragging it over hell's half-acre, so he didn't have to tell me who was crook.

"I'll take your word for it." That was always Bluey's line. His eyes were as bad as they could get.

There'd been a guy in Bluey's shed called Wilf who'd gone into the hospital with a cough like his lungs were going to fall out, and he'd asked me to look after his record player, run it a couple of times every day so that it wouldn't break down in the humidity, that had been Wilf's biggest concern. I know — a record player, a big event! Cable the prime minister! But I'll tell you what records he had: The Singing Stockmen. Art Leonard. Tex Morton, The Yodelling Boundary Rider. I could read record labels, unfortunately; my problem was that I couldn't see distance. I couldn't see eight feet.

The Japs didn't mind a record player — the guards there were all

Korean, incidentally, a guy could pick them out from a star on the collar if a guy could see that far — it was a *radio* that we weren't supposed to have, the same as in Pelayaran, and I knew we had a radio at Changi but no one would tell me where it was hidden. Anyway, when Wilf died his regiment had come in and claimed the record player as their own.

When he heard us coming in Bluey sat straight up in bed, squeaked all his springs. Yeah, a whole bed! Some Aussie who was being shipped away with F Force had given it to him when we'd first arrived. Michel was going on H Force — if they ever needed me and Bluey, Jesus, it would have to be XYZ Force.

"That's the Marshal, is it?" said Bluey. He wiped his mouth with the back of his hand. "I know what's going to happen to you."

"What is it that will happen to me?"

Michel sat across from him on Damian's bed — Damian who'd crept through the fence to the native village down on the beach and brought back a bunch of dried fish. Michel had bought all of them. Damian was on H Force too, he must've left for the gate already.

"They're trading the lot of you for Aussie wool," Bluey said. "No, I'm not off my nut! They've no textiles in Japan any longer. The BBC said that! Oh, cripes." He whispered it. "BBC said that. Won't be long before the Nips'll be running around starkers. No, you'll do all right."

Michel smiled at me.

"They will send me to Australia?"

"No, no. Never. Portuguese East Africa they'll send you. Neutral port there, that's where they'll do the switch."

"That's the new borehole?" I asked.

"Harry? Didn't see you. Lord, no, it's more than borehole. It'll happen. They picked these lads to go free."

"They told them that they're getting on a train," I said.

"Aw, they tell them a whole lot of things."

"I got news about the women's camp," I said.

"Have you?" asked Bluey. "What's the time now? Don't let them shift without you."

Michel got up. I could see the outlines of guys walking past the hedge.

"Best of luck," said Bluey.

The front gate of the camp was open so we walked right out across the pavement. There had to be two dozen trucks parked in the road, and I could see from the waving arms that most of them were full already. Guys lined up for *tenko* behind the truck in front of us, and some guy seemed to be walking around them taking pictures — I could hear the clicking every time he wound his film. He wore a fedora or something, and he was taller than any of the Japs who stood around. A truck pulled out of line and went off down the road. The guys in the back cheered.

"So you won't need those things?" I asked.

He was leaving half of his stuff behind — his shaving brush and the mosquito net and his *Town Talk* tobacco tin that the ants could never break into.

"No, of course not."

He was looking up at the coconut palms.

"Well, you come back here anytime," I told him. "You've been a real good customer."

"It is too bad. Your leg."

We shook hands — we didn't hold our elbows or anything, we just did it like two white men. Everybody else seemed to be in line already. His hand was twice the size of mine. I'd never noticed it before.

"*Selamat jalan.*"

"Oh, *tinggal*," he said. "You know, I have been thinking that you have been a better friend to me than Mills."

I looked at the marks my toes had made in the dirt.

"How's that?" I asked.

"Because you have stayed alive all of this time. You have tried very hard."

"Thanks for going to find her," I said. "That was awfully good of you."

"Yes," he said. "Okay."

He nodded a couple of times, then walked across and stood in *tenko*. None of the Japs seemed bothered that I was standing there. After a second he clambered up into the truck with the rest of them, their canteens all banging against each other, but I couldn't tell if he was looking in my direction. The guy with the camera kept backing up, taking pictures of the whole road full of trucks. It looked like he was a white guy. The tires started to roll over the asphalt and the Aussies hollered unkind things about Changi. I listened to that for a minute, then the engines faded away and all I heard was bugs. The Japs stood around beating the dust off their uniforms. The guy with the fedora came closer.

"Look at this," he said. "Harry?"

You'll never believe who it was. Take a second to think, but you won't ever guess. It was Jimmy off *Asia*. He wore a grey suit and white shirt and black tie and that grey fedora.

"Why, it's Jimmy," I said.

"Harry, you look like a heap of shit. I mean that genuinely."

His accent sounded grand no matter what he said. He looked at me through his camera like he was going to take a picture, then brought it down again. Gave me a wink.

"Wouldn't do to waste film. I'm on the *Shonan Shimbum* now."

"The which?"

"Didn't suppose you could read yet. Lord, won't you take a look at you." He peered through his camera again. "I write articles telling the liberated peoples how the British root in their own filth."

I dragged my stick over the gravel.

"That's dandy."

"And if I'm ever at a loss for material I only need to think back to your bloody underclothes hanging over my head. You might've washed them in soap and water, couldn't you? Bloody animal."

This from the guy who'd vomited across the cabin floor! I went on squinting at him.

"It is a *treat* to see you," he said. "I'd never have reckoned you could come any further down in the world."

"I've looked out for myself all right."

"Bwa-hah!"

He turned around and went back to the Japs, then he must've been pointing me out, telling them about me, it was all in Japanese but he said, "*Empress of Asia*," I caught that. They all had a laugh. A couple of Japs were pushing the gate shut so I had to go back in and then I couldn't tell which of them was Jimmy anymore.

It took me half an hour to get from the front gate all the way back to the garden, and in the meantime guys with amputations were passing me right and left. There must've still been a couple of thousand of us, some living in the old prison building that the Limeys had used in their time; a few hundred guys lived in there with the doors flung open and the rest of us were camped out in huts and lean-tos for a mile around it. It was a hundred times bigger than Pelayaran and a hundred times better, because Elephant hadn't bashed any of us over the head as we came through the gate. I tried to tell some Changi guys about that but they didn't want to hear it, they were too busy telling us about one time when a Korean got drunk and slapped them on the arm.

But they emptied their *benjo* onto the garden the same as at Pelayaran, and you should've seen those tapioca plants take off — they would've made your wisteria look anemic. The garden was on a hillside with the edge of the jungle across the top. I started in our regular row. I didn't mind weeding, it was fresh air if nothing else, and there were bugs but the bites didn't usually swell up too badly.

We had a committee to divvy them up once the plants were full-grown, but I hadn't ever been too concerned about that. Michel had provided.

A pair of feet in wooden sandals walked by in the next row.

"That Changi Dave?" I asked.

"It's *David.*"

"Changi Dave."

I'd chatted with him before on days when Michel had been elsewhere. He hunkered down, his back tanned as dark as a Negro's.

"Has your accomplice departed then?"

"They've all buggered off," I said. "You hear this thing about the wool?"

"Portuguese East Africa? Who fed you that one? He's having you on. They've gone north to build a bloody great railroad."

"How come you couldn't go, you crook or something?"

"They had me out at Outram Road and broke both of my arms. I mended. But they don't look to me anymore. Most likely they don't want any more officers mucking things up."

"You're an officer?"

"Lieutenant Putnam."

"I didn't figure you for one."

"Thanks very much."

"I ought to call you Outram Road Dave."

"I imagine you'll do what suits you."

He kept going up his row and I stood for a while to stretch out the knee. He came back down the next row. He was probably the best weeder in camp.

"My mates have gone north too," he said. "We enlisted together and all of it."

"I met Michel way over on Celebes. Hell of a long time ago."

"Dutch, is he?"

"He's a Frenchman."

"Is he really?" He stood up with weeds in his hands. "How'd he get out here, came down from Indochina?"

Of course Michel had given me the names of the shipping line and the boat and everything, but I couldn't remember them.

"He came east because his grandpa had come east," I said. "That was how he made it sound."

I hunkered back down in the tapioca. I was out there to keep busy after all.

"Didn't he ever bend your ear about it?" I asked.

"No, I never knew him. Huh."

"He could spin quite a yarn, Michel Ney."

"What, is that his name?"

"That's his name, sure."

"The same as Napoleon's marshal?"

Jesus, it was heart-breaking that the two of them had never met, they would've hit it off like gangbusters.

"That's him," I said. "The one who retreated."

"Oh, certainly not every time! *Imagine* having the same name as him, I've seen the statue on the Boulevard St-Michel! But I must tell you — I actually went to school with a boy who was on that retreat from Moscow! No, God no, sorry — let me think about it."

He stood there with his chin in his hand.

"A boy called Philip Conrad, whom I was at school with, his *great-great-great-uncle* was on the retreat. You must know Joseph Conrad, who wrote all the books about the sea, that was his *grandfather*."

"What about Gordon Sinclair?"

"I'm not familiar with him."

"He wrote *Cannibal Quest*."

"Joseph Conrad's great-uncle served in one of these Polish regiments Napoleon took into Russia — of course the Conrads themselves are Polish — and on the retreat they starved out in the snow like Ney and the rest, lunacy to invade at that time of year —"

"So this Conrad shook hands with the Marshal or something?"

"No, his uncle *ate a dog*! Came across it in a village, didn't have any choice, cooked the thing up, and *I* went to Regent Street Polytechnic with his, what was it?" He counted on his fingers. "His great-great-grand-nephew, what do you think of that?"

"I ate two seagulls."

He smeared the dirt between his hands.

"Did you."

He kept going down the row and after a while I heard him talking to another guy. Lieutenant Dave must've figured that the only good story was the one he was telling. Michel would've liked that one about the dog, though, even if I couldn't quite piece it out. Dave came back along the hill — he was three rows across by then.

"What's the buddy of yours doing now?" I asked. "The school chum or whoever he was."

"Who, Philip? I suppose he might have enlisted — what form was he in? No, he'll enlist next year. Wanted to go in the navy. Out to sea the same as his granddad."

Boy, that would've tickled Michel all the way to Portuguese East Africa.

"But still, a *dog*," said Changi Dave. "Wait on a moment." He stood up. "I feel like my head's come off — you said Michel Ney?"

"Just like the marshal."

"Well, bloody hell! Isn't he the opium chap?"

"I don't have the foggiest what you're talking about."

"The devil you don't! Bald chap, about so high, arrived with the *Tohohashi Maru?*"

"No, no," I said, "our boat was the —"

"He's the one with all of these connections in the town, raiding these warehouses, apparently, informing on his rivals or what have you. Making a fortune from the sounds of it! Barber heard he was even paying some Jap bugger to come and tuck him in at night, and Takahashi came in yesterday and demanded to know how we could let it all go on under our noses! We've just had a lovely chat, haven't we? You've been laughing up your sleeve all this time!"

That did make sense. Koon Eng and Eu Chin and the rest of it — how else had we got meat with every meal? I'd thought we'd just been lucky. That people had felt generously disposed towards us.

"No, sir," I said. "It isn't the same guy."

"Winslow," he said, "how can you sit there and lie to my face?"

"Well, I can't exactly see you, Lieutenant. My eyesight is —"

"Get out of my sight. Go."

That was just as well. The knee was seizing up and I needed to eat. Needed my vitamins. I went down the row with the plants brushing my ankles.

"And fancy your saying we'd be great chums!" he said. "Now, hold on, Winslow. What have you got in your pocket?"

A guy wasn't technically allowed to take the tapioca leaves whenever he needed them — they had their committee, after all.

"Doctor's orders," I said.

"Holmes will hear about it."

I carried on down the hill. I walked back past the prison building and got a whiff of the cigarettes they were smoking in there. I needed to reach our hut and just shut my eyes. My stick was starting to crack at the bottom — I'd have to find somebody to cut me a new one. I should have got Michel to bring me a dozen right off the bat.

We'd had a pot and a coal burner but I'd made Michel take them with him. They had a hotplate in Bluey's they could run if the electricity came on, I could boil the tapioca leaves there but then that would mean sharing them out, or I could just borrow a pot from someone and build a fire underneath it on my own.

Koon Eng and Eu Chin and the rest of it. Generously disposed.

Then I wondered what you'd be eating over there in Women's Camp. I felt light-headed when I thought of it. He'd never told me if you were sick or still pretty or one-legged or what. Women's Camp. I pictured lacy curtains in all the windows.

Our hut didn't look right as I came around the corner, though I couldn't see why exactly until I came right up to it. Half of the roof was gone. The thatch lay scattered all over the ground. I looked in the doorway. Two guys were crouched on either side of a fire right in the middle of the floor, fanning it with a piece of roof.

"What are you doing in here?" I said.

"No bloody business of yours," said the one on the left. He looked at me from under the brim of his hat. "You've got a hell of a lot to explain yourself."

The one on the right had a bandage around his head. He kept watching the pot.

I leaned hard on my stick.

"You two are going to hit the road," I said.

"Nobody wants to tackle *you*, mate," said Hat. "Lord, no."

The one with the bandage chuckled.

"You'll have the place back when we're done with it." Hat looked up towards where the roof had been. "Our place needs some patching."

I took a step inside. The *Town Talk* tin lay on its side with the lid beside it.

"What was in that?"

"Want me to bash you?" asked Bandage.

"That's been ten minutes, easy," said Hat. "They'll be done."

Bandage reached into the pot with his fingers and pulled out an egg, dropped it on my mat to cool, then he pulled out two more. Three eggs.

Michel had left them in the tin for me, a surprise, and does anything in the world have more vitamins than an egg?

"Those came out of my tin," I said.

"Look, mate, he told you it wasn't your business."

Hat shook an egg beside his ear. "They're good."

Our *chi-chack* ran down the wall. He'd lived in the ceiling while we'd had one.

"Oh, and mate?" said Bandage. "I don't reckon you came by any of this honestly, so we won't ask no questions, all right?"

He pulled the bundle of mosquito net out of the corner, and all of a sudden I thought I might be in the wrong hut — there were tins of bully beef, tins of coffee, tins of fruit. I couldn't take it all in. Michel had left all of that behind.

"And what you got there?" asked Bandage.

I looked down and saw the greens hanging out of my pocket. He stood up and I turned to get away from him, but I felt a thump on my ear and down I went. I landed in the stubbly grass, it wasn't so bad. Nothing like Sintha's back yard. I felt the greens slide out of my pocket and heard his feet walking back to our hut. Where was Glad Tidings when I needed him?

I went to Bluey's but Don was in there too, so I plunked myself down on their front step. Two seconds of breeze would've made all the difference in the world. I could hear Wilf's record player going in the next shed over: Tex Morton, The Yodelling Boundary Rider. I couldn't get my head around it — hauling a record player all the way from Australia just to listen to music like that. I peeled a bit of wood off the step. We must've sailed over my Waller records when the *Tohohashi* came in.

"Remember when you've castrated the young sheep," Bluey was saying. "And you cook up the testicles?"

"Mountain oysters," said Don.

"Delicious," said Bluey. "My word. Out of the pan."

"Full of vitamins," I said.

"Harry, can't you bloody shut up for one minute?" Don was getting up from his bunk. "Evening, Lieutenant."

Changi Dave stood over me. He'd put a shirt on.

"Is that Putnam?" asked Bluey. "Evening, Putnam."

"At ease, Harrison, thanks. Just here to speak to Winslow."

"Get up for the Lieutenant!" said Don. "Christ Almighty!"

I leaned on the stick and got to my feet. Saluted Lieutenant Putnam.

"Winslow," he said.

"Lieutenant," I said. "I thought about what you said about my friend."

"Have you."

"And even if I benefited from what he was doing, I promise you I didn't know the first thing about it. He won't be my friend if he comes back here. You have my assurance."

"Fine. That's all well and good. But nonetheless, Holmes will speak to you this evening regarding what I witnessed in the vegetable garden."

"Okay." I wanted to sit down again. I felt like a damp rag. "What time?"

"Just go around and see him."

He saluted Don.

"That's all."

I watched Changi Dave walk away until he turned into a blur.

"Harry, old man," said Bluey. "What's this?"

But I didn't have to answer, thank Christ, because Georgie ran up and squeezed through the door. He stood stock-still in the middle of the room and said something slowly and quietly, like he did every afternoon.

"The ... little ... bird. It's good. Bloody good."

"No bloody hoax," said Don.

"The Krauts," Georgie said, "surrendered in North Africa."

"That's borehole."

"BBC Delhi, mate!"

Then they made a hell of a noise, Bluey and Don giggling and smacking each other on the arm and Georgie standing there shushing them. North Africa. It was wonderful. All of those goddamn Limeys I'd left at Suez would be on their way home. Everything was in full swing, as Waller had once said. Happy days.

It wasn't hard to believe that H Force *was* going to Portuguese East Africa on a wool exchange; Michel could've engineered the whole thing. At heart he was a thief and a dope fiend and all the rest. All those cans of beef — who had he strangled to get those? Maybe I should've been tickled that he'd thought of me to the last, my welfare had been at the forefront of his mind, but I knew it was a hell of a lot more likely that it had just been too much for him to carry. So he'd left me holding the bag. He'd done whatever he wanted to, and they hadn't caught up to him. But they'd caught me. That was the second strike. At the rate I was going, I figured a third would do me in.

I pulled myself to my feet. I stepped inside the hut, and even Don was excited enough to shake my hand.

"Six weeks till we're back home." Bluey crinkled up his forehead. "And not via bloody Africa either."

"Naw, three months," said Don. "Be a realist. Three months."

"All right, Harry," Bluey said. "How long do *you* reckon?"

I was still bunking with Bluey eight months later when the guys who'd been trucked away as F Force came back to Changi. They told us that they'd had to build a great bloody railway up north, yes, just like Outram Road Dave had said, and that it had taken eight trains to cart them all up to Thailand and only two to bring them back. A guy named Puden set up a shop making false legs for them out of exhaust pipes. There'd been a couple of hundred amputations due to tropical ulcers — that was the clinical description. All I knew was that I looked strapping and robust beside those guys.

Out of curiosity I asked if any of them had seen a big bald Frenchman up there — well, a Frenchman who didn't have much of an accent so they might not have known he was French. But they always asked what unit he was in.

Bluey had passed away by the time Damian came back with H Force, though it was only a week after F, so he could move straight back into his old hut. Of course Damian had known Michel to see him, so I asked him the minute he staggered in.

"They had us a thousand places at once. Leave fifty at one place, righto, take the rest on up the line, then cholera comes through, kills all fifty blokes but for three or four, and where do they end up? Nobody can know that, I have no bloody idea."

He weighed 94 pounds, he said that he'd weighed 161 when he left

Australia, and it took me the rest of that day to figure out in my head that he'd lost 58 percent of his body weight — I kept getting hung up on the fact that 94 was not exactly three-fifths of 161 but was close enough to distract me. Georgie and I walked out to the gate around sundown just in case there was still a truck or two straggling back in.

"I know what they say about him," I told Georgie, "but a guy should be allowed his own defence, right? If I know my buddy he had a hell of a good reason."

"You've a heart as big as all outdoors," said Georgie.

"Nah, if he's not here now," I said, "he's probably in Portuguese East Africa."

That would've been January 1944. By then Georgie had invited me to move into a cell in the prison because he'd inherited the famous radio from a guy named Howells and said he'd need a hand running it. That meant I had to spend the next year and a half keeping watch in the corridor while Georgie listened to the piece of surgical tubing in the cell, and I was a pretty decent lookout — yeah, me! I'd traded Ferguson's gold tooth for a pair of glasses by then, so all of the Aussies told me that I looked like Prime Minister John Curtin. My eyes had improved with the sweet potatoes too.

Georgie had moved the radio from the water tank at Birdwood Camp and bricked it right into our wall so that he just had to put one end of the tubing over the nail in the wall and hold the other end to his ear and there was BBC Delhi. If a Jap or a Sikh or a Korean came along the corridor I'd just tap my fingernail against the metal door frame, Georgie would pull the tubing off, ball it up in his palm, and all the guard would see would be a six-foot Australian with different-sized nostrils sitting beside a nail in a wall.

I leaned against the rail and looked down on the courtyard but there wasn't a soul around. A lot of them had gone down to Selarang for salt water. The roof on the prison was solid so we never got wet, but cockroaches still bred in the drains in their millions. I turned around to say something to Georgie and a roach the size of a plum flew past my head, and I swung my stick and knocked it right out of the air. He fell the twenty feet down to the courtyard. I wished that somebody had been around to see it because that was the best thing to have happened to me in a month.

That metal door frame felt cool but it stunk of something.

"What you got?" I asked him.

"Just the bloody music. She's clear out there?"

"Did they say what song?"

"They said it's 'Rhapsody In Blue' by Paul Whiteman And His Orchestra."

"Christ Almighty."

He gave me his look so I went out again. There was no one in sight so I took off my glasses and cleaned them on my loincloth — it covered my mister and crotch and that was about all. For a while the Java Balls had made a return engagement but the good old Limey doctor had smeared sulphate on them and that had ushered them from the stage.

When I put the glasses back on Georgie had taken the tubing off the nail. He sat there with his hands on his knees.

"Still empty." I went in. "What's the word?"

He was breathing slowly like he was trying to keep off a fit.

"Didn't it come through? You want to scrounge up those valves?"

He stood up all of a sudden and pulled the tubing out of the pocket of his shorts. He looked down at it.

"Americans dropped those bombs on Japan," he said.

"You mean the one last week?"

"The Japanese have capitulated."

"What does that mean?"

"It bloody means the war is over," he said. "It means the war is bloody over."

He lifted his head and looked at me like I ought to do a handstand.

"The hundredth time we've heard that," I said.

"BBC Delhi says that the Japanese have capitulated."

I stared at the end of my stick. I was no better than him, was I?

We went downstairs like we did every time and told Chester and Nelson and Oldham, and when they heard it they just nodded. They didn't seem to find it any more exciting than when the Americans took the Solomons.

We heard them walk off through the camp — of course we couldn't hear Chester or Nelson or Oldham but now and then we'd hear a shedful of guys shouting back, "You'll never get off the island!" Whenever a guy talked about going home that was what we had say to him, because of course that guy was a fool to even dream about it. I thought he was too. So we heard *you'll never get off the island* a thousand times a day.

Georgie started walking. I didn't mind going with him because he went slowly. We went all the way back to the gardens then all the way around to the front. The gate was shut tight with the Jap flag hanging slack from the pole. It was almost time for supper.

"I'll see my wife," Georgie said.

"Back in Coolangatta."

"That's it. You'll see yours too, I reckon."

"You've got that right."

But even though Michel had gone to all the trouble of finding you and I should've had it cemented in my mind that I would clap eyes on you the minute that gate stood open, in the two years since he'd seen you I'd been doubting more and more that he really had. It had just been another of his schemes, or if he really had seen you then that was no guarantee you'd still be there. For all I knew you were in New York City living under a different name. If you really were in the women's camp that would be fine, it would be the best thing imaginable, and if I found a thousand dollars in cash that would also be fine, you know? But in either case I'd be better off not to plan on it. I could go quietly go home to my folks and see what was left of Canada.

A couple of days later a four-engine plane dropped a load of leaflets over the Changi end of Singapore. I expected them to say *Nippon Army! Your Friend Forever!* but they didn't say that. Georgie and I tacked one on the wall and lay on our bunks looking at it:

Official/Sarkari Elan/Japan Has Surrendered Unconditionally To The Allies/Japan Ne Bila Shart Ittihadion Ke Age Hatyar Dal Die Hain.

We looked at it all day long.

A week after that the guys ran past the railing, hollering that the gate was wide open, so Georgie and I walked over — the Jap flag was gone, and some guy had strung up a Union Jack flag made out scraps of towel. The gate *was* standing open.

We took a couple of steps out onto the asphalt, fifty or a hundred of us. There was nothing on the road in either direction. Somebody said that they could see a bloody Nip leading a cow away — I couldn't see that well — so a lot of guys went chasing off down the road and their arms and legs looked like pipe cleaners. I walked in that direction too. It was a side of the fence and the hedge that I'd never seen before; it was the outside. A red bug flew through the wire and across the road and up into the trees. I stopped to look at some purple flowers down in the grass, and all of a sudden I didn't want to be out there anymore. It was hot, and I couldn't help but think it would be cooler in the camp.

"We should trot along to that women's camp," said Oldham.

"Chester's been down the beach," Georgie said.

Chester wiped his nose.

"Six dead Japs stuck in the sand," he said. "And a bloody mess."

Everyone stood around smiling, looking tired. Nobody wanted to miss anything.

"You look at this," said Georgie. "Here's something."

Another plane flew over and a white blob dropped out of it and swung back and forth. I could see the shape of a man hanging from the bottom.

"Paratroops!"

"What's the colours on the bird?"

"That's the Poms. Look at this, he'll come down on the aerodrome."

"Let's get over and wave him in! A good Changi hello!"

"We ought to."

But instead we all walked back to our sheds and hunkered down in the shade.

A dozen planes dropped barrels full of chocolate and cigarettes on us. I could bend my bad leg up behind me and put a Philip Morris between my toes, take it out, have a puff, put it back, like I just happened to have an ashtray at my hip. Oldham and the rest all loved it. There were Yank soldiers walking through the camp who looked like Flash Gordon crossed with a boxcar, and apparently some nurses were coming to look at us so everybody wanted to comb their hair.

"I don't want any of those," said Chester. "I want one of those Camels."

"They're going to the hospital, they're not coming to see us."

"They might stop in."

"We should go and find that women's camp," I said.

"That sergeant with the cigars said where it was," said Oldham. "Poms guarding that place too." He lit a new cigarette off his last. "And the girls'll soon see the Poms aren't much to look at."

"Not like us, hey, Nelson?" said Chester. "You'll be the new man."

"They'll love it," said Nelson. "They'll go mad for it."

He pulled off his fake leg and rang his knuckles against the side of it. Steel. The ulcers had come back on his stump and the stink was so bad that I had to leave the hut.

"I know what you'll be about," said Georgie. "Find yourself a bloody Fats Waller record."

"No records," I said. "I'm going straight to Harlem and see him face to face."

"Oh, beauty," said Don. "That'd be me with Tex Morton."

"I'll go with you and have a look," said Oldham. "I knew this girl before surrender."

"Our surrender, this was, or theirs?"

"*Our* surrender. Aw, you buggery."

"Who's got a shirt to give me?" I said.

Because all I had was that loincloth. It would be nice if I could tell you that I had no doubts whatsoever, that I had every confidence you'd run into my arms that very afternoon, but that wasn't the case. I just didn't know who we'd run into out there. Maybe the king had come to see the liberation.

"You know what mine looks like," said Georgie.

"Hell, I'll take it."

Someone had left a vehicle outside our gate, a *jeep* — this American thing without a roof. We didn't even hesitate, we just piled in, because what could they do, lock us up again? Oldham drove it like hell under those trees along the East Coast Road. I leaned across him to honk the horn. Of course it was better that he was driving because I could've only worked one pedal. We both liked the Ink Spots, so he kept hollering

I don't want to set the world

On

Fire!

But it sounded like he did.

Another jeep came up the road toward us and Oldham almost steered us in the ditch. The jeep was full of nurses in dark-brown uniforms, even a nurse driving, and they were all holding their caps down on their blonde heads. They went by quickly. Oldham steered back into the middle of the road. He pointed out a line of straight white trees. They looked like birches to me, and it had been years since I'd seen one.

"Rubber trees!" he shouted.

All of those years in Asia, and that was something new to me.

We saw wooden towers off to our right. Wire fences and that. Two and a half years, and it had only been a couple of miles away.

He pulled over a hundred feet before the gate and we got out and walked the rest of the way. Chinese women dressed in black stood all over the road, talking to white women dressed in potato sacks. There was a stubbly field opposite the gate where white kids dragged around newspaper kites.

There were forty or fifty white women standing at the gate, smoking Camels and crushing the butts under sandals that looked like they'd been cut from rubber tires. They all had scraggly hair hanging over their ears and brown dresses that must've been made out of curtains. I couldn't figure out how so many women could look so similar. I'd never realized that Caucasian women had such big noses. I hoped they didn't think that I was staring. I'd seen nothing but starving people for months and months, sure, but those had all been men, and I'd imagined that when I finally saw a woman she would resemble one. The Yanks who'd walked by our hut had looked in like we were a carnival act — look what's on show! free of charge! — and of course we hadn't seen what there was to stare at. But when I saw those women I realized.

Oldham just walked straight through the gate like he'd been into that camp a hundred times. I couldn't see what was beyond the crowd, maybe it wasn't even the right camp, so I stopped to lean on my stick for a minute — no, my stomach wasn't turning, I wasn't dizzy, none of that. I just knew in my heart that you weren't there.

The women stared at me too, though it seemed like some weren't looking at anything at all. One wiped her hands on her dress and walked out of the crowd towards me. She had a pink ribbon across the top of her head.

"Can I help?" she asked. "Are you looking for anyone?"

The way that she pronounced each word sounded absolutely beautiful. She had blue buttons the size of quarters down the front of her dress.

"Are you looking for your wife?" she asked. "Sister?"

"No, no. Don't worry about it," I said. "Lily Brown."

"That's her name?"

I didn't want to be looking for you. I didn't want this woman to come back and tell me no, you weren't there.

"That's her name," I said.

She went back to the group and spoke to the nearest ones, and they watched me over her shoulder and mouthed your name. She looked from one face to another, then she shrugged. She came back to me.

"There are a number of Lilys and a number of Browns, certainly, but we can't think immediately of anyone who's both! Why don't you come inside and ask the commandant? I could show you."

"I'm all right," I said. "I'll just get my bearings."

"Shall I show you?"

I didn't want the women to think that I was standing there just to stare at them, so I watched the kids fly their kites for a while. One fell on his face and got up without a sniffle. Why was I standing there? For years I'd been wanting to go into a store and buy a pencil, that was what I should have been doing.

"Hello?"

There was a woman standing there, a different one, though she had the exact same dress as the one before — the buttons and everything. She had deep lines on either side of her nose.

"Would you like chocolate?" she asked. "They've given us heaps."

She held out a square of wax paper.

"Oh, thanks anyway," I said. "I've had too much already."

"You look as though you ought to sit down."

It had already been a much longer day than I was used to. She led me over to the fence, where there was long grass next to the posts.

"That's nice," I said. "Thank you."

I sat down with my back against a post. Who knows what kind of display I was giving underneath my loincloth. That wood felt hot against the back of my neck. I drew my knees up to my chest and just like that I must've fallen fast asleep.

"Hello?" a woman said.

She was looking down at me. This one had a brown pigtail on either side of her face and her eyes stuck out like a Siamese cat's.

"What is it?" I asked.

"Harry?" she said. "It's me."

It was you — the nose was the same. And your front teeth. You held out your hand and I took it. Your palm felt like a catcher's mitt. I pushed up with my stick and then there I was. Standing next to you.

Is that how you saw it? Maybe you remember us saying different things.

You put your arms around my neck and squeezed. I had to lean hard against my stick. I put my face against your collarbone. You were all collarbone. Jesus, you smelled like a barn!

"Harry. Oh, my God," you said. "I wouldn't have known you."

You held onto my hand and looked me over. Touched my chin. You sniffled over and over until it was like you had a twitch down the side of your face.

"You have glasses on," you said. "That's what it is. Can't you say anything?"

A guy ran up the road with his tie flapping, and when he came to the gate he fell to his knees in front of a woman and two kids. He hugged the kids, and while the woman's nose ran like a faucet she pressed his head into her belly. You and I stood there watching. I ran my thumb over your calluses.

"You know, my buddy told me you were here," I said. "But it was so long ago, I didn't know what to think about it anymore. Jesus, it was ages ago."

"Why, what did he say about me?"

You squeezed my hands.

"Just that he saw you."

"Who were you out here asking for?"

"What do you mean? I wasn't looking for anybody else."

"I know that — I mean what *name*."

"Lily Brown!"

You grinned. Your teeth were still white.

"But my name is Winslow!"

You turned your hand over. You were wearing the black *R* ring on your thumb.

"They didn't confiscate it. Called it worthless."

You had it all sorted out. It was like you'd never had a doubt. But had I really been doubting? Hadn't I got myself to the women's camp?

"They came and asked me if I knew a Lily *Brown*, that an old man was asking for her. Said it must be her father."

I let go of the stick and held your face between my hands and kissed you. After all of that time. Your lips were so dry. I moved my hand to the back of your head — I could feel all the vertebrae in your neck.

"I want to go to the Raffles now," you said.

Planes flew over the field and the kids ran underneath them. We held hands and walked down the road to the jeep, but there was grime between our fingers so I had to tug my hand free and wipe it on Georgie's shirt. I led you around to the passenger side, but then I remembered.

"Oh. I can't drive," I said. "I have a bad leg."

"I'd been meaning to ask you."

So I held onto your arm and walked you around the front of the jeep like we were at a dance, and you stepped up onto the driver's side with those tire-tread shoes. You sat and held the steering wheel.

"Where's your mother?" I asked.

"She died."

Then you reached down and started the engine.

You drove so fast that I had to hold my glasses against my face, and you didn't seem to like the clutch — you got it up into fourth and left it there.

We didn't see a single Jap except for one little encampment as we drove along the sea, but there were Chinese everywhere as we drove into town, little kids waving their hands, grown-ups running around with these red and blue flags, not the Union Jack, I couldn't figure out what they were. We passed a couple of mosques that I hadn't noticed the first time in Singapore.

Then we came to the Raffles.

Two Japs in spectacles sat on wooden chairs in the driveway, next to row after row of filing cabinets. A gigantic paper sign covered in Japanese writing hung out of an upstairs window; the other end lay on the steps. You parked on the sidewalk and ran ahead of me across the driveway — I moved slowly despite my best intentions. The two Japs stood up and saluted you. You got to the top of the steps and spun around again, furrowing your brow and tugging on a pigtail.

"I don't have any money!"

"They don't look open for business anyway."

"Oh, it won't take more than a minute."

You marched past me and climbed back into the jeep, and twenty-five seconds later we pulled up outside of Ricky's church. There were leafy vegetables growing on the front lawn.

The inside of the church didn't smell too different from the last time — there weren't any soldiers on the pews, of course, but it looked like water had been running down the walls since 1942. A few Chinese gals sat on the back pews and a white gal knelt at the front. You marched past and straight up the steps towards the pulpit, and she turned her head to watch you go by.

"He's answered our prayers!" she called to you.

And He really had — you reached through the organ pipes and pulled out a brown envelope. I was only at the bottom of the steps by then, and you came running back.

"It's pound sterling." You tore open the end and peered inside. "I knew that they would never look there."

"How much is in there?"

"A few thousand. What Mum had."

Someone had written *Brown* on it in a careful hand.

"Blazes!" you said. "I've just remembered Ricky!"

We stood there on the steps and gazed around the church, as though he might have been reclining in the choir stalls. You kept turning the *R* ring around your thumb.

"Ricky?" called out the woman. "Gone!"

"Where exactly?"

The woman kept her head bowed and hands pressed together.

"Run away!"

"Away?" You bit your lip and smiled, as though you ought not to be smiling. "If that's the case, then I have every confidence that the Ricky I know has been fighting alongside the guerrillas these many years."

"I shouldn't think so," said the woman.

You smiled again — I'd forgotten how it went right across your face. You held up your left hand, slid the *R* ring off your thumb and onto your ring finger. It hung down over the knuckle.

"Watch that it doesn't drop off," I said.

The two Japs by the filing cabinets stood up and saluted us again. We went up the steps and into the lobby. There were no more chesterfields or pianos or even potted plants, just two long rows of rolltop desks. More signs covered in writing hung from the balconies.

"Can I help?"

It was a Limey who looked like he was twelve years old, with a holster at his side and the hair shellacked to his head.

"We've just come out of Changi," you said. "Could we stay here?"

"You can see it's awfully cluttered."

"We stayed here on our honeymoon. Can't we have a look round?"

"Have a look round then." He read from a stack of papers, then glanced back up at us. "See if anything suits you."

"There are two Japs sitting outside," I said.

"Heavens, I'd forgotten about them."

I watched your legs go up the stairs ahead of me — your dress had a belt that tied at the back. I leaned on the banister and hopped from one step to the next. You watched me from the landing for a minute. Then you stamped your foot. *Bang!*

"Are you not in any hurry?" you asked.

So for the first time in a long time I put some weight on that left foot, and it did not too badly. When I had one step to go you leaned down and gave me a long kiss. Your lips weren't as dry as they had been. You straightened up.

"I do feel ill."

"You've been going like a blue streak," I said.

"This is true."

My knee didn't seem to know what part of the body it was supposed to be, but it held up one step after another. We got up to the hallway and looked down into the courtyard. It was a jungle. You gave my hand a squeeze.

"Thirty-nine," you said.

The numbers were still on the doors.

It was unlocked, and I smelled smoke as soon you turned the handle. The room was empty — no furniture — but there were moths or something flying all over. The window was wide open and the curtains flapped at us. There was a burn mark on the floor the size of a dart board.

"They had a corn roast in here," I said.

One of the moths caught on the front of your dress. You picked it off — a flake of ash, but we could still see a Japanese letter on the paper. It looked like a little house with a chimney. You smeared it between your fingers.

"I'll tell you what *I* want," you said. "A bath."

We went into the *mandi*, and the jar was full of water but had a hundred moths floating on top. Real moths. You scooped some of them out and peered down into the water.

"No tadpoles." You scooped more moths onto the ground. "That's a start."

It stunk of mould in there and I could see spiders running in the slats near the ceiling. The toilet needed a cleaning.

"I can scrub that if you like," I said.

You unbuttoned the front of your dress.

"I'll get towels," I said.

"Don't be long."

I went next door to thirty-eight. It had a bed frame without a mattress, and a stain on the wall that might've been blood. There were framed pictures of Japanese men on the wall.

I went back into our room and tore down one of the curtains, then I took it into the *mandi*. You were standing there dripping wet with your hands over your breasts, but you weren't the least bit shy about showing the hair down there. You held out one of your legs.

"See? Shaved this morning. I saved the blades for two years."

You put your foot back down.

"And look! Hip bones."

I offered you the curtain, but you grabbed my head and started kissing me. I backed against the doorway.

"I don't want to fall," I said.

We kissed and kissed until you'd got me soaking wet and Georgie's shirt had come apart down one side. But we still weren't entirely naked because I had the loincloth on, and you had the curtain.

"What's this tattoo?" you asked me. "Japanese give you that?"

"I got that from the Aussies two camps ago."

We spread out another curtain and you put my glasses on the windowsill. We lay down without any clothes on. Your ribs felt hot against mine. You touched my tattoo with your fingertip, and we kissed and kissed. My mister didn't work.

You got up and hung your dress on the door.

"I have three more of them in camp. Blazes, I would make one and take it apart and start all over again, do you know why?"

"They made you."

"Yes, that would have been very like them — no, because it was easier to wait for a dress to be finished than the war, how do you like that? But I kept this one aside for today, I imagined how I would put it on and walk outside and *breathe*."

I liked being in that room with you. I did. I realized all at once that I wasn't thinking about anything except for what you were saying, and my stomach felt fine, and I believed — maybe it was the burn mark, maybe it was just that enough days had passed — that the Japs really were done, that they weren't going to burst in and hack us to pieces.

If the twelve-year-old Limey with the hair had burst in, well, I wouldn't have minded him, and he'd already seen me in my loincloth so I knew he wasn't likely to.

"I did have *one* better one. I worked months on that."

"Why didn't you wear that one?"

"I put Mum in it."

You lay down with me again.

"Don't you want anything to eat?"

"No." You threw your leg over me. "I've at least had a *meal* in four years."

We watched the flakes of paper fly around until the sun went down. Planes flew over all night. You said that they were American, from the sound. The girls had figured out all off the different makes.

"Do you remember the fifth of February?"

"Um. I don't have much of a memory for —"

You smacked my belly.

"Our anniversary! Honestly! Every girl had a jar of flowers for her anniversary, and a piece of pineapple and a good cry. I'd say, 'Harry, my darling, this is our anniversary. I haven't any idea where you are but someday we will go off together hand in hand.'"

"And that's what's happened."

"That is exactly what has happened."

You weren't there in the morning. I found my glasses, and on the wall someone had written

BREA

KFAST!

I lay there watching the gap under the door for somebody's feet, but I smelled you coming even before you appeared.

"Fresh bread! Can you imagine? Baked on the ships!"

You took off your dress and we ate breakfast. There were three loaves of bread but we only ate one. You dragged my loincloth over with your toe.

"Now is this what the prisoner of style cannot be without? Where exactly does one — *Exclusively For Robinson's Singapore*? Oh no. This was not the tuxedo you had on that night!"

I hadn't read that label in all of those years. Ten thousand hours spent thinking about nothing and I never once thought to read my own pants.

"But wasn't it your friend's that you had borrowed?"

"Bunny."

"Bunny. That's right. Did *he* buy it at Robinson's?"

"I got it at Robinson's."

"It was open in the evening?"

"I smashed the window with a rock."

You sat on my lap and put your arms around my head so that what was left of your breasts pressed against my neck. I kissed across your collarbone, down the row of bones in your chest, then out on the red nipple. It tasted like paint. Your fists tugged my hair.

I lay down, and you stayed on top of me so that your pubic hair went into my belly button. You started to rock back and forth, and I could feel my hips dig into the bones in your legs. We were like a pair of sawhorses.

"When we first went into camp my hands took a bad infection." Bits of hair hung in your face. "Mum thought I would lose them entirely."

I took your hand and kissed it.

"How did you get a bad infection?"

"From the bits of glass on our wedding night. And there's a mystery solved — they were all over the jacket you'd pinched."

"Oh no," I said. "If I'd —"

"Shush. It reminded me of you."

You shoved your hips back and forth.

"Sorry about that," I said.

You kept moving on me. You leaned all the way back.

"Christ," you muttered. "Don't fret."

We stayed at the Raffles for two more weeks and ate ten chocolate bars a day. By our second day there were white guys typing up forms at every one of those rolltop desks. We spotted those two Japs with the glasses filling in a trench on the cricket field, and one afternoon we went to pick up free soap and towels and saw a line of Korean guards piling bricks. There were soldiers running around everywhere — Aussies, Limeys, Yanks. I went to buy a pencil, remember, when we heard that they'd accept sterling, and the little Chinese guy dropped the change into my hand and said, "There you go, Joe!"

Everybody was chewing gum like their life depended on it.

We went down to the docks to look for a boat going anywhere, and there were a thousand troops who'd been there since the night before, waiting for anything leaving that afternoon. The Aussie prisoners looked like umbrellas, with those big hats on their beanpole bodies.

In the meantime we had our room at the Raffles, and most times of the day or night I had some line or other from "Honeysuckle Rose" in my head, if you catch my drift. Though you never liked it if I was on top of you, do you remember that? I tried it once and the next thing I knew you were on your feet, looking down at me as if to say *Who the hell are you and how did you get in here?* So I came to understand that you didn't. like to do it that way. There were plenty of other ways though. I'm sorry, I'll quit with the smut now. A guy never forgets his glory days.

We found your dad's battalion headquarters and the kid at the desk said that according to the forms Colonel Brown had been declared missing in action somewhere up in Malaya but that your mother must have never received the telegram, it had been a month before surrender. Our surrender.

You seemed to take the news pretty well — he had already been missing, so in a way it wasn't really news. A red-headed officer who remembered you came out to the desk and we asked if he knew of any boats that weren't just for military personnel, and the red-headed guy said it might be a few days yet. Which I figured meant never. But the next day your dad's battalion headquarters got you on the phone at the Raffles and told you that a Yank plane was leaving for Manila in a half-hour if we eventually wanted to end up in Vancouver. Our twelve-year-old Limey was watching from across the lobby and he said he'd give us a lift. You wore a nice blue dress and I had a suit from the Red Cross that made me look like a parcel of bacon.

"Rashers," you said. "Parcel of rashers."

It was a seaplane, floating out in the harbour, so we walked along the pier and down a gangway. An American sailor, a Negro, stood in the shade under the wing smoking a cigarette. He was also chewing gum.

"Say, look there!"

He pointed at something behind us. We saw a long cloud over the post office, getting longer — it was like watching a line on a chalkboard. I rubbed my glasses on my sleeve.

"That's a jet airplane," he said.

You looked pale. We hadn't eaten.

"Isn't it lovely," you said, then you stepped up through the door.

"We get to Manila," he said, "*then* you'll have a good time."

"I'm not going to any nightclubs," I told him. "When we get to the States we're taking a train across and we're seeing Fats Waller in Harlem. That's the first thing we do. Then we decide what to do next."

He quit chewing.

"I'm sorry to tell you," he said. "He died."

"What's this?"

"That was '43. I remember, it was Christmas time. I'm sorry about that."

He grabbed my arm. I must've looked unsteady.

The seats in that plane all looked like chesterfields. You sat there with your hair tied behind your head.

"I forgot to say goodbye to Pia," you said.

She'd been your buddy in camp. I hadn't said goodbye to Georgie, either, but that might've been because of his torn shirt. The green water started moving past us. You turned your head toward the window, but I didn't lean my head on your shoulder or peer out to look for *Empress* lying under all of that clear water. I just didn't think to.

"Say," I said. "Did you ever hear of a guy named Fats Waller?"

"No." You blew your nose into your Red Cross hankie. "I certainly haven't."

Three

I wake up and listen for your breathing, picturing your hair glued to your poor sweaty head, and I can't feel you beside me but plenty of nights when you're bad I end up away on the other side of the bed, so I know to just listen and wait for you to find that breath. But after a couple of seconds I still don't hear you and my heart takes that funny beat. And then I remember everything that's happened. I'm in Bangkok, Thailand.

I can't see much without my glasses, of course, but I left the curtains open and I can at least tell that the sky is still dark and I can hear diesel engines bawling down below. I put my face right up to the clock radio, 3:25, so I've slept five hours. That's the longest sleep I've had since you've gone. That's some kind of record. Only four hours till the train leaves for Kanchanaburi. And then what? On to Sangkhlaburi, where I'll hug and kiss Michel. He helped me find *you* once, so I guess it's all fair.

My bad knee is stiff as hell after the flight, it's pinned under the bedsheets so that I have to reach down and find my ankle to tug my leg back into shape.

Is this how you did it, sweetheart? Would you stay a night in Bangkok before you carried on to see him? If I was a crazy guy I'd go down to the desk right now and demand to see their guestbook, and every guest-book in every hotel until I found the name Lily Winslow.

The room is bright when I wake up again. The river looks yellow with the sun shining on it. Then I go into the bathroom and turn on the faucets so I won't have to feel for them with my glasses off. A strange shower can be one of life's great mysteries. You always preferred baths but I don't want to get overheated and end up fainting.

By the same logic I won't need my sportcoat today, but there's no room for it in the suitcase. I figure that the hotel can hold onto it. I put on my green polo shirt and the yellow trousers that I always used to wear when we went across to Bowen Island, then I cram that whole mess of papers into the pocket — passport and traveller's cheques and that.

Some of the hotel guys in copper-coloured trousers stand around the lobby dusting lampshades, they tell me that the only restaurant open before 7 a.m. is the Author's Lounge at the other end of the hotel.

"Do I have to be an author?"

"Ha, ha. No, sir."

In the hallway I find an old picture of Tsar Nicholas of Russia sitting with the royal family of Thailand. They should've have those Siamese Twins in there with Tsar Nicholas too, that must've been about the same time. Imagine two people twisted in a knot their whole lives.

All of the furniture in the restaurant is wicker, and there's a tableful of Italians telling the hotel girl all of the places they've been — Florida, they loved Florida. I ask her for a fried egg and a coffee and when it comes the yolk is rubbery.

I want to leave the sport coat with them at the check-in desk but they say that they have to know when I'll be coming back.

"Sir, a reservation is always recommended."

"Well, I don't know how quickly I'll be back."

"Do you fly out of Bangkok?"

"That's the twenty-sixth. The twenty-sixth. But, I'm sort of a loose cannon, I — you go ahead, you can help her first. No, go ahead. Can you hold onto it?"

One of the hotel guys manages to bow to his ankles and hold open the big glass door for me at the same time, and as I walk out of the air-con into the outside world the smell just about knocks me down all over again — it nearly took my head off outside the airport. That tropical armpit. The first time I came to the Orient was by sea, of course, so it didn't hit me all at once.

A traffic cop in a blue shirt and peaked cap sits in a booth down at the foot of the driveway. It's more of an alley leading up to the hotel than an actual road, and guys in their undershirts and women with their hair going every which way push carts up the middle of the pavement, wooden stools and tin pots clattering against the wheels. Maybe they're on their way to fix breakfast. I know that we're right near the river but I honestly have no idea which direction it's in, so I knock on the glass and the traffic cop gets right down from his stool.

"Bangkok Noi," I say. "Bangkok Noi?"

"Bangkok Noi."

"Where do I catch the boat?"

I know I should say please, but I honestly can't see where to fit it into the conversation.

"This way," he says.

His takes off his hat, smoothes down his hair, puts his hat back on, then waves his arm down the road, the direction the guys with carts are going.

"Maybe, oh, one minute walking. Cost is eight baht. Where do you go?"

"Bangkok Noi," I say.

"Bangkok Noi? This is Thonburi. You want a boat going this way." He waves both hands away from the hotel. "From the left, okay?"

"Okay."

"Eight baht."

"Thank you."

See, there — aren't I good? I pick up the suitcase and start up the alley, letting it thump against the good knee. There are a lot of kids in blue shorts and white shirts coming towards me in a hurry. Something smells like garbage, and not just the mould smell, it's something rotting.

"Sir!"

The traffic cop runs after me, waving his hat. What have I dropped? I put the suitcase down and check my pants pocket.

"If the boat has a red flag or yellow flag, you don't get on, okay? These are express boats, okay? You will miss your station."

He's already turning around.

"Oh," I say. "I'll keep an eye out."

I know, you would've said something much sweeter. You would've given him a present. Some kids in white shirts are sitting against the brick wall, eating what look like noodles out of plastic bowls. Melmac bowls. Maybe those are their school uniforms. One of them says something to me that I don't understand. A guy picks up a frying pan from a tin stove on wheels. He waves me over, points at a green plastic chair.

"Where's the boat dock?" I ask him.

"Maybe fried rice."

At seven in the morning? At the end of the alley there's a squat little cement bunker that might be the ferry terminal, it might also be a squat little cement bunker, but the air feels like it's dropped about two degrees so maybe the river's on the other side. I feel with certainty that I won't make the train on time.

I shuffle through the bunker and sure enough there's the river, all of the buildings on the far bank lit up in the sun. From up close the water's grey, like a kitchen sink that's never been emptied. Long skinny boats float up and down the river but nothing's coming in our way. I'm on a cement platform with a passel of other people: more kids in white shirts, guys with ties and moustaches, women who look like secretaries with long skirts and high heels, and two monks in the bright orange robes — monks in bright orange robes! But it's easy to pretend that they're just ho-hum, like they're a couple of mailmen, because nobody else is even looking at them sideways.

A schoolkid carrying a soccer ball sidles over and stands up very straight in front of me. He's trying his best to grow a moustache.

"You are going to the Grand Palace?" he says.

"No."

"Here. This boat is to Grand Palace."

"I want Bangkok Noi."

"You go to Thonburi? Here, this is your boat."

And sure enough there are boats coming in from three directions, each of them louder than a chainsaw — there must not be such a thing as a muffler in the whole country. Another kid comes up and tries to wrestle the soccer ball away from the moustache kid.

"No, no!" he says. "This one!"

So I don't want the boat on the left, I want the one on the right. I hustle down the ramp to the dock. A kid in a Hawaiian shirt hops off the back of the boat and holds the rope while a couple of dozen people jump onto the dock, and he never once stops blowing his whistle. They make a racket every chance they get. That dock lurches up and down and a lot of the kids in white shirts hop on ahead of me, I have to jump over the tires that are chained to the dock and after coming down the ramp my knee's not sure if it wants to. But then the two monks hop on and the kid with the whistle blasts it in my ear and I know that my train is just about leaving, so where does that leave me? I grab the steel rail and swing myself over but the suitcase trips me up, I just about fall backwards into the water but this fat Chinese guy grabs me. Then just like that the boat is pulling away and almost tosses me in again. I want to thank the Chinese guy but he's already gone under the roof to sit down. I ask a women with a crocodile-skin purse if she knows the time. I have to shout over the wind.

"I'm catching a train!"

She just looks down at the water. A girl in a denim shirt stops beside me so that her head is in my armpit; she's shaking a can full of money like she thinks it's castanets and she's working for Ricky Ricardo.

"Eight baht?" I ask her. "Is that what it is?"

She says something but I can't make it out.

"What's that?"

"You get off at Wat Pho?"

I try to fish some money out of that mess in my pocket and the wind tries to pull it all out of my hands. All I can find is a hundred. She rolls her eyes. All this because of your grand plans, sweetheart.

"Small, small," the girl says.

She shakes the tin can over her shoulder and gazes around at everybody. I find a twenty folded up at the back of my passport.

"I want the train station."

"This one?" She tilts her head in the direction we're going. "Bangkok Noi?"

We're almost across to the opposite bank and the schoolkids start pushing against me. I'm going to be right in their way when they get off. The wind slips behind the lenses of my glasses so my eyes start to water but I manage to scuttle the suitcase and myself into the middle of the boat and out of the way. Every building along the bank is either a white-washed apartment building or a barn with a gold roof, except for the odd silver tower that must be a church or a monument or something. It really is like nothing else I've ever seen. It takes my mind off things. I hadn't thought of nasturtiums until just now.

We bump into the next pier and the kid starts in with his whistle again. Everyone else stands around like they don't even hear it. It's just a bosun's whistle, isn't it? He's just doing his job. A couple of white guys with briefcases hop onboard, having a good laugh about something. The girl with the tin can acts like she knows them. We go under a bridge and miss one of the pilings by all of a foot — guys in their underpants hang off it with fishing rods. Tin shacks hang over the water on either bank. And what would you say? "What a shame, the children that must live in there."

"This is *Tha Phran Nok*," says the soccer kid. He points ahead of us.

"Thank you."

His buddy reaches around him and punches the ball.

There's a rush at this one for everybody to get off so I make sure that I stay right behind him. I make the hop across with all of the kids but the knee doesn't like that. I wonder if I should sit down for a minute. I hold onto the railing and go up the ramp.

"No, no!" The soccer kid turns around. "You want Thonburi Station! The next stop."

"Where?" There's a long white building to our right. "Is that the station?"

"This is university."

People push to get past us. The boat is already out in the river. I turn back up the ramp and the soccer kid is long gone.

I climb up to the sidewalk and step around a lot of fruit that a lady has spread all over the sidewalk, and all of a sudden I realize that I've left the suitcase behind and my heart gives a little jump, but no, it's still in my hand. The sweat runs down my back, the polo shirt is stuck right to me, and it can't be any later than half past seven in the morning. I walk in the same direction that the boat had been going but after thirty feet the sidewalk stops and they just have plywood laid down over the mud. A skinny guy wearing what looks like a doctor's coat comes towards me, and maybe he is a doctor, because there's a stethoscope hanging out of his pocket.

"Excuse me, buddy," I say. "Do you know the time? Do you have a watch?"

"The time?" He has a big silver Seiko. Squints at it. "Seven thirty-five."

"How can I find the station?"

"Oh, through here. Straight on and a left."

I can't tell what he's pointing at. He waves at another guy in a white coat.

"You'll be all right, sir?" he says.

It seems to be a driveway between two cement buildings. That egg yolk is sitting in my chest. Doctors dolled up in white keep coming at me so that I have to duck between them, nurses too, and one of them looks just like the Chinese nurse who gave you your sponge baths. Carol. She looks up and gives me a big smile — Jesus, it might even be the same girl!

"Can I help you?" she says. "You are Professor Bluman?"

Can you believe this? I'm out of breath.

"I want the train station."

"Oh, I'm sorry! Through here," she says. "Orthodontics. Then, um, when you are outside again, turn right."

That takes me into a building with all kinds of wood panelling that smells like the back of a church, swarming with those kids in white coats — I ought to ask for a shot of Temazepam in my knee. A shot of Tasmanian. How long have I been walking? It feels like twenty minutes since the doctor gave me the time.

I find the exit at the end of the hallway but a guy's coming in just as I'm going out and the suitcase whacks him in the shin and I apologize and stumble out the door sideways so that the suitcase slips out of my hand and tumbles down the steps and winds up standing on end down on the sidewalk.

The building next to the medical school is made of corrugated tin and plastic tarps, and it stinks like fish — I could smell it from inside but thought it was formaldehyde — and people in shorts and flip-flops keep ducking under the tarp with about a hundred plastic bags in either hand, and things seem to be slapping against the inside of the bags, especially this one old lady. I guess this must be a Thai fish market, sweetheart, something else I've never seen before, though for all I know you worked part-time here. The suitcase and I stick to the boards over the mud but then they end and there's a concrete slab, and I must be watching the planks a bit too closely because I trip right over the slab and crash straight onto the ground. I come down hard on the knee and skin my hands a little bit. It's for the best that you weren't here to see it.

A guy in black gumboots with all kinds of tendons showing in his legs tugs at my shoulder to help me up. The wind's knocked out of me, though, so that all I can do is prop myself up on my elbows while Gumboots says soothing things. Two red plastic bowls sit right in front of me, each about two feet across and half a foot deep, and one's full of snakes and the other of turtles. Of course the snakes just slither around in the bottom but Jesus, the turtles are stacked one on top of the other and in the fifteen seconds that I'm watching one of them drags himself to the top and flips onto the pavement! Gumboot leaves me alone for a second and plunks him back in. Then he and another guy set me on my feet — they've both got faces that are wrinkled in a thousand places but they're patting me, brushing off the front of my pants like they were Boy Scouts.

"Thank you." I feel exactly as old as they're treating me. "Thank you."

I stagger on toward the station and the next turtle takes his turn over the side. And if they're all going to end up in the soup anyway, why should the ones on the bottom give two shakes if the ones on top have a little more ambition? In the meantime the snakes just lay there wondering which minute is going to be their last, so which bowl would you rather have been in?

That's straight out of Michel's playbook. He and I can discuss it over beer.

It's another fifty feet to the end of the tin shed, then I look to my left and there's the station, cream-coloured with a brown roof, but the big clock on the tower says that it's eight o'clock. So I've missed my train.

I stop under a palm tree and put down my suitcase. A guy in uniform steps out from under the archway and waves me over, and he could've just as easily stepped out of Pelayaran — the brown uniform, the black boots, even a rising sun on his shoulder! My first thought is that it's some kind of costume for the trip out to the Death Railway, he's paid to dress that way or else he's some kind of fanatic. But I stagger over to the archway and he shows me a ticket window with a little guy peering out — Jesus, maybe he works for the railroad! In that outfit!

"When's the next one?" I ask.

The guy in the window lifts a pencil off the counter. That's all he does.

"River Kwai," I say. "Kan — Kanchanaburi."

"Kanchan-*a*-buri," says the guy in uniform.

The guy in the window keeps staring at me.

"Kanchan-*a*-buri," I say. "When's the next one?"

The guy in the window points into the station — there's a train at the platform!

"*Yee-sip ha*," he says.

He holds up two fingers. Then five fingers.

"That's when she goes?"

"*Yee-sip ha.*"

He rubs his eyes, then opens a drawer and holds up two bills, a twenty and a five — money! He wants money. A door opens beside me and another guard comes out carrying a green flag and a red flag. He blows a whistle and strides off towards the train. I spread my papers across the counter until I find a hundred-baht note. The guy in the window types on his computer, then he hands me back a bunch of money and a little white ticket.

"Kanchan-*a*-buri," he says.

The first guard picks up my suitcase and I hurry after him. What do you figure the odds are, sweetheart, that I'll end up where I actually want to go? One in five, I'd say. We skirt around the dogs lying on the platform and I almost run headlong into a monk reading a magazine, and by then the guard's a mile ahead of me. I hustle past one yellow passenger car after another as the train hisses and clanks — honest to God, I keep expecting it just to rumble past me out of the station — until the guard slides down the steps out of a car and gives me this big salute, clacking his feet together. He's got metal plates tacked to his heels so it makes a hell of a noise. At least the Japs never had that. I get a good grip on the handle beside the steps, and as soon I've got a foot up the train starts moving.

I go down the aisle in the car and my suitcase is on the very first seat. The whole train seems to be made of wood, except the seats are covered with the same green vinyl they used to put in the '71 Mustang. Trim code 1R. The train gives a couple of good lurches so I flop onto the seat, then there's a long sound of steam releasing, but it can't be a steam train, can it? Across the aisle there's a soldier in fatigues, drinking a can of beer with a straw — Tiger Beer! Like we had for breakfast. I wish to God he was drinking something else. His beret's stuck under one of the straps on top of his shoulder, what do they call those? He swings around in his seat and Jesus, he has a thing the shape of a brick growing out of his neck. A goitre. He pulls the metal shutter down over the window and leans his head against it.

So I face forward too, and who's in the seat opposite me? A Japanese guy! Not three feet away! He's got headphones over his ears and he's picking a scab on the back of his hand, gazing right at me, and I know he's not Chinese because he doesn't have that sleepy look — remember even Mike Wong told us to look for that? Hell, maybe Mike was just getting back at me. Except for the three of us the whole car's empty, with the window panes rattling like mad on either side as we roll along. I feel for the handle of my suitcase so I can hustle to the back of this car or maybe to the next one, but he's too quick for me. He takes his headphones off.

"Hello," he says.

The soldier eyeballs us.

"Morning," I say.

The Japanese guy puts the headphones into his bag and takes out a pad of paper. I just watch him. The car sways back and forth.

I'm trying to picture him in a uniform but honest to God I really can't. His posture is too awful.

"You're going to the River Kwai?" he asks. "It is beautiful."

He looks out the window.

"What is?" I ask.

If he looks away for more than a minute I'm going to run to the next car.

"You see the water lilies?" he asks.

All that I see is a lot of cement going by. A building, a wall, another building. Warm air comes in the window.

"The dogs?" he says. "Oh, very cute. May I ask some questions?"

He must be one of these guys who wants to practise his English. Rudy had one come onto the lot a couple of times, a Korean.

"It is for my newspaper," he says.

"Japanese newspaper?"

"Yes. You were a prisoner on the River Kwai?"

"Was I a what?"

"A prisoner on the River Kwai."

Jesus!

"No," I say, "I wasn't. Not me, but my buddy was."

"But you are going to see the grave? From what country?"

"I'm Canadian."

He writes that down.

"Your friend — captured in Hong Kong?"

"My buddy? No. He's from France."

"Really? Oh, lotus flowers." He peers out the window again. "Listen now." He pulls a little hardcover book out of his bag. "Listen."

"I'm listening."

"This is an official book. 'The countries who have graves at Kanchanaburi are Britain, the Netherlands, Australia, Malaya, India, New Zealand, Canada, Burma and unknown Allied.' No France."

Maybe he sat by the soldier so that no one would throw him out the window.

"But my buddy isn't dead," I say.

"Ah. Most people don't know that Japanese soldiers found the

Allied graves in the jungle and brought the dead men to the cemetery. The Japanese did that."

"What'd they do that for?"

He spins the pen between his fingers.

"Do you harbour anger toward the Japanese for what they did to your friend?"

"What *you* did?"

"Sir, I am not old enough."

"And I told you the guy's still alive, I don't —"

"You go to the site of his incarceration?"

"No, I —"

"Are you are angry at me because I am Japanese?"

I have to wait a second.

"No. Hell," I say, "I just met you."

He writes that down. The soldier crushes his beer can under his foot.

We stop at a little station. The benches on the platform are blue tile, just the shade that you like. An old couple climbs on, hollering out some kind of singsong; he has cans of soda in a bucket and she has plastic bags filled with some kind of food. The soldier buys one and the old girls sees me watching. She has Snoopy on her T-shirt.

"Chicken," she tells me.

The soldier leans out in the aisle while he eats, pulling chicken off a skewer and stuffing it into his mouth, then a cube of rice, chewing with his mouth wide open and never giving either of us so much as a glance. You'd probably be a bit nauseated by it, but it really is funny. The Japanese guy puts his hands over his eyes and once or twice he peeks out between his fingers. The soldier drops his skewers on the floor and puts his head back against the wall, and I can hear that rhythm in the wheels: *you want it, you got it, you want it, you got it.* The Japanese guy sits up and smiles.

"You talk to a lot of guys?" I ask.

"Oh, a few each day. Most of them are not angry. But some are *very* angry."

He pulls out a little radio that's all taped together.

"An Australian man smashed my recorder. You see? Mitsubishi Electric. They made fighter airplanes."

"I know that."

"A shame," he says.

I don't know if he means the planes or the radio. A guard in a brown uniform comes along and checks our tickets, clattering his hole-punch like he thinks he has castanets too. He's all smiles but doesn't have a tooth in his head, and if you could get a look at him you'd see once and for all why I'm so deadly serious about dental hygiene.

"Let me ask you," the young guy says, "do you wish that the Japanese people would say sorry to you?"

I have to stop and think about that. My armpits start to itch.

"Yeah," I say. "I can't see what harm that would do."

He sits up straight and gives a quick little nod.

"*Sumimasen*," he says.

"And what's that mean?"

"It means 'sorry.' What do you think?"

"I don't know."

He writes that down. If he really wanted to make recompense he'd let me slap him, and then kill his wife's parents. But I have no urge to. He doesn't have any scars around his mouth. He puts the notebook back in his bag and looks out the window.

"Oh, everyone is farming rice, you see? And the cows? Oh, they run away —"

It's hot as hell but as long as we keep moving there's a breeze from the window. I pull out the itinerary so that I'll have some idea of what's coming, it says *Apple Guest House is recommended*. I try to keep my eyes open. We stop at another station where kids play on a pile of dirt. A horse is rolling out in the middle of a field. Palm trees do their best not to fall over.

The sky has turned grey and the air smells like pig shit and smoke, like driving through Chilliwack. Kanchanaburi is another little whitewashed station but its platform is overflowing with guys in motorcycle helmets and yellow pinnies. They wave pamphlets in front of me while I try to get the suitcase down the steps.

"River Kwai Hotel. You see? Very good room. Good price."

"I have a room," I say.

I dig out the itinerary and they gather around me, bumping their helmets together. *Apple Guest House is recommended. Take a taxi. I have not made you a reservation. It may be possible to arrange transport to Sangkhlaburi from here for the same day but you may also wish to rest.*

"Apple Guest House," I say.

"Oh, *App-el.*"

They run to their motorbikes and roar off blowing smoke. Hondas. Every vehicle's Japanese — they've invaded more effectively now than they did back then. Economic invasion. But no one's getting hurt, are they? Everybody's getting fed.

I walk down the driveway from the station to the road, shrubs on either side, it's a long walk but the air doesn't smell as bad as it did from the train. I watch trucks fly by on the main road, but now a horn is honking behind me — some kid in a Datsun pickup with a canopy. He's in luck because I've walked fifty feet and I'm tired of it. He slides out and I let him put the suitcase in the back. He has a Band-Aid in the middle of his forehead and Jesus, he can't be more than thirteen years old.

"Where do you stay?"

"Apple Guest House."

"Twenty baht."

There are a couple of two-storey houses built of breeze block on the main road, but everything else is one storey high, like an Old West town, and he has to steer around a lot of chickens. At every intersection he keeps the clutch in and works the gearshift back and forth — it has a golf ball for a knob. I make sure that I have a twenty and it turns out that I have lots; they all show a skinny guy in big glasses. Maybe the Thais think I look like him. We drive over gravel and park under a great big tree.

"Here is Apple," he says.

The sun is poking through the clouds. I hand him my twenty.

"Where else do you go? See a waterfall?" he says. "Wampo Viaduct?"
"Sangkhlaburi."
"Sangkhlaburi? Okay."

After five hours on the road the kid's taking corners so fast that we rattle around like a couple of dice. We drive beside a silver-coloured lake and dark green hills rise on either side of us, their tops nestled in cloud. But we're returning to civilization now — a lot of yellow statues with hands shaped like fly swatters sit beside the road, big as a row of condominiums.

"Buddha," the kid says.

We turn onto a street with mildewy awnings and park in a lot full of red mud. The kid slides out and lights a cigarette.

"Sangkhlaburi."

I take out your paper and unfold it.

"Coudreaux Guesthouse?" I ask.

"*Cood-row*?" He comes around from the back of the truck and sets my suitcase down. He takes the paper and points over the hood in the direction of the lake. "That way, sir."

I clamber down and my shoes sink into the mud. The air feels cold though I'm sweating as much as ever.

"Well, thank you, fella," I say. "I sure did appreciate the ride."

As though I'm from Texas. I'm just trying to keep a level head. He jumps back in and slams his door, and the truck circles around me. The kid's face goes by.

"Good luck," he says.

Schoolgirls in blue skirts say things to me as I walk down the street, but of course I don't understand, though I imagine they're saying, "That's him, that's Lily's husband." It's raining and I can feel the damp money like a lump in my pocket. An orange-headed chicken runs out into the road and looks at me. Dogs bark from behind a bamboo fence, but with that exception Sangkhlaburi is a very quiet town. A guy on a motorbike goes past with a folded-up umbrella tucked in his armpit, and I know that if you were here you'd say he looked like a knight on horseback. *Ivanhoe*. Maybe in years past you've seen that exact guy and thought that very thing. There's a bulldozer parked at the end of the blacktop and a girl in work boots and a hardhat crouches on the tread, putting on lipstick.

I'm on a path through thickets now that creeps down a steep hill, which my companion the bad knee does not enjoy, not as long as we're with my other friend, the suitcase. I hold onto the wet bushes so that I won't slide onto my behind. You must have pictured this when you were lying in 407. You must have had a good laugh. But I don't begrudge you a good laugh.

When I get to the bottom I'm still not at the lake like I thought I'd be, there's just a big veranda in front of me carved out of dark brown wood, though I can hear a boat motor whining from somewhere beyond it. I'm in the middle of a muddy road that curves along the hillside in the direction of town, so even a moron would've known that he didn't have to fling himself down that embankment. There's a fern stuck to my suitcase.

A sign on the veranda says:

Coudreaux Guesthouse
Inexpensive Bungalows & Rooms
Rafting, Trekking & Tours
Sawasdi Khap

I can't understand that last bit and there's more written underneath that I don't understand one letter of. I figure it must be Thai. The inside of my mouth tastes terrible. I should turn around and go home now. I've made it here but I don't see anyone around. But the veranda is full of tables and chairs, and chances are that if a guy sat in one of them he could look out over the lake, and I do need to sit down. I can hear women talking, so if I sit down maybe they'll give me something to drink. You've sent me here old and infirm, that's all; if that wasn't the case I'd turn on my heel this minute. But I walk up the three steps and set my suitcase down.

It's a long room with a high ceiling and a thatched roof. To my right there's a bar with beer taps and a goldfish in a tank and Christmas lights that aren't lit. To my left there's a little desk with maps in nice little stacks and pens and books, that looks like where a guy would check in if he were going to spend the night, and behind the desk there's a set of those saloon doors that probably lead to a kitchen.

I don't see any sign on the desk that says *Michel Ney, Proprietor*, or so much as a picture of him on the wall. Two small brown women are pulling chairs back and sweeping under the tables. They haven't noticed me. Beyond the tables there's just a long railing, and beyond that a lot of branches hanging down, then the grey-green of the lake. I leave the suitcase by the desk and go and sit down beside the railing.

Both women look like they're about forty. They wear long black skirts; one has a white blouse and the other's is blue-and-grey checks. Blue-and-grey looks up at me and smiles but carries on sweeping.

"How you?" she asks.

"I'm fine," I say. "How you?"

They have their jobs to do. They keep moving chairs and sweeping. At the end of the bar I see a flight of stairs leading down, maybe to the guest rooms. I move my chair closer to the rail. Little brown ants run along it. There's a forest below us, all green and slick in the rain, the drop must be a hundred feet, and there are little peaked roofs down among the trees. The lake looks flat and grey, and with all this cloud I can't even make out the far shore. There are houseboats off to the right and one has a flower garden on its roof, you'd love that, wouldn't you? A wooden bridge crosses over the houseboats and disappears into the cloud. Someone with a pink umbrella is starting across. Roosters are crowing but I can't see even one, and there are a lot of other noises that might be coming over the water from a hundred miles away — barking dogs, a chainsaw, a puttering boat.

Is this what you intended for me to see and hear? Am I just supposed to sit? Was someone supposed to jump out with balloons and say, 'Surprise, Harry, she hasn't passed away — here she is!' If that's the case then I won't mind that I've come all this way. But if there is a surprise I don't think that will be the one. I can only delude myself so much, sweetheart. I've gone to the effort of sitting down, though, so I can't see the harm in waiting around a few more minutes.

"There!"

Blue-and-grey throws a coaster onto my table — it looks like the Carlsberg logo but of course the words are all different.

"How you? What do you want, a drink?"

"I won't say no to a drink. And after that I'd like to see the owner of this place."

"What for?" she says, looking back at the other woman. "Bad service?"

The other woman laughs and keeps sweeping.

"Okay, what you want? Beer?"

Will her face light up if I mention your name?

"I don't want beer."

"Okay, Fanta. I am teasing you just now." She touches her chest. "I am the owner."

"Well, of course," I say. I hadn't expected that. I'd have as much expected for her to punch me in the nose. "It's a beautiful part of the world."

"With my husband. It is his place too."

"Your husband too? I see. Is he from around here?"

"Yes, sir. Before that in Singapore." She walks toward the bar, the broom propped over her shoulder. "He is running errands now but he will be here in five, maybe ten minutes. He can check you in if you want to stay."

She *might* be talking about Michel. He grew up a little bit in Singapore, I guess, though he didn't accomplish anything there outside of getting us a Japanese manservant and lots to eat. And I profited by that, didn't I, even if I never knew what was going on. Maybe I wouldn't feel ill when I think of it if he'd told me in the first place what was going on. And now you've co-opted his practice of leaving me in the dark.

The co-owner goes behind the bar and I hear a cap pop off a bottle. The other woman disappears down the flight of stairs, sweeping as she goes, and two little girls come up the three steps from outside and walk right in, but they stop in their tracks when they see. They're five or six years old; one's wearing a red T-shirt with a panda on it and the other has a striped shirt like a referee's. She cradles a toy car that looks like a Ford Aerostar and Panda Bear holds a remote control with an antenna four feet long.

"Hello there," I say.

The co-owner comes out from behind the bar with a bottle of bright red pop. It looks enormous in her hand. She says something to the girls and Panda Bear holds up the remote control and the van's wheels start spinning in the referee's arms. Flecks of mud spray across her sleeve. Panda Bear laughs up her nose. Her mother says something that sounds pretty sharp, so Panda Bear sticks out her bottom lip and the referee takes the remote out of her hands. The woman sets the bottle beside my coaster and says something else as the referee goes down the steps into the rain.

"I don't need a nap!" says Panda Bear.

Her mother talks to her in Thai or whatever it is and waves her toward the stairs, but the little girl goes the long way around, touching the back of every chair. Maybe it's part of their beliefs over here to say good-night to every piece of furniture, or maybe she's just one of those kids. She blinks at me as she goes past.

"I won't fall asleep."

"I wouldn't either," I say.

The pop is cold but so sweet it makes my fillings crackle. Did you drink this Fanta when you were over here?

"Aha!" The woman looks at me over her shoulder as she ushers the girl down the stairs. "Here is my husband."

A Suzuki Samurai pulls up to the front steps — yes, the model that always tips over, another of Japan's gifts to the world. All I can see of the driver is that his head's right against the ceiling. Even though the knee feels a little shaky I stand up and walk around the table. The car door opens and a rubber sandal steps out onto the mud. The driver hops out and slams the door, swinging a blue bucket in his hand, then he bounds up the steps. It's not Michel. This guy is big and tall enough, but his face looks Thai and he has salt-and-pepper hair cut just above his eyes.

What did we call that? A bowl cut. I don't know how old he is, maybe forty-five? He stops when he sees the suitcase and looks over at me.

"Afternoon." He sounds British. "Braved the wind and the rain, have you?"

"It's treacherous," I say.

"Oh no, did you take the path? Did you not see the sign on the road? That is a shame." He circles behind the desk and throws some keys in a drawer. "I was just in town to get a bucket for the boat. I would have picked you up had I known."

He stands up very straight and puts his hands on his hips.

"Now, did you wish to check in right away? Have you had a drink? Good, good. May has looked after you."

"I'll check in," I say. "I might as well."

He bends over some kind of ledger. I shuffle one table closer and drum my fingers on the back of a chair.

"As a matter of fact," I say, "I was hoping you could tell me if somebody's staying out here."

"Well, at this time of year only a handful. Or did you mean someone in particular?"

"Yeah," I say, "yeah." I swallow hard. "His name's Michel Ney. A Frenchman. Somebody told me he might be out here."

He clicks the end of his pen.

"Grandpa Michel? You heard correctly, certainly. He built this place when there was nothing around here. But he left us some years ago. It's just been May and I and the children for the last while."

I hold onto the back of the chair.

"Where's he gone?"

"Oh, he passed away, what, five years ago? Six, nearly. It was quite a blow, really. He was my stepfather. Still getting used to it." He writes something in the book. "Every week I get people asking after him."

"Beautiful part of the world," I say.

"Where are you from, then?" he asks. "The States?"

"Vancouver."

"Oh? I know people in Vancouver. Did you say you *knew* Grandpa?"

"Yeah, yeah. But ages ago."

"He might have mentioned you — what was your name, sir?"

"I'm Harry Winslow."

"God."

He stands up straight and the pen slides out of his hand.

"I'm sorry for your loss, sir," he says.

"What's that?"

He steps out from behind the desk but doesn't come any closer.

"My, uh, my dad did talk about you," he says. "And fondly, too, very fondly. Winslow. From the war?"

"That's right."

"Well, I am sorry for your loss." He wipes his nose with the back of his hand. "I mean, I'm sorry because I was told that your wife had passed away, and I am really, terribly sorry to hear that."

"Someone told you Lily died?"

"I *thought* of going to the memorial, you know, I did, but the, the letter just came the other week, and —"

"Hold on," I said. "Somebody wrote you about her? Who wrote you?"

"Well, yes, and I just didn't know if ..."

"She used to stay here, is that what it was?"

"Your wife did. She certainly did." He wipes his nose on the shoulder of his T-shirt. "You'll have to excuse me for just one moment, um, Harry. I'll do better if I have something to drink."

He starts toward the bar.

"Can I get *you* anything?"

"I'm fine," I say. Though my heart is beating a mile a minute.

The woman yells from downstairs — it sounds like *day mi* — and he yells something back down to her. He goes behind the bar and takes a glass from the shelf. I shuffle back to where I was sitting. I take a pull on the bottle but the pop's gone as warm as bathwater. I look through the trees for the houseboat with the flower garden. He's about to explain it all to me. I just need to keep my head screwed on and stay out of the wet. Michel has been dead six years. That's an awfully long time for this guy to still need a drink.

"Could you tell me your name?" I call out.

He comes around the bar with ice tinkling in his glass. He seems happier. He has dimples in his cheeks.

"It's Kwan," he says. "Simon Kwan." He sets his drink on the next table. "Have you never heard that name before?"

"I haven't, no. Listen, I —"

"No, hold everything. Please. I promise. All will be revealed."

He trots off through the saloon doors, and I sit here watching them swing back and forth until they've stopped entirely. Maybe he's gone to get the balloons after all. Simon Kwan. Kwan? It sounds Chinese, but he doesn't look the least bit sleepy. I thought he was a Thai who had an English accent. If May is his wife, is Panda Bear his daughter? Is this an exercise to keep an old guy's brain active, like when you said I should take up bridge?

He hurries back out, eyes on the ground.

"We've had this for you for some time."

He holds out a yellow 8 x 11 envelope, and I take it. It says *Harold E. Winslow* in your handwriting, the way your writing used to look. From the weight it feels like there's a magazine inside.

"We've kept it locked in the safe all this time in an effort to keep it from falling apart. I've heard paper does much better in temperate climes."

"Does it."

"I really am trying to go about this in as straightforward a way as possible." He leans back against the railing and folds his arms. "Just the other day I said to May that with both of them gone there was no chance whatever of Harry Winslow still coming."

There's nothing written on the back of the envelope. The flap is still glued down.

"What's in here exactly?"

He smiles. He takes a pack of cigarettes out of his shirt pocket.

"I've no idea. I was about to say that every morning when I take out the petty cash I have an overwhelming urge to tear it open. That has happened every day since she left it here in '74, so I'd appreciate it if you'd carry on and read it."

He walks to the next table over and pulls out a chair. *Harold E.*

Winslow, you've written. What was I doing in 1974? Buying a Chevy Nova and selling it to someone else.

"Go on." Simon shakes out his match and drops it in the ashtray. "I'll be quiet as a mouse."

The envelope smells like an old newspaper. I slide my finger under the flap.

"No, no. Wait on." He stands and takes a jackknife out of his pocket. "There."

I reach across and take it. I unfold the blade and slice the flap open very neatly, then I close the blade and toss the knife back to him. Are you watching all of this carefully? Did you imagine, when the day came, that I'd smell like a wet dog?

There is a stack of papers inside, and I slide them out onto the table, keeping clear of the ashtray. They've come off a writing tablet, written in blue ink, and you've numbered each one in the top right corner. I flip to the back. Eighteen. At the bottom of the first page there are all kinds of loops and scribbles like you had trouble with the pen. Simon is tapping his sandal against the table leg.

"Don't let me keep you from anything," I say.

"Oh, I reserve this time of day for mooning about." He quits tapping and folds his leg over his knee. "They're all asleep. And I feel I ought to be here while you read it."

"Even though you don't know what it's going to say."

"But I have an inkling. And suppose you need a drink? I'll leap up and get it. Please, Mr. Winslow — this has dragged on for *so long*. Please just carry on."

"All right. I'll dive in then."

I stand the pages up and straighten them so they're nice and square. He's still watching me, and from the look on his face his stomach must be flipping and flopping just the same as mine is. A bird is tooting out a little tune — he must be in the branches just off the railing. I can hear women singing, just snatches of it, and somebody shaking out an umbrella.

Harry my love,

For thirty years I have been thinking of what to say to you, and now that I am trying at long last to put it to paper it is as though I never once in all that time had considered what I would say. In truth I have, but all of the wonderful coherent things I had thought of have flown out of my mind. It has taken me ten minutes to write the last two sentences. I do hope that you will never have to read this, that what I am writing now is only practice before I am able to tell you in person. But if it is so hard to get these words down, how could it be any easier to say them to your face? Your poor face, I can't imagine how it will react. I want to cry just thinking of it. Oh dear, and here it is, splatter on the page. You see what I told you? For Simon there has never been a secret, he always knew about you, I would tell him when he was small that never in a thousand years would I want what happened to me to happen again, and never in a thousand years would I ever wish that he had not been born. It has been the same with you, my love. I have wished that the war had never come because if it had not then I would not have lost my entire life, but for all that I have never wished that you and I had not met. Someone up above us decided that I would have to trade one for the other, and once that choice had been made my only job was to be happy with it. Not that our life together has been a job. Not entirely, anyway. You know that I love you. I love that you love your business and it keeps you so very busy, and we need money to survive so it is all very commendable, but there is one thing that you should know about yourself that I am sorry to be the one to tell you: you are a very easy man to fool. One reason for it is that you are not a very good listener, my love, you really are not sometimes. I know how you will react to anything I might say about the Japanese. About anything that anyone might say about them. That is one example. I suppose that does not make you a bad listener necessarily. But because I <u>can</u> talk about the Japanese, and I go to Nitobe Gardens now and then, and I will drink green tea at a restaurant, you have led yourself to believe that I had an easier time with the Japanese than you did. I have heard you tell people so. I wish that you had never done that, Harry. It made me want to kill you so that you would never say such things again. You can tell that I am still angry about it. I love you, I say again, but you are ignorant, and in general I do not like a person who goes around believing that they have had the worst of everything.

I have just looked over what I have written, and rather than crumple it up like all of the other ones I will only say that if you are ignorant it is my fault. I have told myself every day for a very long time that I should tell you, if for nothing else than that it might make your own view of the war a little sunnier. The way Simon has mine, I suppose. As though the present were capable of changing the past! Now I have gone too far along, it is a danger of writing things down in that the pen can get too far ahead of me. I know that the things I ought to tell you now will make nothing sunnier, Harry. They will only make you suffer. How could I have ever thought to say this to your face?

Here is the thing that I must tell you. I was attacked by a guard in Changi and afterward I found I was pregnant. I was in the wrong part of the camp and there it was. Raped is really the proper word for it but I have decided that <u>attacked</u> sounds somewhat better, though I imagine that if a husband hears that his wife has been attacked it must conjure up every possible horrible image in his head, and whatever has just now come into your head is very possibly correct, and that is all I wish to say about it. And if that had been the extent of it I would certainly not be telling you or anyone about it now or ever. But because I became pregnant it would not end. I wanted very badly for it to end, you should know, but my lovely mother would have none of it. My lovely mother who thought that having a baby while other women were dying would be as lovely as a fairy tale, and thanks to her, though it would never have crossed her mind, it sometimes feels as though the man who attacked me is still lurking around us, beaming with pride at what a good job he made of it. His son just brought me tea and a plate of biscuits.

<u>Biological</u> father, I ought to have said. I have asked Simon to sit still and ignore the telephone so that I will be able to describe to you how little of him is really Japanese. He is trying to read my scrawl but it is upside-down to him and I do not think he will get anywhere. His skin is darker than mine but most people would think him an Italian or a Spaniard. I think of him as Italian. His hair is straight black hair like a Japanese but it falls in his eyes which strikes me as very Italian. He has my father's long neck and, most remarkably, my father's Adam's apple. Poor Simon! As though he has swallowed something that he should not have done. His eyes are not Japanese, but they are not my eyes either. They are brown rather than blue. The telephone started ringing again a moment ago and Michel came crashing up the stairs to answer it with a bedsheet over his shoulder. He said "hello" at first, as you or I would, but now I don't

know what language he is speaking. He looks over at us as though he is annoyed. Simon makes a gesture of helplessness. Michel winks. Only in the time that I have been writing these last few words have I realized that they have the same eyes, Simon and Michel. You might remember that Michel has large brown affairs with a pinched sort of look in the corners, from scowling or laughing I'm not sure. Simon's are identical. It must be nurture overtaking nature. He looks puzzled now because I cannot stop from smiling at this medical discovery and he is wondering what in this letter I could possibly have to smile about. But I do have things to smile about. It has been many years since that thing happened and once you, Mr. Winslow, have been told all about it then every trace of unpleasantness will be behind me. Gloomy things happen in one's life, certainly, but that does not mean that life is by definition gloomy. You ought to be flattered, love, that for a long time you have been my only source of anxiety.

Simon has put his elbow on the table. I think that perhaps his nose is out of joint. Perhaps he has been able to make out what I wrote further up the page about his looking so wonderfully Italian, and that in saying so I am trying to reassure you. Because what if he had good old-fashioned Japanese buckteeth and a pair of myopic spectacles, would I have given up on him entirely? I must admit that perhaps I would never have considered writing this letter if that had been the case. Not once have I said to Simon that the reason he has yet to be introduced to his stepfather is that his stepfather does not like Japanese people. He knows that part of him is Japanese but never for a moment have I wanted him to feel that this situation between you and me is his fault. Instead I have told him that his stepfather does not like to travel, and I cannot help but feel that this describes you very well. You will not go west of Oak Street! This is my sense of fairness: rather than make it Simon's fault, I have made it your fault. Never is it my fault. He has given up trying to read my upside-down scrawl. The German family that checked into the bungalow below mine has come in and their little boy is absolutely frantic. Simon is crawling under tables now, helping them to look for something. Which brings me to another way in which this is your fault. I have never felt that you wanted children, though it was not as though we did not try. We never took steps to _not_ try. But whenever we saw friends who had been more successful, and it seemed that most were, I would coo over the child and you would say, "What would we want with one of those things?" I suppose you meant to make me feel better but after a dozen times I must admit I took it to heart, and when we went to see one horrid doctor after another it was almost in spite of myself. Simon is 31 years old now so my conviction that you abhor babies is no longer relevant even if it were true. I realized once and for all that it was not when Rhonda came over with her daughter the other week and you sang the Lulu song to her. But in those early days when I began to write to the Kwans and ask after Simon, I told myself a hundred times each day that you could not be told because you simply did not like babies. Even though he was three or four by then. I had a box at the post office that I would run up the street to check every time I went to Woodward's, and you may remember that there were times I was going downtown to Woodward's three and four times a week. I loved you as ever, that has never wavered, I promise you, but in my mind's eye I saw you smashing my Simon to bits. I may have even told the Kwans that if my husband in Canada ever saw the baby he would kill him, though Simon claims to have no memory of me saying anything of the sort. But I found it much easier to slander you than to dwell on the fact that I had been attacked. I hope you will understand that. Sometimes, yes, but only for the briefest of moments, it is as though the man who did it is here with us, like a shadow, and other times when I am very low and I try to imagine him as a human being I cannot decide if I would rather imagine him alive now or dead. But he is only with us for a fraction of the time, and for the rest I consider myself the sole parent of my miraculous Italian baby, as though we were refugees from a Renaissance painting with little haloes hovering over our heads.

Remember Ricky? Any thought of church makes me think of him. I daydream about him during the sermon. It is <u>such</u> a <u>shame</u> you never met my father. I was thinking of our wedding night just now and how he was very probably dead already. Another excuse I often entertained was that you and I drank too much to be able to look after a child properly, I would think that when I was back in Singapore and had to tell myself that Simon was better off with the Kwans. Also that you were away at work for too much of the time and that we had too many card parties and that our friends drank too much. If we raised a child it would grow into a felon. But then I remembered that my mum and dad drank a tumbler of gin each day after breakfast so that was one argument at least I have been able to shake myself of.

I have just read down from the beginning and realized that you will have no idea who the Kwans are and that my claim that I was or am Simon's sole parent does a enormous injustice both to them and to Michel. Our friend Michel to whom Simon and I owe everything. You know that M. saw me in Changi. He came in when Mum was still there and I must have been six months pregnant, enough for it to be as plain as day. I asked him not to tell you. That was the first of the thousand favours he has done us. The women told me that he was a rum sort, a collaborator, because he seemed to have an understanding with the Japanese, and that I should have nothing to do with him so I was wary, but when one of the Koreans came into the hut and handed me a bottle of cod liver oil, should I have poured it out? Or the box of eggs? Smashed them over his head? I took them and as a result the goldfish inside me was born. He could not have weighed five pounds, but there he was. Now I may have given you the idea that Michel was the only one to help us, but half of the women must have dropped food into my hand at one time or other, some rice or a black banana. They were all the ones who had come around to Mum's way of thinking that having a baby in that place was something other than an act of utter stupidity. When I had one month to go Mum stopped eating entirely, she would sneak it all into my bowl. She starved herself for Simon. If I refused to eat her food she would leave it for the ants until I decided that Simon had as much right to it as they did. I told you that she died of cholera but that was only at the end.

I did not tell you how she initially convinced me, did I? She slapped my face and she lay in the dust and screamed. I thought that she had gone mad because she behaved like a madwoman, but when Simon answers my letters or meets me at the bus from K'buri I wonder whether she really had gone mad. Perhaps she knew there would be no children after him. Madwomen have a sense of these things. She became more and more ill, though, and one night I held her in my arms as though I could hold her on this earth or go along with her if that was what it came to. She kept shaking, and I said to her, 'Stop shaking, Mum.' And when morning came she neither shook nor breathed nor danced the fandango. I have told you about that morning but I never told you that I was nine months pregnant at the time. I think now that she might have very well died from the cholera even if she had not been starving to death, and that if she had to go she was happier believing that she was going for Simon's sake and not because a few men far away had decided they had better overturn the world.

While I am thinking of Changi I will tell you that I saw Michel only the once while I was there but I knew that the eggs were from him. When S. came

*up here permanently Michel finally admitted that the condensed milk and all
the rest had indeed been from him. For years before that he had been scratching
his head and telling me they must have come from someone else. Ha! As well
there were two nurses from the General Hospital who managed to pull me
through the delivery. For the entire first day he would not nurse, and the nurses
and girls in my hut went all around camp trying to find any sort of milk, any
animal would do the trick they said, and the best we could do for him was
<u>coconut</u> milk. Which he would not take. The nurses came to me and said that
if I did not want to see my nine months of work undone I should consider
sending him out of camp. A woman across had lost her two year old and told me
the same. I am ashamed to say now how easily I was convinced that the best idea
was to send him away. But if I had not saved Mum how would I be able to save
him? There were no white people in the city left to send him to and the only
Chinese I knew were the Kwans. The cook and her family had gone out to the
kampongs but I did not think Kwan had, so we sat around the child trying to
think how we could possibly get word to them, and in walked the Korean guard
who had brought my cod liver oil! He told the nurse in Japanese that the
Frenchman had told him to help with the baby when it came, he had been well
paid so he meant do it. I gave him their address and told him to ask the Kwans
to come to the camp. It is quite unbelievable to me now that we should have
trusted him. It must have had a lot to do with the tiny sound Simon was
making. I also must confess that somewhere in my deep dark mind I did not
want to have him with me on the day that you and I walked out of our
respective jails and resumed our life, which only goes to show what a stupid girl
I was because there was every chance you could have been sent up to the railway
and never come back. If he had been healthy I would have kept him, I have no
doubt of that, and told you that I had adopted him after his mother had died,
which would not have been far from the truth because his <u>grand</u>mother had died.
There were hundreds of children in the camp and if he had been healthy he
might have melded in with the rest of them, but he was not healthy. I have lain
awake beside you a thousand times and argued with myself but I know that it
was not a mistake to send him away.*

*On the second day Simon ate rice gruel off the end of my finger and we
applauded him, and I wondered how we could tell the Korean that we would not
need the Kwans after all. He walked in and said that they were waiting on the*

other side of the fence. My legs were resolute if the rest of me was not, and they carried me out after him. A track ran through the bushes behind the camp and I saw the Kwans sitting there in a cart being pulled by a tiny pony. Kwan had been our chauffeur. They had a load of paddy rice in the back and I could only assume that they were going to hide Simon there if they ran into trouble. S. was only dressed in a rag from a pillow slip and I had no toys to send along with him. Kwan reached between the wires, and I gave Simon to the Korean and he knelt down and placed him in Kwan's hands. They went to the cart and drove off and his little starved cry never quit, which made me feel somewhat better because that was the reason he was going. Feeling much better being a relative term. August 17 is his birthday by the way, which he has proudly told me is now independence day in Indonesia. After he had gone I debated whether or not I should tell you when it was all over. For an entire year I had decided that I would and that we should walk through Singapore together on the way to fetch our son. I thought that it would be lovely. But the war showed no sign of ending then so it was easy to forget that I would have to tell my husband about the child I had conceived in his absence. Even if he had been a blond child I couldn't have claimed that he was yours because we had never even been to bed together! I really did love you, Harry. I find it quite daunting to think of. I had known you for the space of a day and I must have loved you more than my own poor child. My immaculate conception. And after two years I decided that if the Kwans had kept him alive for all of that time then it would only be a hindrance to them if I appeared at their door. So it was their fault that I did not tell you right then, and also your fault. It could never be my fault.

Simon has been taking dinner orders from the tables and has facetiously asked if I require a menu. I am having the spareribs and fried rice. <u>Burmese</u> spareribs. I had it for three nights straight until last night when I had the chicken for a change and found myself missing the Burmese spareribs rather badly. You remember that I went back to Singapore in 1951 for Simon's eighth birthday, though you didn't know it was for his birthday. I had told you I was going to visit Pia, and I did stay with Pia for the first night. The Kwans would not have forgiven me if I had not spent every night from then on with them in their <u>tiny</u> house, you really should have seen it. Yes, I should have brought you to see it. A cinema stands there now. Simon came back into my life at that time because of Myrtle and Eva in England, though they know as little about him as you did.

I had written them from Vernon so that they would know about Mum and Dad, and a few years later they asked in a letter if I was still in touch with any of the girls from the camp. That prompted me to write to Pia care of the college in Singapore where she had been studying before the Japanese arrived. I did not mention Simon in my letter, I was not ready to, but I was also terrified lest she mention him in her reply which you might read over my shoulder, so I went out and rented my post office box and gave her that address on the back of the envelope. And after a few letters I took the step of asking if she might try to locate Simon for me, that she might look in the school listings, and after a month she wrote to tell me that a Simon Kwan was in the second level at Radin Mas School, which was in the neighbourhood where I remembered the Kwans living. That night I insisted you take me dancing and I got very drunk. Dear Pia contacted Mrs. Kwan and learned from her that S. knew all about me but they had assumed I was dead, so I began to write him and from then on we wrote each other faithfully twice a month and his were full of sweet little drawings. I cannot imagine how it made the Kwans feel to finally hear from me, and in all the years afterward it was never mentioned. I sent S. all of the dividends from a little portfolio of stocks I started and never mentioned to you. I suppose I could feel bad about that but we never suffered without it, did we? I did show you Pia's letters from time to time, you will remember, because I did not mind if you knew that I had a girlfriend. Only the ones that did not mention Simon, though, and I had already burnt the envelopes in the grate so you would not see my address. If it was summer I would burn them in the vegetable garden. It was an exhausting process. But I needed you to know about Pia if I hoped to ever see Simon, and when his eighth birthday was approaching I convinced you that there was enough money in the bank for me to visit her. You will recall that due to the expense there was never a question of you coming, and you were sick to death of Asia besides that, and the lot could not spare you for so many weeks, or even hours, if the truth be told, and in the twenty-three years since I have never expected you to feel any differently. Your single-mindedness has always played into my hands.

Now from the first page of this I am expecting you to swallow a brand-new view of the world in one gulp. Though perhaps you have not made it this far. Perhaps these words are burning in the vegetable garden. The last leg of that trip was Malayan Airlines from Bangkok to Singapore, and you know what that plane looked like from the postcard I sent of it which you have had pinned behind your desk ever since, so that I feel sick each time I step into your office. The same phrase always comes into my head: <u>a symbol of my duplicity</u>, as though I lived in an overwrought French novel. Because I am not with Simon then, I am with you, and that is when I see how stupid I have been yet I can see no way out of it. You must remember how many times you have retrieved that poor card from the wastebasket. I burned Simon's letters in our vegetable garden as well, even the drawings. Now that I think of it, that may be the crux of it: for one moment in time my dignity suffered and I have been suffering for the sake of my dignity ever since, and by suffering I mean this subterfuge.

If you must know I am terribly sleepy. Michel and his girlfriend Noi ate with me, she is the daughter of his previous girlfriend which might be scandalous if we were elsewhere in the world. Her mother still lives in the kitchen and is a marvellous creature, older even than Michel, in fact Noi must be my age and Simon tells me that her daughter may soon be too old for Michel and when the time comes for him to move on he will have to go to the granddaughter, whom I have seen and is very lovely. They are Karen people, and except for Noi's granddaughter all are widows as their husbands were killed when the lot of them lived next door in Burma. That seems to be a very common situation around here and Simon and Michel do very well as a result. S. also has an accent which I am sure is much stronger than mine, and I believe he may only have it when I am here because Michel has been giving him some strange looks. M. himself has an accent that he has said no country on earth could call its own. He has been in S'buri all this time, and his accent is certainly stranger now than when I first met him.

I have used up a great deal of ink while avoiding what I must tell you next: Michel wrote to you when we lived at McGintys' and I never showed you the letter. I stood on the porch of that house, staring at his name on the envelope, and convinced myself that his only possible purpose in writing was to tell you about Simon. So I opened the letter that was not addressed to me and found that he was only writing to tell you that he was alive and still in Thailand. He had written the Canadian Seamen's Union, who had found our address for him through the Manpower office. He asked after me but knew better than to ask after the baby. When you came home that day I could have told you that I had opened it out of sheer excitement that your old friend was still alive but I did not trust myself to be able to do so convincingly, though I *realize now that the thrill it would have given you would very likely have kept you from reading the <u>duplicity</u> in my every word. I was not thinking clearly. I actually fainted dead away and Mrs. M. found me there! You were at Fairfax then and our lives had been going so well that I had been telling myself that in a few years I would forget I had ever had a sick little baby. But seeing Michel's name made me feel as though I had only left S. the day before. I cannot describe how sick at heart I felt. I should rephrase what I wrote earlier: it was not that I did not trust myself to lie to you convincingly but that I did not trust myself not to break into hysterics.*

Certainly I told myself that I would tell you before long, that I would retrieve the letter from the bottom of my makeup case and tell you that it had just arrived that day. But if I have learned one thing over these years it is that despite one's best intentions it is nearly impossible to take back a lie and suddenly begin telling the truth, because it is much easier to carry on living with the lie, especially if it is a lie you have been perpetuating for a month and then a year and then twenty years, and that keeping silent about something so ridiculously important is as much a lie as telling you something patently false. I kept Michel's letter secret from you one afternoon twenty years ago, on the surface that might seem forgivable, but the fact is I was also busily keeping it from you yesterday. And I say <u>nearly</u> impossible because at least I am telling you now. I will relax the moment you have read this.

I think we are nearly full circle. I will carry on telling you. Via my P.O. box I wrote Michel myself and told him that the Winslows and Simon were all well though separated by much distance, and I babbled some explanation as to why you had not written yourself, and in every correspondence and conversation since I have told the poor man that I <u>must</u> tell Harry the whole truth, I am about to tell Harry the whole truth, and obviously he has respected my decision though he recognizes I have made it out of weakness rather than strength. You really must come and see him. He mentions "the Java Sea" as though it were the greatest time of his life. I wrote to M. every year to tell him how you and I were getting on, and when I went back to see S. in '58 I invited him to come down as well so that Simon could finally meet his Uncle Michel. They got on wonderfully because M. (a grown man!) would play football with him at any hour and S. was in the middle of a term paper on Wellington which M. promptly co-authored. Poor Kwan had died only the year before and Mrs. Kwan was *looking very frail so I mentioned quite casually that it might be a nice treat for everyone if S. went up to Thailand on his holidays to stay with his new uncle, a plan which said uncle heartily endorsed. He came up here that Christmas and every one after, and when poor Mrs. K. died in '61 he came for good.*

I think I am coming to the end. Now I am wondering how you will react, despite my congratulating myself at how clever I am to not have to weigh every word as it comes out of my mouth, for I have already weighed it here on the paper. But now that is nearly time for you to put the paper down and look up I must resign myself that you are going to be looking at me, and then I will most likely not feel quite so clever. Assuming that I have had the stomach to be there. Having finally put words to paper and full of momentum as I am, I see no reason why I should not give this to you the moment I am back at our kitchen table. Maybe something has already shifted in your mind and I am no longer the same person I was when I gave you this to read. Are you going to smash something, break something, take me in your arms? There is a record that Simon has been playing that says people often change but memories of people cannot change. Wouldn't that be nice? But I know that your knowing all of this must colour everything that has come before. You must think that you have not known me at all, that the Mrs. Winslow you know cannot even lie to the tax people. I can only guess that I have kept the secret this long because it is <u>mine</u>. I have been writing too long now. Too much supposition. My poor hand will not be happy come tomorrow. What else? I love you deeply. I have not done this to hurt you, though you may well feel that I have. My one hope is that you will come over to meet Simon and to finally see Michel, because none of this is their fault. I am finished now so throw this away and please take me in your arms.

your L.

But I do not throw it away. I keep the pages in my hands. The dark wood of the deck seems very dark and the trees all around us look very green. Almost yellow. The roosters are cackling and probably have been all this time. How much later is it? An hour? Simon is still at the next table, staring at the ceiling. Moths fly around the rafters. He holds a cigarette near his face, one elbow on the table, the smoke drifting straight up, and his other hand is almost resting in the ashtray. He brushes a fleck of ash out of his hair, and belches at the same time. Now he knocks his fist against his chest and taps the cigarette off. He shifts in his chair and looks out past the railing. Finally he looks over at me.

"Oh, you've finished." I think he's trying to smile. "What does she say?"

My mouth is full of glue.

"Quite a lot," I manage to say. "She says quite a lot."

"Anything specific?"

I hear a car horn echoing from miles away. And yet everything seems so quiet.

"She says that you're my grandson."

"Stepson," he says.

"That you're my stepson."

"She's told me that as well."

I push my chair back. I get up and offer him my hand. He stands up too, and shakes it.

"I'm pleased to meet you," I say.

"Same to you, Harry."

I think he's smiling but it's almost a frown. My knee's so stiff I have to sit down again.

"Did it answer all your questions?"

"I don't know," I say.

"We knew Mum had been sick." He gets up and skirts around my suitcase on the way to the desk. "She'd phoned us when she first went into the hospital. Talked to May for a long time. And a letter came a week ago, when it was already over. That wasn't easy, let me tell you. That was how we knew."

He holds up an envelope and reads the back of it.

"'Yuriko Ikebachi, St. Paul's Hospital.' Do you know her? She seems very sweet." He tries to smile again. Those dimples. "Is it safe to assume you'd like a drink now?"

It's as though I'm hearing everything he says from behind a waterfall.

"I would love another of these soda pops," I tell him.

"You'll have to drink it in a hurry. Before Ita sees. She's a terror with too much sugar."

I keep busy watching the mosquitoes land on my arm. Then I brush them away. If you'd like to know how I'm feeling about all of this you'll have to wait. But the one thought that's been creeping in is that I haven't lost you quite as much as I'd thought I had. I haven't lost you because as it turns out the you that I lost wasn't a real person. A guy can't have lost what didn't exist in the first place, right? No, she did exist, but I only saw half.

But in another sense I haven't lost you as much as I'd thought because you're still here. The pop Simon brings is orange this time.

"Let me ask you," I say. "Did you miss the funeral because of this stuff she'd said about me?"

He shrugs. A big one, like a comedian.

"I don't remember anything like that. I always knew that you existed … God, this is *strange*. It hits me now and then how strange this is. While you were reading I told myself I'd gotten used to the idea, but, wow, here you are again. Are you getting that too? I always thought you'd be big and fat."

"All I thought was Michel might be here."

"Oh. That is a shame. I'm sorry if I didn't put it very gently, it's just I'm still getting used to Mum, whereas Michel I'd, you know, accepted. It's a long time he's been gone."

"She told me I had to rush over here and see him."

He sits on a table and lights another cigarette.

"She was having you on. That was the last time she was here, the memorial we had for him. She tipped his ashes off the bridge herself."

"Is that right?"

"Yes."

He blows a smoke ring up to the ceiling. The longer he goes on talking the more it seems like we're talking about someone who isn't you at all. Your sister or somebody.

"Using Grandpa Michel as bait. She was cunning, wasn't she?"

"I hadn't realized," I say.

Which you ought to jot down as one of the greatest understatements of all time.

"In the back of my mind," says Simon, "I always thought you *did* know about me. But evidently she never told you anything."

"The old girl never had much time, did she? I'm mean, you're only, what, fifty years old?"

"God, fifty-two in a couple of weeks."

"Well, over there in Vancouver our lives were just chop-chop-chop. She never had a spare minute for a little thing like this."

He grins. Whatever I'm doing is working; I feel like grinning myself. But just you wait, sweetheart, in about two minutes I'm going to turn around and kill him just to prove you right.

"*Kai! Kai!*"

A lanky teenage boy stands on the steps, holding a blue crate with two brown chickens in it. One pokes its head out the top and looks at the desk and wall, wondering where the hell he's ended up now. Simon rattles off a hundred different languages as he takes the crate. They bow to each other, the boy goes off, and Simon hustles the crate through the saloon doors. A brown feather flutters down to the floor. I wonder if you know what any of those words meant.

Simon hurries out and past me, nodding at the bottle on the table.

"If you could finish that I would very much appreciate it."

He yells something down the stairs, it sounds like *dung di dow, dung di dow*, then stands there with his hand on the banister, waiting, until the woman's voice calls up, and a second after that loud music starts playing downstairs. I can feel it against the bottoms of my feet. It's tinny piano and a cruddy drummer, and some sad sack guy singing in yet another language I don't know. But I should make the best of things, shouldn't I? So I finish my bottle of Fanta in one swig. Simon strolls over, picks it up and carries it over to a wire rack by the bar. Dad used to have one just like it in his store.

"Now, what are your plans?" he asks. "Do you have to get back right away?"

"I fly out of Bangkok in a month."

We have to shout over the sad sack singer.

"No, no! Not long enough. Mum only ever came for two weeks, it was ridiculous! We'll ring the airline and have them change it."

It sounds as though he's inviting me to stay indefinitely, which of course is awfully big of him. Maybe he can tell that I'm too banged up to move more than ten feet.

"Only if I can make myself useful."

The song gets louder for a second but then it finishes, and the sounds of boat motors and twittering birds come back.

"I don't want to sit with my feet up," I say.

"No, no. If Mum and Michel were watching us from on high they would not be impressed with that at all. I'll tell you what, if you have a moment now we can walk down to the clinic and see if the tetanus serum has come in, and if not I'll place a call to the Baptists in Bangkok."

"The Baptists."

"Yes, they're wonderful. Even better than the Buddhists in Buriram."

"So you *do* have a phone."

He looks at me like I've farted.

"Yes," he says, "we have a phone."

The mother appears at the top of the stairs with Panda Bear on her hip, both of them looking bleary, and the woman in the white blouse comes up behind her followed by two tall girls wearing T-shirts and jeans. Simon puts an arm around May and steers her towards me.

"May," he says. "My dear. You met this gentleman earlier?"

"Yes." She stifles a yawn. "Excuse me. Hello, sir."

The little girl rubs her face against her mom's shoulder. Simon reaches over and takes her as the other three women squeeze by on their way to the kitchen. Another song starts to pound against the floor — a lot of drums and electric guitar. Simon swings the little girl in his arms.

"This gentleman is someone we have talked about many times, but never *dreamed* that we would ever meet. Do you know who it is?"

May glances at me, strokes the child's arm with the back of her hand.

"May, this is Harry Winslow."

She glances at me again. She looks worried.

"This is Harry. This is Mum's husband. Who she always said she would bring with her one day."

She peers at me for a second, then her eyes get wide.

"Yes?"

She's grinning now too, bowing with her hands pressed together. It's the happiest sort of bowing I've ever seen. I stand up and my chair falls back with a bang, and that makes the little girl look up.

"Oh!" says May. "But Mum has died, yes?"

The look in her eyes makes the truth of it seem so much worse, worse than the fact of it tossing and turning in my head or what anyone said at your funeral. Because you were important to these people and yet you were always apart, so that even when you were living they thought of you with sadness.

"Yes, she has," I say. "She got very sick."

"Oh, but I am very sorry!"

She puts her small hand on my arm and I see Simon blinking. All of a sudden his chin crumples up, and then I think that I must be crying too, sweetheart, because it feels like I'm breathing through the roof of my mouth and something drips onto my arm. I have to prop myself up against the table, and Simon puts his arm around my shoulders, and I know that on one level it's good, we are all people who loved you and it's good that we should feel sad together, even with that music thumping against our feet, but even so I can't help feeling how futile it is to be sad, because your life was so unfair at every turning, it should have been so much better, but instead you got very sick and died. And though I loved you I could not save you, which I really should have, because you must have preferred your unfair life to what you have now. But I'm picturing your face with the tubes coming out of it. How tired you were. That's the only consolation we can take. How tired you were.

"I'm all right," I tell them.

Simon and May aren't much better, blowing their noses and wiping their eyes as they pick the chair up and sit me down. The little girl's wandered off. May gives me some paper napkins and I try to clean myself up. The older girls watch us over the saloon doors. Simon carries my suitcase down the stairs and the music stops. A dog is barking somewhere below us and May crawls around the restaurant, lighting mosquito coils under every table. The smell sends a shiver up my spine.

Feet thud on the front steps — three white boys with backpacks. They're all trying to grow beards. They look at May and me.

"Any beds?" They sound Australian.

"Yes, yes." May hurries over. "Bungalow?"

I hear something in the kitchen being dumped into a hot pan; it's a very distinctive sound. I ball up the last of my napkins. Simon appears beside me, holding the little girl's hand.

"I found Ita," he says. "Would you like a walk? It's stopped raining."

I get up and follow them to the front. I still feel muddle-headed, as you would say. May has the Australians writing their names in the book. Simon and I go down the steps but the little girl stays up on the veranda, where she executes a pirouette.

"Ita," says her father, "have you been introduced to this man?"

She puts her hands behind her back and looks from him to me.

"Do you remember Grandpa Michel?"

"No," she says.

"No. The other girls do but you were too little. At any rate — are you listening? This is Grandpa's friend," says Simon. "You should call him Grandpa."

She pirouettes again. He turns to me.

"And Grandpa, this is Marguerita."

"Marguerita?" I bend down. "Did you know, young lady, that my dear old mother-in-law had just that name?"

"I should hope so," says Simon. "That was what Mum said it was."

"And who are these other girls you mentioned?"

"Oh, they're both hard at it in the kitchen. I ought to have introduced you. Mol has been running the restaurant since she was twelve, and I must say that Grandpa Michel was beside himself with joy about that, especially when we had Chinese guests in, from New York or Toronto actually but they were Chinese as far as he was concerned, and he took me aside and said it fit exactly with a theory of his —"

"*Faw!*" says Ita.

"— that she should be cooking for the Chinese. Mysterious, wasn't he? But she makes our *tom yam*, she makes everything."

Ita sways back and forth on her tiptoes. Something seems to be weird about her feet but I see now that she's tucked her sandal straps under her little toes.

"Do you want to hear a joke?" she asks.

"Sure I do," I say. "Shoot."

"How did the dog decide, um, decide which poop it was going to push out *last*?"

"Oh, God," her father says. "Ita —"

"Do you mean to say a dog can *decide* which one comes out when?"

"Yes." She sinks back down on her heels. "He *can*."

"Well," I say, "then I don't know. How does he do it?"

"He decides ... he decides by *process of elimination*!"

"Let me make sure I have this straight," I say. "He decides —"

"I made it up myself!"

She leaps up and down.

"Isn't she a bright bulb?" Simon asks. "Okay, Smalls, I forgot to stop at Nurse Sang's today, so can you show Grandpa where it is?"

She stops hopping.

"I want to go to Suri's."

"On the way back, but only maybe. You'll have to ask Grandpa."

She looks at me and picks something out of her ear.

"Hurry on," says Simon. "I want you back before the people come for dinner."

She jumps off the top step and starts skipping up the driveway.

"Please just ask Sang if she needs me to place the call, will you?"

"Isn't this lady going to wonder who I am, just walking in with this one?"

"Oh, not at all." He's already going back inside. "Ita takes a guest down to her most days in the week. They all imagine they have malaria. But do please introduce yourself. Sang knew Mum very well."

It's still sinking in that by "Mum" he means you.

"Dad!" Ita calls. She's already at the bend.

"Here he comes," he says. "You wait!"

When I get to the bend she's pulled all of the leaves off a poor branch that's hanging into the road. She starts to skip again.

"Do you know jokes?" she asks.

"What kind of jokes?"

"How *many* do you know?"

I'm trying to remember the ones we used to tell Rudy.

"I know two."

"Only *two*?"

"Let's go. 'Knock, knock.'"

She stops to pick up a stick and starts peeling the bark off it.

"Who's there?" she asks.

"Cantaloupe."

"Cant — cantaloupe who?"

"Can't elope, my father's got the ladder."

For such a small person she gives a very withering look.

"Ready for another?" I ask. "Okay? 'Knock, knock.'"

"Who's there?"

"Interrupting cow."

"Interrupt —"

"Mooooo!"

She throws down the stick and skips off ahead of me. Interrupting cow? That joke used to be like money in the bank. You remember. I try to keep her in sight but I can't help looking down through the trees at the green lake and the rusty roofs of all the houseboats. There's that one with the flowers on the roof again. I can't imagine anything that you'd like better.

"Wait for me, Ita," I call.

Should I run to catch up with her?

Two hours ago it had never crossed my mind that these people even existed, this family. Tucked away up here in the boondocks. I was still busy realizing that you were gone, that there wasn't a piece of you left in the world, and that before long I would have to stop talking to you. But now I think I'll just carry on.

I've caught up to her, skipping on the spot.

"I get it now!" she says. "It's funny!"

"Isn't it?"

"I'll ask you, okay? I'll be the cow?"

"Shoot," I say.

Two brown dogs come running at us from around the end of a chain-link fence, barking their heads off. They stamp their white feet in the mud.

"Settle down," I tell them. "Where's the fire?"

The one with black ears quits barking and starts to growl in earnest, showing us his teeth. Both of them start circling to our left.

"*Rawang! Bay si!*" Ita yells.

She kicks a foot in their direction, then grabs my index finger and starts to pull me up the road. The dogs have already hustled back behind the fence but she hasn't noticed, she's tugging me for all she's worth.

"Run, Grandpa!" she yells. "Run!"

Acknowledgements

I AM INDEBTED to the many writers whose books saw me through the writing of this one: Noel Barber, Pierre Berton, Milton Caniff, Peter Elphick, Raymond Horricks, C. O. Jennings, Agnes Newton Keith, Gretchen Liu, Eric Lomax, Anton Lucas, Hank Nelson, John Sandilands & Lavinia Warner, Gordon Sinclair, Robert D. Turner, Alfred Russel Wallace, and plenty of others.

Thanks to James Baker, Taryn Gunter, Karen Handford and Madeleine Thien for their advice on early drafts. Thanks to Tom O'Malia for stories of the merchant marine, to Derek Fairbridge and Mike Holcomb for jazz history, to Willem Atsma and Madeleine Thien for Dutch translation, and to Patsy Baxter for stories of the Raffles. Thanks to Philip Conrad and the Joseph Conrad Society UK, the staff of the Singapore National Archives (they give out candies!) and Dorothy Ng of the Singapore History Museum.

Many thanks to the Canada Council for the Arts for their financial support during this project.

Thanks to Steven W. Beattie for being a shrewd editor and lovely guy, and to Helen Godolphin for her scrupulous copy-edit. Thanks to Joy Gugeler, Lynn Henry and Michelle Benjamin for their unswerving support. Thanks to Jesse Finkelstein, Teresa Bubela and Monica Bisal at Raincoast for their diligent and enthusiastic work, to Anne McDermid and Jane Warren at the McDermid Agency for their excellent advice, to Angela Cameron and Hannah King for the printer, to Carol Handford for the chair, and thanks especially to Rick Maddocks, who looks after his friends.

Boundless thanks and love always to Nicole D. Handford, LLB.

ADAM LEWIS SCHROEDER grew up on an apple orchard in Vernon, British Columbia, and has since traveled widely, publishing stories in more than a dozen journals and anthologies. His story collection, *Kingdom of Monkeys,* was shortlisted for the Danuta Gleed Literary Award, while *Empress of Asia* was a finalist for both the Ethel Wilson Fiction Prize and the Amazon.ca/Books in Canada First Novel Award. Adam lives with his wife and sons in Penticton, British Columbia.

Visit his Web site at www.adamlewisschroeder.com.